I will shatter
gates of bronze
and cut down
iron bars.

Isaiah 45:2

GATES OF
BRONZE

· *Philadelphia* ·
The Jewish Publication Society of America

Translated from Hebrew by
S. Gershon Levi

GATES OF
BRONZE
HAIM
HAZAZ

Introduction by
Robert Alter

English translation copyright © 1975
by The Jewish Publication Society of America
All rights reserved
First English edition
Taken from the final revision of Daltot Nehoshet,
published by Am Oved, Tel Aviv, 1968
ISBN 0–8276–0059–3
Library of Congress catalog number 74–15463
Manufactured in the United States
Designed by Adrianne Onderdonk Dudden

Translator's Preface

It is not true that translation is impossible. It is just very difficult. In the instant case it is doubly difficult because there is so much of Hazaz that is necessarily lost in the transfer to English—not only overtones, but whole tones, images, allusions rich and complex, even ideas.

This is said, not by way of apology, but of warning. Let not the reader imagine that he holds in his hand anything like a facsimile of the original. It would be more appropriate to call these pages an echo, a reverberation of the novel from which they are drawn.

The reasons for this are many, but the principal one is alluded to in Robert Alter's Introduction. The author chose for his own voice, even more than for that of his Jewish characters, a Hebrew neither classical nor modern, but what might be called scholastic—the language of the study house. Even within that tradition he leans more on the legal style than on the moralistic, more on the Mishnah than on the Midrash. Paradoxically, this style provides a kind of poetic (and ironic) charm, which is just what gets lost in translation.

Lost, too, is the unabashed use by Hazaz of Russian, Ukrainian, and Yiddish words and idioms. Only a limited number of these could be refracted through the prism of the translation offered here.

S. G. L.

Introduction by Robert Alter

Paris in 1923 hardly seems a likely place for the gestation of a novel written in Hebrew that would offer a searching panoramic vision of the *shtetl*'s disintegration in the historical maelstrom of the Russian Revolution. The last volumes of Proust were still coming out; Gide was working on *The Counterfeiters;* Surrealism was about to be born out of the aftermath of Dada; and at that time and place, a twenty-five-year-old Ukrainian Jew, who—having fled

Russia two years earlier—had arrived in Paris by way of Constantinople, began to ponder the fate of Jewry and Judaism in the age of revolution, using a mode of fiction that harked back to Dostoevski and to the cognate traditions of social realism of the nineteenth-century Yiddish and Hebrew novel.

Haim Hazaz had nearly half a century of activity as a novelist still ahead of him, and after his emigration to Palestine in 1931 his work, with varying artistic success, would eventually reach out to encompass other continents, other cultural spheres, other communities of Jews. The traumatic events that he had witnessed in Russia in the fateful winter of 1917–18, however, were to remain at the heart of his imaginative world, for he would continue to brood over the Jewish hunger for redemption and the modern attempts to realize redemption through politics. In 1923 the Revolution was still being almost universally celebrated by the intellectual avant-garde in the West. Hazaz as a Hebrew writer was, one might say, acutely advantaged to see not only the vastness of the Revolution's messianic hopes but also its murderously destructive possibilities. If the Revolution, catalyzed and to an appreciable degree implemented by Jews, meant the end of the Jewish people, it might also mean the end of humanity as we have been accustomed to think of it. Over the years, as historical experience confirmed the rightness of this grim perception, Hazaz returned to the fictional material he had conceived in that distant Paris, working and reworking it.

The kernel of his novel, *Gates of Bronze,* first appeared in print in 1924 in the periodical *Ha-Tekufa,* as a series of fictional vignettes entitled "Revolutionary Chapters." In 1956 Hazaz radically revised and expanded these chapters into a short novel. In 1968, four years before his death, he published a new version of the novel, almost twice as long, with certain significant additions to the historical picture presented in the earlier material. As the book grew in length, Hazaz's conception of how he must handle his subject became firmer, moving away from effects of decorative elaboration through imagery and flaunted grotesquerie in the first version (qualities he would remain addicted to in other works) to a spare, concentrated presentation of the conflicts between classes, generations, and ideologies in the second version, finally rounded out with greater novelistic specification of scene and subsidiary characters in the final version. Specific episodes and characters, however, remain substantially unchanged through all three treatments of the subject; and there is one scene, retained from the 1924 story, that is, I would like to suggest, the vital central point from which this whole Hebrew imagination of the Revolution radiates.

A small knot of young comrades in the Ukrainian village of Mokry-Kut has just emerged from a political meeting held in the heady period of fervid debate and confusion of tongues that marked the first winter of the Revolution. At the meeting there has been a collision between Communist and anarchist views of the revolutionary situation. As these Jewish revolutionaries make their way through a midnight blizzard, the town itself seems to disappear in the storm. Then a spectral voice reaches them from behind the clouds of wind-whipped snow. It is, we will learn in a moment, the drunken chanting of Heshel Pribisker, the pathetic, uprooted Hasid, a religious instructor by profession with no children to teach any more, who has left his own wife and children and now dangles in desire for one of the young Communist girls while the iron wheels of revolutionary change move rapidly down upon him. At first, however, Heshel's voice alone is detectable, as though this sorry representative of the twilight of traditional Judaism were a mere sounding board for visionary words first intoned 2,500 years earlier. The words chanted by the stranded Hasid through the all-enveloping storm are those of the prophet Ezekiel: "One-third of you shall die of the pestilence . . . and shall perish of hunger in your midst, and a third shall fall by the sword round about, and a third will I scatter to every wind, and the sword shall pursue them."

Hazaz, let me hasten to say, was by no means a symbolic writer, and the midnight encounter between Heshel Pribisker and the young comrades is in context entirely continuous with the verisimilar representation of historically plausible figures and actions out of which the whole novel is shaped. The very choice of the Hebrew language to enact the clash between two generations of Jews in the throes of the Revolution, however, produces certain symbolic overtones, the words themselves sometimes leading us to see the paltry events of a few months in this forsaken *shtetl* through the magnifying prism of ancient visionary perspectives. It is precisely this peculiar feature that gives Hazaz's account of the crisis of Jewish values in the Revolution unique worth as historical testimony.

Hebrew literature on European soil had rarely been very subtle in the nuanced discrimination of character and motive, largely because it had no vocabulary for such fine discrimination and perhaps also because there was little in the culture from which it derived that might have trained writers to Jamesian or Flaubertian niceties of perception. (Hazaz is no exception to this general rule.) By way of compensation, Hebrew, because its own adaptation for secular literary ends sharply reflected the contradictory struggle with modernity of Jews steeped in tradition, provided an ideal instrument for probing the pathologies and potentials of historical Judaism in the modern era, and also for measuring the modern world against the values of historical Judaism. The effectiveness of this recurrent literary focus on a critical stage of historical transition was enhanced, for Yiddish as well as for Hebrew writers, by an accident of sociology—the fact that the

Jewry of Russia and Poland typically (though by no means exclusively) lived in *shtetlach,* provincial townlets predominantly Jewish in population. The *shtetl* was for the Hebrew and Yiddish writer more or less what the ship was for Melville—a ready-made microcosm, a social unit of limited scope, with established hierarchies and conventions, within which opposing views and conditions could be set in coherent relation as part of a cohesive fictional structure. Thus the imponderable forces of modernity could become fictionally manageable in the microcosmic conflict between the study-house hangers-on and a local *maskil,* or proponent of Enlightenment, in the grudging decision of a pious householder to bypass the matchmaker and allow his daughter to choose her own husband, and so forth. This concentration on the microcosm of the *shtetl* leads Hebrew and Yiddish writers in precisely the opposite direction from the European novel, which is impelled by the titanic aspiration to embrace, encompass, and dominate in language the vast inchoate reality of the modern metropolis, from Balzac's Paris and Dickens's London to Joyce's Dublin and Biely's St. Petersburg. The two novelistic traditions are, one might say, ways of scrutinizing the dynamics of history from the two opposite ends of the telescope.

Historical change is generally a corrosive presence, inexorably encroaching on the enclaves of piety, in the late nineteenth-century Hebrew and Yiddish fiction about the *shtetl.* In the revolutionary moment in which the action of Hazaz's novel occurs, such change becomes literally explosive: the first illumination of the *shtetl* in the book is from the flames of the aristocratic manors put to the torch by Sorokeh, the Jewish anarchist. *Gates of Bronze* explores the tensions and discrepancies between two competing views of the Revolution, one messianic and the other apocalyptic, both rooted in the language and concepts of Jewish tradition. The most dramatic expression of the messianic construction is voiced by Sorokeh at a New Year's party held by the young revolutionaries to inaugurate 1918. As the midnight hour strikes, Sorokeh announces that "at . . . this very moment, the whole world is crossing a frontier, traversing a line that divides all of human history into two. . . . The sun of capitalism has set —a new world has come into being—a world of social justice, of freedom and happiness, a world celebrating the grandeur of man." Sorokeh's image of history cut through by a critical dividing line at the point where he stands, with "everything that has gone before, the entire past for two thousand years, four thousand years . . . on one side," is central to the novel and to Hazaz's general perception of the modern predicament. What is at issue is whether the other side of the line hides the *atkhalta degeula,* the dawning redemption, as Sorokeh imagines, or universal doom, as the Ezekelian vision of Heshel Pribisker darkly intimates.

With an allusion to Dostoevski, Lionel Trilling once suggested that because the old conflicts between social classes had become blunted and blurred, the future of the novel might lie in the study of conflicting ideologies. *Gates of Bronze* is a rather pure example of this sort of ideological novel. Hazaz in fact sharpens the focus on ideological conflict by devoting so much of the novel's bulk to dialogue, with a bare minimum (particularly in view of his narrative procedures elsewhere) of authorial obtrusion around and between the long exchanges among the characters. What makes this book especially distinctive as an ideological novel, however, is the way in which the ideologies articulated by the characters repeatedly impose themselves as theologies in political guise. The choice of Sorokeh, the utopian anarchist, as the central character is wonderfully effective in precisely this connection because Sorokeh in himself is "a one-man party," a busy intersection of different ideologies with their sundry theological freight. It would have been temptingly easy for Hazaz, a Hebraist and a Zionist, to have introduced a clear spokesman for his own commitments in the novel, a Zionist Positive Hero anchored in the Hebrew heritage who could reprove the waywardness of the young Jewish Communists. Something of this is in fact done through Sorokeh, but in a historically complex, psychologically convincing way, because Sorokeh embodies so many of the baffling contradictions and ambiguities of trying to persist as a Jew on the other side of that great dividing line of history.

The young Communists who quickly become the administrators of the local revolutionary government have only a tenuous connection with their Jewish antecedents, while their professed ties with the Russian people are even more dubious, as Hazaz made clear in the final version of the novel by confronting the Jewish comrades with anti-Semitic Russian peasants (there are scarcely any gentiles to be seen in the two previous versions). Sorokeh, by contrast, recapitulates the various stages of ideological modernization undergone by Russian Jewry without really abandoning the earlier stages as he goes on to later ones. He is, then, the son of a yeshiva director, the grandson of an illustrious talmudist. Trained from an early age in rabbinical lore, he had lost the old faith, seized upon the new secular Hebrew literature, afterwards Russian literature, then the Social Revolutionary party, as modern instruments of salvation. But when, on the verge of World War I, the SR renounced terror as a weapon of revolution, Sorokeh turned anarchist. Psychologically he is a new kind of Jew, measuring the length and breadth of the *shtetl* with a machine gun tucked under his arm, answering a demand from the local Revkom chairman to show his arms permit by coolly drawing his pistol and pointing it with a smile at the head of the Bolshevik authority.

And yet we are reminded that his revolutionary fervor is continuous with the mystical fervor of his pious forebears; he quotes Yehuda Halevi as passionately as he does Kropotkin; and the interludes to his dreams of sweeping the world with a cleansing fire of destruction are the idyllic fantasies he entertains of going back to a sun-drenched, bucolic haven in the Land of Israel. Sorokeh's fitful imaginings were the only voice of Zionism in the two earlier versions of the novel. In the book's last revision and expansion, there is actually a Zionist movement in Mokry-Kut, the Tseire Tsiyon, and its presence gives greater substance and balance to the conflict of ideologies among the young generation of Russian Jews. Nevertheless, Hazaz remains true to the soundness of his first intuition in keeping Sorokeh with his confusions at the center of vision, so that in this historical maze of contradictory longings Zionism is plausibly an alluring—perhaps quixotic—possibility, not a pat solution.

Sorokeh the anarchist is driven on an unchartable zigzag course by passionate impulse; his Communist rivals follow a straight line of murderous abstraction. In the foreground of the novel, we see the purity of Sorokeh's motives; in the background, we get an occasional glimpse of the awful consequences of his utopian activism—in the rape and destruction unleashed upon the countryside by the anarchist bands he has helped to organize. As a voice in the ideological debate, what sets him apart from the Jewish Bolsheviks most decisively is that his feelings are still palpably in touch with the living Jewish people caught between the millstones of the Revolution. The older generation of that people is almost entirely a gang of bourgeois counterrevolutionaries, running-dogs of capitalism—that is, they are more or less the *shtetl* Jews of Mendele and Sholom Aleichem only a little more prosperous, not *schnorrers,* petty con men, and ne'er-do-wells but small shopkeepers, grain merchants, economic middlemen of varying sorts. They still have the same verbal mannerisms, the same comic nicknames, the same daily regimen of pious practices as the Jews of Mendele and Sholom Aleichem, but now they flounder in a bog of desperation, for everything on which they lived is being destroyed, with their own children zealously executing the iron purpose of the new regime. Incomprehension is their primary response to the revolutionary moment, and it is in its way a historically illuminating incomprehension. They simply cannot understand why their shops should be closed and their stock confiscated, why their homes should be invaded for a general search on the holy Sabbath itself, why some among them should be summarily arrested, beaten, even shot.

The Hebrew words they use in the novel to express their bewilderment impart to it a special historical resonance. In point of fact, such Jews would of course have been speaking Yiddish to one another. Hebrew literature in Europe, following the masterful example of Mendele, made the most of a supreme gesture of stylization, putting Hebrew in the mouths of speakers of Yiddish, exploiting the older language's rich texture of literary associations while trying to simulate in Hebrew the nuanced liveliness of the actual vernacular. Hazaz's novel is a culminating instance of this peculiar literary tradition, which means that even though the book was completed by a writer who had been living for decades in the new Hebrew-speaking cultural milieu, it is by no means modern Hebrew that the characters use with one another but the language of the Mishnah, the Midrash, the medieval exegetes, and the Bible, as it would be imbedded in a Yiddish consciousness.

This exchange between two study-house faithfuls at morning prayers is typical: " 'They just don't want us to live,' said Yankel Potchar hoarsely. 'I've heard that their *rebbe,* Karl Marx, was himself an apostate and a Jew-hater, and said all kinds of terrible things about Jews, as renegades always have. They say he left the Bolsheviks a *torah* called *Kapital,* where he preaches hatred for man-

kind, and permits stealing and bloodshed.' " The translation clearly suggests the unbridgeable chasm between the
mental worlds of, say, Rashi's commentary and Left
Hegelianism, though certain important overtones are
necessarily lost in the English. "Apostate and Jew-hater"
is *meshummad v'sone yisrael* in the original, two Hebrew
terms naturalized in Yiddish usage, habitually invoked in
both languages with a kind of spitting emphasis of contempt that could only be guessed at by speakers of a gen-
teel language like English. The conversational "said all
kinds of terrible things" is in the Hebrew *amar dilatoria
kasha 'al yisrael*—roughly, "viciously maligned the people
of Israel"—a turn of old-fashioned literary phrase that,
with the key Latin loanword, *dilatoria,* calls to mind early
rabbinic contexts and thus suggests that Karl Marx is only
the most recent version of an archetypal line of plotters
against Jewry going back to Hellenistic times. Yankel
Potchar's Hebrew formulation of revolutionary Marxism
is obviously a terrible simplification, but it is a simplification that firmly catches a brutal historical truth which
somehow continued to slip through the fine mesh of im-
measurably more sophisticated intellectual vocabularies
even during the Great Terror, the Doctors' Trials, and
more recent barbarities.

The response in context to Yankel's observation then
moves the argument from rabbinic lore and law to the
Bible and its exegesis: " 'Ye shall sow your seed in vain, for
your enemies shall eat the fruit thereof,' quoted Reb Avrohom-Abba, holding his beard and swaying mournfully.
'Scripture is talking about our children. We toil to bring
them up, and they turn around and choke us.' " In the
Hebrew here every single phrase, except of course for the
biblical quotation, is in perfect Midrashic idiom: the men-
tality nurtured by a long tradition of exegesis naturally
applies biblical texts to the present predicament, though
there is sour irony in that mental operation, in the use of

that vocabulary, since the present predicament threatens both to extirpate the tradition and to hound to death its upholders.

Sorokeh, as the chief focusing device of the novel's historical vision, provides a lucid perspective on these Jews of the Old World under the shadow of extinction precisely because his feelings about them oscillate between critical distance and intimate identification. Broadly, his sense of solidarity with the Jews is expressed in dialogue, in his debates with the other revolutionaries, while the angry criticism is generally reserved for his interior monologues, his debates with himself. This socialist-anarchist has no use for the Jews in their stance as "otherworldly spectators of history," alienated from nature, enmired in petty trade, adept in a thousand varieties of verbal ingenuity but impotent in the realm of practical action. His indictment is one that had been familiar in Hebrew literature since the days of the Haskala; it shares the vehemence of those early Hebrew-Enlightenment critiques, but the vehemence is now qualified with compassion. The obvious and sufficient reason for that change is the fact that in the historical moment of 1918 these idlers and obscurantists of the *shtetl* culture are catastrophically threatened by forces whose ruthlessness is infinitely more pernicious than their own shambling impracticalities. Indeed, Sorokeh is able to perceive in the Jewish fathers a kind of quixotic integrity that seems almost noble in comparison with the motives of their revolutionary sons and daughters. If the traditionalists with their long-deferred messianic hopes have an imperfect knowledge of their complicity in history, the revolutionists, giving their own lust for power the name of humanitarian idealism, exhibit an even more disastrous lack of self-knowledge.

I have been speaking of *Gates of Bronze* as an instructive historical testimony, but its assault on the contradictions of Jewish revolutionary universalism also makes it a compelling monitory text still relevant in the last decades of the twentieth century. The ideological debate between universalism and particularism is at the root of all modern Jewish history, and it is a debate that has had literally deadly consequences. Because this debate involves a collision between general ideas of history and concrete, individual human predicaments, perhaps the most effective formulation it could receive is in fiction, where fully imagined personages can struggle with ideas against a background of highly specified human situations. In the novel Sorokeh himself has universalist aspirations, and feels torn between them and his persistent Jewish loyalties, but he serves primarily to confront the young Jewish Communists with an inexorable historical fact: that national consciousness remains a stubbornly potent element in all human identity, including that of self-professing universalists; and therefore the Revolution, in which the Jews imagine they enjoy an equal role, is as Russian as the spires of Moscow or the knout.

"In the end reality will catch up with you," Sorokeh tells the Bolsheviks. "You'll have to pay for your illusions. The bill will be paid by the Jew each of you carries hidden within himself. These *goyim* will take it out on him with axe and pitchfork, as they have from time immemorial!" These words were first devised for the 1956 version of the novel; in the 1968 revision, Hazaz underscored this general emphasis later in the book by having a Russian peasant fire into the Revkom office, killing a Jew, with the cry, "Down with the commune of the *zhids*! Long live the rule of the Soviets!" The basic insight, however, was already present in Hazaz's first conception of the novel a scant half dozen years after the Revolution, and subsequent history has proven to be a series of terrible footnotes to this observation, from the countless Jewish universalists who died as Jews in the gas chambers and before the firing squads, to the hundreds of thousands of Russian Jews in the 1960s and 1970s desperate to leave the country at any cost because there is no place for them in Soviet society.

Both Sorokeh's special interest as a psychological type and his peculiar value as a voice of ideological critique derive from his cool confidence in the rightness of his own perceptions. This confidence is unshaken even when his perceptions lead him to be stigmatized with the labels that modern Jews fear above all else: chauvinist, nationalist, reactionary. He is, in other words, impervious to that force of moral blackmail which in our century has so often cowed intellectuals into positions of base political conformism, and consequently he is able to bring to bear a fine lucidity in the debate with the party-line Marxists.

One exchange between Sorokeh and Leahtche Hurvitz, the rather conventional Jewish girl turned Bolshevik who is the erotic center of the novel, brings us to the heart of his quarrel with the universalists. The dictatorship of the proletariat, he has been arguing from his twin vantage point as anarchist and self-respecting Jew, is a dictatorship like any other, and its moral character is especially transparent in the way it has set about crushing the pathetic, befuddled Jews of the *shtetl.* "These poor people have to pay for the sins of the bourgeoisie! Tell me, what hope is there for these poor lost Jews, what have they got to look forward to?" Elsewhere, Leahtche Hurvitz, like the other Communists, is willing to contend that the Revolution is beyond all considerations of morality, that if it requires colossal injustice, its redemptive power lies precisely in thus trampling upon the jaded values of the dead past. (The claim sounds like a late echo of Sabbatian theology.) In this particular discussion, Sorokeh's polemic insistence on the suffering of the Jews, always an irritant to Leftists, triggers a classic Leftist response: " 'I'm not a nationalist.' She shook her head solemnly. 'I'm for humanity as a whole.' " This grand declaration induces a peal of laughter in Sorokeh, then a dismissal of her words as foolish cant. Leahtche, much offended, reaffirms her position: " 'I don't care what you say . . . but I'm not a nationalist. I'll go further, I'm an anti-nationalist. I'm a Communist.' 'What a Jewish answer!' Sorokeh laughed again. 'No *goy* would say, "I'm not a Russian, I'm not a Ukrainian." Only Jews talk like that.' "

Certain words and ideas find uncanny echoes in unexpected places, perhaps because of their inevitability as historical perceptions. Cynthia Ozick, in a grimly powerful essay on the Jews, the world, and past and future holocausts, evokes a ghastly vision of the universalist victims of the Nazis, refusing to be categorized as Jews, their "charred bones . . . cry[ing] out from the gut of the ovens, 'You cannot do this to me! *I am a member of all humanity!'* " To this Cynthia Ozick adds, "Only Jews carry on this way," and then a devastating epigrammatic summary: "Universalism is the ultimate Jewish parochialism" ("All the World Wants the Jews Dead," *Esquire,* November 1974).

What a novel like *Gates of Bronze* might well do is lead us to reconsider the meaning of parochialism. If to be parochial is to be hedged in by the mental assumptions of your own limited parish, whether geographical, cultural, or ethnic, that in turn implies some grotesque, perhaps calamitous disparity between the terms through which you conceive of the world and the way it really is out there, in the historical moment which is yours to confront. The study-house Jews of Hazaz's novel are obvious and familiar parochials, almost comically so when they talk of the Bolsheviks' *rebbe* Marx and his *torah,* or when they imagine writing a letter to their Jewish brother, Lev Trotsky, to redress the injustices done them. Their Communist sons and daughters are far more self-deceived in their parochialism, but they, too, apply to the alien world a grid of assumptions unwittingly taken from their own group's experience and needs, and so in certain crucial respects they are even more incapable than their elders of seeing what is actually going on in the movement of history around them. Sorokeh angrily accuses them of being all too eager to make themselves the lackeys and mindless functionaries of a Revolution that is not ultimately theirs. As a point of historical fact, when the nativist managers of the Revolution no longer needed such a class of "universalist"— that is, non-Russian—zealots to do their administrative dirty work, that class was ruthlessly eliminated. The iron boot of Cynthia Ozick's epigram fits these young Jews of 1918 with painful precision.

The issue of revising notions about parochialism is raised not only within the novel itself but also by the anomalous facts of its composition in Hebrew. Hazaz's commitment in the Paris of 1923, after his flight from multilingual Russia, to go on fashioning an imaginative world in Hebrew—an eminently "parochial" language and at the time hardly a spoken one—must surely seem a peculiar choice to conventional ways of thinking. (It might be worth recalling what an illustrious line of East European expatriates—playwrights, poets, critics—has gone to Paris in this century and adopted French as their means of expression.) When "Revolutionary Chapters" first appeared, Hazaz could have hoped at best for a couple of thousand readers—a few brave coteries of Hebraists in Paris, Berlin, Vilna, New York, and the new, small centers in Tel Aviv and Jerusalem. Even by 1968 the probable readership for a Hebrew novel would not have increased by more than a few thousand. Yet after half a century this fiction first conceived in an almost-lost language for the perusal of the not-so-happy few possesses a cogent timeliness, and from our own vantage point seems to render the fateful historical juncture which is its subject with a persuasive fullness of vision. The same could hardly be said of the now quaint reams of effusions by "progressive" intellectuals in the sundry European languages during the twenties and thirties written to celebrate the achievements of the Revolution.

Hazaz, as I have tried to suggest, needed Hebrew in order to define his Jewish material with some profundity of historical dimension, to take its measure through and against the accreted meanings of its own distinctive terms; and, of course, he needed his Jewish material in order to describe the full impact of the Revolution at the point he knew most intimately and could probe deeply. Historically and imaginatively, there is a way of seeing out and around by first seeing within very keenly. The translation of *Gates of Bronze* offers readers of English a valuable opportunity to observe the operation of that paradox in fiction, for it is a novel which, by making scrupulous use of its inherited cultural and verbal materials, vividly shows how a supposed backwater of history could be a point where the most portentous historical currents converge.

BOOK ONE

1

It was not the biggest town in that part of Russia, and it was not the smallest. Mokry-Kut was an ordinary *shtetl*, huddled between the river and the forest, surrounded by peasant villages and fields. Chmielnitski in his time had passed this way, and later Gonte and his Haidamaks had come and reaped an equally bloody harvest. But still the big old wooden synagogue stood, its tiered roof giving it the appearance of a Hasid with a hat perched on top of his skullcap. There it stood, a grim reminder of days gone by, a warning of what was yet to come.

Mokry-Kut had always been a town of shopkeepers and peddlers, artisans and other plain Jews, each after his own kind, but all of them poor. To be sure, there were usually two or three who were a little better off than the rest. These would generally be appointed by the townfolk as community leaders.

Poor as the town was, it was rich in study houses, each the home of a *hevra,* a brotherhood dedicated to one beneficent purpose or another. There was a society for the study of the Mishnah, a *hevra* of Psalm-readers, a brotherhood for visiting the sick, another for dowering the bride, and of course the most powerful of all—the burial society, the mighty *Hevra Kadisha.*

At any rate, that is the way it used to be. But now times were changing. The study of Torah had declined, and Hasidic virtues were in eclipse. The ambitious young men of the town were becoming *externes,* busily preparing for the entrance exams to the *gymnasia,* the coveted Russian secondary school, and then going on their way. Those who stayed behind were the simpler types, tailors, cobblers, harness-makers, and the like, and when the Revolution came to Mokry-Kut, they eagerly took up its cause. "It's just like during the Yizkor service," quipped Reb Simcha Hurvitz. "All the young people have abandoned the synagogue."

His own daughter, Leahtche, had thrown her lot in with the young revolutionaries. She was a sharp-witted girl, with reddish-blonde hair and a captivating manner. Now she went about proclaiming the slogans of the day: "End the imperialist war!" "No more confiscations!"—and so on.

"What are you raving about?" Reb Simcha would storm. "Stupid girl! Silly fool! Who asked your opinion?"

"People ask," she would fling back, her cheeks aflame

with revolutionary fire. "They ask, and they'll keep on asking!"

Agh, a plague on the lot of them, may the cholera carry them off!

2

Those first days of the Revolution were heady days filled with promise, like blue spring skies, like distant hazy fields. People rushed about from demonstration to demonstration, their heads abuzz with dreams and hopes of peace and plenty, of a world of freedom and ease everlasting.

The people of Mokry-Kut knew little about what was happening in the distant centers of power. They heard that a man called Kerensky had become Prime Minister. They knew that a certain Lenin, who had spent his days in exile, had come back from Germany in a sealed train and had joined up with Trotsky—"one of our own." But they knew more about what was happening in the nearby towns and villages. In one place a policeman had been killed, in another an officer, here the peasants had burned down the landowner's house, there they had killed the squire and his family.

Sorokeh joined hands with the peasants, egging them on, even though they had no need of his advice, for they themselves knew what had to be done. But there he was, nevertheless, not only inflaming them with his words, but actually leading the mob into the fray.

Night after night the fires burned. Tchopovsky's estate

went up in flames, and so did Kovalevsky's, and Graf Bra-
nitsky's. The nighttime sky glowed like the dawn, the
smell of smoke was everywhere. The stars were hidden,
the moon could scarcely be seen. In Varnitsa the flour mill
heaved and groaned and church bells tolled throughout
the countryside, in Sloboda the dogs set up a howling.

Mokry-Kut stood alone, afraid, surrounded by the night.
Its people gazed at the flames on the horizon, and fur-
rowed their brows as at a difficult passage in the Talmud,
sighing, muttering, "Such things going on in the world!"

"It's all Sorokeh's doing," said Reb Simcha, standing in
the middle of the street, his eyes fixed on the red sky.
"He's stoking the fires of the Revolution, apostate that he
is! He has to take up the cudgels of the gentiles!" And
even as he spoke a great cloud of red smoke billowed up
to the sky.

So it went from night to night, for days and months on
end, all that summer long, until finally the landowners
were wiped out, and the peasants had looted their estates
and divided the lands among themselves. Whereupon they
began to turn on each other, neighbor against neighbor,
village against village. As for Sorokeh, who tried to make
peace between them, they sent him packing.

"Go to the devil's grandmother," they shouted, "don't
mix in our affairs. This is a matter for us *pravoslavi,* for
true believers, and no business of yours!"

One day the peasants of Bielosuknia attacked Mokry-
Kut and burned down the market. The flames touched off
many houses in the streets nearby, and they too went up.
And so Mokry-Kut was the first of the Jewish towns to feel
the hot breath of the pogroms, for this was before Petlura,
and Denikin, and the Polish hordes, and all the rest of
those roving bands that ravaged the Jewish communities
in the old Pale of Settlement.

3

One cold wet day, after the High Holy Days, Sokoreh came to town, a young fellow of medium height, intense and quick-moving, with tiny honey-colored, self-assured eyes. He sauntered down Post Office Street in an old greatcoat, a black lambskin hat jaunty on his head, dragging a machine gun and whistling the marching song of the anarchists.

His pals greeted him with great to-do. "Hey, Sorokeh," they shouted, sticking out their hands and slapping him on the back. "So you finished off feudalism, eh?"

The older people came toward him, scowling like black thunderclouds. "You!" they shouted. "You're the cause of our troubles! All your pity was for those hoodlums, kind soul that you are. But they had no mercy on us, they came and burnt us out!"

The womenfolk wept and wailed and cursed the *goyim* and Sorokeh and the Revolution, all in one breath.

"Who needed this Revolution?" they cried.

Sorokeh looked about for a room, but there was none to be had. Any rooms there might have been were all taken by the victims of the fire. Then he had an idea.

"Is the old bath-house empty?"

"It is, may the world be emptied of our enemies."

Sorokeh grabbed his gun. The crowd separated. "Off we go," he said, and headed toward the bath-house.

He turned down a narrow street, dragging the gun and

piping his song of the Revolution. A bunch of young boys trailed after him, joining in the song.

"Hey, comrade, where to?" said a sharp-faced youngster with impudent eyes. "Are you going to the old bath-house?"

"Yes, comrade."

"What a miserable place! It's full of ghosts and goblins. They'll keep you up all night."

"What? Ghosts?" Sorokeh pretended to be frightened.

"There aren't any ghosts," chimed in a pale youngster with a frost-reddened nose.

"There were, but they ran away to the capitalist countries," put in another, a freckle-faced boy with buck teeth.

"Right you are," said Sorokeh. "That's where they've gone."

"They were scared," laughed buck-tooth.

"That's it. Tell me, what are you doing out here?"

"It's recess."

"Students, eh?"

"What else?"

"And what do you learn?"

"Hebrew, Russian, math—the works."

"Do you have books?"

"We will."

"Notebooks?"

"We'll have them."

"Do you get anything to eat?"

"What a question! Whatever you want—jam, goosefat, cream, chocolate. Only, we have no appetite."

Sorokeh burst out laughing. "Nothing but the best."

"It's meant for the best," said the pale-faced boy, his nose redder than ever.

One of the boys pointed his chin at the gun. "Is that a Maxim? Give us a few bullets. Let's have just one."

By this time they were at the bath-house. A thin rain had started to fall.

"All right, fellows. Off to school."

The boys gave a shout and ran off pell-mell, like a tribe of savages on their way to war.

4

Sorokeh stayed in Mokry-Kut only a few days at a time. Once in a while he would show up, and then be off again. The townsfolk didn't know him, or what he was doing in their midst. They did know that he came from Novoselt-sovo, some distance away, and that he was the son of the head of the yeshiva there. They heard that his grandfather had been the great Rabbi Yitzchak-Eisikl, author of a learned Bible commentary. It was also rumored that Leahtche Hurvitz, Reb Simcha's daughter, was in love with him, and that was why he would return to town.

When Leahtche was asked about this, she denied it. "I swear," she laughed, "there isn't a thing between us."

"And what about those midnight prayers the two of you conduct by moonlight?"

"Just prayers," she grinned.

She sang his praises at every opportunity, saying that he was a wonderful fellow, one in a million.

"Really?"

"Oh yes. A pillar of the Revolution, an idealist."

"What do you mean?" they tried to draw her out.

"I can't explain. You'd have to hire an orator to tell his life story. All I can say is, he's a wonderful young man."

"Well, tell us, what party does this paragon belong to? That you surely know, Leahtche."

"What party?" She thought a bit, her lovely face prettier

than ever, with only a shadow of uncertainty passing over her lightly freckled cheeks. "He's a party all by himself."

"How do you mean? A one-man party?"

"Just what I say. He's an anarchist, and not just an ordinary anarchist, but an anarchist-individualist-internationalist."

"Quite a stew."

"Just wait and see. He'll be heard from. You'll see."

The bath-house had become a meeting place for the younger generation of Mokry-Kut. Young men and women would gather there every evening and listen while Sorokeh expounded his ideas. They would argue with one another in excited debate. Sometimes they would pass around a bottle of vodka in the fashion of their Hasidic forebears, or perhaps after the fashion of the *goyim,* to whom strong drink was no stranger.

5

The last generation of Jews before the Revolution suffered from an ever-increasing number of official restrictions. Among other things, the doors of the *gymnasia* were closed to Jews. Young Jews would study by themselves, take the state examinations, and promptly be disqualified. They would study some more, try again, and fail again. Meantime, most of them eked out a living by giving private lessons to Jewish children who seemed destined to repeat their teachers' fate. As time passed they became frustrated intellectuals, unemployed and embittered, spiritually footloose. Some of them joined one or another of the various illegal political movements and devoted themselves to underground work. Many were arrested and served time in prison, finding fulfillment in their dedication to revolutionary activity. That they abandoned the ways of their fathers goes without saying.

Sorokeh had studied Torah as a lad with his father, the head of the yeshiva. At the age of fifteen he had decided that the traditional Jewish way of life was not for him. At first he was attracted to the new secular Hebrew literature, then he became enamored of Russian culture, and finally he succumbed to Marxism, not surprising for a Jewish lad who had dreams of a better social order. Sorokeh then joined the Social Revolutionary party, the party closest to the common people and the most activist. Indeed, the SR's, as they were called, were the spearhead of the underground, fighting the czarist government not only with words but with deeds, with acts of terror.

But then, just before the First World War, the party had a change of mind, turning from terror as a weapon of revolution. Sorokeh was unhappy with the change. At secret meetings down by the river or in the forest, at the central committee, at celebrations where the young revolutionaries gathered to drink and to sing, he would give vent to his fiery ideas, demanding action, self-sacrifice, immediate revolution. When he saw that he was getting nowhere, he began to think about the anarchist parties. Finally he decided: "At heart what I really am is an anarchist."

In the meantime, the past began to stir in him. The Torah he had studied in his youth, his one-time love for the Hebrew language, these memories drew him back to the Jews and their problems. Moreover, the pogroms, the mass migrations to America, the outbreak of war and resulting expulsion of thousands of Jewish refugees forced from their homes by government decree—all combined to change his views. Now that the Revolution had been achieved, he looked for a political party to match the new needs of the hour and the scope of his dreams. Unable to find one, he sat down and composed his own manifesto, a heady mixture of Hasidic fervor and socialist doctrine and of indignation over the sufferings of the Jews and the poverty of the downtrodden *muzhiks,* the whole suffused with utopian idealism.

People listened; but only a few were convinced. Most remained skeptical. "That's because it's for real," Sorokeh would say. And truth to tell, he wasn't interested in attracting the masses, only a select few. One plan he shared with only a trusted handful: he would muster a hundred or a hundred and fifty young Jews, anarchists all, and they would sally forth to scour out the evildoers of both the Right and Left, and uproot the villages that had conducted pogroms, and frighten off the rest.

"One of these days," he confided to Leahtche, "I'll go to the Jewish farm colonies in the south, and recruit the followers I'm looking for, tough young farmers, as sturdy as any Russian peasant, and I'll turn them into an anarchist fighting force!"

That's what Leahtche meant when she said, "Just you wait, you'll be hearing from him."

Sorokeh was in Mokry-Kut for only a short time. Then he disappeared. Mokry-Kut stood forlorn, even more so than before.

"If only Sorokeh were here," the young men and women grumbled.

Leahtche went around like a lost sheep, and cried when she was alone.

The day after he left, word came that Bielosuknia had gone up in flames.

"Sorokeh's handiwork," the people of Mokry-Kut whispered to one another, without being sure whether it was good news or bad.

6

The townsfolk had not yet clapped eyes on a real live Bolshevik. Before there was an opportunity to do so, a band of Russian army deserters on their way back to the villages showed up in town. They lost no time in breaking into the houses and helping themselves to bread, liquor, and whatever else they could lay their hands on. They grabbed chickens and cooked themselves a meal in the marketplace over a bonfire they had made out of tables and chairs. Then they started chasing after women and girls, singing drunkenly, and shouting till the very heavens rang out. The soldiers professed to be Bolsheviks, but nobody in Mokry-Kut believed them.

"Huh! They're Bolsheviks like we're Bolsheviks, these sons of Esau!"

But a few weeks later Polyishuk arrived, and then they saw the real article. He came in an armored train on which a slogan was painted in big red letters: "Death to the bourgeoisie!" Nobody in town knew who he was or where he came from, but there he stood, a short thickset fellow, with broad shoulders, a heavy face, gray wrinkled eyes, and a nose like a driven nail. He wore a shabby old army greatcoat with a red patch on the breast, high boots, a rifle slung over his shoulder, and a revolver on his left hip.

Right away he called a meeting and made a speech. It wasn't a well-ordered speech, but he made himself clear. He told them in no uncertain terms that the provisional government had fallen, and the Bolsheviks had taken over. He himself, he said, was a representative of the Bolsheviks, and he had come to take charge of Mokry-Kut and environs. The war was finished, there would be peace all over the world. The social revolution was on, under the dictatorship of the proletariat. War on the palaces of the rich! Peace to the hovels of the poor! "Despoil the exploiters! Only those who work will eat!"

His listeners were stunned. "Did you hear?" they whispered to one another. "A born devil! May he rot!"

"Pheh!" they told each other. "A Jewish robber."

Just before dark Comrade Polyishuk walked into the house of Reb Simcha Hurvitz. Leahtche was there, and she jumped up in confusion.

"You have a vacant room," he commanded. "I'm taking it."

"Taking it? What do you mean, comrade?" Her tone was uncomprehending.

"Confiscating it for my own use." He didn't look at her, his eyes roving around the house.

"But comrade, didn't you say no confiscations?" He paid no attention, but unslung his rifle and banged it down in a corner.

After evening prayers, as Reb Simcha was returning from the study house, Leahtche went out to meet him. She whispered: "*He* is in our house. He has taken over the living room."

"Who? What?"

"The Bolshevik. Be careful what you say. Don't lose your head, for God's sake."

Reb Simcha went in, and found Polyishuk lying on the sofa. His greeting was ignored.

"Where is a Jew from?" Reb Simcha sat down at the table. Still no answer. Reb Simcha waited a few minutes, and tried again.

"And what brings you here?" He might as well have been taking to a stone. Reb Simcha wavered. "Have you come to pluck a shorn lamb?" he tried to jest. Still no answer.

"Well then," said Reb Simcha, getting to his feet. "You're a roomer in my house, a regular tenant. Nu, enjoy it. I wouldn't have given the parlor to anybody else. But you . . . well. . . ."

7

A few days later four or five young toughs, arrived and put themselves under Polyishuk's command. The people of Mokry-Kut described them as scum. These fellows seized power in all the neighboring villages, and proceeded to impose the decrees of the Revolution. Some of the local young people, seeing which way the wind was blowing, joined up with them.

There were three who opposed them, who became known as Mensheviks: Hirshel the clockmaker, Nachman the tailor's apprentice, and Avremel Voskiboinikov, who had been a helper in Pomerantz's store. They had never had anything to do with politics or intellectual matters, but now they opposed Polyishuk out of sheer contrariness, and having taken the step, they held fast to their course. They came to every meeting the Bolsheviks called and shouted and heckled, though what they said was often a confused jumble and nobody knew what they were driving at, even they themselves. But there was one point that everybody did understand. "Where's the Constituent Assembly? Power belongs to the Constituent Assembly!"

The Bolsheviks and their followers would heckle back. "Noodles!" they shouted. This was because Hirshel the clockmaker and Avremel Voskiboinikov had traded in noodles during the war. They had hoarded the stuff, and driven up the price. Now they were greeted with the mocking chant "Noodles!" every time they opened their mouths.

Polyishuk raged against them. "In-tel-lec-tu-als!" he spat out the syllables. "Yes indeed! Friends of the people! We've got your number!"

He swore that he would tear them up by the roots, he would leave no trace of them, meantime exhorting his hearers to guard the dictatorship of the proletariat in the Jewish ghetto, to defend the banner of the Revolution to the end, to the last drop of blood.

Leahtche got caught up in the matter, too. At first she disliked Polyishuk. He paid no attention to her, never greeted her, but kept to himself, like an enemy in the house.

"An odd fellow," she would say to the neighbors. But bit by bit she won him over, and soon the two of them were taking walks in the moonlight. "They have important matters of state policy to discuss," people would say to one another with a knowing wink.

Occasionally at the meetings Leahtche herself would get up to make a fervent speech, always ending with the slogan: "No confiscations! No forced levies!"

It got to be a joke. Every time she rose to speak she was greeted with, "Nu, when do we get to the confiscations and the levies?"

The people of Mokry-Kut submitted to every new restriction and ukase, as their fathers had before them. As usual, they tried to blunt the edge of catastrophe with wry humor. "The same old Torah," they sighed, "only with a new commentary."

The Revolution was not turning out the way they had expected. They had thought it would improve the lot of the Jews and usher in a time of equality and freedom, but it turned out to be harsher than anything their forefathers had experienced.

"A revolution?" they muttered. "It's more like a pogrom, God forbid."

What shocked them more than anything else was that this was being done to them by young Jews, their own flesh and blood. "Good God! Where did they come from? We never raised our children to be murderers!"

The first thing the Bolsheviks did was to close off the Jews' source of livelihood. They took over the marketplace and made every kind of trade illegal. For a while some stores were open, some closed; then open at the back door but closed at the front. You could see the storekeepers flit furtively in and out.

Next, the Bolsheviks demanded an inventory of the miserable stock that was left, and confiscated most of it. But worst of all was when they started making arrests. Hayyim-Meir Shklianka was caught trading in a bit of sugar, and was sent to jail at the district capital. Then they picked up Reb Yakov-Yosef Lifshitz in his house at midnight, and took him away too, to be dealt with as a *burzh-uk,* an enemy of the people.

The townsfolk were thrown into a panic. After all, they were just like Hayyim-Meir, petty traders who eked out a living from dealing in a bit of this and a bit of that. They could all be arrested as *burzhuks!*

Now was the time when the people of Mokry-Kut desperately needed a spokesman. They couldn't send any of the old community leaders, who were the very ones in trouble. They talked it over, and picked two spokesmen: Kalman the baker and Bunem the tinsmith. They reasoned that these two stood a good chance, since they were both workingmen, proletarians you might say. They added the Rabbi to the delegation, and sent the three to see the commissar.

Kalman the baker was in good spirits, his face glowing as though he had just baked three oven-loads. Bunem looked like a chicken that had just been nabbed in the barnyard. The Rabbi walked with bent head, like a man burdened under a heavy weight, fear reflected in his eyes. Kalman was the chief spokesman, with Bunem to back him up, while the Rabbi rolled his frightened eyes, smiled wanly, nodded his head, and said nothing.

Kalman the baker began addressing Polyishuk and his henchmen.

"Comrades! We are the emissaries of the Jewish community, good hard-working people who deserve to be well-treated. . . ."

Polyishuk cut him short. "What's all this about?"

"About? You mean you don't know? Why, it's about the men who were turned over to the authorities!"

"So?" Polyishuk glared. "What business is that of yours?"

"Business of ours? What do you mean, are we Jews or aren't we? Whose business is it if not ours? Have a little mercy, treat us like brothers."

Gates of Bronze | *18*

"Redemption of captives," murmured Bunem the tinsmith with downcast eyes.

"Yes, friends, that's it. Redemption of captives is a great *mitzvah,*" Kalman added, with a learned air.

"It'll save you from purgatory," Bunem put in helpfully.

"He's right, you rascals, you'll be saved from Gehenna. Nu, fellows, don't turn us down, you have the power, you can do anything you like. Comrade Polyishuk, I know that everything you have done has been for the sake of the commandments, that is, for the *mitzvah* of Revolution. Now I beg you, set aside your good intentions and save two Jews. Go against your principles; that should be easy for you, since you are a heretic, a deliberate sinner."

Polyishuk paid no attention to what was being said. He looked at the ceiling and spoke slowly. "Do you know who you're pleading for? For two dyed-in-the-wool counterrevolutionaries, one a trader and the other a *burzhuk!*"

A change came over Kalman the baker. Now he looked like a cantor chanting the Kol Nidre confession.

"Ah, Father in heaven," he sighed. "Hayyim-Meir a trader! All his life he's been dirt-poor, his whole crime is two pounds of sugar. And as for Reb Yakov-Yosef, he's a fine Jew, charitable, scholarly—I wish we had more like him. And what if he had a little money, he's no Brodsky. His million was certainly short by a few kopecks. And when you consider that his store was burned down, and he's been left with nothing, nothing at all! So there, you see, he's broke now, like the rest of us."

He might as well have been spitting into the wind. It was no use, no use at all. The three of them left with their tails between their legs.

"That's it," sighed Kalman the baker. "What a fix we're in! Look who's lording it over us."

"Worse than the *goyim,*" said Bunem the tinsmith. "Hard, cruel men. The likes of them haven't been seen since Sodom and Gomorrah!"

The Rabbi trailed after them, each hand stuck into the opposite sleeve. "Oy, *Ribbono-shel-Olam!*" He looked up into the flurry of snowflakes. "O Master of the Universe, what can we do? Who will take pity on us? Where can we turn?"

9

On those nighttime walks with Polyishuk, Leahtche learned all about the Revolution. She was instructed in the fine points of Marxist theory, the reasons for the split between the Bolsheviks and the Mensheviks, not to speak of the SR's, the internationalists, and the rest of the petty-bourgeois democrats. She heard about the teachings of Lenin and Trotsky, and to her it was all a revelation.

"Now I understand the whole thing!" she exulted. "Now everything falls into place!"

She found out from these talks that Polyishuk had grown up in the Party. When he was still a youngster, working as a helper in a flour mill, he used to distribute underground leaflets. Later, when he had become a locksmith, he had joined the Party. "I've been a member of the Party for a long time," he said, with just the proper tinge of pride.

She learned that he had been wounded twice during the war, and still carried a bullet in his thigh. He had been court-martialed for propagandizing among the troops, and the Revolution had saved him from a death sentence in the nick of time.

Leahtche swallowed his teachings whole. She worked hard at fitting everything that had happened into his theories. He kept up the indoctrination, until she understood that the fate of humanity was being decided now, right now. The Bolsheviks were in a life-and-death struggle, no half measures would do, there was no such thing as a half revolution, and there could be no revolution without suffering. She ought to realize that things were going to get much worse, that everything that had gone before had to be swept away like so much rubbish—all the past with its certainties, all the old ideas of right and wrong.

"Look," he explained, "the Revolution doesn't care about the dignity of the individual. The individual doesn't count, and that includes the whole middle class, with most of the intelligentsia thrown in. The proletariat is the only master, it will rule the world, its time has come."

But the victorious Revolution still had work to do. Its enemies were many, they were everywhere. It had the workers behind it, and the soldiers, but the army was now breaking up. As for the villages, they were unreliable. The SR's were undermining the Revolution in the villages, the Ukrainian nationalists were doing their dirty work, and the more affluent peasants were out for themselves. The situation in the villages was one of counterrevolution through and through. It was no place for decrees, for expropriation. No. And especially now, when the soldiers were returning from the front with weapons in their hands.

"Do you think I came here to bother with your miserable Mokry-Kut? I came because of the villages around here, that's why!"

It was then that Leahtche blurted out, "There's a comrade here who's been working with the villagers."

Polyishuk stopped in his tracks. "Who?"

"Sorokeh, a fellow called Sorokeh."

"A Bolshevik?"

"Almost." Leahtche hesitated, a bit afraid. "Actually, an Anarchist. An interesting fellow."

"Hah! An enemy of the people." Polyishuk spat out the words.

"You must be fooling. Sorokeh an enemy of the people?"

"A rotten intellectual!"

"No, no, he's a hundred-percent revolutionary, as sure as two and two make four. Why, he's well thought of by all the peasants. Together they burned out the landowners all around here."

"So what? In 1905 didn't they burn out the landowners?"

"That was a long time ago. Look, he may come to town soon, you'll get to know him."

"We know that bunch, we know them."

10

Reb Simcha and Polyishuk were like two cats tied up in a sack. One wore a constant scowl, the other ignored him. Reb Simcha kept out of the way, while Polyishuk made himself completely at home. After a while, Reb Simcha decided that this was no way to do things. He went into the parlor to see Polyishuk.

"Tell me," he said, half asking, half protesting, "is all trading illegal from now on?"

"Exactly."

"Then what do we do with the stock we have?"

"It's not yours any more. We've confiscated it." The tone was measured and ominous.

"What, may one ask, will we eat?"

"You'll eat the fruit of your evil deeds," answered Polyishuk.

Reb Simcha wouldn't let go. "But listen, we're human

beings, living, breathing people. We can't just sit and starve. How are we going to make a living?"

"How does that concern me?"

"What do you mean, how does it concern you? You're the ones who cut off our livelihood and seized everything we had. What happens to us now is your responsibility."

"All right," said Polyishuk, adopting a tone of reasonable compromise. "All right. We'll figure out a nice death for you people."

Reb Simcha puckered up his lips. "You people? Who does that mean?"

"All counterrevolutionaries, all the *burzhuks* and enemies of the people."

Reb Simcha thought that one over. After a few moments he asked quietly, "Is that the law?"

"That's it," said Polyishuk with finality.

"And who is a *burzhuk?*" asked Reb Simcha. "Everybody who has been robbed and had his blood sucked out?"

Polyishuk waited for the rest of it.

"And I suppose everybody who commits assault and robbery qualifies as a proletarian, and he's the man for whom the world was created?"

Polyishuk fixed his cold eyes on Reb Simcha without answering. It was a terrifying gaze. Reb Simcha seemed to shrink, his hands helpless at his sides. He shook himself and left the room, his head bowed, his heart pounding.

From then on he was deathly afraid of Polyishuk.

"An evil beast," he would whisper to people, "chief of all the devils. A cruel, murderous, ruthless robber!"

He was incensed at Leahtche, who danced attendance on Polyishuk, cooked his meals, made his bed, and swept his room.

"Sweep, sweep! Crawl for him!" he raged at her. "God willing, he'll bring you great honor. May I be a false prophet when I say that we Jews will shed oceans of tears on account of him, God forbid."

People began to talk about Leahtche. The womenfolk would ask her about her boarder, and she would praise him. "A utopian fellow!"

"Really? Utopian?" They had no idea what the word meant.

"And how does he compares to Sorokeh?" This a little slyly.

"Sorokeh can stand on his own two feet," she answered with a quick little laugh, "and Polyishuk on his."

"Aha!" they mocked. "One a sheep and the other a goat. Best comes first, and last is best."

Some of the women were pleasant, but others gave her an argument.

"The world is burning, everybody's in trouble, only you are happy. Look at her, rejoicing like a Kotzker Hasid!"

When she heard that, Leahtche launched into a speech, as if she were on a soapbox. She lectured them about the Revolution, its laws and commandments, and told them that Polyishuk was a fine person, a good social democrat, a regular revolutionary saint, a *tzaddik*.

"Tzaddik, tzaddik," they flung back at her. "He's a *tzaddik* like you're a *tzaddik.*"

11

Things got worse and there was talk in the community about declaring a public fast, but the leaders kept postponing it. "There's time," they told one another. "This is one bit of business that will keep."

But time went by, and the three arrested Jews were not released. In fact, three more respected members of the community were seized and taken away. Then all kinds of new decrees were announced, one more oppressive than the other. There was a shortage of food. Everybody was cold and hungry. Finally, the leaders of the community proclaimed a day of fasting.

It turned out to be a beautiful day. There had been a blizzard the night before, and the sun shone brightly on the newly fallen snow. The houses were white mounds, here and there an eave or rooftop showed through. There was no sign of streets or crossroads. Everything was a solid blanket of white, stretching beyond the town across the fields clear to the forest, a shadowy bluish tinge in the distance. A few narrow footpaths wound their way through the quiet drifts, while here and there a grotesque fencepost stuck out its head in the surrounding stillness. The sky seemed higher than ever, bluer than ever, with only a few fleecy clouds overhead.

In the old synagogue a handful of Jews had gathered, in heavy furs and sheepskins. Some were sitting, others were walking up and down. There was a low hum of conversation, the usual small talk worn thin by constant repetition. Each said to the other what the other would have said if he had gotten in the first word.

"People are late," said Yankel Potchtar, tugging at his impressive goatee, his eyes darting around the room.

Reb Ozer, nicknamed "Hagbeh" because he had a habit of tugging up his trousers, interrupted his own chanting of the Psalms. "They'll get here!" He pulled up his belt with both hands and gave Yankel Potchtar a sidelong glance over the top of his spectacles.

"What do you think, will the fast day save us?" Yankel wagged his beard at him with a grin.

"It—will—save us!" Reb Ozer retorted firmly, drawing himself up to his full stature, hands on hips. "We'll make it a regular little Yom Kippur, with penitential prayers and everything."

"A little Yom Kippur?" This was Kalman the baker, standing there in his icicled sheepskin. "We'll make it a full Yom Kippur! We'll storm the heavens! Because if we don't get mercy from on high, why then, God forbid, 'Man perisheth,' as the Good Book says."

"If only," sighed Yankel, "if only He would plant some good thoughts in the hearts of those comrades, so that they would cancel all those evil decrees."

"They'll never do it!" burst out Kalman the baker, as though he were quarreling with his fellow Jews. "They'll never change their minds, no, not ever. Why, when I went to see them with the Rabbi and Bunem—"

Eisik Koysh turned to them, his massive beard covering his face, and stamped the snow off his feet. He was wearing high felt boots.

"Gevald! . . . gevald!" The syllables dropped like water into a rain barrel. "Gevald! Woe! Beasts of prey, flint-hearted murderers! If only the earth would swallow them up!"

"Oy, oy!" Yankel Potchtar brought his palms together in despair. "How can we survive? How can we ever survive?"

"We'll survive," Kalman the baker told him. "We have a Father in heaven."

"Good God!" Yankel Potchtar was jittering from the cold, and his breath came in frosty puffs. "How good life would be if it weren't for those nasty little Bolsheviks. Ai, ai, ai! Bread and meat and milk, a herring with potato, and even a glass of tea, with a fire burning in the stove."

The congregation was beginning to gather. In came Reb Itzia Dubinsky, followed by Reb Simcha and Reb Avrohom-Abba.

"Late," Yankel chided.

"You're the early birds." Reb Simcha hardly threw him a glance.

"Early is what a *mitzvah* calls for," Yankel grinned.

Reb Avrohom-Abba stopped to have a word with them.

He was a tall thin man, with a pale face and a scraggly beard. There was something about him reminiscent of an autumn day before sunup, when the air is heavy with wisps of fog, and the roosters are crowing, and there's a smell of stagnant puddles all around.

"Well, Yankel, how are things?" he asked, knowing full well that Yankel was engaged in a little forbidden trading.

"Alive, but not making a living," answered Yankel. "You know what Scripture says, 'I shall not die but live.' Well, the first part I'm managing; as for the second—like trying to part the Red Sea."

"And what about the special tax?" interrupted Kalman the baker, presuming on his new status as community leader. Reb Avrohom-Abba let the question hang in mid-air.

"We'll pay up, as our fathers did before us." The answer came from Ozer Hagbeh, pulling himself erect, hands on hips.

Yankel Potchtar jumped up. "We'll steal from *them,* and pay it back to them. What else can we do?" Reb Simcha turned away and went to his regular place in the synagogue.

Reb Itzia Dubinsky stood heavy in his bulky foxskin overcoat, caracul hat, and galoshes, a bewildered expression on his face. "Fast days," he mumbled, shrugging his shoulder.

"Heh . . ." Yankel took the cue. "These new fasts of ours."

"What do you care?" cut in Reb Avrohom-Abba. "Either way there's nothing to eat."

"The shame of it!" groaned Eisik Koysh from behind his huge beard. "What troubles made us declare this fast? Who's the enemy that brought this on us? Haman the villain? Titus the wicked?"

"Our own children did it." Ozer Hagbeh nodded mournfully. "Our very own! Shall we cry out to the Good Lord and say, 'Our children have sinned against us'?"

"Who ever heard of such a thing?" breathed Eisik Koysh. "A fast because of persecution of Jews by Jews!"

Reb Itzia Dubinsky opened his mouth as though to speak, but said nothing. Instead he walked over to his prayer stand and stood before it with his head bowed.

Heshel Pribisker came in, and Yankel Potchtar rushed over to him. "Ah, Heshel! What do you say, Heshel, hah? What honor the Holy One has brought to us! A public fast. . . ."

Heshel Pribisker walked into the circle. He was a tall handsome man, head and shoulders above the rest, dressed in shabby old clothes, a woman's scarf, unraveled at the edges, about his neck.

"The public and the individual are one and the same," he said glumly, his eyes roving around the group.

They didn't take his meaning.

"It's a decree in the Torah of Marx," explained Yankel Potchtar with a learned air. "According to Marx we don't qualify as God's creatures. Sodom, that's what it is. So-dom! That stands for So-cial Dem-ocrat—So-dem!"

"In the past," said Heshel Pribisker, "we had penitential prayers when there were conflagrations and wind-storms. Now we need *selichos* on account of the Revolution."

At that point several members of the congregation banged on their prayer stands. "Time for prayers!" they called out.

"Yes, yes," the members of the group nodded. "It's a fast . . . a fast."

"The first of its kind in all history," threw in Reb Avrohom-Abba.

Three or four members of the congregation banged again on their prayer stands. "Nu! Nu!" they moaned, as they wound their *tefillin* around their arms, and wrapped their prayer shawls over their heavy coats.

12

Polyishuk was something new for Leahtche; she couldn't figure him out. What's this fellow got? she asked herself.

On the one hand, he was not good-looking, no intellectual, neither a thinker nor a speaker, no poetry in him; a thorough child of the Revolution. Power!

Power, that was it. He was a man of action, getting things done, giving orders, making decisions, and punishing anyone who disobeyed the iron will of the Revolution, contemptuous of the majority, of their pleas and even of their hatred of him. He alone, against all the rest, the take-charge man; always on the job, spreading his forbidding authority over the villages, setting up village councils, binding them to the Revolution. Never quiet, never at rest. A regular seething Sambatyon River. That was Polyishuk.

All right, that's what he was. But what was he like inside, in his heart? She thought about it for a week, for ten days, for two weeks. Meantime his mouth uttered words, his feet walked alongside hers. How they walked! She heard every crackle of the snow under their feet.

Several times she found herself alone with him at headquarters of the Revolutionary Committee, the Revkom, but she never heard one personal word, not even a hint of one. All he talked about was the Ukrainian villagers, the Revolution. That's all that mattered to him. Not that she had anything against him. Goodness, no! Not at all. But he certainly bore no resemblance to the man of her dreams.

This was nothing like the hero of her imaginings, certainly not in appearance. Oh well! . . . but still . . . what a man of ideas, what flawless ideology, what persistence. And yet . . . there is a time for everything. Surely there must be a time for casual talk, for personal exchange. Doesn't everybody need to confide in somebody, to talk about his sorrows, his hopes, his longings, his inner feelings? But no! That was not for him.

There were times when they fell silent, and you might have thought there was some sense of intimacy in their silence. There were times when his hand seemed to touch hers, touching yet not touching. But then, back to the struggle against the SR's, the Ukrainian nationalists, the anarchists. For him, the only happiness in life was the total victory of the Revolution.

She would have liked to know what he thought about love. Had he ever loved a woman? She doubted it, and she felt sorry for any girl that might fall in love with him. It wasn't easy to fall in love with such a man. It seemed to her that he never gave a thought to women. He certainly didn't know anything about them. Come to think of it, he didn't know anything about people in general, male or female. Maybe he had no love for anybody, for the whole human race, workers and peasants included. What were they to him? Human beings didn't count for anything with him. The main thing was the idea, and the act that fulfilled the idea. For the sake of the Revolution he was ready to take life, even the lives of masses of people. She recalled what he had said: "The Revolution doesn't care about the dignity of the individual."

"But that's a mark of greatness," she defended him to herself. "It's what the times call for. It's a revolutionary virtue!" Whereupon she reproached herself for this whole train of thought. What business did she have mixing love and revolution? These were no times for a man to busy himself with romance. After all, the individual can wait, but society can't wait. At least, not until the Revolution was securely in power.

And yet, she said to herself half complaining, there are things he doesn't understand. . . .

Once, when she was alone in the room, sitting bent over a sheet of paper, he came in and asked her something or other, glanced at the paper, put his arms around her, kissed her on the lips, and was gone. Just like that.

The incident didn't affect her much; it certainly didn't excite her or set her heart pounding. But it did leave her sitting with an odd expression on her face.

"So"—she wiped her lips—"that's something. Even a bit more than something." She ran the back of her hand over her mouth again, and laughed.

Nu-nu. All beginnings are supposed to be difficult, but here's one that was easy. She laughed. What an artist! Done like a real Bolshevik. I suppose it's a good sign for a Bolshevik to be brazen.

And now she was eager to know what lay in store for her. Her imagination brimmed with romantic thoughts. Scenes from novels she had read by Turgeniev and Tolstoy, by de Maupassant and Hamsun flitted through her daydreams, as she pictured what was going to happen to her. Her reveries raced ahead to a mixture of happiness, little crises, gay ones, soon past; to jealousies and hurts and final reconciliation in true love, a mighty love that would take her by storm and sweep her away.

She waited for things to happen. Surely they would happen soon. No, no, a determined hell-bent fellow like Polyishuk would not waste himself on nonsense. She knew him. He would come, and fall down at her feet . . . who knows what he might do . . . he was drunk with love. Ah, in affairs of the heart she was smarter than he. Besides, she was rational about the whole thing, she was not carried away, because after all, he wasn't her type.

"All right," she thought, "we'll see."

And see she did. Polyishuk didn't come. On the contrary, he seemed to have lost interest. He ignored her, he didn't even greet her. Leahtche had her own interpretation for his behavior. It only proved, she told herself, that something was bothering him, and she was sure she knew what it was. Day after day, when he cut her dead she would laugh inwardly, confident of the end result.

Polyishuk became busier than ever, always on the road haranguing the peasants, trying to get them to set up village councils. He always came back bone-tired and in a dark mood. Whenever he returned, the atmosphere at Revkom headquarters would change. The comrades would fall silent, bending over their paperwork with special diligence. He would stalk about the place, barking at this one and that.

Oh, my dear, Leahtche would whisper to herself, you're overdoing it, overdoing it!

She was quite sure that all this turmoil was on account of her. He was fighting her. But she would prove stronger than he, in the end he would give in. So let him rush around like a wild man, seething and storming.

"The fellow has lost his heart." She sat there, sorting her cards and files, smiling to herself.

13

Four of the town's Jews were arrested as hostages, because the community had not paid the collective tax. They were Reb Yitzhok-Yakov Kleinman, Reb Osher Zaslavsky, Reb Shimen-Yosef Liberman, and Reb Nachman Spektor. They were sent under guard to the district capital.

Mokry-Kut was stunned. People stood in little knots in the street between the piles of snow and talked about the new blow that had befallen them.

"One evil decree follows another," sighed Reb Itzia Dubinsky, stamping his feet in the cold. "Barely a week since Reb Yakov-Yosef and Reb Hayyim-Meir were taken, and here's a new catastrophe! Gevald! What will happen next? It's on account of us they were arrested! Yes indeed, 'All Jews are responsible for one another.'"

"*Sloboda,*" said Reb Ozer Hagbeh. He meant *svoboda*—freedom—but his Russian was not very good. He tugged at his trousers, and a puff of vapor issued from his mouth.

"Such is the Revolution and such its reward," remarked Reb Avrohom-Abba, adding two steamy wisps to the frigid air.

Yankel Potchar dropped his voice and wagged his beard like a wise old billy goat. "They'll finish us off, God forbid. They'll skin us alive. Oh, I see it coming. They'll choke us one by one." Then, frightened by his own words, he lowered his head and glanced up and down the street.

"Gevald, gevald, who will take our part?" moaned Reb Itzia Dubinsky, still prancing in the snow.

"The Revkom has the power," said Reb Ozer.

"Nu?"

"Nu!"

"Agh! A wasted effort," said Kalman the baker with a wave of his hand. "Who runs the Revkom? Polyishuk! No, he'll never revoke the order. I know the fellow. When I went to plead for Reb Yakov-Yosef I was taking a big chance, believe me! I nearly got myself hauled before the *shtab,* the staff to combat counterrevolution."

"Yes, he's the one," agreed Bunem the tinsmith, stabbing the air with a half-frozen finger. "It all comes from him, he's our sworn enemy."

"It was bad enough when we were persecuted by the *goyim,*" complained Reb Avrohom-Abba with a deep sigh.

"Yes, we were pushed around by the Czar's policemen. But to be under the thumb of this one. . . ."

Reb Simcha stood off to one side, perplexed and fearful, his hands thrust into his sleeves. "Nu-nu," he whispered to himself sadly.

One by one they drifted off. The street was empty. Behind the houses, draped in icicles, the snow banks rose up sharply. All was silent. The sun lay hidden, and the whole world seemed one damp chilly gloom. It was as if earth and sky no longer existed, and the world had ceased to be a place of human habitation. From somewhere deep within a narrow street, a sound broke the stillness, a woman's scream, as though coming from a house where someone had just died.

14

The community sent another delegation to Polyishuk, this time to explain why they had been unable to pay the collective tax. The delegation came back empty-handed.

"A heart of flint," they reported.

"Let me tell you what I said to him," said Eisik Koysh. He had been picked because he was a wagon-driver, and his sons were tailors and shoemakers. "I said, 'Boys, you can't get blood from a stone, or manure from a pile of clinkers. They simply don't have the money. You know they don't have it. They'd be glad to pay if they had anything to pay with.' "

"Nu?" his listeners pressed.

"Nu! I was preaching to a deaf man, the devil take him!

We thought we could bargain with him. Hah! He wouldn't listen to a word. Just dismissed us, kicked us out. Now, you know me, I'm an old horse, the whip doesn't scare me. 'What?' I said. 'Can't we bargain a little? What is this, a one-price store, a pharmacy?' "

"And he wouldn't give an inch?"

"Not an inch," boomed Eisik, "not a kopeck."

It seems the delegation had kept on trying to get the tax reduced, until Polyishuk had pulled out his revolver and yelled at them, "I'll let you have it with this gun unless you get out of here right now!"

The community leaders, which is to say all those respected citizens who had lost their livelihoods, called a meeting. They made another assessment on the town's Jews, and raised the amount each would have to pay. This gave rise to arguments. "Highway robbery!" the people complained. "What are we, grist for the mill? Where are we going to get the money? We've been burned out, and the government has confiscated whatever we had left. We're not earning anything. Where are we going to get the money?"

On top of that, the wives of the those arrested came and protested. "Give us back our husbands! Robbers! Murderers! Their blood will be on your heads! Pay whatever the government demands, and get us back our husbands!"

Reb Simcha left the meeting in a rage. He didn't find Leahtche when he entered the house, but he could hear her voice from the parlor, talking pleasantly to Polyishuk.

"Where are you there, may the black year carry you off!" he shouted toward the door.

"Just a moment," Leahtche called out, standing up and continuing her conversation.

"Not just a moment! Right now!" Reb Simcha stormed. "This instant!"

"What's the matter? What happened?" She came out, bewildered, her palms a question mark.

"What happened indeed!" Reb Simcha's mouth was twisted with anger. "What are you doing in his room?"

"What am I doing?" She was completely taken aback. "Nothing."

"I said, what are you doing in his room?" Reb Simcha clenched his fists and took a step in her direction. "I don't want you anywhere near him. Do you hear what I'm telling you?"

"Sh-sh-sh!" Leahtche was frightened. She put her finger to her lips.

"You heard me!" Reb Simcha was trembling with rage, his arms were waving wildly. "You're to keep away from him!"

"What's the matter?" Polyishuk had come out of his room.

"Nothing, nothing," said Leahtche, desperately trying to calm things down.

Reb Simcha turned his face away from them and muttered angrily, "A plague."

"What's wrong with you, old man?" grinned Polyishuk.

"Plenty," growled Reb Simcha.

"Calm down."

Reb Simcha reacted as though he had been stung. He turned on Polyishuk. "What's that you say?" he shouted.

"Come away, father, come," Leahtche pleaded.

Reb Simcha brushed her aside. "Calm down, is it? You rob me of my store, you take away my living, you arrest decent Jews, you levy a tax we can't possibly pay, you treat us like our worst enemies never did—and then you say calm down!?"

"Nu-nu, old man." Polyishuk dropped the word of warning coolly, almost absentmindedly.

"Father . . . listen, father. . . ." Leahtche was clutching

at his sleeve, and signaling Polyishuk to go back into his room. Reb Simcha pulled his arm away from her.

"Nu-nu you say? Nu-nu what? Are you threatening me with a pogrom? Go ahead! Break up the furniture, smash the windowpanes, rip up the featherbeds! What, you'll kill me? Kill! It's not much of life anyway. Get out of my house! Criminal! Hooligan! For the time being it's my house! Get out! A plague on the whole business! A cholera!"

15

Word of the incident spread. The townspeople could scarcely believe it. "Did you hear?" they said to one another.

"I heard."

"Nu?"

"Nu-nu!"

"What do you say about Reb Simcha?"

"What do you want me to say? He did a beautiful job!"

"Imagine, he said those things to him, and the fellow kept silent!"

"He said what had to be said. What a contrast with his daughter's behavior! He must have gotten away with it on account of her."

A few at a time they would slip over to Reb Simcha so they could hear the story again.

"What's new, Reb Simcha?"

"Nothing."

They would sigh deeply. "Troubles."

"We have no lack of those," Reb Simcha would sigh in agreement.

"What about that tenant of yours? He could be useful. . . ."

"Let him be useful to a draft of poison!"

"Why? What's the matter?"

And so, bit by bit, they would draw him out, and he would repeat the whole story, while they stood glued to the spot, wide-eyed and open-mouthed.

"That's what you said to him?" they would gasp.

"Just like that!" Reb Simcha was beginning to enjoy his role.

"You mean you said those very words to his face? And he didn't grab you, he didn't arrest you? He didn't do a thing?"

"He acted deaf, dumb and blind. He wiped his mouth, and sh! Not a word!"

Three days later Polyishuk moved out of Reb Simcha's house into the house of Reb Mordkhe-Leib Segal, which he declared had been confiscated for his own use. Reb Mordkhe-Leib didn't understand what was going on.

"Are you dispossessing me?" he asked.

"Possession belongs to the dictatorship of the proletariat, and to nobody else," Polyishuk decreed.

Mordkhe-Leib still couldn't understand. He started to argue, he asked for justice and fair play, then he pleaded for mercy, and finally he demanded his rights. Polyishuk drew his revolver and shouted at him, "Twenty-four hours! After that I don't want to see hair or hide of you or yours around here."

Sheindel, Reb Mordkhe-Leib's wife, ran out into the street and raised a hue and cry. She would uproot graves in the cemetery, she screamed, she would tear open the ark in the synagogue.

The people were sorry that Reb Mordkhe-Leib had been thrown out of his house and wondered why Reb Simcha had gotten such different treatment. Nobody would put the answer into words, but they rolled their eyes knowingly.

Heshel Pribisker had been rooming with Reb Mordkhe-Leib, so he too found himself out on the street. Not having any choice, he moved in with Reb Simcha. The fact is there wasn't a corner of living space available in all of Mokry-Kut, except for Reb Simcha's parlor.

16

The comrades turned the long, boring winter nights to good purpose. They entertained themselves by playing cards and dancing to accordion music. They danced the polka, the quadrille, the *krakoviak*, the five-figured lancer, and the Ukrainian *hopak*. Finally Shimtze danced the *lezginka*, skillfully employing his hands and head, his shoulders and hips, leaping into the air with a click of his heels, swirling around in a storm. Everybody applauded.

"Devil take him!" the young men said admiringly. "He's better at the *lezginka* than at political economy."

"A real artist," said the girls, their eyes shining as they fanned their flushed cheeks with their kerchiefs.

Polyishuk frowned on these nocturnal festivities. He preached serious behavior, befitting revolutionaries. They ought to be studying Marxism, not enjoying themselves. His words went in one ear and out the other. In any case, they had no Marxist books, and no one to teach them.

From time to time Polyishuk would call a meeting and deliver a lecture. He would launch into current politics, attacking the Rada—the Ukrainian National Council—for backing the Social Democrats, and he would denounce the Social Revolutionaries, the Social Federalists, and other middle-class parties, enemies of Bolshevism. These, he said, were propagandizing the villagers, fighting the agrarian policy of the Bolsheviks as laid down by Lenin in his theses, and were distorting the class consciousness of the workers. From the very start, he argued, the Rada had joined hands with the Provisional Government of Kerensky in order to preserve the status quo, and to establish autonomy for the Ukrainian bourgeoisie.

"They're using hunger to stifle the Revolution," he shouted, waving both fists. "Remember what Lenin said: 'The struggle for bread and the struggle for socialism are one and the same!'"

He informed them that revolutionary committees of soldiers had been set up, to fight counterrevolution and to establish proletarian democracy everywhere. In Kharkov, he said, the council of workers and peasants had expelled those of its members who were Mensheviks and SR's, and had appointed Bolsheviks to fill the vacancies. In Tchuguiev a revolt of junkers had been put down by force.

Then he went on to tell what was wrong in the villages. The supply of grain was disappearing from the farms, and what was left was being turned into home brew, *samogon*. The work of political education was being neglected, the peasants didn't understand their role in the Revolution. He demanded that the comrades go out to the villages to take charge of the struggle against counterrevolution.

They argued with him. "What do we townspeople know about village affairs?"

"The only effective leaders would have to be peasants themselves."

"Besides, there's Karpo, and Ilko, and Zabolotni, and the others."

The argument went on, until Shayke and Mayerke jumped up and volunteered to go out to the villages from time to time, and look the situation over. Having disposed of the matter, they shuffled the cards, and started several games of *oka* and *stukalka*.

Polyishuk stopped Leahtche on her way out. "Mere talk," he said. "They won't really do it."

Leahtche looked surprised.

"Sit down," he said.

"Why, what's the matter?"

"Sit down."

She did so, reluctantly. "But on condition that you behave yourself."

"Haven't I been behaving myself?" He acted surprised.

"No."

"In what way? Because I kissed you?"

She didn't answer.

"How can a kiss spoil things?"

"When it doesn't involve the heart."

"A kiss doesn't decide anything."

Leahtche was offended. She gave him a hurt look. Seeing it, he said, "That only proves how young you are."

His last remark stung her deeply, and she looked at the floor. They were silent for a few minutes and then he gave a laugh. "Forget the whole thing."

"I'm willing to forget a lot of things, with one exception."

"And that is?"

"That I'm a respectable girl."

"You're a sentimental girl," he answered. "You're a romantic."

He began to pace up and down the room. Leahtche looked up at him. "Comrade Polyishuk. . . ."

He half turned toward her.

"Tell me," she said innocently, "is it true that you don't love anybody in the whole world?"

He let the question hang in midair, as though giving it thought. Then he walked over to her, seized her, and held her tight. At first she was frightened, helpless. But when he pulled her up she began to struggle with him. He tried to kiss her, but she twisted her head wildly from side to side.

"No!" she cried out. "I don't want to! No!"

He took his hands away from her waist, seized her face, and kissed her savagely.

She straightened up and slipped out of his grasp. She stood at the doorway panting, hair disheveled, cheeks aflame, hat in hand.

"A lot of nonsense," she breathed, wiping her hand across her mouth.

Polyishuk stood there bewildered.

"Yes, nonsense," she repeated. "You kissed me, comrade, all right, you kissed me. So what?"

He looked as though he were about to pounce on her.

"You started at the end," she laughed in his face, and ran out the door.

17

Before the Revolution, while the war was still on, Mokry-Kut had been a place of refuge for men who didn't want to serve in the Czar's army. The local authorities had made a good thing out of it, collecting a monthly fee from them, but otherwise leaving them alone. As a result, Mokry-Kut became a favorite hideout for these "rabbits," as they were called, and nobody raised an eyebrow. When Heshel Pribisker was called up, he too became a "rabbit." He came to Mokry-Kut as a temporary resident, and took up his regular calling, for he was by trade a teacher of Jewish children, a *melamed.*

He was a tall man in his thirties, with bright eyes and a longish brown beard, an active type, mercurial by temperament. He had left his family behind in Pribisk, since after all he was only a temporary fugitive. But when the war was over, and he didn't seem in any hurry to go home, tongues began to wag. People speculated that he was unhappily married. Some even went further, and suggested that the devil had him by the earlock. "The *melamed* has lost his heart to Leahtche," they winked. To be sure, the gossip was confined to the womenfolk and the lower orders, who would add in shocked tones, "A *melamed,* a Hasid, a married man and a father—what's he doing involved in a love affair?"

Then they would settle the matter to their own satisfaction by sagely quoting a Russian folk proverb: *"Liubov nye kartoshka,"* which is to say, "Love is not a potato."

Since he had come to town, Heshel Pribisker had made a habit of dropping in on Reb Simcha, sharing a drink with him on special occasions, and a glass of tea on every occasion. The two of them had plenty to chat about— words of Torah, Hasidic talk, tales of the Besht. Often they would sing a *niggun* together, as Hasidim are wont to do.

In spite of all this, Reb Simcha was not very happy when Heshel moved into his house.

"We're crowded as it is," he grumbled. "There's no room to turn around in."

Now and then he would question Heshel. "What keeps you in town? How is it you don't go back to your family?"

Heshel always managed one way or another to turn the question aside. But Reb Simcha persisted.

"The war is over. There's no more conscription."

"Don't press me," Heshel answered in a distracted tone. "Don't press me."

"What do you mean?" Reb Simcha countered. "Don't you see I'm only asking because I'm interested in your own good. . . ."

"Do me a favor," Heshel interrupted, "and don't take pity on me. I hate pity. Just be kind enough not to be sorry for me." And before Reb Simcha could answer, Heshel went on. "You're not really being kind, you're being a judge! You're passing cruel, harsh judgment on me because I'm a lowly creature, full of troubles and faults, good for nothing!"

All Reb Simcha could do was shrug his shoulders and whisper to himself, "Ah, good God in heaven!"

18

It was cold in the big parlor. The two double windows were partly boarded over and stuffed with rags. The clock on the wall was silent, its idle pendulum leaning at an odd angle. Under the clock stood a shabby old sofa with the stuffing coming from between the slats. Nearby was an ugly old bookcase, slightly askew. It was loaded with books of all sizes, worn and moldy books, obviously much used. A painted *mizrach* hung on the wall above the bookcase. Its lions and reindeer looked like no creatures ever seen on earth.

Between the sofa and the bookcase there was a mirror, cracked and discolored. One glance into it was enough to turn your stomach.

Reb Simcha sat with his back against the cold stove, hunched up in a fur coat that was coming apart at the seams, each hand thrust into the opposite sleeve. On the table in front of him stood a bottle and two small glasses, along with several potatoes in a deep dish. Meanwhile, Heshel Pribisker was pacing up and down, his overcoat and scarf wrapped around him. The floor creaked with every step he took.

All day long Heshel had been disturbed, filled with gloom and foreboding. All sorts of thoughts had been nagging at him. Sometimes they seemed to be getting him somewhere, but most of the time they only added to his gloom and confusion. He paced the floor up and down, muttering to himself in a barely audible singsong.

"But is it not written . . ." He repeated the words, only now the emphasis shifted, and the tone changed, as though he were arguing with himself.

"Is it not written, 'Man is like unto vanity'?" And again: "Is it not written, 'If we willed it, we could vanish from the world'?" And finally: "Is it not written, 'A single purely spiritual hour is better than all the material pleasures of earthly existence'?"

He came to a stop in the middle of the room, one arm limp at his side, palm open. "Ah! Go blow the shofar in the graveyard!" he muttered despairingly, as though he were talking to the floor.

He straightened up and went over to the table. "Nu. . . ." His beard flicked at the bottle and the potatoes, and a sardonic gleam lit up his hungry eyes. "Thank the Lord, we've got everything we need. As Scripture says, 'Thou hast made man master of all creation'!"

He comforted himself with a glass of whiskey. His whole expression changed, as though life were now worth living. "There we are!" He dried his mustache with two fingers, and added bitterly, "Fine! Like the High Priest in all his glory!" Then he took up his march around the room.

He was talking to himself, his head hunched between his shoulders. "I'm sorry for you, brother. Spending your days so uselessly. . . ."

"What are you mumbling about?" Reb Simcha looked up.

"Who's mumbling?" Heshel retorted, still pacing the

floor. "That's not mumbling. That's the cry of a drowning man . . . out of the depths."

"Nu. . . ." Reb Simcha sounded unconvinced.

Heshel went over to the table again, and poured himself another glass. A smile tangled with his mustache, and the wicked gleam came back into his eyes.

"Tell me," he said, "this Heshel Pribisker, what do you make of him?"

Reb Simcha rolled his eyes. "I would say, the fellow's tipsy."

"Bah!" Heshel gestured the thought away, and started his pacing again. "You're talking nonsense."

Reb Simcha looked straight at him and made a pronouncement: "The commandment says that a person should behave properly in everything he does."

"Good God!" Heshel shouted. "Don't pick on me!"

"Who's picking on you?" Reb Simcha looked away. "I only said it was a commandment."

"Commandment! Don't I know?" Heshel exploded. "The whole world is falling apart, everything has gone haywire, and he and the likes of him go on as if nothing had happened. They keep gnawing at tired old words that have long since been chewed to death. Bury themselves in Torah until you can almost see the mold! Don't talk to me about commandments!"

The outburst shocked Reb Simcha. "So things have gone that far!" he said in a queer whisper. "You've lost heart! Why, you . . . you're as bad as them . . . no! . . . worse . . . like Korah and his rebels!"

Heshel dropped into a chair and gulped down the whiskey. "Korah . . . the world's first Bolshevik." He showed his teeth in a nervous grin. "Him the earth swallowed up. But now. . . ."

He broke off, and began chanting, "A psalm of the sons of Korah. . . ." He stopped short, closed one eye, and winked with the other. "Who knows what they are cooking up right now."

Reb Simcha shrugged. "I'm surprised you sit here, huddled up to my cold stove. Why don't you go and join them? Go ahead, get in on their robbery and bloodshed. Enjoy yourself while you're still alive."

"I might have done just that, if the Torah didn't forbid murder. 'Thou shalt not kill,' you know."

The two of them sat there for a while, silent, each buried in his own thoughts. Heshel had his head in his hands. "What's becoming of us?" he muttered. "What's going on? Is it real, or is it all just a nightmare?"

Leahtche came in from her job with the Bolsheviks. Her cheeks were rosy from the cold, her eyes sparkled cheerfully. She took in the scene, her father, Heshel, the bottle between them. "Aha," she said. "Been making *Kiddush,* I see. For most folks once a week is enough."

"Be quiet!" Reb Simcha scolded her.

As for Heshel, a change came over him. He straightened up, he brightened. His face, pinched with hunger, took on a touch of color, and his beard arranged itself around a gentle smile.

"Maybe you can tell me," he said, "what's happening to us? What's to become of us?"

Leahtche had no reply. She took off her coat. "You're quite drunk, Reb Jew," she said. "Feeling no pain, I see."

Heshel gave her the friendliest of smiles. "Well, I guess I am jollier than my situation calls for." Leahtche burst out laughing, and Reb Simcha chimed in.

Heshel suppressed a pleased smile. "Tell me," he said, "what's new? What are you people planning to do next?"

"You're better off not knowing," she evaded the question. "If folks told everything they knew we'd all be in a bad way."

"I suppose so." He looked at her with a mixture of bewilderment and affection. "But tell me, what's it all leading to? Our rulers hold us in fear, and they're downright atheists as well. Right, Leahtche?"

She stood with her hat in her hand, so that you couldn't tell whether she was coming or going.

"Now you're taking up the cudgels for God. Very nice of you."

"Not for God," Heshel shot back, pouring himself another glass. "For myself."

Leahtche grinned. "Now you're talking. I suppose that calls for another drink."

"Chatterbox!" Reb Simcha flung at her. Then he turned the full force of his anger on Heshel.

"Look at him! He's taken over the whole parlor. A person hasn't got room to turn around in the house!"

Leahtche left the room. Heshel went over to the window and stood staring at the opaque patterns of thick frost.

Reb Simcha sat there, huddled up in his shabby fur coat. A deep sadness covered his face, like the look on the face of a Jew when he chants the haunting melody of the weekday evening prayer.

19

As a Hasid, Heshel was used to strong drink. Every day he downed a glassful at the synagogue, and if not there, with his meal. Occasionally he would sit with a group of Hasidim around a bottle while they told stories about their *rebbe.* But now he began to drink to excess, not for the sake of a *mitzvah,* or to celebrate an occasion, but on account of his troubles. He was trying to forget his tangled problems. His world was cracking up, a world that had been all of one piece, compounded of Torah and prayer, reverence and piety, and Hasidic exaltation. The truth is that there were cracks in his armor even before the Revolution. His piety had cooled, his faith had diminished, his learning had begun to fade. Now the Revolution had shaken the whole structure of the traditional Jewish community. Its loyal adherents were now old men on the edge of the grave, treated like so much excess baggage, not to be reckoned with. They were pushed off into a corner, like those torn pages of holy books that are stored away until they can be given decent burial.

Heshel was caught in the middle. Willy-nilly he was affected by the atmosphere of the Revolution. The old and the new struggled within him, the past and the present. Still, he could not throw off his past, and he remained outwardly what he had always been—a Hasid in dress and deed and everything.

It pained him to see Jewish loyalty and solidarity disappearing. Above all, the central support on which everything else depended—faith in God and his Torah—was crumbling. More than once he had engaged in conversation those young Jews who were tyrannizing the community, and tried to reason with them. "Easy, fellows, you don't have to be overbearing. After all, we're not a people of looters, we're not murderers. We're the seed of Abraham our father."

They brushed him off. "Leave us alone!" they shouted, raising their fists.

There was a further affliction, an unexpected one. He was smitten with love for Leahtche. It was a first love for him, a secret love, and it gave him no peace. He knew full well that it was hopeless, Leahtche would never give a thought to a Jew with beard and earlocks and a long black coat. Of course, he never whispered his love to her, as lovers do. He never gave a sign or a hint.

Just the same, the thing was talked about, it was common knowledge. How? That question is easily answered. There were simply no secrets in Mokry-Kut. The townsfolk themselves admitted this. They used to say that they knew what was going on in Gehenna itself.

Heshel suffered in secret. He was tormented by his yearning for Leahtche, and devoured by jealousy, first of Sorokeh, and then of Polyishuk. A number of times he had intended to tell her how he felt. But he could never find the words. He would stand there helpless, a look of supplication on his face.

"What is it?" she would ask. "What's happened to you?"

"Leahtche," he would stammer, at a loss for words.

She could see that something was amiss. He looked like a drowning man.

"Queer creature," she said in Russian, her tone a mixture of pity and puzzlement. *"Tchudak tchelovek."*

20

Leahtche began to avoid Heshel. She would slip away whenever he came around, and shy from the slightest exchange of words. But she didn't stop preparing food for him, or making his bed. She was sorry for him.

Heshel pretended not to notice, although he knew why she was behaving this way. He even tried to change her attitude.

"What's the matter?" he asked. "Why are you so unfriendly?"

She didn't answer.

"Is it because I'm beneath you?" he asked with a bitter smile. "Because I'm not a proletarian, neither a shoemaker nor a laborer nor a murderous *goy?*"

She kept quiet, and brushed past him. He followed her out of the room to where Reb Simcha was sitting.

"I suppose we are now considered flax," he said in a strained voice, "while *they* are pure wool, and the two can never mix, since the Torah forbids it."

Reb Simcha looked up. His glance went from Heshel to Leahtche, who was standing at the open sideboard. "Don't worry," he said, "linsey-woolsey is allowed in making shrouds for the dead."

Leahtche, busy with some household chore, joined in. "How a person sleeps depends on how he's made his bed."

Reb Simcha wasn't sure whether this was an idle remark, or whether it had some meaning he hadn't fathomed. In any case, he scolded her. "Keep quiet! The devil knows what you're cooking up."

"Well . . ." Leahtche began to speak, then shrugged, and started out of the room. On her way she glanced at Heshel, whose eyes were fixed on her. "What are you staring at me for, like a turkey at the slaughterer?"

The remark cut through the air, and she was gone.

Reb Simcha sighed and murmured to himself, "Impudent girl, may God preserve us!"

He closed one eye and dropped his lower lip, lost in thought. After a bit he spoke. "A world gone lawless! Brazen girls, crazy . . . they do whatever comes into their heads!"

Heshel began to pace the floor. The house was heavy with silence, filled with gloom, dim in the twilight. Outside a winter storm moaned, the wind rising at times to a screech.

Heshel came to a halt in the middle of the room. "Ah,"

he said to Reb Simcha. "If you only know how low I have fallen, how I suffer in body and spirit."

Reb Simcha was seized by a fit of coughing. "Satan is after you," he managed to choke out.

Heshel bit his nails. "What I need now is a *rebbe,*" he said softly, sadly. "One who would draw me close to himself. But the truth is, there isn't a real *rebbe* left in the whole of the Ukraine."

Reb Simcha sighed deeply. Slowly he got up and went to fetch some kindling for the stove.

A dim half light, streaked with some color from the setting sun, filled the parlor. Heshel rubbed off a small space in the frost on the windowpane and began to recite the afternoon prayer. When he came to the words "Forgive us our Father, for we have sinned," he bent low, and a tear fell on his beard.

21

The time came when Heshel Pribisker was earning next to nothing. Indeed, the demand for his services had begun to dwindle even before the Revolution. The parents of his charges had been satisfied with a few chapters of Bible with Rashi commentary, or at most a bit of Talmud. But even with this reduced instruction the boys had been unwilling students and would duck out of classes whenever they could. Now that Polyishuk had turned a baleful eye on religious education, the Hebrew school had closed down completely, and Heshel was left without work.

He didn't seem to mind. He had already decided that there was no future in being a *melamed.* His needs were limited, and he eked them out by tutoring on the quiet three or four boys of good family. "Grit your teeth and hang on!" he said, downing a glass to bolster his courage.

"Hang on, hang on," Reb Simcha mimicked, shaking his head. "Look, you've got nothing left here. Why don't you go back home?"

"Leave me alone!" glowered Heshel. "I'm not going back! I had fifteen years of hell there. Even sinners in purgatory only suffer twelve months. I had fifteen years!"

Reb Simcha sighed. "Well then, what's the solution?"

"Solution? What makes you think there's a solution?"

"Ai-ai," Reb Simcha intoned sadly. "Look at you—homeless, down and out, drowning in strong drink. What's to become of you? Before you know it you'll be pawning your prayer shawl for a bottle of whiskey."

The room fell silent. Reb Simcha sat in his place beside the stove, looking lost. Heshel was at the table, supporting his head in one hand and gazing woefully into space. After a while he straightened up and said with forced cheerfulness, "What's the good of all this gloom?"

He filled two glasses, one for himself and one for Reb Simcha. "We've been talking a lot of nonsense!" he said with a wave of his hand. "The thing is, hang on!"

They lifted their glasses, recited the blessing, repeated "Amen" one to another, and drank, each in his own fashion. Heshel downed his drink in one gulp, Reb Simcha sipped slowly, closing his eyes and smacking his lips after each swallow.

"That's it." Heshel Pribisker wiped his mustache. "After all, thank God, I'm not a murderer, or a robber, or an adulterer. I'm a man who spends his time on Torah and prayer. I've been a God-fearing man all my life. I put on *tallis* and *tefillin* every day, and fulfill the rest of the commandments. True, I haven't accomplished much, but still . . . *lehayyim!*"

He poured himself another drink, tossed it off, and

started pacing up and down, chanting to himself, "Even though . . ." He stopped, thought for a minute, and took up his chant, ". . . just the same . . ." Several times he repeated the phrases, as though engaged in a dialogue with himself.

Bit by bit his face clouded over, his brow wrinkled, his eyes widened as thoughts chased themselves around in his head. He began to mutter Aramaic phrases from the Kabbalah. "*Raza da* . . . this mystic truth . . . even as in the upper regions. . . ." It sounded like a delirium. "Male and female . . . this is the hidden truth . . . male and female as one . . . the mystery of all mysteries. . . ."

Reb Simcha stared at him. "What are you saying? It doesn't make any sense".

Heshel didn't seem to hear. He stopped and bit his fingernail. "That's how God runs His world. He created everything for the sake of that, and that for the sake of everything else." He started to pace rapidly.

"Poor restless man!" said Reb Simcha. "Look at him, a torrent like the Sambatyon River."

"What's that?" Heshel focused on him. "All you can see is that I'm in deep trouble. You have no idea, brother, what's in my heart."

He stood still, bathed in rue, staring at the floor. "Something . . . has been revealed to me," he stammered, "but I don't know . . . what it is." Reb Simcha turned away.

"God in heaven, give me strength!" Heshel was pacing again, furiously. "Now I'm . . . now all of us are coming to the end . . . of everything . . . to the last frontier, where Israel is finished, God forbid."

Another drink, and then another, and he began to quote. " 'The end hath come, an end hath come. . . . Behold, the day of tumult is nigh, and not of joyful shouting upon the mountains.' Great words, hah? 'Let not the buyer rejoice, nor the seller mourn.' "

He turned on Reb Simcha with a bitter laugh. "Ezekiel is talking about you! 'Let not the seller mourn.' That's you!

'For wrath is upon all the multitude thereof.' Ezekiel, the very essence of prophecy, my friend, the penetrating eyes of the world."

Reb Simcha was shaken. He clutched his head to his hands. "Stop running around the room!" he shouted in a high-pitched voice. "Stop! You're driving me crazy!"

22

Reb Simcha stayed home. He earned his bread by a little secret barter with bits and pieces salvaged from the inventory of the store he had owned. He wouldn't go out, for fear of the Bolsheviks. Most of the stores had been burned out, and in the marketplace you hardly ever saw a peasant, drunk or sober, much less a sack of grain, or potatoes, or a cabbage, or anything to sustain life. Besides, Reb Simcha was afraid for his life. How was he different from Reb Yakov-Yosef, or any of the others who had been hauled off by the Bolsheviks? Wasn't he the same kind of respected pillar of the community? His blood ran cold when he remembered his last conversation with Polyishuk, the way the fellow had looked at him with that murderous cold rage, God preserve us!

Nobody knows how the rumor got started that the Bolsheviks wouldn't last beyond the summer. Reb Simcha heard the rumor and made up his own mind; he gave them only till Passover.

"Their regime can't last," he comforted himself. "They'll soon come to a bad end."

Heshel Pribisker didn't agree. "No, you'd better brace yourself. A lot is still going to happen here."

"What's the matter with you? Don't aggravate me, you hear? I'm only flesh and blood. Everybody has his limits, I can only take so much!"

"What's wrong?" Heshel seemed surprised.

"Now that's *chutzpah!*" Reb Simcha was in a rage. "You and your idle chatter! The devil knows what you're saying! You don't even listen to your own words yourself!"

Three or four of Reb Simcha's cronies would drop in from time to time, and they would sit around cursing the Bolsheviks. The lowest of the low, subhumans, really, said one. "When a slave becomes master," said another, quoting the old proverb. The epithets grew stronger when the talk turned to Polyishuk—bastard, apostate, Haman, boor, ignoramus.

Yankel Potchtar applied the midrash on Canaan, son of Ham, who was said to have instructed his descendants to observe the following five commandments: "Love one another, love thievery, love whoredom, hate your betters, never speak the truth." He claimed that the Bolsheviks fulfilled all five to the letter.

"Theft and robbery in their purest form," he went on, "as permitted by the bible of Marx, their master, even as it is written. 'Exploit the exploiters, rob the robbers!' "

Yankel was in full swing, savoring his own sarcasm. "They're simply carrying out the doctrines of Marx, their *rebbe,*" he said, grinning with enjoyment at his own ingenuity. "The Bible says, 'Turn aside from evil,' and they've given it a brilliant new interpretation. As for their reading of 'and do good'—what's the use of talking, they've come up with a new gloss, a stroke of genius! An extraordinary new morality!"

When Reb Simcha spoke up, he sounded the way the revolutionaries once did, when they poured fire and brimstone on the government of the Czar. "Robbers is what they are! Gangsters!" His beard trembled, the wrinkles on his pale face twitched. "They're shedders of innocent

Gates of Bronze | *56*

blood! Enemies of the people! They're the ones who are the enemies of the working class! They rob, they do violence, they abolish trade! Who put them in charge? Did they ask the people? Did anybody vote them into power?"

"Not everything has to be voted on," said Heshel Pribisker quietly. It wasn't clear whether he was expressing his opinion, or just being contrary."If the Ten Commandments had been put to the vote at Mount Sinai, I'm not sure they would have gotten a majority."

"Pheh!" said Reb Simcha contemptuously. "Three thieves and two loafers and one lame watchman set to mind the garden patch! A handful of men have made themselves masters of the whole country!"

He continued shouting in this vein until he was spent. Then, with a sigh that shook his whole body, he lapsed into his former state. "Ai-ai," he moaned, " 'The Lord is nigh unto the brokenhearted. He will save them that are humble of spirit.' "

Heshel Pribisker gave an ironic grin. "What good sense can't handle, time will cure; and when neither will work, a verse from the Bible comes to the rescue."

23

Reb Simcha had mixed feelings about Heshel Pribisker. He was bothered by the fact that Heshel didn't go back to his wife, and he resented the bouts of drinking, the strange mutterings. On the other hand, he was glad to have company in this frightening time of troubles, of hunger and cold and loneliness. It was especially good to have him there at twilight, between the afternoon and evening prayers, when sadness lay heavy on the heart, and one choked back bitter tears. And most of all at night, when the two of them sat alone by the light of the little wick, while the wind howled outside, rattling the shutters and the shingles and moaning down the chimney, so that the whole world seemed to be storming against that little house.

But now Reb Simcha sat alone in the room, head down, his beard spread out over his old fur coat. Everything that weighed on him had already passed through his mind. It all added up to the fact that the world around him was reduced to poverty, there was no bread to eat, no wood for the fire, life was a misery, and even at that was only sustained by a miracle.

Again and again he thought about Leahtche. In normal times she would have been married by now. What was he to do? Where could he find her a suitable husband? There wasn't anybody in town worth considering. The young fellows had all become wicked toughs, enforcing a regime detrimental to the Jews. This was no time for matchmaking. Who? What? Where? His thoughts turned repeatedly to Heshel Pribisker, who hated his own wife, and wouldn't go back to her.

So he sat there, huddled in his fur coat. Agh, so let it be. His eyes reflected stale despair, his face bore the look of defeat.

The pallid gray light in the parlor was a reflection of the snow outside. The silence, too. It was like the calm of death.

Heshel came into the room in high spirits, his face glowing with the cold, a satisfied smile on his lips.

"How dull it is in here!" His breath came white.

Reb Simcha glanced at him from behind half-closed lids, and said nothing.

"With every step I take"—Heshel strode over to the middle of the room—"I enter a different world."

"Drunk again?" rumbled Reb Simcha.

"In a manner of speaking," said Heshel, rubbing his

hands together. Reb Simcha shrugged sadly. Heshel sat down facing him. "Look," he said, "whiskey-drinking is a low thing. But the desire to drink—that, my friend, is something lofty." He raised his palm as high as it would go.

" 'Let the drunkard alone,' " quoted Reb Simcha. " 'He'll fall down even without your help.' "

"Drink," answered Heschel, "makes some people feel bad, and others feel good. A learned man always feels good. He studies a little Torah, and it calms him down. A little more, and he's a regular lion, on top of the world. But when he studies a lot, he becomes humble and serene. Today I'm serene, at peace. We sat and studied in the *bes-medresh*."

He went on with a full account of the Talmud they had studied, the questions and answers, the discussion and dialectic. Reb Simcha looked as if he couldn't care less.

"Did you eat anything?" he growled.

"I ate, I ate."

"I've got half a *taranka* and a little oatmeal."

Heshel picked awhile at the dried fish and the cold left-over porridge. Then he recited the grace after meals and stood up.

"It was nice of the Good Lord to give us grace after meals. Otherwise we'd be eating all day!"

24

It was the next day. The room was silent, as though still asleep. Reb Simcha sat cramped over, near the stove. Heshel sat opposite him, leaning aslant at the table, his feet stretched out on the heels of his worn-out boots. Now and then he glanced sidelong at Leahtche, who was sitting alone by the window. The tattered pamphlet she was reading was lit up by colored rays of sunlight, refracted through the frosted pane.

"What's that you're reading, something political?"

"Yes, the Erfurt Program." Leahtche didn't look up.

"About improving the social order?" asked Heshel.

"They'll improve it all right!" growled Reb Simcha. "Just you leave it to them! They'll fix it for good!"

Heshel tried to draw Leahtche out. "An important work, I suppose?"

"Very."

"Ver-r-y," Reb Simcha mimicked. "It would be a lot better if you found a husband instead of wasting your time with the programs of those hoodlums of yours."

"Marriage?" Leahtche looked up from the page. "Now that's a subject you don't grab at, and anybody that tries to gets his knuckles rapped."

"Fool!" Reb Simcha's face was contorted with anger. "Much good those books will do you, them and those fine comrades of yours!"

"Here we go again!" Leahtche turned the book face down on her knees. "What do you want from the comrades? They're doing their job, looking after the welfare of the workers."

"Let them look after the devil!" Reb Simcha interrupted angrily. "If they're so interested, why haven't they fixed up marriages for old maids?"

Leahtche burst out laughing. "You want the Communist party to find me a bridegroom? That's a good one!"

"You laugh?" Reb Simcha looked her full in the face. "All right then, laugh. Soon enough your head will be full of gray, and you'll be laughing out of the other side of your mouth. That's about all the social improvement you can expect from them."

Having gone so far, he was not to be stopped, but moved on from the curse of Leahtche's spinsterhood to the plague of the Communist comrades, those wicked apostates, those tailors and shoemakers who were now in charge.

"They've broken us like so many clay pots, may God shatter them. And especially that chief devil of theirs, that unclean reptile, that robber and murderer who bathes in Jewish blood."

Heshel looked at him, and Reb Simcha turned away. "Jews aren't villains," said Heshel, "and even if they are, they'll repent some day." Before Reb Simcha had a chance to answer, Heshel grinned, and added, "That's why it's the custom to buy a new Haggadah every Passover, just in case the wicked son has repented and become a saint."

"*You* wait for them to repent!" Reb Simcha's voice was mocking, contemptuous. "Jews not villains? They're worse than anti-Semites, they're apostates for spite!"

Heshel was not to be deterred. "There is such a thing as a person who is righteous for spite. These fellows are on fire with godly passions. They're out for truth and justice."

Reb Simcha stared at him, astonished. Heshel looked over at Leahtche, who was reading her pamphlet and paying no attention to them. "Well," he said, "what does the program say?"

She didn't answer.

"I hear you people are going to abolish money. Is it true, Leahtche?"

He waited for her reply. When none was forthcoming, he grinned and said, "It should be easy. Look at me, I haven't got a penny but I'm still around."

Leahtche stood up, took her pamphlet and three or four others off the windowsill, and headed for the door. "They don't give you a minute's peace around here." On her way out she turned on Heshel. "Why do you keep pestering me?"

Heshel sat, his eyes fixed on the door she had closed

behind her. "Reading, always reading, every free minute she has."

"And what's the good of it?" sighed Reb Simcha. "No man is going to step out of her books and ask for her hand. Tolstoy and Maxim Gorki aren't going to take her to wife."

Heshel smiled bitterly. "Yes, Tolstoy, Gorki.... That was a bad bargain our father Jacob made when he sold the mess of pottage to Esau. Esau ate and was satisfied, while Jacob is left scraping the empty pot."

25

It was the hour when Leahtche returned from her job. She found her father asleep, covered with his fur coat. He was curled up, his face pale and wrinkled, his hair tousled, his lower lip slack. Suddenly compassion welled up in her, to see him there so helpless, like a little boy. Then she took hold of herself and busied herself with the housework. After all, that's the way it is with fathers. They become sorry figures, old and gray.

Soon she went into the parlor.

"Cold!" She blew on her fingertips. "God preserve us, it gets into your bones." She went over to the mirror, hanging between the sofa and the bookcase, and took a quick glance.

Heshel spoke up. "We might have expected that this new era that we've waited for for so many generations would have arrived on a lovely summer day, with food and drink and gladness—and instead we have cold, darkness, no crust to eat or rag to wear, not even a stick for the stove."

Leahtche went to the kitchen and came back with a

pitcher of water for the plants. "Papa's asleep," she said, half to herself. "He's angry at the whole world."

"Well, after all, he's been robbed." Heshel was eager for conversation. "He's lost all his merchandise."

"Robbed?" Leahtche echoed. "He's no different from anybody else. It's happened to people a lot poorer."

"The new order is pitiless," said Heshel with a tentative smile. Leahtche ignored the remark. "Papa eat anything?" she asked.

"I didn't see him eating. You know, those frozen potatoes—"

Leahtche kept her eyes on the trickle of water from the pitcher. "And you? Have you eaten?"

"Yes, yes," said Heshel, his face lighting up. "I ate, I ate."

Leahtche took the pitcher back into the kitchen, and returned with the wooden mallet of a kitchen mortar. She sat down and busied herself with her shoe. "This darkness of ours will light up," she said, meanwhile turning her shoe around and examining it carefully.

"You believe in miracles?" Heshel smiled.

"I believe in the miracles we'll bring about by our own efforts," said Leahtche, hammering with the pestle on the sole of the shoe. "Things will be better for us than at any time since the world began, and I don't mean only materially, but morally as well."

"Morally?" Heshel's eyebrows shot up.

"I mean it. Great saints would have been pleased to reach such a level of morality."

"Really?"

"Really!" Leahtche hammered at the sole. "Why are you so surprised?"

"If only we kept the moral rules we already have." Heshel ran his fingers through his beard. "Say, at least, the Ten Commandments—thou shalt not kill, for example."

"The Revolution will hand down a new Ten Commandments." Leahtche's eyes were shining. "It will be a great innovation. You can't imagine." Her fingers poked around inside the shoe. Finally she put it on and walked over to the window.

"The ravens are flying low. It's going to snow."

Heshel stood up and looked as though he were going to say something.

"How short these days are," she said, as though speaking to herself. "It'll soon be evening."

"Leahtche . . ." Heshel's voice was a hoarse whisper.

"Why are you so talkative today?" She was looking out the window. "You know you're not supposed to talk much with women."

"Leahtche . . ."

"What's the matter with you?" She turned around and saw him standing, supplicant like a beggar.

"There's something I want to say to you . . . something . . . you must have noticed. . . ." He was pale, his eyes fixed on the floor. "I know I have no right . . . I know . . . but . . . I'm tormented . . . day and night. . . ."

Leahtche brought her palms together in dismay. "Woe is me!" she whispered in terror, her cheeks flaming. "Something told me this would happen! Good God, what is this! Go! Leave this house right away! For God's sake, go!"

"No, no!" Heshel walked into the middle of the room. "I must stay here. I have to see . . . to hear your voice. It's all I have left."

"What? You're in love with me?" Her palms were spread out in amazement. "It's beyond belief. . . . It makes no sense. How could you think of such a thing? You, my *uk-hazhor*—my suitor? A married man, with children? And besides, you're a God-fearing Jew, a Hasid! Do Hasidim get involved in love affairs?"

Heshel stood there humbly, a sad grimace on his lips.

"Nu-nu, what a catastrophe!" She clasped her hands over her bosom. "For God's sake, leave the house right away. This is not only painful, it's shameful. Have pity on yourself, go! Run for your life! Just think what's happened to you."

The sound of a cough came from the next room. Leahtche tiptoed toward the door. "Take pity," she whispered.

26

Now that Heshel had revealed his feelings to Leahtche he saw how hopeless the whole thing was. Before, it had been his own wonderful secret, a world of exquisite torture raging within him. But now all that was gone, and he felt empty.

He had been too ashamed to look her in the face, to say anything. It was as if the revelation itself had been the whole thing, and there was nothing more to say or do.

He sat alone in the parlor, sprawled out over the table, his head resting on one chapped hand. His whole life passed before him, and it added up to a loss. He felt that he was the lowest of the low.

What's happening to you, he whispered bitterly, as though he were talking to somebody else. What's to become of you? You're in exile, that's what, sunk in darkness and evil. Satan has got hold of you. Matter has gotten the upper hand over spirit.

He pictured his wife, pale and sad, her eyes dripping tears. Try as he would, he couldn't get the image out of his mind. Then he thought of his children, and the thought was painful. He wept inwardly.

"Ach, God in heaven!" He clutched his head and rocked to and fro. How can I be strong and hold my ground against this torrent of troubles? Gevald!—"To keep, to do, and to fulfill—to keep, to do, and to fulfill!" He repeated the Scriptural injunctions, his eyes closed, as though reciting the *Shema*.

Again he thought of his children, and this time the tears would not be held back. "My children, my children! God have mercy on you!"

Pity for his children stirred the anger toward his wife, and he sat there blaming her for everything that had gone wrong, for ruining his life. It was all her fault.

So he sat for a long time, seething inwardly, until he was emotionally spent, helpless. Then he got up, took a book of Psalms from the shelf, and sat down again.

The main thing, he told himself, is not to let your thoughts get the better of you. Fly from them, take refuge with the good Lord. Through the path of suffering—through the path of suffering—nu! He coughed and started chanting the first Psalm. "Happy is the man who hath not walked in the council of the wicked . . . oy, oy, oy! . . . nor stood in the path of sinners. . . ."

But this was one time when the Psalms were no help. Gone the usual fervent inner glow, the efflorescence of the soul. No, it was a routine mechanical recitation, bored, detached. His own thoughts began to steal in behind the Bible verses.

"Where did all this come from?" He had interrupted his chant, gazing blankly around the room. "What has made you reject the wife of your youth? What? Isn't she a decent woman? Is she ugly? Hasn't she borne your children? Or is it possible that she isn't the one destined for you, so that God has turned your heart away from her? And if that's the case, why hasn't God made her willing to accept a divorce? And how do you know that another woman is the one for you?"

"Oy, oy, oy!" He shook off his train of thought and resumed his chant. " 'My voice cried unto the Lord, and he answered me from His holy mountain, Selah.' " But it was no good. "Is it simply by accident that Leahtche crossed my path? Maybe it was fated? Who knows the secrets of the universe? You know so little about the visible world, much less about the mysteries of life."

A black fog enveloped him. His thoughts became blurred. For two or three minutes that seemed an eternity he sat still. Then, "Ach, ach!" He spread out his hands as though begging for mercy. "My soul longeth exceedingly—"

27

Mayerke and Shayke were buddies. Mayerke was a tall young man, with a pistol strapped to his hip and two black leather belts crisscrossed on his greatcoat. A red star, front and center, decorated his gray lambskin cap. There was an audacious twinkle in his brown eyes. The leather straps and the weapon added to his air of authority.

Shayke was the opposite, short and chunky, with a soft round face. He wore his coat sloppily, and his pistol seemed out of place. But he too was quite a fellow in his own way. He had been a dealer in eggs for export, until the war came along and put an end to his business. Besides, he had been drafted, and remained a foot soldier until the Revolution.

They were very fond of one another. Mayerke was the dominant one, while Shayke followed him like a shadow, and hung on his every word, like a Hasid in the presence of his *rebbe*. Sometimes Mayerke would tease him unmer-

cifully, while Shayke would look at him sidelong, attentively, until he would get the message, and laugh along at
his own expense.

From time to time the two of them would venture forth
to the surrounding villages. Mayerke had dealt in garden
produce, and he knew many of the peasants. They would
go on foot to the nearby villages. To the distant ones they
rode horses, which they obtained from Eisik Koysh. At
first, Eisik was doubtful about entrusting the horses to
them.

"Look, fellows, treat them gently. Kindness to animals,
you know. Give them a little oats, some cut straw. You
know how hard it is these days to make a living. The railway station stands idle, nobody comes, nobody goes,
there's no traffic between the villages. And it's winter.
Where am I going to get fodder? The poor things are suffering, they're in a bad way."

By his own account Mayerke was a socialist from way
back, even before the Revolution. He said he could prove
it. Once, long ago, a speaker from the Bund had come to
town. He had accosted Mayerke in the street, and asked
him, "Can you see God?" "No." "That proves He doesn't
exist." Then, "Do you see the Czar?" "No." "That proves
that he shouldn't exist." Mayerke was impressed. From
then on, ideas chased around in his mind like rabbits. He
began to ask people questions, to look into books, to get
notions. That's how he became a socialist.

He talked it over with Shayke, and taught him what to
say to the peasants. The main thing for a propagandist was
to talk about farmlands. That's what the Revolution was
all about, that's what was on their minds. If they got
possession of their farms from the squires, then the Revolution was a success. If not, write it all off.

"You better be prepared what to tell them," he warned.
"You say the wrong thing, and you're in the mud."

Not all the villages were alike. Some were poorer than

others, in some the villagers were tougher than in others. For reasons of their own the pair avoided Podberezhnoye, and bypassed Sokolichi. They headed for Skolotina, where the peasants were the poorest of the poor.

"Well, here we are," said Mayerke encouragingly. "Every hen knows its own eggs." He was hinting at Shayke's old occupation. The first person they met was an old woman filling two wooden pails at the well. Then they saw another woman standing in a doorway. She wore birch-bark sandals, her head wrapped in colorful kerchief. She greeted them.

"Don't you know me?" said Mayerke, grinning.

"The gardener's son, is it?" She hesitated, then her face lit up. "Mayerke!"

"Himself in person, Uliana. So you did recognize me!"

She stepped back into the house. "Come on in, let's have a look at you. And who's this, your brother?"

"My pal." They stepped into the yard and entered the house. Three pigs in the house were feeding at a trough, while five or six chickens pecked at some grain, clucking softly.

Uliana hastily wiped the bench with her apron. Mayerke and Shayke sat down. The ikons on the wall were covered with an embroidered towel, and a red lamp glowed in front of them.

"And you, you married?"

"What do you think? An old woman, and you ask such a thing!"

"Old? Why, you're a sapling! Prettier than when you were a girl."

"Come on, idle chatter. I'm not going to get back my youth on a well-ridden horse."

"Who's your husband?"

"Don't you know him?" She reddened a little. "He's a soldier."

"And where is he?"

"Where do you expect a soldier to be? At the war, of course, right from the start."

"Never mind. He'll come back. Soon. The war's over."

They talked a while about the village. So-and-so had been killed in the war, another wounded, a third taken prisoner. Certain girls had been married and had children.

"Nastia, what about her?" Mayerke asked.

"Nastia? Which Nastia? You mean Semyen's? So you remember her! No, she's not married. No."

"How come?"

"Who knows? She just refuses to get married, not till the war is over."

"A pretty girl," said Mayerke.

"Very pretty," Uliana agreed. "One of her kind in the whole village. And what about you? You married, or what?"

"Single."

"Well then, what's holding you back? Come on and marry her. It's revolution now. Permitted, as you might say."

"Sure, permitted. Why not?"

"Tell me, what brings you to the village? You got something to buy or sell?"

"No, Uliana, we're here for the village Council."

"Commissars?"

Mayerke looked around the room, at Uliana who had been standing the whole time, at the wide, bare bedboards, at the loom that was leaning in the corner. He stood up, exchanged a few friendly words with Uliana, and gave her a quick hug. She slipped out of his embrace, shouted at the pigs, and shooed them away. Mayerke and Shayke said goodbye and left.

At the village Council House Mayerke made a speech about the Revolution. It had come from the power of the people, and for the sake of the people. When he was finished, they discussed village affairs, and made their decisions. Then Mayerke and Shayke went off to visit Semyen Bodarenko, to see whether they could get any vegetables from him, cabbage or beets, and what is more to the point, get a look at Nastia. Semyen wasn't home. They found Nastia there, together with old Motria, who was sitting over the stove. They chatted awhile with the two women, and went on their way.

"Did you see Nastia?" said Mayerke. "What a beauty! I know her. I know all the women here. Most of them used to work for us in the vegetable plots. I used to have fun with them. With Uliana too. But Nastia . . . none like her!"

Shayke allowed that Nastia was a great beauty.

"It's permitted now, there's a revolution," Mayerke quoted. "That's the way it is. Permitted. Why not? What do you think?"

Shayke faithfully took the cue. "Permitted," he agreed.

28

It was rumored that the government was going to seize all the merchandise left in the padlocked stores. Some said it would be on account of the levy. Others said no, it would be straight confiscation, and the levy would stand. That's the way it had happened, they said, in Krasilovka and in Kamenka and in Verkhny-Brod. They had simply loaded the stuff onto wagons, and carted it away.

At first, before the Revolution was firmly established in Mokry-Kut, some of the storekeepers had heard whispers of the impending doom from relatives who were petty officials. They went ahead and hid their merchandise, leaving only token odds and ends. But there were many who weren't tipped off, or refused to believe that the government would do such an unheard-of thing. Even when the stores were closed down, they comforted themselves that their property was still intact, and the day would come when they would again be men of substance. Now, when the rumor was confirmed, they took fright, running around like scared mice, asking one another's opinion, standing and staring at their padlocked stores, not knowing what to do.

Reb Simcha was in despair. "Let be what will be," he muttered. "We're out of luck, devil take it." He wrapped himself in his *tallis,* put on his *tefillin,* and began his morning prayers with many a sigh and groan.

Heshel Pribisker stood by, watching him. "His children are in deep trouble," he said, nodding upwards with a sad grin, "while He sits up there on His heavenly throne."

"Devil take it," growled Reb Simcha into the open prayer book, and returned to his prayers.

Later in the morning the men gathered at Reb Moshe-Meir's, also called "Ladder" because he was so tall. They came in furtively, and stood around, all talking at once.

Reb Mordkhe-Leib Segal, gray-bearded and defeated, spoke fearfully. "They say that a week from today they will empty out all the stores. Brothers, what shall we do?"

"What can we do?" sighed Reb Avrohom-Elya Karp, a roly-poly type, as broad as he was tall. "We're helpless."

"How can you say that?" broke in Pesach Yossem, waggling his scraggly yellow beard, his eyes darting in every direction. "We have to find a solution, come what may."

"For example?"

"How should I know?"

"But you said a solution."

"Of course!"

"Well then, tell us. We're all ears."

Pesach Yossem hesitated. Then he said, "We'll write to Trotsky!"

"Aha!" Reb Itzia Dubinsky exploded sarcastically.

"Or else," Pesach added quickly, "we'll send somebody to see the district authorities."

"Ha-ha-ha!" Chatzkl Kanarik's derision sounded like the blast of a *shofar.*

The more they talked, the less they could decide what to do. Reb Simcha sat alone, bowed, silent. Reb Moshe-Meir turned to him. "What's your opinion, Reb Simcha? Why don't you say something?"

"My opinion?" Reb Simcha looked up at him absently. "My opinion? I've made up my mind that whatever we do won't matter. Whichever way we turn, we won't get out of their clutches. Their rule is crueler than the rule of Gehenna, of hell itself!"

"What have they got against us?" pleaded Reb Avrohom-Abba. "What do they want from our lives?"

"They just don't want us to live," said Yankel Potchtar hoarsely. "I've heard that their *rebbe,* Karl Marx, was himself an apostate and a Jew-hater, and said all kinds of terrible things about Jews, as renegades always have. They say he left the Bolsheviks a *torah* called *Kapital,* where he preaches hatred for mankind, and permits stealing and bloodshed."

" 'Ye shall sow your seed in vain, for your enemies shall eat the fruit thereof,' " quoted Reb Avrohom-Abba, holding his beard and swaying mournfully. "Scripture is talking about our children. We toil to bring them up, and they turn around and choke us. Ai-ai-ai! What a curse! That our children should be our enemies! They choke us from within, while the foe surrounds us without—"

"This doctrine of theirs," Yankel Potchtar continued, meanwhile breathing on his cupped hands to warm them, "this doctrine permits robbery and murder! What am I saying! It commands robbery and a murder! A positive commandment, you understand, like from the Torah!"

"What's the use of all this talk?" grunted Reb Avrohom-Elya Karp, without removing the bedraggled cigarette from his lips.

"No use at all," chimed in Chatzkel Kanarik. "But I can't help thinking what luck some people have. Those others, they saved their merchandise in the nick of time, right when it was between the mortar and the pestle."

"That's right!" said an aggrieved Pesach Yossem. "Where's the justice? If you say they're poor people, well so are we. And if you say, we're *burzhuks,* well so are they!"

"Let's say they were lucky, they got theirs." This from Reb Moshe-Meir the Ladder, shaking his head like an ox trying to escape the yoke. "Granted, but then let them pay up the levy, and get the rest of us off. They can't have it both ways."

It was an old argument that had been chewed over time and again. But they went at it once more with gusto, getting themselves red in the face.

Reb Avrohom-Elya Karp bent over and whispered something to Reb Itzia Dubinsky, who listened and nodded. Then Reb Avrohom-Elya went over and whispered to Reb Avrohom-Abba, who answered him with a shrug of the shoulder. Reb Avrohom-Elya straightened up and approached Reb Moshe-Meir the Ladder.

Reb Simcha saw that something was going on. He stood up, cracked his knuckles, and turned toward the door. "Talk, talk," he grumbled to himself. "Chewing over old bran." Reb Avrohom-Elya hurried over and tried to stop him. "Listen," he hissed, "it's time for a *mitzvah.*" But Reb Simcha didn't turn around. He put on his fur coat, opened the door, and went out, his head hunched between his shoulders.

29

A little while later Reb Avrohom-Elya knocked on Reb Simcha's door. "You come to me?" Reb Simcha asked, surprised.

"To you, to you. There's something I want to talk about." Reb Avrohom-Elya stepped in, looking like a mound of jelly in his lambskin coat.

"About what?" asked Reb Simcha. Reb Avrohom-Elya eased himself onto the bench beside the table, stretched his fingers a few times, and rubbed them together.

"Cold!" he said. "Seems to me this is the coldest winter we ever had." Reb Simcha waited.

"I've come to you for a *mitzvah*," Reb Avrohom-Elya began, "and out of respect for you."

Reb Simcha threw him a suspicious glance. "What's this all about?"

"It's about—wait, I'll explain in a moment. Are we alone here?" He looked around the room furtively. "Your Leahtche isn't home, is she?"

"There's nobody else in the house."

"Well then," Reb Avrohom-Elya fumbled, "uh, uh—I have something—something nobody knows about—yes, that's it."

"Then for goodness' sake speak up, and don't keep me dangling. He takes one step forward and two steps back. Speak up!"

Reb Avrohom-Elya rubbed his pudgy little fists together. "Briefly," he said, "I've come to talk to you on a matter of business—yes, that's it. You were at the meeting today. You saw, you heard."

"I heard you stuffing one another with useless talk."

"Nu, that's not all that happened, there was more. We decided to take action—yes. And we want you to have a share in it."

"What are you talking about?"

Once again Reb Avrohom-Elya glanced around the room. Then he whispered, "We'll take the merchandise out of the stores."

"Take out?" Reb Simcha looked at him sharply.

"Uh-huh."

"You'll take it out? How?"

"With keys," Reb Avrohom-Elya whispered, "and where there is no key, we'll break in."

Reb Simcha sat silent for a few minutes. "Nu?" Reb Avrohom-Elya pressed.

"I don't know," said Reb Simcha doubtfully, "I can't give you an answer."

"Why not?"

"Well, I wish you luck, but I'm afraid it's too dangerous, and we'll all get into worse trouble."

"What, they'll catch us, God forbid? Well, first of all, there's no watchman in the market, especially after midnight. Second, there's a God in heaven. And in the third place, if they do catch us—may it never happen!—what can they do to us? Take off our heads? We're dying anyway —no livelihood, nothing to eat."

"Still—" Reb Simcha was mulling it over in his mind.

"Still what?" Reb Avrohom-Elya interrupted. "Whatever happens will happen. A merchant is like a hunter. If we live, we live. If we die, we die. Come on in with us. We'll all lend a hand and help you salvage at least part of your stock."

"That's all well and good," said Reb Simcha hesitantly. "But wait. Let's say we don't get caught in the act, still, we'll be found out in the end. Don't you remember? They've got the whole inventory itemized in their ledgers."

"So what? Are we responsible for what happens to it?"

"Easily said. But I hate to think of what will happen if the whole thing comes out."

"So they'll call us bad names!"

"I'm sorry," said Reb Simcha with a sigh, "I can't come in with you. No, it's no kind of business for me. Go ahead without me. I'll have to sit right until this tyranny passes away."

"All right," nodded Reb Avrohom-Elya. "You do as you see fit, but we wanted you to know about it. Only remember —don't be sorry afterwards. We're in a desperate situation, up against gates of bronze and bars of iron, as the Good Book says. No doubt the good Lord will save us, but in the meantime, what will happen to your merchandise? They'll be clamping down in a week or two, there isn't much time! Anyhow, now you know the whole story, you do what you think best."

"No, no," said Reb Simcha, finally deciding. "Apart from everything else, the whole thing is too much like a childish prank. Imagine me at my age stealing merchandise from the store in the middle of the night!"

"What are you saying?" Reb Avrohom-Elya protested. "Would you be taking anything that doesn't belong to you? It's your own property!"

"Just the same," said Reb Simcha.

Reb Avrohom-Elya got up to go. "Nu, as you wish. But remember, I didn't say anything and you didn't hear anything." He opened the door, then turned around, one finger to his lips. " 'Guard thy tongue. . . .' " he said, and was gone.

30

Heshel Pribisker disappeared, without a word to Reb Simcha or to Leahtche. One day, he simply wasn't there. The house seemed peculiarly empty.

"What's happened to him?" Reb Simcha worried. "Where's he disappeared to?"

"Ran away," Leahtche suggested.

"Ran away? What do you mean?"

"Just what I say."

"But why should he do a thing like that?"

"Why? Because he's a confused man."

It sounded reasonable to Reb Simcha, so he dropped the subject. To himself he whispered, Queer person . . . vanishes . . . without goodbye, without anything. . . .

But three days later Heshel returned. Reb Simcha was glad to see him.

"What happened to you?"

"Nothing."

"Where were you?"

"In Pribisk."

"Nu!" Reb Simcha was taken aback.

"Nu." This calmly.

"So why did you come back?"

"What have I got there?"

"Well, what have you got here?" No answer. At this, Reb Simcha's pleasure evaporated.

"What's new in Pribisk?" he asked, sighing heavily.

"Nothing new. Same as in Mokry-Kut. Same business, same troubles."

"Is the marketplace idle?"

"Just about."

"And the stores, are they shut down?"

"Not exactly."

"Are they open, then?"

"Hmmm."

"You don't say! Nu, and the stock?"

"What stock?"

"You mean, they took it?"

"Took it, didn't take it—the stores are empty."

"Here they're planning to take everything away."

"Oh, they'll take it all right. The real point is, the marketplace has been closed down for good. No more trade, no more bargaining. The whole thing has been abolished."

"Nonsense!" said Reb Simcha angrily. "You're getting too smart for yourself. Tell me, how will people make a living without trade, without the necessities of life? Hah? What will the peasants do with their produce? Who'll supply them with a scythe and a sickle, with yard goods and kerchiefs and boots and all the other things they need? And what about the rest of us—do we sit at home and get manna from heaven? Smart fellow indeed!"

Heshel answered him quietly, seriously. "The government will take care of supplying people's needs."

"Aha! The government! And you don't seem to mind!"

Heshel offered no reply, and Reb Simcha stormed on. "I suppose the government will wait on customers in the store, and sew up clothes and shoes, and fix plows and horseshoes?"

"They'll set up cooperatives."

"Enough!" shouted Reb Simcha. "Do you hear? Don't talk to me!"

They sat there in silence, one smiling and the other enraged. After a while Reb Simcha calmed down. "Tell me," he said, "did you say the Bolsheviks confiscated all the stock in the stores of Pribisk?" Heshel murmured something, and Reb Simcha continued. "That's what they propose to do here." Then he told him about the plan of the storekeepers to hide their merchandise.

"Reb Avrohom-Elya was here," he said. "He asked me to join with them. I didn't agree." He waited a few seconds. Then, "Maybe I was wrong. What do you think, hah?"

Heshel let the question dangle, and asked instead, "Which Avrohom-Elya?"

"Reb Avrohom-Elya Karp."

At that moment they heard a racket outside. Heshel jumped up and ran to the door, with Reb Simcha at his heels. Three men were running down the middle of the street, Avremel Voskiboinikov, Hirshel the clockmaker, and Nachman the tailor. Avremel was carrying a big red flag, and all three of them were shouting, "Long live the Constituent Assembly!" Chasing them at a distance of fifteen or twenty yards was Polyishuk, accompanied by three other men, all with drawn revolvers. Men, women and children stood in the doorways watching the scene.

"Woe is me!" wailed one of the women fearfully. Scarcely had she cried out when Polyishuk fired three shots in rapid succession. In a flash the people disappeared into their houses, terrified. The pursuers caught up with the three demonstrators, and began to beat them unmercifully with fists and revolver butts. Now the people emerged out of their houses once more. Reb Simcha stood on the steps of his house and shouted to the world at large, "Murderers! Jewish criminals!"

Polyishuk waved his pistol at him, but went back to beating Hirshel the clockmaker on the nape of his neck with the revolver butt. Hirshel's face was covered with blood. He bent over, screaming, "Jews! Help!"

The spectators gathered in little knots. The womenfolk clasped their hands and wept, filling the air with imprecations. Slowly the sun sank behind the forest, and the western horizon glowed red. The piles of snow stood silent. From a distance the alleyways seemed to be enveloped in a bluish fog.

With a heavy heart Reb Simcha went back into his house. He started to light a fire in the stove, but the sticks were damp, and he couldn't get them to burn. Try as he would, he couldn't get the fire started.

Night fell. The house was dark and gloomy. Reb Simcha wearied of the stove and the wet kindling. He straightened up and went over to the window. Standing in the darkness, he began to murmur the evening prayer.

31

It was the middle of the night. Reb Simcha awoke to find Heshel Pribisker standing at his bedside. "Wake up, Reb Simcha!" he hissed. "Get up! Get up!"

Reb Simcha sat up, shivering. "What? Who?" He pulled the fur coat around his shoulders and scratched his head with both hands.

"Sh! Don't make any noise." Heshel lit the lampwick. "Is Leahtche asleep?"

"What?" Reb Simcha was still scratching himself awake. "What do you want?"

"Take a look. What do you see?" Heshel poked his toe at a bundle lying on the floor.

"What's that?" Yawning widely, Reb Simcha looked at the bundle.

"Not so loud! Whisper, or you'll wake up Leahtche. This is your merchandise—part of your stock."

"What? What?" Reb Simcha jumped up, stuck his feet into his big boots, and put on the fur coat. "What did you do? How?"

"Sh-sh!" Heshel grabbed his hand. "Keep your voice down. I went in through the roof."

Reb Simcha couldn't contain his excitement. "What a favor you've done me, what a favor—you've saved my life. I was afraid, I trembled at the thought, I couldn't do anything—and here you come along. It's an act of Providence!"

He bent over and took some of the goods out of the bundle, holding them up to the light of the wick. *"Seitz!"* he exclaimed. "Good, good!" All excited, he pulled out some more pieces of fabric. "Look! *Bayko!* Oy vay, *bayko!*" He repeated the performance with *kort* and *tchortova kozha* and *madopolam.* "You even brought *modipilan,"* he mispronounced, nodding in wonder. "Nu-nu, who can find *modipilan* these days? Maybe somebody who needs comfortable shrouds. Well, well, my dear and loyal friend, I certainly owe you a lot!"

"All right, all right," Heshel cut him short. "Now get the stuff out of here."

"Yes, yes," said Reb Simcha, all business. "Nobody must know about this, especially not that chatterbox of mine." He thought for a moment. "The garret! For the time being the garret, then we'll see, hah? What do you think, Heshel?"

They dragged the yard goods up to the garret and stored the stuff in the cupboard that held the Passover dishes. They came back down breathing heavily, in high spirits.

"I'll never forget this act of kindness!" Reb Simcha's eyes were sparkling, as he rubbed his hands together. "At first I thought you were making fun of me—"

"Nu!" Heshel waved him off. "Back to sleep! It's getting late."

"Right away, right away," Reb Simcha panted. "But—

what was it I wanted to say?—oh yes! If they come and accuse me of breaking in to the store—"

"Nye zhuris!" Heshel clapped him on the shoulder. "Never fear!"

"But what does the roof look like? Did you close up the hole?"

"Yes, yes. Don't worry."

"I see. Well, good. May the good Lord reward you. And listen—you can live in my house as though it were your very own. And may God restore peace between you and your wife."

Heshel hardly seemed to hear him. He stood there, thinking, And all this time Leahtche is fast asleep.

32

It was time for Leahtche to leave for work. She came out of her room, glanced at Heshel, and tossed a remark over her shoulder. "You still around?" That's all. It was plain that she paid him no particular attention. She hadn't been bothered much by his disappearance or gladdened by his return. Still, she didn't go right off to work, but kept puttering around. Reb Simcha was impatient for her to leave. He wanted to go up into the garret for another look at his merchandise.

"What are you poking around here all morning for?" he growled.

"Why? What's up?" She glanced around the room.

" 'What's up! What's up!' " he mimicked sarcastically.

When she was finally gone, Heshel said, "I think she knows."

"What makes you say that?" Reb Simcha was taken aback.

"Oh, I don't know. All kinds of hints and things."

"I didn't sense anything."

"Well, she hung around unusually long."

"Fiddlesticks, it doesn't mean a thing," said Reb Simcha, and disappeared up the ladder into the garret. He stayed there quite awhile.

When he came down Heshel looked at him. "Nu?"

"Nu-nu!" answered Reb Simcha. "You certainly did a good job on the store." Heshel didn't reply, and Reb Simcha went on. "You saved my life. If it hadn't been for you, who knows what would have become of me. I might have died of hunger one of these days, God forbid." He paused for a moment. "The main thing," he said, "is to get the goods out into the market. And that's not easy. Well, we'll see. And I hope nobody points the finger at me, and gets me caught. Come on, are you coming?"

The two of them went off to the synagogue for the morning prayers.

Reb Simcha put in a busy day. He came home in good spirits, his face wreathed in smiles, his hands blue with the cold. "I did some business," he started to say to Heshel, when the door opened and Leahtche walked in. The two men promptly washed their hands and sat down at the table. Reb Simcha picked up a piece of cold potato.

"Where were you last night?" he asked, his eyes on the potato. "When did you get in?"

"Now there's a new question!" said Leahtche, with a shrug. "What time did I get in? Let's see, you weren't even asleep yet."

"Wasn't I?" Reb Simcha nearly choked on a piece of potato. "Funny, I didn't hear anything."

"It was early, around nine or ten."

"You don't say." Reb Simcha was perturbed, but he tried to hide it.

"These frozen potatoes are simply awful. I woke up around midnight, walked around a bit, lit the lamp. Heshel woke up too, we sat around and talked. Did you hear anything?"

"Not a sound," answered Leahtche innocently. "I fell into bed like a log. My feet were like two blocks of ice. By the time I got warmed up under the covers I was dead to the world."

Reb Simcha glanced at Heshel, and the shadow of a smile crossed his face. "Nu, so tell me, what's new with your crowd? What are the comrades saying these days?" He sighed, more or less out of habit, yet he seemed strangely at peace with the world. Leahtche glanced at him sharply.

"Seems to me you're acting a little peculiar today," she said slowly, deliberately.

Reb Simcha turned to Heshel Pribisker. "You hear? Last week you weren't here, seems to me. Or, wait a minute! Yes, you were here! Polyishuk and his buddies chased those three wise men, Avremel and Hirshel and Nachman, and shot at them with their revolvers. Nu, what do you say to that, eh? Murderers, plain and simple murderers. They shoot, hah? They shoot! Now I hear the three are in prison, and who knows what will happen to them."

"Serves them right!" said Leahtche. "What business did they have with demonstrations? No demonstrations! We won't permit them!"

"You don't say!" Reb Simcha cocked his head. "And according to you, the boys were in the wrong?"

"The soviets are better for us than any Constituent Assembly," answered Leahtche. "The Constituent Assembly will only attract all the reactionaries, all the bourgeoisie and the social renegades! No! All power to the soviets!"

Inwardly, Reb Simcha was proud of her, her articulateness, her intelligence, her air of authority. Oo-wah! he said to himself. What a sharp knife she wields! Aloud he said,

"But what business is it of yours, if you will be so good as to enlighten me? What do you care? How come it doesn't matter to me, but matters to you?"

"People have different natures," she answered calmly. "It's my nature to care."

"What a baggage you are," sighed Reb Simcha. "Just be sure that you won't be sorry, that's all. You'd be better off giving up all this nonsense—"

"Oh, absolutely!" Leahtche interrupted, sarcastically.

". . . and I don't think it's such a good idea for you to be so involved in politics, so arm-in-arm with a bunch of tailors and shoemakers and beggar boys scraped off the floor of the town flophouse."

Leahtche had heard all this before, more than once. She answered calmly, "Look, father, you might as well realize that work is no disgrace. It's not work that demeans a man, it's the man that demeans the work. And as for beggars and poor people, just remember that everybody is born without a shirt to his back."

"Agh, what's the use of talking to you!" Reb Simcha ran his hand over the frost on the windowpane and started to whisper the grace after meals.

After a while he stood up. "I'm going out," he said. "Who knows? Maybe I'll run across the day before yesterday."

33

Now the two of them were alone in the house. Leahtche and Heshel sat silent, not looking at one another, uncomfortable in each other's presence.

Leahtche was the first to break the silence. She looked at

Heshel sharply and addressed him like a policeman questioning a suspect. "Speak up!"

Heshel looked at her, astonished. "Do you take it back?" she persisted.

"Take it back?" Heshel had no idea what she was talking about.

"Yes, take back those things you said. They're still stuck in my throat like a bone."

Heshel blinked. So that was it. Leahtche went on, a faint touch of friendliness creeping into her tone. "You'd have been better off not to say such things."

Heshel was surprised. "What's the matter? Did I do you wrong?"

"That's it exactly. What fault of mine was it that you fell in love with me all of a sudden? Still, I *am* partly to blame. I'm the cause of what happened to you."

Heshel opened his mouth in astonishment. "You're not to blame at all," he answered, "and as for me, I can't take anything back. Believe me, I'm more to be pitied than envied. If you only knew what I go through every day. Still, whenever I see your face—that's a great kindness to me, an unmerited grace."

"Stop it!" said Leahtche with an impatient wave of the hand. "You were in Pribisk. What's the latest at home?"

"At home? At home there is sadness and joy, weeping and song. That's it. You wouldn't be able to understand more than a fraction of it."

"I don't understand a single bit of it," she shook her head. "What's the joy and what's the sorrow?"

"Both," said Heshel, not explaining. "Deep waters flow over a man's head, torrents. . . ."

Leahtche looked at him and kept her peace. After a while she gave a deep sigh. "How are your wife and children?"

"Thank God," he replied, without taking his eyes off the floor.

"The children well?"

"Thank God."

"Were they glad to see you?"

"Naturally."

She sat for a while, thinking, then nodded her head. "You went to give her a divorce, right?"

"Uh-huh."

"And she refused to accept it. She must be in love with you."

"What? Who? Nonsense."

"Well then?" she tried to draw him out.

"Nothing."

"Why doesn't *she* ask for a divorce?"

"A woman you can't live with is one you can't get rid of."

Leahtche was astounded. "You mean she's such an evil woman? It's unbelievable."

"Oh no. There are lots of women like her."

"Well then?"

"It would take days to tell."

"Just the same," she pressed.

Heshel reflected for a little while. Then he said, "What can I tell you? She blocks off my light."

"She blocks off your light—" half to herself. "Unfortunate, how unfortunate we are."

Heshel reached over and touched her hand. "Sit, sit." She recoiled from him. "Still, I can't understand what happened to you. How did you fall in love with me, and why do you love me?"

Heshel gave no answer. He sat there with his eyes downcast.

"Is it for my body?" she persisted. "All right. It's my body you want. You religious fanatics don't understand a woman's soul; you simply lust after her body."

"I don't know, I don't know," mumbled Heshel, as though out of his mind.

"But maybe you've stopped being a fanatic. What if I ask

you to shave off your beard?" She waited for an answer and, when none was forthcoming, went on slowly, emphasizing every word. "All right, then. I tell you to shave off your beard."

"Shave off my beard?" Heshel was astonished. A tortured smile passed over his lips.

"For God's sake!"

"What's the idea?" Heshel gave a forced laugh. "Are you trying to make a clown out of me?"

"Not a clown, a human being!"

Heshel picked up his chair, brought it over, and sat down near her. Before he had a chance to open his mouth she looked him full in the face and commanded, "Move away, keep your distance!"

"Leahtche—" he put his hand over hers.

"They grow themselves beard and earlocks to fulfill the commandment, out of religious conviction," she said, gradually disengaging her hand, not looking at him. "You know it is forbidden to touch me; you're supposed to regard me as dried straw, as chaff."

Heshel took hold of her hand again.

"'Like chaff which the wind doth blow,'" he quoted with a smile. "But the trouble is that when the wind blows, the chaff gets into your eyes and your nostrils and your throat."

Leahtche made a move to get up, but sat down again. Her face was flushed, her shoulders slumped, her breath came fast. "The time has come for you people to leave the study house." Her hand trembled as Heshel held it between both of his. "It's time you gave up the world to come, and paradise, and all such fairy tales."

"My darling, my darling," whispered Heshel, putting his arm around her.

She took his arm away, and went on. "A wonderful new world is coming into being." His arm was around her again. "Great happiness is in store for humanity! I'm so glad to be alive at this time, in the same generation with real men, heroes of the Revolution."

"Beloved, dearest." Heshel drew her close and whispered, "Dear heart, light of my life."

Bit by bit she was drawn to him. Her arms fell slack, her eyes were half closed. She made a few weak efforts to push him away. She twisted her mouth to escape his kisses. And then, despite herself, she was entangled with him in a passionate embrace. In a moment, she opened her eyes, and saw somebody there looking at them. She jumped up in confusion, eyes wide, cheeks aflame. Then she realized that what she had seen was her own image in the mirror.

Heshel came toward her with arms outstretched, and whispered hoarsely, "Leahtche—"

"Madman!" she cried out. "Crazy! What do you want from my life? Go!"

34

Heshel was in a state of confusion. He wasn't quite sure what had happened to him, how the encounter had come about. Was it his doing or Leahtche's, were things now looking up for him or the reverse? He began to feel remorse, and to blame himself unmercifully.

"Oy, oy," his conscience wailed, "you fake Hasid, despicable and disgusting, lower than the dust, than the nethermost level of hell!"

But then he would bounce back, and feel that he was walking on air, everything was turning out right for him.

Before long he was downcast again, thinking things couldn't be worse. Between these two extremes he vacillated, up and down, down and up.

Reb Simcha sensed that he was acting even more strangely than usual. Two incidents in particular caused him to wonder. Once Heshel walked up to him all aglow and said, "Today I'm the happiest man alive."

Reb Simcha fastened a beady eye on him. "What? What's this all about?"

"I'm happy! Happy!"

Reb Simcha was left to wonder.

Another time he discovered Heshel, bent and broken, sitting over an open psalter, his face dark with agony. He interrupted his reading long enough to say, "Gevald, gevald! If you only knew what things go on in the world!"

"As if you're the only one who knows!" Reb Simcha feigned anger. "Robbery and violence and murder! Cold and starvation and disease, typhus and cholera and fever, weeping and wailing in every back alley, in every house!"

"No," said Heshel, swaying to and fro, his eyes downcast. "That's not what I mean. I'm talking about the exile of the spirit, the darkness of the soul."

Reb Simcha drew back. He passed his hand over his beard, and pursed his lips. "Ah that, my friend, is your own doing. It comes from within you."

Heshel went back to the Psalms, his voice wracked with sobs. He came to the verse, "A broken and a contrite heart, O Lord, Thou wilt not despise." He chanted it three or four times, and then added, "A broken heart, yes, but not when it's brought about by the evil inclination, by things of no worth."

As before, Leahtche paid no attention to him. It was as if nothing had happened. Only once he sensed that she was standing there looking at him. As soon as he turned in her direction she walked away, shaking her head and

whispering to herself in Russian, "*Eto dyko, dyko—*
strange, strange."

35

Whenever Mayerke and Shayke came to a village, they
gathered the peasants together, addressed them, discussed
their problems, issued instructions. But there were some
villages that didn't accept their authority. Sometimes
there was a cantankerous peasant, or even a social revolutionary, who gave them an argument. Sometimes there
was a seminarian in the crowd, who had come looking for
a bride, or for a parish. In such cases, the two emissaries
of the Revkom had their hands full. The peasants buzzed
around them like a beehive in the springtime.

"All right, comrades, suppose you explain it all to us.
What do you mean by property of the state? Does that
mean that we and our wives and children and everything
we have will be reckoned state property, or what? Now
you, comrades, feed us with what's going to be tomorrow
and the day after. What about today? Where can we get
makhorka for a smoke or a chew? How about a plow or a
nail or two? And we need work boots! It's winter now.
Nothing from our harvest is left in the house, and there's
no work for hire, either. Not in the forest, or the sugar
factory, or the glass factory."

At Horoshchina the precentor of the church took the
floor and asked the audience, "Tell me one little thing,
brethren. Who are you for most of all?" After a long silence
a voice called out, "The Rada." Someone else hazarded,

"Hrushevski" A third said, "Lenin-Trotsky." The precentor shook his head.

"No, my brethren, you have not spoken well. Dear above all to us is Saint Mikola, the man of God, he who founded the Pravoslav faith, who intercedes for us at all times—he and not Lenin-Trotsky. I ask you, my brothers, is it for nothing that the holy Orthodox Church has set aside two holy days in his honor, Saint Mikola's in the spring and Saint Mikola's in the winter? You find him wherever you find the people of Christ— in the holy Lavra Monastery in Kiev, at the Uspenyi in Moscow, at the Kazanyi in Petrograd, and in the famed city of Amchensk. In all these places he stands in prayer for the whole Christian communion. On Mikolshchina Day all the saints gather. Elias himself in all his glory is there. You won't find Lenin-Trotsky there. No, they'd be out of place. And now, my brothers, let me ask you one question. Do you know what is written in the Holy Bible? I'll tell you, and listen well and understand. In the Book of Esdras it is written: *Behold, the days shall come when there will be great turmoil in the land, and wickedness shall multiply, such as thine eyes have not seen before, nor thine ears have heard. And the land shall be desolate, the trees shall drop blood, and the stones cry out. The sea of Sodom shall spew forth fish. Understanding shall be hidden, and truth shall not be found.* There, that is what is written in the Holy Bible! And now all these signs and portents have come upon us. Lord, have mercy on us! Mikola, sainted one of the Christian people, appear unto us! Lenin-Trotsky and all the *zhids* with them have done this to us. Is it right that *zhids,* the pernicious Jews, should jump up in front of Christ's folk, considering all the turmoil they have caused?"

Mayerke and Shayke were lucky to get out of there alive.

In the village of Razdorozhye they happened upon an ex-soldier who had picked up a lot of ideas from attending revolutionary meetings. They took him along with them, and he turned out to be an effective speaker. He always opened with the same words: "The sun of liberty, backed up by the bayonets of soldiers, has risen over the Tauride Palace!" This made a strong impression on the villagers, and they began to understand that it was for them that the Revolution had dawned, and now all the fields and forests and factories and stores and the state itself, all, all now belonged to them. From this point on the boys found the going much easier.

From time to time they would stop again at Skolotina. Mayerke had made Shayke at home in the house of Semyen Bodarenko. He explained what a favor he had done in giving him a free hand with Nastia. Now there was a girl, hah? Only out of friendship had he done it. After all, Shayke wasn't very handy with women, while he, Mayerke, was quite an expert.

"Well, then," he pressed, "it's up to you. Make up your mind, will it be me or you?" Shayke looked at him sheepishly, at a loss for words.

"So what will it be?" Mayerke kept after him. "Are you ready? After all, I'm taken care of. I have Uliana. I have only to snap my fingers."

"Ready," stammered Shayke.

"All right, she's yours," said Mayerke, with an air of finality.

Mayerke accompanied him to Semyen's two or three times. After that, Shayke started coming on his own. Semyen was a friendly, slow-speaking peasant. He sat Shayke down and engaged him in conversation. "What's new these days?"

Shayke was not an articulate fellow, but now his tongue loosened up, and he launched into praise of the new social order, quoting Lenin and Trotsky, even offering his own opinion. Occasionally two or three neighbors would drop by and join in the talk. It gave them pleasure to recall the squires and landowners, now a thing of the past. They especially liked to talk about the ones they had done to death, and to review the killings in lip-smacking detail. "Hey, remember how they split open so-and-so's skull with an axe?"

They also spoke about farmlands, and about goods that were in short supply, oil, salt, boots, tar. They recalled the market days, now no more, and the Jewish peddlers who used to come around with goods for the farmer's wife, needles, thread, patterns, little crosses, brass rings, and the like, which they would barter for eggs, pig bristles, tallow, and the skins of cats and rabbits.

"Those days are gone," sighed one of the farmers.

"Listen, hurry up and get the Revolution over with, get it off our perishing backs," said another, adding a string of obscenities.

And so they went on, until the talk turned to hunting, which is to say, rabbits.

"It's been a bad year for rabbits," said Semyen Bodarenko, himself the best hunter in those parts. He remembered the year before the war, when he had shot rabbits in droves all through the winter. Every night he would find them, next to the piles of stubble in the field, near the cabbage roots in the furrows, or in the old clover field, sometimes even beside the silo.

"But last year we had a dry summer, and it's always the same—after a dry summer the rabbits disappear."

Shayke also made friends with Semyen's wife. Motria was a tall woman, thin and wrinkled, quite a contrast to her vigorous husband. She told Shayke how worried she was about her three sons, all of them away in the army. She complained about the scarcity of household needs, no oil or salt, no kerosene for the lamp. Her only consolation was Nastia, a lovely and capable girl, thanks be to God;

first with the pitchfork on the heels of the reapers, leading all the other women in binding the sheaves, handy on the loom and with the needle and everything. The only trouble was, there were no real men left in the village, only children and oldsters.

"God grant that the fellows come home from the war, then we'll all be happy."

Shayke watched Nastia at her chores, pulling pails of water out of the well, carrying them on the yoke slung across her shoulders, mixing feed for the cows, boiling potatoes and mashing them into the trough for pig swill with a wooden pestle. Warm vapor enveloped her from head to foot.

She was a chunky girl, big-breasted, red-cheeked, earthy, with a sly twinkle in her brown eyes. Around her neck she wore a chain of colored glass discs, supporting a little brass crucifix. Once in a while she would glance at Shayke and smile to herself. Was she encouraging or mocking him?

Once she asked him to get her some colored thread. "Look for some among your own kind, and bring it to me."

Another time he found her alone in the house. Seizing the opportunity, he put his hands on her breasts. She gave him a cool stare. "Hands off. That's not yours."

Evenings she would go off to the house of a certain old woman, where the boys and girls of the village made merry. The girls were grown up, while as for the boys, the oldest of them was barely sixteen. Even so, Shayke was no match for them when they started making fun of him, while the girls roared with laughter. Two of the fellows warned him not to lay a finger on their girls. "Buzz off!" they said. "Don't hang around here."

When he still persisted in coming, they decided to get him. One night, on his way to the party, he was chased by three peasant boys armed with picket slats. Shayke ran for his life. From then on he stayed away from Skolotina, and that was the end of his rosy dreams.

Mayerke promptly spread the news, and the comrades took to teasing Shayke about his Nastiushka. "Tough luck! Too bad for you."

"Too bad," Shayke agreed, and joined in the laughter at his own expense.

36

Conditions grew worse daily. There was a scarcity of bread, salt, sugar. Vegetables and other farm products were a rarity. People ate when they could and what they could, some of it barely fit for human consumption.

Heshel subsisted on bits and scraps. Now more than ever he threw himself into study of the Torah. "When I'm half dead with hunger," he would say, "I sink my teeth into a passage in the Talmud."

To be sure, it was not only hunger pangs that drove him to the study chapel. He was also trying to master his illicit desires, even as the sages have taught: happy are the people of Israel, for when they busy themselves with Torah and with deeds of kindness, then their instincts are in their power, and not they in the power of their instincts.

He hinted at this to Reb Simcha. "I'm not doing it for the sake of Abaye and Rava, or even for the good Lord Himself. I'm doing myself a favor."

From time to time he would approach Reb Simcha with a wink and a grin. "Got anything?"

"Nothing! Nothing!" Reb Simcha would snap back.

Undaunted, Heshel would press on. "Nu?" This would infuriate Reb Simcha.

"What nu?! What nu!!" And his beard would start to tremble. "Where am I going to find anything for you? Tell me, where?! So far I haven't clapped eyes on a real live kopeck."

"Still, in the end you'll have to give," smiled Heshel confidently, "because I have the upper hand. I'm poor, and I have nothing."

"I should give you money to spend on drink? Don't drink, and don't sin!"

"A little vodka is no sin," he said in a placating tone. "Just to cheer up my poor soul." Reb Simcha turned his back on him. "A little liquor," Heshel went on, "makes for harmony between body and soul."

And so the argument continued until finally Reb Simcha pulled out his purse and handed over a couple of tattered bills.

"This'll be the last time! I'm telling you, the last time!"

Before very long the two of them were sitting at the table drinking together. After a few drinks Heshel began chanting a phrase from the Torah: " 'Thou shalt keep thyself from every evil thing, oy-oy-oy, thou shalt keep thyself from every evil thing.' "

Reb Simcha sighed, shaking his head sadly. He thought, Poor fellow! Sits at the table making merry, while all the time he's in anguish. God have mercy on him!

Sometimes a few of Leahtche's friends would drop in, comrades from the Bolshevik bureaucracy, impressive-looking young fellows, with their smart military breeches and fur tunics, red star on the cap and revolver at the hip. If Heshel was there they would have a little fun at his expense, arguing with him about anything at all, dripping arrogance and contempt.

Once it was Shayke and Mayerke who came to visit

Leahtche. They started right in on Heshel as soon as they saw him.

"Nu, what's the good word, you idle *melamed?* How much soap, sugar, and flour have you got socked away?"

Heshel said that he was not in business. "Now if there was a market for Torah, I'd be sitting pretty for some illegal trade."

"All right, but what about cigarettes? I'm dying for a smoke."

Heshel spread out two empty palms, a smile on his face.

"Come on, look around, I bet you'll find some," Shayke pressed.

"That Holy One of yours has all kinds of good things," Mayerke put in.

"You can't get cigarettes from Him," answered Heshel. "What you can get from Him is truth and justice."

"Truth and justice?" Mayerke retorted. "From your kind? We're the ones who supply truth and justice!"

"Tzaddikim," Heshel murmured, smiling to himself. "The kind of righteous men that the good Lord Himself is afraid of."

"So let Him be afraid!" Shayke exploded with laughter at his own wit.

Reb Simcha had been sitting in a corner by himself. Now he glared across the room.

"What has the Holy One got to do with an idiot?"

Shayke was struck dumb. He sat there with a foolish grin on his face.

"Tzaddikim!" Reb Simcha fumed. "Thieves and robbers, gluttons and guzzlers, dressed in their fine clothes . . . Righteous men! Don't be such *tzaddikim!* Be human beings! Live, if you want to, but not by squeezing the life out of other people!"

Mayerke and Shayke shrank like beaten curs, Heshel and Leahtche looked at the floor. But Reb Simcha was not finished. His lips flecked with white, he raised his fist at the two young Bolsheviks.

"And anyhow, who do you think you are, coming into my home and insulting me? How dare you come into my house with your pistols on your hips? I won't have it!" He jumped up, beard atremble, cheeks like chalk, his eyes flashing fire.

"Sh, sh!" said Leahtche fearfully.

"Keep your mouth shut!" Reb Simcha didn't even look at her. He clenched his fists and rushed out of the room.

Shayke and Mayerke lingered for a few more minutes, exchanging words with Heshel. Then they got up to go. Leahtche called out after them. "Wait for me. I'll just get a kerchief for my head."

She stood in front of the mirror tying the kerchief. "Leahtche. . . ." Heshel turned to her. Tucking the ends under her chin, she looked at his reflection in the mirror.

"Leahtche," he whispered, "what's become of us? What's happening to us?" Calmly she adjusted the knot over her throat, a fleeting smile of triumph on her apple-red cheeks. She addressed the mirror.

"A kiss doesn't lead to love. It's love that leads to a kiss." She tossed her head, and was out the door.

37

There was no feed for the cows in Mokry-Kut, and one by one they had to be slaughtered. The last one left belonged to Kalman the baker.

Kalman moved heaven and earth to keep his cow alive until the spring, when he would be able to put her out to pasture. He tried to board her in the village, but the peasants turned him down. They were hard up themselves, they said. Once in a while he brought her a little straw, but the poor thing got thinner and thinner. She would stand in the yard sad-eyed, her bones sticking out, and moo pitifully.

"She's lowing again," said Tzeitl, Kalman's wife.

Tzeitl couldn't bear the thought of slaughtering the cow. Why, the animal had been born right in their barn, and Tzeitl had raised her from a calf. Every morning she used to lead her out to pasture, and in the evening she would always have a nice supper waiting in the manger.

Finally Kalman came home with a couple of sacks of chaff he had picked up in the village.

"Another day or two," he sighed, "then what?"

Tzeitl looked as though she were about to cry.

"Why do you love her so?" Kalman argued. "Milk she doesn't give, her calf was born dead, she has no strength left. How long do we keep on suffering for her?"

"But I've known her all her life," Tzeitl pleaded.

"Can't you see, she's not long for this world? Sooner or later we'll find her on her back."

Tzeitl knew that he was right, but she just couldn't consent. She ran her hands over the skinny flanks of the poor creature, feeling a slight tremor beneath its hide. "My pet," she whispered, and the cow turned its eyes on her and gave a pitiful moo. Half blinded with tears, Tzeitl stumbled back into the house.

Her mother, the widow Golda, sided with Kalman. The animal should be put out of its misery, but on one condition: "The tallow belongs to me."

When the butcher finally led the cow away, Tzeitl stood watching from the window, her tears a steady drip on the sill.

Golda got her tallow. She heated the fat in a big pot, and dipped in the wicks she had made from shreds of her late husband's clothing. By dint of repeated dipping and cooling, dipping and cooling, she made herself a whole basketful of candles.

On Friday she went from door to door, handing out her candles to the housewives. The women blessed her, and she replied in kind.

She was stopped on the street by Comrade Shimtze.

"Tell me, granny, what's in the basket?"

"Real contraband," she answered with the sunniest of smiles. "I've got *Shabbos,* I've got light."

He looked blank. "Just a little light, to brighten up your soul," she said.

"To brighten up my . . . ?"

"Yes, for the repair of your soul!"

Now he caught her drift. "Not for me, granny. Me, I'm a Bolshevik."

"Come on, silly boy," she smiled gently. "Even if you don't deserve it, the good Lord in His great kindness will have mercy on you, and let you have your share in the world to come. He is very charitable, blessed be His Name."

He laughed at her and started to walk on.

"Wait a minute!" she called. "How's your father?"

"Sick."

"The Lord send him full healing. Listen, do you want to do me a favor? Take these two candles to your mother."

At sunset, when Golda had blessed her candles, she wrapped herself in her shawl and stood outside her front door. All up and down the street she saw the Sabbath candles, twinkling from every window. "Thank God," she whispered, at peace with the world.

38

The days were short, and there was so much to do. Shayke had no stomach left for their work in the villages, partly because of Nastia, partly because of the unfriendliness of the peasants, but especially because their speech-making soldier had left the boys and taken to the bottle. "What!" he growled at them drunkenly. "Jews rule over us? I'll see you dead first!"

Shayke kept urging Mayerke to get them home before dark.

"What good is our work?" he grumbled. "We grind away, without results to show for it."

"Results, no results," said Mayerke. "We're doing our revolutionary duty."

Mayerke tried to keep up Shayke's spirits. He talked about the more promising villages, he talked about Uliana, and how much he enjoyed a night in her bed, he talked about Nastia and said she had asked after Shayke, and had wondered why they didn't see him around any more. Yes, and Semyen and Motria had asked after him, too.

In his mind's eye Shayke saw Nastia's face, her firm body and deep lush bosom. He remembered her stirring the swill for the hogs; he remembered the row of ikons on the wall, the poppies and artificial flowers peeping out from behind them, the spacious oven and the bed boards. He remembered especially the smell, the strong alien smell. "The devil take her!" he said out loud.

"Now don't say that," chided Mayerke. "She's an all-right girl, good-looking, juicy. Take her into your arms. Look, I cleared the way for you and you stumbled, that's all."

On their way to Kalinovka they passed Skolotina, and who should be at the well but Nastia, in a sheepskin coat, a colored kerchief on her head, her cheeks aflame in the crackling cold. They stopped, ostensibly to water the horses, but really so that Mayerke could show Shayke how one talks to girls.

"Hello there, Nastia."

"Hah, it's you." She lowered the yoke with its two empty pails. "What ill wind blew you in?"

"I knew we'd run into you."

"Very good," she laughed. "Look while awake and see in your dreams."

"Exactly," said Mayerke, "awake and asleep."

"And have you looked at your own face lately?" she hooted.

"What are you whinnying for, like a filly at the fair?"

"Go on, water your horses. I haven't got all day."

"What are you so puffed up about?"

"And you, what are you staring for?"

"Looking you over. Don't you understand?" Mayerke took a step toward her.

"Keep away," she said. "Take a look and move on."

"What, you can't be touched? You'll fall apart or something?" His foot slid on the icy strip in front of the well. She giggled.

"I'll come to you tomorrow right after dark," he said lowering his voice. "Wait for me behind the cowshed."

She batted her eyelashes. The next moment she raised her voice at him. "Get going, you horned devil. Let a body get to the well. I haven't got time to stand around and listen to you beat your gums."

"I'll whistle for you."

As soon as they left, Mayerke said to Shayke, "See, that's the way to talk to them."

At Kalinovka, Mayerke made a speech. There was one fellow there, a village healer with sharp tiny eyes and a droopy walrus mustache, who addressed him half in Russian, half in Ukrainian.

"I see you're a sharp young man. Good. That's the kind I like. With fellows like you we'll soon brew a good keg of beer. Good. Politics. Very fine. There's politics and politics. Here we plant our vegetable garden without politics. Yes indeed."

He smiled a little to himself and fixed his eyes on Mayerke. "And you, sir, what kvass barrel do you come out of? A Jew, right? Seed of Abraham, Isaac, and Jacob? Very well, then let me ask you: How does the first chapter of the Book of Psalms go?"

He looked at Mayerke slyly, all the while smiling into his walrus mustache. "I'll tell you: *Blazhen muzh izhe nye ideh na soviet netchestivikh.* Right or wrong? See, it says *soviet.* The soviet of the wicked. That's the way King David said it. So what are you doing trying to get us to support the soviet? Making us all kinds of promises? Not nice! No sir, it's a bad business."

This started the ball rolling, and the complaints poured forth. What about the land they were supposed to get? How about jobs? Did he realize that their cupboards were bare, and their cattle dying of starvation?

"Not enough we haven't gotten the upper hand, we're worse off than before. Some revolution!"

This was nothing compared to what happened to them at Privoloki. When they came out of the meeting they found their horses harnessed backwards. The crowd stood around and guffawed. The loss of face was compounded when they started to set things right, and in their embarrassment got the straps all mixed up, much to the amusement of the villagers.

Shayke began to hate his job, and to be really afraid of the peasants. Especially when he had to go out alone. The village seemed alien and baleful. The white fields, the sharp rays of the sun, the whole scene looked menacing. He swallowed his fear, pulled his cap over his ear, and spat to one side.

"Never mind," he told himself. "The Revolution is stronger than they are. It will get them into line."

39

One fine day Sorokeh showed up. The comrades rushed out to greet him.

"Sorokeh! Back again!"

After exchanging a few words with them, he turned to go.

"If you're heading for the old bath-house, it's cold there, Sorokeh, even on the top bunk."

Polyishuk didn't go out to meet him. Instead, he asked Leahtche, "That the anarchist you were talking about?"

"Yes," she answered, reddening.

"A counterrevolutionary," was his verdict.

"Sorokeh a counterrevolutionary? Why, he's the most revolutionary of all!"

"No anarchist is a revolutionary," he declared with finality.

Leahtche forced herself to keep quiet.

"And you better keep away from him."

"Really? Why?"

"Just like that."

"Is this advice you're offering?"

He didn't respond, but said with a trace of venom, "What's he doing here?"

"How should I know? I suppose he has some business here."

Leahtche was in a state of confusion that day. She felt drawn to Sorokeh, but then Polyishuk's warning held her back. "That warning of his," she told herself, "is proof positive."

That was the trouble with him. You had to put two and two together. Nothing was explicit. On the other hand, Sorokeh's explicitness wasn't leading to anything either. How different the two men were! The one a strong personality, a Communist through and through, clear about what he had to do, knowing which way he was headed; the other sensitive, excitable, a poet and an orator, a man who treated every woman as though she were a princess. Which, then, of the two? Who could make such a decision? Meantime, neither one was getting her anywhere. This romance of hers could end up as a tragedy. She tried to laugh to herself.

That evening the young people gathered around Sorokeh in the old bath-house. He had lit the stubs of two candles, but their guttering light did little to dispel the darkness. Grotesque shadows chased themselves in ghostly fashion around the walls, rising, falling, intermingling, subsiding. Sorokeh had seated himself on a board in front of the semi-circular old furnace, into which he was poking dried branches left over from the time when the people of Mokry-Kut used them as switches on Friday afternoons. Long thin tongues of flame leaped up, licking the soot-covered rim of the oven.

The young men and the girls crowded around Sorokeh,

some of them crouched on their toes in front of the flames, their faces glowing like coals. Sorokeh held forth, expounding the doctrines of Marx and Engels, and criticizing the acts of Lenin and Trotsky. The comrades remained unconvinced, the die having already been cast in favor of Lenin and Trotsky.

"Your God is Kropotkin," they told him, "while we are followers of Trotsky."

When Sorokeh got the best of the theoretical argument, they discounted him anyway.

"What you're saying is just high-flown speculation, it has nothing to do with the world of reality. Nothing will come of your fine-spun rhetoric."

Leahtche felt that the debate was fruitless, so she broke into a Yiddish song. Everybody seemed to enjoy it, and she sang on, with childlike abandon. When she had exhausted her repertoire, Masha took over, with a group of Gypsy melodies, accompanied by the appropriate gyrations.

After that, everybody burst into a Ukrainian song. Then the boys started telling jokes and doing imitations, and everybody laughed and had a good time.

When the crowd broke up around midnight, Sorokeh walked Leahtche home. They walked slowly, by the light of the snow and the twinkling stars. All was quiet in the empty street. The only sound was the crunch of the snow beneath their feet, and the murmur of Sorokeh's voice as he talked of longing and of love.

"I knew you'd come back this winter," Leahtche murmured.

"You knew?" Sorokeh whispered. "How did you know?"

"Something told me."

He put his arm around her and drew her closer. She felt the sweetness of the moment, the happiness. Polyishuk was completely absent from her thoughts. She was alone with Sorokeh, there was no one else in the world. What a dear fellow! How lovable! How good to be walking with him, listening to him! How spacious the sky, how unusually bright and brilliant the stars! Ah, God in heaven, what a fellow was this! She could go with him to the ends of the earth.

40

Sorokeh went to have a look at the little streets adjoining the burned-out marketplace. He stood gazing at the gaunt chimney stacks, bereft of the houses which they had been part of; at the single surviving stucco wall of a house, with its useless doorway in the middle; at bits and pieces of iron and tin sticking out of a pile of snow; and at the snow piles themselves, in every shape and size, covering God knows what wreckage.

He proceeded down the miserable little streets, and began going into houses where he didn't know a soul. He just walked in, sat down, and started talking to the people. How were things in Mokry-Kut? What about the new government? He learned that some of them had sons in the army, or at the University, and that some of their sons were commissars in Kiev, in Zhitomir, in Odessa.

A few borrowed money from him. To some he made a gift without being asked, just put his hand in his pocket and handed over whatever coins and bills came up, without counting, as though he were trying to lighten his load.

At any rate, that's the way people described it. "Would that there were more panhandlers like him, *Ribbono-shel-Olam!*"

There was one person of whom he made a request, Freyda the widow, whose husband had died of typhus the year before. She was a pale young woman, her eyes permanently downcast. She had two little boys and an old mother who lived with her. Her house was filled with all kinds of useless glass objects, because her husband had worked in the glass factory. Sorokeh asked if he could eat his midday meal regularly at her table.

Freyda was perplexed by the request. She sat, not looking at him directly, her hands slack on her lap.

"Where will I get food?" she said.

Sorokeh was not to be put off. He answered that he wasn't choosy about what he ate, he would be no trouble at all, he would share whatever she and her family had.

"But what?" she wondered aloud, turning the thing over in her mind. "The market has been wiped out. The butchers slaughter only once in a long time, there's no poultry at all, you can't find a potato or a glass of milk."

Sorokeh answered soothingly that he would make do with whatever there was. He turned to the grandmother.

"What do you say?"

"Any way you like," the old woman shrugged.

He stood up, took a bundle of Kerensky bills from his pocket, and put them on the table. Freyda stared at him as though he had gone out of his mind.

Outside, he made his way to the pharmacy that was a sort of boundary mark between the Jewish and the gentile neighborhoods. The pharmacist, Yosef Piltch, had been a student long ago at the yeshiva of Sorokeh's father. He was a bachelor, eight or ten years older than Sorokeh. He had fallen in love with a Russian woman, the doctor of Mokry-Kut, and having followed her there, had remained in town, and was still a bachelor.

Piltch gave Sorokeh a cool reception. How, he wanted to know, not getting up from his chair, how was the Rabbi? "Still breathing?"

The conversation lagged. A whole world had come between them.

"Foul atmosphere," said Piltch with a grimace.

"Foul?" Sorokeh was surprised. "Why, it's a bright sunny day."

"I mean, the atmosphere of events, of current history."

"The Revolution?"

"The Revolution." Piltch looked as though he had tasted something bad. "And what's to follow? Truth? Justice? International brotherhood? A regular idyll. . . ."

Piltch's eye strayed to the apothecary's jar that glowed with a red light in the window.

"A jar full of foulness," he whispered, as though to himself, "borne by folly. . . ."

Sorokeh laughed.

"And you've stuck your neck into this filthy swamp," Piltch went on in a deprecatory tone. "Making history, I suppose!"

He kept on in the same fashion, not waiting for an answer, and finally summed up, "I don't get involved in this mess."

Sorokeh started to leave.

"How long will you be here?" asked Piltch.

"Oh, I don't know. Not very long."

"Tell me, do you play vingt? Come around in the evening, and we'll go over to Dr. Stephanida Dmitrievna's. A small group of us are meeting at her place this evening for cards. Her husband, of course, and the priest, the teacher and two or three others."

Sorokeh went on his way. He had found the encounter both amusing and sad. A good man gone to seed, making a virtue out of his own decay.

41

Polyishuk ran into Sorokeh on the street. He stopped and looked him over.

"Comrade Sorokeh?"

"Present," answered Sorokeh, military style.

"Polyishuk." He stuck out his hand. "Head of the Revkom in Mokry-Kut."

"Aha," said Sorokeh, a note of contempt in his voice.

"No doubt you've come to help us run the Revolution. Very good. We need men like you."

"Like me?" Sorokeh feigned surprise.

"We're shorthanded on the cultural side, comrade. I'm ready to appoint you. We can get the school going, organize courses, lectures. I know that you and I don't see eye to eye on a few matters, but in culture the Revolution can accept you. I've heard of you. You're an anarchist."

"Right. An anarchist."

"Very well, then a Communist too. We both eat from the same loaf."

"Aha." Sorokeh looked him up and down. "And you spit the whole thing out in one wad."

Polyishuk's face clouded, but he controlled himself.

"I see you're carrying a revolver. By official permission, I presume."

"Want to check? Go right ahead." And with a polite smile, Sorokeh pulled the weapon out of his pocket and pointed it at Polyishuk.

Polyishuk walked away. He realized now that the two would never get along. The truth is, he had disliked Sorokeh even before they met, partly because of Leahtche, but mostly because he hated everybody who was not a Bolshevik. He was especially hostile to those young Jews who had fallen for the anarchist line. A bunch of wastrels and windbags, he told himself; their fancy spouting was good only for attracting romantic young girls.

Later that very day Leahtche brought Sorokeh to the Revkom. She wanted to show him how things functioned, how well they were organized. She tried to introduce him to Polyishuk, but neither one put out his hand. They stood glaring at one another.

Her embarrassed smile disappeared. "What's wrong?"

"We've met," snapped Polyishuk, drumming his fingertips on the table.

"More than just met," grinned Sorokeh.

Leahtche shifted a surprised glance alternately between the two men. "What! You know each other?"

Sorokeh looked at the pictures of Lenin and Trotsky hanging on the wall. "The red gendarmerie?" he asked.

Polyishuk clenched his fist, his eyes flashing balefully. "Watch out what you're saying!"

"What's going on here?" Leahtche wanted to know. "Why are the two of you standing like two roosters ready to fight?"

Sorokeh was not deterred. "So that's what the Revolution is all about," he said, "so that you people can have authority to tyrannize the public."

"What are you saying!" Leahtche looked astonished. Her lips were trembling. "It's the dictatorship of the proletariat!"

"Let him alone!" Polyishuk ordered. "Don't you see who you're dealing with? A counterrevolutionary!"

"Ah-nu," Sorokeh addressed Leahtche. "Dictatorship of the proletariat. So that kind of dictatorship is permissible, eh?" He put his fingers gently under her chin. "Daughter of a learned Jew, lift up your eyes and take a look at what you people are doing. How much unnecessary hardship and suffering you're causing. Even here, in this God-forsaken little town. What for? What purpose does it serve? These poor people have to pay for all the sins of the bourgeoisie! Tell me, what hope is there for these poor lost Jews, what have they got to look forward to?"

Leahtche straightened up. "I'm not a nationalist." She shook her head solemnly. "I'm for humanity as a whole."

Sorokeh burst out in uncontrolled laughter. "Shame on you," he said when he got his breath back. "You used to be a nice innocent girl, and now you've been spoiled by this nonsense."

"I don't care what you say," she answered, offended, "but I'm not a nationalist. I'll go further, I'm an anti-nationalist. I'm a Communist."

"What a Jewish answer!" Sorokeh laughed again. "No *goy* would say, 'I'm not a Russian, I'm not a Ukrainian.' Only Jews talk like that."

Polyishuk stood up, head crunched between his shoulders, jaw jutting out, lips curled with rage, and shouted, "Get the hell out of here, you lackey of the bourgeoisie, you leftover of the clergy! Out!" And he pulled his gun out of its holster.

Without hesitation Sorokeh thrust his hand into his pocket and pulled out a huge key, pointing it at Polyishuk.

"Stop it!" Leahtche rushed in between the two. "What are you, *goyim* or something?"

"Clown!" Polyishuk muttered between clenched teeth, putting the gun back in its holster. "Just wait. We'll take care of the likes of you. Your time will come."

Sorokeh stood there, twirling the key around his finger. Leahtche burst out in hysterical laughter.

"With a key? Holding him up with a key?" She doubled over, gasping for breath. "With a key!" she choked out, "I'm dying! Oy mama! With a key!"

She got control of herself and started to lecture them. "What are you two quarreling over? Your grandmother's legacy or something?"

42

Sorokeh tried to make himself useful. He busied himself with the schoolchildren, whose attendance had fallen off for want of food and proper clothes. He worked with a Zionist club, firing the young members' imagination with his fervor, with his vision of a restructured Jewish people, imparting to them his enthusiasm for the Hebrew language and culture.

He would go to the marketplace and observe the paltry activity, a handful of townsfolk, mostly women, trading with the few peasants who showed up with some cabbages, half a sack of potatoes, a few beets. These would be bartered for a clock, a copper tray, some glass object or other, a frayed silk dress.

Or he would drop in on the poorest Jews, leaving behind a bit of saccharin, some toffee, a spool of thread, flints and matches, not to speak of the money he distributed. It was rumored that he had a pile in the old bath-house, a sack full of Kerensky money, and another one stuffed with Romanov currency.

Some people said it was tainted money, probably looted. Others took a more lenient attitude. "It's just money," they said.

"What do you mean, just money?" the doubters retorted. "Do you suppose it's his own, or a legacy from his father, the head of the yeshiva? Come on, it's loot, downright stolen."

"We go by the rule 'take what's offered,' " came the answer. "Money has no odor." This argument carried weight with most of the womenfolk, who bore the brunt of trying to keep their households together. "As long," they said, "as it doesn't come from the Bolsheviks, those robbers and murderers, those apostates."

"Wine and vinegar are one species," said the more finicky types. "You can choke on either one. The anarchist is also a kind of Bolshevik."

Yankel Potchtar offered to explain the whole matter.

"There are three parties," he began. "There is the Bolshevik party, the Menshevik party, and the Anarchist party. The terms explain themselves. *Bolshe* means big, so the Bolshevik is the big fellow, who has infested the whole country. Menshevik means the little one, and so he has been from the very start. The Anarchist is the *archilistos* mentioned in the Talmud. For them there is no mine and thine, it's all one big pot."

The women especially liked Sorokeh. These pitiful souls, crushed by poverty, some pregnant, some nursing their infants or frantic with the care of numerous children, all of them unhappy and constantly bemoaning their lot, full of sighs and imprecations—for them it was a comfort to talk with Sorokeh.

He would listen attentively to their woes and their problems, and his answers were always comforting.

"A fine young man," they would whisper, as they watched him leave. It was as though his bright face and warm manner had brought them back, if only for the moment, to better days, when they had been young brides, to days of goodness and blessing before all this bitter misery had descended upon them.

43

In a way, Sorokeh was envious of young Jews like Polyishuk who had cast off their Jewishness and joined the general populace. For them life was much simpler. They followed the Party line; Jewish problems were no concern of theirs. For him it was different. He was torn between his universalist humanitarianism and the woes of his own people.

Not that he didn't have his accounts to settle with the Jewish people. He was highly critical of many of their customs and habits, of some of the petty rituals to which they clung. He railed against the immutability of their Torah, against their faith in miracles, their messianic hopes, while all the time their fate was decided by others, not by themselves. Inwardly he characterized them as "empty bags," "dried out old branches."

Ach, he thought, these otherworldly spectators of history, these peddlers and petty traders of the world, for whom creation with its fields and forests and rivers scarcely exists; all they know about is the miserable penny. This poor and bitter people, excitable, complicated, wordy. Yes, they were sharp and clever talkers, but their talk was like their action, not proceeding in a straight line, but jumping rabbitlike from one clever phrase to another, from one jest to another, and settling matters with a biblical verse or a wise saying from the Talmud. They were, he told himself, like beggars going from door to door, nourishing themselves on what scraps could be had, economically and spiritually uncreative.

But he didn't only play the prosecutor. He had something to say in defense of his people, though this too was tinged with mocking bitterness. Just think, he ruminated, here is a Jew, dirt-poor, evicted from his house because he hasn't got the rent, his wife is pregnant and his children are crying for bread, and what does he do? He stands outside reciting the benediction for the new moon! "May it be Thy will, O Lord my God and my father's God, that the flawed moon be restored to fullness." That's his only worry —the fullness of the moon! We Jews are the Don Quixotes of history!

From time to time he would forsake the big cities, Kiev and Kharkov and Odessa, and return to the region where he had grown up, to be with "his Jews," to experience their lowliness and poverty, their despair and bitterness of soul.

"What's new with you?" he would ask.

"Thank God," they would sigh, "everything as usual. Those who are starving are starving, and those who are suffering are suffering. Everything is in its proper place. So we're drowning in the whirlpool? Thank God, as long as we still have the strength to drown."

If he raised the subject of Eretz Yisroel, of the Land of Israel, they would sigh deeply, and say, "But we're in *golus,* in exile."

If he persisted, "Do you want to go to Palestine?" they would sigh again and answer, "Certainly, if it were up to us."

"Well, who is it up to?"

"The Messiah, may he come soon."

"Maybe we should go out to meet him halfway?"

"Oh no, that would be improper. It is written that the Holy One came down on Mount Sinai, and not that Mount Sinai climbed up to the Holy One."

When the Revolution came, at the same time that people heard about the Balfour Declaration, they began to think that maybe some good would come out of the war and its attendant suffering.

After all, they said, the Land of Israel is desolate, and the people of Israel is in ruins. They make a good pair. But when Sorokeh suggested that now was a good time to think about going to Palestine, they looked at him as though he had gone out of his mind.

"Now?" they said. "Now, just when the law of the Pale has been abolished, and we're allowed to live in Kiev, Moscow, Petrograd?"

Then, when the hand of the Bosheviks was heavy on them, they sighed, "The *golus* itself is in *golus*."

44

What had been a gap between the generations before the Revolution now became a yawning chasm. It happened without fireworks, without arguments or recriminations. It was as though the parent generation had been dismissed, forlorn characters with no more roles to play. The young people seemed to belong to a new species, for whom the burdens and sorrows of their parents were of no concern, and the values of their parents of no interest. This was true for the young Bolsheviks, as well as for the group that called themselves Tseire Tsiyon, the Youth of Zion.

There were not really any Zionists in Mokry-Kut, except for this handful of boys and girls. Polyishuk detested the little group and all that they represented. His hate was mixed with contempt, the contempt of a man of action for a powerless group of ineffectual talkers. They, in their turn, were afraid of him. The worst Bolsheviks, they said, were the Jews.

Even the parents of these young people didn't take the impractical enthusiasms of their youngsters seriously. Better become Bolsheviks, they said, than waste time on talk that could lead nowhere.

The Youth of Zion spoke Hebrew to one another, in the Sephardic accent. They took turns delivering lectures on modern Hebrew literature, and dreamed of settling in Palestine. They spent a lot of time debating what they called "ideological fundamentals." Some of them sought a synthesis between Zionism and Marxism, others were firm in their adherence to the principles of democracy. The most clever among them invented new social theories.

Sorokeh's contribution was unique: he advocated a combination of Zionism and Anarchism. His idea was rejected by all the others, who declared the two ideologies incompatible. But Sorokeh defended his invention with great skill, until Dena spoke up in a deliberately little-girl voice. "Does your grandmother's merit prove you right?"

She was only sixteen, this Dena, a short girl not yet fully developed, still a bit bony at the shoulders and elbows. Her hair was pale straw, her face white, with a touch of red in the cheekbones, her eyes like two drops of blue seawater. Most of the group thought her pretty. They said she reminded them of a nasturtium.

But the main thing was, everybody was fond of her, even the Bolsheviks. They were attracted by her quickness of wit and tongue, by her childlike vivacity, and most especially by her constant laughter. The least little thing would send her into gales of mirth and double her over gasping for breath, until finally she would straighten up, wipe the tears from her eyes, and pant, "Oy, these Jews of ours!"

For another thing, she liked to recite before the group,

and to take part in the dramatic productions put on jointly by the young Bolsheviks and the Tseire Tsiyon. She would get up and sing modern Hebrew songs, like "How Delicate Her Hand Was," and Bialik's " 'Twixt the Tigris and Euphrates," and Tchernikhovsky's "Laugh at All My Dreams, My Dearest."

The Bolsheviks tried hard to win her over, but she would fend them off. "You don't argue with a sixteen-year-old," she would tell them.

"That's just it," they would answer. "You're young, you don't understand."

"And how old is the Revolution?" she would counter. "If youth is a defect, it's a minor one; if it's a virtue, it's soon gone."

Sorokeh took pains to explain to her the theory of Anarchism. She grasped it all quite well. Others in the group who stood by confessed that they couldn't see what Anarchism had to do with Zionism.

"What don't you understand?" she asked, adopting her little-girl pose. "Come, I'll spoon-feed it to you. They use either Marxism or Anarchism as fuel to heat the pot of Zionism. Now do you see?"

Whereupon she burst out laughing, and everybody joined in.

Sorokeh decided not to press his argument. "Very well," he said. "You stick to your own opinion."

"Right," she answered. "Period. Enough said."

Sorokeh didn't share the general opinion that she was pretty; after all, her eyelids and eyelashes were so pale as to be almost invisible, and she was short-legged, somewhat thick from the waist down. But that didn't make any difference to him; he was quite fond of her.

They had an interest in common. Together they spent a lot of time with the schoolchildren, in school and out, since the teacher was sick more often than not. Sorokeh and Dena took over, teaching the children Hebrew and Jewish history, telling them about modern Hebrew literature, and about the Jewish settlements in Palestine, about such places as Kinneret and Degania. Then, if it was a bright night, they would all go sleigh-riding down one of the steep streets, flying over the snow on little sleds, filling the street with gay shouts and laughter.

45

In the synagogue, all was desolation—books piled helter-skelter on the shelves, benches awry, lecterns leaning on their sides. The clock had stopped, as though waiting for the Holy One to repent of His anger. There was no light in the brass candelabra, only an occasional metallic glint to punctuate the dullness of the room. A sharp ray of daylight slanted from the top of the window down to the laver that stood near the doorway.

The morning service was over, and a group of men, still bound in their *tefillin* and wrapped in their prayer shawls, sat at the eastern wall, to the right of the holy ark. They were talking things over, the old times before the Revolution, the war, the uprooted Jews wandering everywhere, Germany and England and America, Czar Nikolai, who had been deposed.

"It's the same old story," said Reb Mordkhe-Leib Segal. "Four kings against five."

None of them knew what he was talking about.

Reb Ozer Hagbeh, hands on his stomach, put the question. "What do you mean, four against five?"

"What do I mean?" Reb Mordkhe-Leib stroked his mustache with a tired smile. "Germany, Austria, Turkey, Bulgaria—there's your four. Russia, England, France, America, Italy—makes five. Four against five."

"Nu?"

"Nu-nu!" with a touch of impatience. "History repeats itself. What do we read in Genesis? 'It came to pass in the days of Amrafel, king of Shiner, Ariokh, king of Elasar, Cedarlaomer, king of Elam, and Tidal, king of Goiim'—that makes four. 'These made war against Bera, king of Sodom, and Birsha, king of Gomorrah, Shinab, king of Admah, and Shemeber, king of Zeboiim, and the king of Bela, which is Zoar.' That adds up to five. And there was another one there, from beyond the river, waiting in the wings. See? History repeats itself."

"Ah!" Reb Ozer Hagbeh sighed admiringly, pulling himself up and smiling appreciatively at the others.

Reb Mordkhe-Leib drove home his point. "Now you understand where this Revolution comes from, and why I've been driven from my home and my livelihood. The serpent gives birth to the dragon."

"Sodom," said Yankel Potchtar with a grin and a wink. "That stands for So-dem—Social Democrat."

Reb Mordkhe-Leib started to pace the floor, softly singing a sad tune to himself. Yankel Potchtar walked up to him and said, "When does a Jew sing? When he's hungry."

Heshel Pribisker looked up from the book he was studying. "Even as it is written, 'At eventide he lieth down weeping, but in the morning, a song.' In the evening he cries because he has nothing to eat, and in the morning he sings because his stomach is empty."

He paused for a moment. "Eating is not an end in itself. It's a sop thrown to Satan. Here, take this and choke on it. Fill your mouth and leave me alone, so that I can study Torah."

Reb Mordkhe-Leib and Yankel continued their separate pacing. Heshel gave a deep sigh. "I'm left with only three things," he said, "my soul, my Torah, and my people." He pulled the lectern toward him and went back to his book.

Jiggling his feet to keep warm, Reb Ozer made a pronouncement. "The synagogue used to be a friendly place. If a wagoner or a porter or any other poor Jew wanted to warm himself up, he only had to come in. Now it's cold in here. Cold."

Reb Avrohom-Abba raised the question of Czar Nikolai and his family, who had been arrested by the Bolsheviks. "What's happened to Nikolka?" he worried. "Where is he? What are they doing to him?"

"They'll fix him," Reb Ozer threw out. "Never you fear!"

"Oh, will they fix him!" chimed in Kalman the baker. "On them you can depend."

Reb Mordkhe-Leib stopped his meandering and faced them with the deliberateness of a judge pronouncing a verdict.

"They'll kill him. And he deserves it. When he dispersed the first Duma, before the war, he signed his own death warrant. As long as he was absolute ruler, sovereignty was his. When the Duma was convened, it became sovereign. When he shut the Duma down, that made him a rebel against constituted authority, and liable to the penalty of death."

46

At that moment Sorokeh was passing by. After a moment's hesitation, he decided to enter the synagogue. Seeing him, Reb Mordkhe-Leib fell silent while Yankel Potchtar jumped up, hand outstretched in welcome, a doubtful smile on his face.

"Ah, *sholom aleikhem,*" he greeted. *"Zdrastie, tovarishch."*

The rest gathered around, each greeting him in turn.

"Where from?" they asked, not unkindly.

"From the big wide world," he answered. "Nu, how are you people here these days?"

"Thank God." It was Yankel Potchtar, answering for all of them.

"Thank God for what?"

"For what?" Yankel laughed, as at an idle question that has no real answer. " 'That He hath not made me a woman, that He hath not made me a *goy'*—and that He hath not made me a murderer."

The others smiled silently, nodding their heads.

"So?" Sorokeh sat down, almost upsetting the bench. Some of the men quickly sat beside him, while the others sat facing him.

"You're the one who lives in the old bath-house," Yankel winked. "I know."

"Yes, in the old bath-house."

"The *mikveh,* the ritual bath there isn't kosher," jested Yankel. Laughter.

"It's not the *mikveh* that counts," interjected Heshel Pribisker, to no one in particular. "It's the going to the *mikveh* that's important."

"The *mikveh* purifies the impure," said Reb Mordkhe-Leib. "But what's to be done when the *mikveh* itself is full of impurity?"

"See what he means?" laughed Yankel. "He's not talking like a religious fanatic."

Sorokeh let that pass. He wanted to know how they were managing.

"Nu," he said, "what's doing? What do you hear?"

"What do we hear? Don't you know? 'Great weeping,' that's what we hear; 'sighing and sorrow,' 'calamity upon calamity,' that's what's doing."

Sorokeh tried to soothe them. "That's how it is with revolutions."

"But there never has been a *golus* like this," sighed Reb Avrohom-Abba.

"Golus is always *golus,"* intoned Heshel Pribisker, as though he were chanting a passage of Talmud. "If the *goy* is bad, your body is in danger. If he's good, your soul is in danger. Either way, your lot is bitter."

"But when you're in *golus* at the hands of Jews," interrupted Yankel. "Ah, there's nothing worse than that, God preserve us!"

"What moves them," said Heshel gently, "whether they know it or not, is the zeal for the Lord that burns in their hearts."

"Listen to that!" Reb Avrohom-Abba pointed an accusing finger at Heshel. "He's defending them. Zeal for the Lord indeed!"

They talked on, but the conversation was halting, the atmosphere restrained and suspicious. In the minds of the Jews in the synagogue there was no great difference between Sorokeh and the Bolsheviks. True, they had heard that he said one thing and the Bolsheviks another, but they were still suspicious, and thought of him as belonging to the enemy camp. What they had against him especially was that he came from a good family, the son of a head of a yeshiva, and was said to be deeply learned in Talmud and the religious codes—and look how badly he had strayed! On top of that, they remembered how he had led the peasants in ravaging the landowners' estates, things that even the Bolsheviks had not done.

Adopting a tone of pretended humility, Yankel Potchtar tried to draw him out. "Look, I'm in the dark about this business, try as I will I haven't been able to understand it. Tell me, what are you? Are you a Bolshevik, or what?"

"An Anarchist," Sorokeh answered.

Gates of Bronze | *126*

Yankel was puzzled. "Not a Bolshevik?"

"No."

"So what's the difference?"

"A big difference," answered Sorokeh, not explaining.

"Are you againt the Bolsheviks?" Yankel interrogated. "Are the Anarchists opponents of the Bolsheviks?"

"Certainly."

"Like Avremel Voskiboinikov the Menshevik? Aiee, Bolsheviks, Mensheviks, Anarchists. The Holy One has left nothing out in this world of His."

"We never dreamed," said Reb Avrohom-Abba, "that our own youth would behave so badly."

"We wanted a revolution," said Reb Mordkhe-Leib. "So now we've got a revolution."

"We must have said our prayers wrong," nodded Reb Ozer Hagbeh.

"We besought the Lord 'who looketh on the earth, and it trembleth,'" murmured Heshel, absently.

"What? What?" Reb Ozer was mystified by the remark.

"When 'the worm of Jacob' turns into 'the strong men of Israel,'" offered Reb Avrohom-Abba, plaintively.

Yankel Potchtar went back to his cross-examination. "Well then," he said to Sorokeh, "it seems that your crowd are against the Bolsheviks. If so, what part do you play in the Revolution? Being an Anarchist, does that make you for us or against us?"

"If the fish has scales, you don't have to examine him for fins," mocked Reb Mordkhe-Leib learnedly.

With a heart full of pain and pity Sorokeh looked around at the Jews before him, poor victims of the Revolution, for whom the future held no promise.

"Don't pin any hopes on the Jewish Communists," he told them. "They themselves are no more than tools in the hands of others. And they're the very ones who will tear up the Jewish people by the roots."

"Then what's the way out?" asked Reb Avrohom-Abba.

"The way out?" Sorokeh reflected for a moment. "Way out, you say? There's no way out."

He waited for their reaction, but nobody spoke, so he went on. "There's no solution for you because you have nothing to fall back on, nothing you can really call your own."

"All right," said Yankel Potchtar, "Granted we have nothing to look forward to from the Bolsheviks. But what about you and your Anarchists?"

Sorokeh launched into a disquisition on the theory of revolution and the classless society, and the distinctions between Communism and Anarchism. They listened politely in silence. Finally, everybody got up to go.

Reb Mordkhe-Leib offered Sorokeh a kindly parting word. "The Holy One, blessed be He, abolished classes long ago, when the Israelites left Egypt. You know, 'a kingdom of priests and a holy people.'"

"Oho, that's it," agreed Kalman the baker. "You can't say that one person is first-grade carrot pudding, while the other is ordinary sour soup. But you people want to abolish all distinctions, and make everybody alike."

"What's the good of all this talk," said Yankel, with a nudge to Kalman. But Kalman the baker held his ground.

"No, I've got a right to speak. I'm a Jew who earns his living by his own ten fingers and the sweat of his brow. I've a right to speak my piece. I don't care if they're *bolshevniki* or not, these young Jews of ours. Let them be what they want. What gripes me is that they are wicked, cruel, overbearing. I'm wise to them, thank the Lord. That time, when I went with Bunem and the Rabbi. . . ."

He was off, describing once again his mission on behalf of the community, and what he said to Polyishuk, and what Polyishuk said to him.

They all left the synagogue, and Sorokeh headed toward the post office. He felt depressed, involved in the sorry fate of these broken, uprooted Jews, whose like was legion throughout the land.

"Is this really the end?" he whispered aloud, his face twisted with pain, his eyes roving over the houses sunk in snow, taking in the dirt-gray skies that lowered over the miserable roofs.

47

Each of the girls in Mokry-Kut had her own particular young man, with whom she would go walking, share her thoughts and sighs and daydreams, discuss the great problems of life. It was fully expected that a time would come when each girl would marry the man of her choice.

This fashion of courtship had developed in the previous generation, replacing the custom of matchmaking by parents and relatives. It was what distinguished a modern, enlightened girl from her old-fashioned sisters.

Malia was such an enlightened girl, who had read Gorki, and Andreyev, and Forel's "The Sexual Question." Her romance with Shimtze contained all the ingredients set forth in the classical novels—dreams, sighs, yearnings—a real affair of the heart. That is, until Shimtze departed from the prescribed form. One day, when the comrades were at some sort of celebration, she saw him off in a corner with Ethel, the two of them talking and laughing.

Malia made it plain that she was outraged. Shimtze came over and tried to appease her, but she wouldn't listen. "Go ahead!" she said, "go to your Ethel, go!"

"What's wrong? Because I was talking to Ethel? That's all it was, just talk. It doesn't mean a thing."

Malia was adamant. Her romance was going to be pure and unblemished, or not at all. "No!" she stamped her foot. "Don't think you can fool me. You want to bite the bread and the onion at the same time? Not with me, not with Malia!"

"But it was nothing! You and I both know that there's nothing between me and Ethel."

"You're a traitor!" Malia flared. She was flushed, her eyes filled with tears. "You have sullied my love, the purest and holiest feelings of my heart!"

"Me? A traitor?" Shimtze was deeply offended. "A traitor? So that's what you think of me. Nu, so be it. Goodbye, then!"

He stamped off, and the two of them spent the rest of the time apart, as though they had nothing to do with each other.

"Just you wait!" he said to himself. "She'll come crawling back, you'll see! I'm not just anybody, to be treated like that! Can you imagine? The pot isn't kosher because a drop of milk fell on the meat! So I spoke to Ethel. . . . Does she think she can stop me talking to people? Nu-nu! She puts in a kopeck and demands a whole ruble!"

As for Malia, she waited for him to come back and apologize.

"Never mind," she comforted herself, "if he's worthy of you he'll come back."

In the meantime she went around downcast and melancholy, like a person who had suffered a great personal tragedy.

48

Leahtche's thoughts raced from Sorokeh to Polyishuk and back again. She was torn, filled with doubts, unable to make up her mind how she really felt. Then suddenly one day at twilight the fog lifted from her spirits, and it became clear that Sorokeh was the one for her. Some inner voice handed down the verdict, and all the turbulent conflict in her heart subsided, to be replaced by great joy, like the sun breaking through heavy clouds. Now the future spread out before her as one unending feast day. She felt as though something decisive had already taken place, radically changing the meaning and flavor of her life.

That evening when she met Sorokeh he sensed something different about her.

"What's the matter, Leahtche?"

She bent her head, and gave no answer.

"Something happen?"

She laughed. "Yes, something."

"What?" He took both her hands in his.

"No, no, I won't tell you."

He looked at her thoughtfully. "Good or bad?"

"I don't know."

"Don't know?"

She didn't respond.

"Tell me, is it something normal, that happens to everybody?"

"No," she shook her head. "It's something that rarely happens in this world."

"Rarely happens?"

"Very, very rarely!"

He thought that over for a while, puzzled. "I don't know what to say." Then he bent over and kissed her. She hid her face in her hands, like a woman blessing the Sabbath candles. "Darling—" She trembled, and burst into tears.

"What's the matter?" Sorokeh was alarmed. "What's wrong, dear girl of mine?"

She bent over, crying uncontrollably.

"Tell me, dearest, what happened? Tell me."

"Nothing happened."

"Then why are you crying?"

"It's nothing." She couldn't look him in the face.

Sorokeh gazed at her reflectively. An expression of sadness crossed his face.

49

The gentile comrades were attracted to Sorokeh, even though they didn't agree with his ideas. They regarded him as a loner.

"Head and shoulders above the rest of the comrades," they said, "and yet, without roots."

They liked him especially for what he had done on behalf of the peasants, when he led them in burning down the mansions of the estate owners, and parceling out the lands to the village farmers. There was one thing he had done for which they didn't thank him—he had set fire to the distillery. Since then, they grumbled, there wasn't a drop of liquor fit for human consumption to be found. Hence this cursed home brew, this damned *samogon*, devil take it.

Then they would make the best of a bad job, and say, "Well, as long as that's the worst of our troubles. Things will pick up, we're not doing too badly."

Comrade Karpo expressed his opinion about Sorokeh. "He's like a windmill on a September day. Round and round with his tongue, round and round."

Comrade Ilko thought, no, Sorokeh reminded him of a wild goose. His meaning was unclear, but he probably meant it as praise, since Ilko preferred wild geese to the domestic variety. He was a hunter, and his speech was full of references to wild geese, ducks, rabbits, and the like.

From time to time these fellows would drop in on Sorokeh at the old bath-house, bringing him firewood from the forest and something to eat. At the same time they would sit around and ask him questions, like students at a seminar. They wanted him to explain what the different parties stood for, the Bolsheviks, the Mensheviks, the Anarchists.

Sorokeh would provide vodka and *samogon*. They praised the vodka and cursed the *samogon*.

"Now, as for your Menshevik," said Karpo, "he smells like vodka and tastes like *samogon.*"

Ilko, keeping to his own terms of discourse, tried his hand. "He's like a crow compared to a hawk."

Sorokeh adopted their idiom. "The horseradish," he said, "is not sweeter than the turnip." He went on to explain his theory of revolution. Whereupon Karpo interposed his objections.

"Wait a minute, now, hold it! This fellow is like a creek after the spring snow! According to us, the Bolshevik party is the right one, the natural one. Why? Because its policies are correct."

Nothing Sorkeh could say would budge them. The two sides were like stubborn rams, with horns locked.

Karpo said the only thing he had against the Anarchists

was that they wanted to abolish the state, which would do him out of being a commissar.

"Everything for them and nothing for me?" he protested.

By "them" he meant the past generations, society under the Czars. They, he argued, had their District Governors and Provincial Governors-General. Now he, Karpo, was the equivalent of a *Gubernator*. That's what a Commissar was—same thing as a *Gubernator*.

"Those days are over," he said, "when Grandpa Yehor was arrested for helping himself to one log out of the forest, and was sentenced to the lash, and used his cane to make crosses in the sand on his way to the village *volost* to be beaten. Those days are gone forever, yes sir! Now we're the bosses! Everything is ours now, all the lands, and the forests and the rivers all ours!"

"Right!" said Sorokeh helpfully. "Everything belongs to the people. It's all public property."

Karpo was infuriated. "You mean, that's all I get after suffering three years in the mines, and being wounded twice? And still nothing in it for me, hah? No, comrade, there's something wrong with your arithmetic, your calculations are way off base. We'll get what's coming to us, comrade, every man for himself. No, our party is the right one, the way it's all spelled out in our program—ours!"

Ilko agreed with Karpo.

"The old days will never come back," he proclaimed. "The old order is gone forever. There was a war. Quite a few people got killed—aiee, dark days they were! And now we've got a revolution, thanks be to God. Now the power is ours!"

"It's all very well for you to talk," Karpo grumbled, "you did all right for yourself. Took over land from the squire up to here"—Karpo put his palm under his chin—"not to speak of a cow, and two of the best horses, and quite a few sheep, and sacks of flour and barley, and all kinds of tools."

"Quite right," Ilko agreed. "I had it coming to me. Seems the Revolution owed it to me."

"Then what about me?" complained Karpo. "How come I get only a little bit of land, and one spavined old mare, and five sheep, and that's all?"

"Luck of the draw, brother," said Ilko complacently. "A lot of things are just a matter of chance."

50

The state of affairs in his village, said Karpo, was nothing short of a scandal. The peasants were drowning in *samogon,* may they drown in hellfire, beating their wives, fighting murderously with one another. All you could hear was shouting, screaming, weeping, quarrels, loud curses on the government. Yes. As bad as that. This people's government is something new, but the people haven't changed; no, they remain what they always were. What am I saying? They're worse than ever, drunkards, the lot of them, thievish, foul-mouthed, covetous, each man hating his neighbor. Look, last week they broke in Kornei Telepen's shed and beat up his cow. A good milch cow, she was. Then some character, devil take whoever it was, made off with a pig from Sidor Piven's barnyard. And one night Kondrat Shchur froze to death in a ditch, done in by his own drunkenness. Zeitchikha's baby was stillborn; Priska gave birth to an infant, but it died. As for the village girls, this one was walking around with a swollen belly, another was having labor pains. The whole village was one stinking mess.

And on top of everything, not a bite to eat, next to nothing. Go find a slice of bread to feed the children. What can you do? Your guts are knotted inside you. How does the proverb go? "Summer work for winter days, winter work for summer days." You figure it out: if there's no planting, where will the harvest come from? All right, the village got its hands on the squire's property. Yes. But what good came of it? Everything disappeared, gone with the wind. Who benefited? A few strong-armed types, that's who. They latched on to the best lands—curse them—took possession of the finest fields, and as for movables, aiee! Mother mine! They grabbed everything that wasn't nailed down. Their houses are filled to the rafters with loot.

"What about the village Council?" Polyishuk interrupted.

"Village Council? You mean you don't know?" Karpo pushed his lambskin hat back from his forehead. "Why, they themselves are the chief looters! They've grown themselves fat bellies, such-and-so on their mothers, and they're the ones who run the show. If you open your mouth about their ill-gotten gains, they bristle at you: What's it to you? Did we take anything of yours?"

Karpo went back to his old refrain. "I was the first to bear the brunt of the Revolution, and I'm the last to get anything for my pains." His fists were clenched, his eyes clouded over. "Three years I did time in the mines, and when the liberation finally came, what did I get? Not even a bone."

"What you're saying doesn't mean a thing," said Polyishuk.

"Doesn't mean a thing?" Karpo was thunderstruck. "Begging your pardon, have you gone crazy or something? Don't I count for anything? My family are the poorest of the poor in our village. Our history is written in welts on my grandpa's back. Yes. So now we have the Revolution, and I'm a Bolshevik and a commissar. And what do I get out of it? Nobody takes my poverty into account. No. It seems the Revolution is no honey pot, either. What happens to me? Nobody gives a bloody damn!"

Polyishuk tried to calm him down, but Karpo was too excited. "What's needed," he proclaimed, "is a new *instruktsia,* a directive to redistribute the land to those who need it, and keep that help-yourself crew out of it. Make them give back all the other property that they stole, too, and divide it among the needy. An *instruktsia,* that's what's called for. Let the Revolution proclaim justice, goddammit!"

"All right," said Polyishuk, "we'll think about it." Karpo's face lit up. He hitched up his *nagan,* his teeth gleaming in a broad smile.

"Khvakt?" said he. "Really?"

51

Malia was a very unhappy girl. Shimtze paid no attention to her, but went around with his nose in the air, as if nothing in the world bothered him. So she decided to make him jealous, and took to walking out with one fellow after another, with comrade Ziame, with comrade Sukhar, and comrade Muntchik.

From time to time she stopped in to see Sorokeh, and to philosophize with him about the meaning of love, and the theory of free love, and other such matters of major importance to an enlightened girl.

She felt that she was wasting her life in this godforsaken town, among ordinary, colorless people, none of whom understood her.

"Nobody in the whole world understands me. Well, they understand me, but not really. I'm not like other girls. I want to do something big with my life, I'm looking for beauty and harmony and great ideals. But here I am, suffocating in this miserable Mokry-Kut, with no way out. I'm simply stuck here, with big ideas and no luck."

What with one thing and another, she told him the story of her life, how her father had disappeared two years after the wedding, leaving her mother a grass widow until the day she died. After her mother's death three years ago, she had gone to live with her paternal grandmother, a sickly old woman. She had been making a living by taking in sewing, only now there was no work to be had. A sorry tale, but that's the way it is. Life these days is a sorry tale, sad, people are in a bad way. And especially women. Ach-ach, those poor women. . . .

"If it were up to me," she said with a grin, "I'd hang all the men on one rope, and send all the women off to summer resorts."

Then there were times when she would sit silent, lost in thought, and finally, with a little shiver, look around her, as though she had been far away and was trying to get her bearings.

"I hear a buzzing in one of my ears." She fixed her eyes on Sorokeh. "Tell me, which one?"

"The left."

"Wrong. It's my right ear." Then, half to herself, "That's a good sign for Shimtze. He never missed. I tested him lots of times, and he always got it right."

One morning Leahtche took it into her head, while she was working at her government job, to slip out of the office and run over to see Sorokeh. She ran excitedly, like one pursued, her cheeks aflame, her heart pounding, her breath short. Some great joy had overtaken her. She saw herself flinging the door open and saying, "Here I am!"

When she did open the door, she found him sitting and chatting with Malia. Her face fell.

"What a perfect idyll!" she gasped, still breathless from her running.

"Leahtche!" Sorokeh greeted her warmly. Malia stood up, red-faced.

"So you're looking around, hah?" said Leahtche to Malia, with a bitter knowing nod and a touch of contempt.

"Looking for what?" Malia pretended not to understand. Leahtche turned on Sorokeh.

"Tell me, if you please," she raged at him. "How many girls must you lead astray, how many dirty tricks do you have to play, in order to keep thinking yourself a superior person?"

Sorokeh sat smiling tolerantly, like an adult who has just heard a bit of childish prattle.

"As I live," Malia whispered to her, "there isn't a thing between us."

"Then what are you doing here?" stormed Leahtche. "What did you come for, to say Psalms?"

"I-I just came," stammered Malia.

"Just! Just like that! You can't fool me! Come on! You have no business here. Do you hear me? Don't come here any more! Out!"

"All right, all right," said Malia meekly. She bent over and picked up her book off the bench. The two girls left together, one stern and angry, head held high, the other downcast, ashamed.

52

Leahtche planned to have it out with Sorokeh. She would tell him off about Malia and all those other girls she imagined must have been stealing in to see him secretly; she would give it to him about all his faults and nasty habits. Yes, she would settle her accounts with him once and for all.

But by the end of the day she was worn out emotionally by all this inner turmoil, and as she made her way to him at nightfall, she was settling accounts with herself, rather than with him. After all, she concluded, he was not her husband, they were not even engaged, and she really had no claim on him.

So when she got there, all she said to him was, "You're a hopeless case."

Sorokeh let the remark go unanswered. He too seemed weary, in a melancholy mood. Leahtche sighed softly, and gave a little shiver. "Cold. . . . The whole world is cold. Where can a body find a little warmth?"

"Yes," said Sorokeh, absently, continuing his own train of thought. "There, there it's warm. The sun is shining, the fields are green, trees are in blossom."

"Where?" Leahtche turned to him.

He was silent.

"Where?" she repeated.

"In Palestine."

"Ah. . . ." she said wearily.

Darkness filled the old bath-house. The walls faded into the murk. It was like being adrift on a boundless sea.

"Just imagine," Sorokeh went on, "a day right out of the Bible—mountains and valleys, vineyards and olive trees, all surrounded by a hot, heavy stillness. Nice, hah? Just to lie resting in the shade of a tree at the foot of a mountain. Good, no?"

"Good," whispered Leahtche. "I wish winter were over. I can hardly wait for spring!"

"Or to bathe in the Jordan. . . ." Sorokeh continued.

"Bathe?" She shivered. "Br . . . rr . . . rr."

"On the contrary, it's good to bathe, because it's very hot. Or how about a hike through the mountains, wandering far out into the desert. Ah, the desert, the desert!"

"You talk as if you had been there." A touch of mockery crept into her voice.

"Yes," he agreed. "If you want to know, I do feel as though I had actually been there, and passed through the length and breadth of the land. I have a vivid picture of every hill and valley."

They fell silent, sitting apart, each sunk in his own thoughts. After a while Sorokeh sighed deeply.

"Ach!" he spoke into the darkness. "If only this people had the will!"

"What? Which people?"

"These Jews of ours."

"Nu?"

"Why, I would shake off the whole confused mess of this Revolution, and go to Eretz Yisroel."

"Enough foolish talk!" She stood up. "Come on, let's go. I'm frozen to death."

As soon as they were out of doors her mood changed. She twined her arm around his and walked with bouncing steps.

"Don't you talk such useless nonsense," she said. "Do you hear? It doesn't become you. Teach me instead about the night sky. How I love those stars! They light up my way, and I don't even know their names, ignoramus that I am!"

He stopped, and began pointing. "That's the North Star, there's Mars, over there is the Big Dipper. . . ."

"My, you know everything!" She snuggled up close, pressing her shoulder against him. "There isn't a thing you don't know!"

53

Freyda treated Sorokeh with all the dignity of a landlady who knows her place. She made no attempt to curry favor with him, or to engage him in conversation. Whenever he came into the house she set the table for him, and he ate.

The fact is, she didn't like his self-assurance, his tempestuous personality, or the raucous way he played with her children, making the whole house ring. He had forced himself into her life, creating a stir, disturbing the peace of her settled lonely widowhood. She said nothing, but kept wondering what she had to do with him, why he had picked on her house, paying her too much, and bringing her things from the village, bread, potatoes, cabbage, even firewood from the forest.

"What is this? What's going on?" she asked herself, spreading her questioning palms to no one in particular.

On the other hand, her mother, Nehama-Itta, saw nothing to be disturbed about. She was a slight, active creature, with a tiny pointed chin and bright clever eyes. Looking at her wrinkled old face, you could still tell that she had been a pretty girl.

"No cause for complaint," she said. "He's a fine man,

with a heart of gold, which is nothing to sneeze at. That's one thing. And for another, what's to question? Does a man have to eat, or doesn't he? Where is a poor lonely bachelor to get his meals? And besides, what do you care? Will he make you lose your grandmother's legacy? Have no fear. You won't lose out on account of him. And listen, don't be ungrateful. So he brings a little extra food into the house. Say thank you, and hold your tongue."

Sorokeh asked whether he could eat at the table with the family, but Freyda wouldn't agree to it. Sitting alone, she thought it over. "No, no!" she said to herself, agitated, signs of a deep hidden sadness visible at the corners of her mouth and around the edges of her eyes.

When he had eaten and left the house, Freyda put her hand over her eyes. "Oh what a headache! He's turned the house into a regular market fair! You'd think it was some kind of holiday, with all this jollity! Quiet!" she yelled at her two little boys, who were jumping around like two puppies, filling the house with their din.

The children stopped their racket, but their faces were still flushed, their eyes shining. Freyda went off to the bedroom and lay staring at the ceiling, her eyes filled with some unfathomable sadness.

Nehama-Itta, unlike her daughter, enjoyed Sorokeh's company. Whenever she had a free moment she would come and sit down, and fill his ear with the latest local news. First and foremost she wanted him to know about her late son-in-law, Freyda's husband. Now there was a fine man, and well-educated besides in Hebrew and in Russian.

"He was a bookkeeper," she informed him, "head book-keeper at the glass works."

Furtively she pulled his picture out from under her apron. "Just look at that man!" she whispered. "What a good-looking fellow. And tall! And those eyes! Died before his time. He wasn't yet thirty years old."

They were so in love, she whispered, that this man had married her daughter without a dowry. Imagine, for love's sake he made no demands. Yes, he was always undemanding in money matters, a golden character.

"Ask around, folks will tell you." Quickly she slipped the picture under her apron. "He was active in community affairs, too. And a Zionist, a fiery enthusiast."

He had intended to take them all to America, because after all, his whole family already lived there, and as for her, Nehama-Itta, all her own sons and daughters were in America too, that is, of course except for her daughter Freyda, long life to her. So what happens? Along comes the war and turns the whole world topsy-turvy! "What do you say to a misfortune like that?" She cocked an eye at him, as though propounding a riddle. "There we were, all ready for the journey, when along comes the war and turns everything upside down!"

Well, the Revolution would be over one of these days, and then they'd all be off for America, God willing. She, Nehama-Itta, was depending on the Eternal One to let her see her children once more in her lifetime.

Her conversation was not confined to her own personal affairs. Far from it. She kept Sorokeh informed on everything that was happening from one end of Mokry-Kut to the other. They say, she told him, that Manya the teacher's wife is getting a divorce. Why? Oh, because their political views are at odds. He's a Zionist, she's been a *Bundovka* all her life, and now, what do you think happened? She took the plunge and joined the Communist party. Imagine, that's the reason for a breakup! Well, that's what they say. But who knows what goes on between husband and wife? Only God in heaven knows. Anyhow, she left him, ran away to Kharkov. All the way to Kharkov! He, poor man, is in a bad way. Hardly ever shows his face at the school. . . . Today she, Nehama-Itta, had gone to the marketplace.

It's like Yom Kippur there, really, just like Yom Kippur. The butchers aren't slaughtering, the bakers aren't baking. Nu, with all the stores closed, what do you expect? By order of the Revolution. There were only three peasants poking around, with a calf and two sheep, a bit of cabbage and beets, three sacks of bran, and a handful of mushrooms. It was all gone in the twinkling of an eye, before you could say *shema yisroel.* Before she could look around there wasn't a soul left in the market. . . . Last night, at midnight Reb Simcha and Reb Avrohom-Abba left town in Koysh's wagon, probably for Zapotozhnoye. Looks like they went for merchandise, or maybe they took merchandise with them. . . . Paula the modiste has made it up again with her intended, Zaslavsky the commissionaire. That's the seventh time they've quarreled and disgraced themselves with the terrible things they said about one another, may those angry words fall on empty fields and forests, *Ribbono-shel-Olam.* Now they're together again and getting ready for the wedding. What a girl she is! Thunder and lightning, fire and brimstone. She walks around the house in a peignoir. Imagine—a peignoir! Anyhow, now they've made up. All right. That's as it should be. But what a situation! Look at Leahtche Hurvitz. What's to become of a girl who's past her teens and still unmarried? Mokry-Kut is full of such girls from one end of town to the other.

Sorokeh was charmed by the old woman. He enjoyed listening to her conversation, so good-hearted and full of shrewd common sense.

"Too bad," he joked, "that the old women aren't young." Nehama-Itta laughed.

"The old ones have accomplished something in their lifetimes," she said. "I gave birth to eleven children. Seven are still alive, God grant them length of days."

"Yes, yes," he nodded, "yes, grandma. You accomplished something. You accomplished a lot."

54

Freyda was not like other Jewish widows. Most of them were active, forceful, taking hold of their husband's trade, becoming full-fledged breadwinners. Not Freyda. She was passive, downcast, completely wrapped in the aura of her widowhood. The other women respected her, as though her demeanor were somehow superior to theirs. She made no attempt to earn a living, but subsisted on what her late husband had left, and sat waiting for the Revolution to be over so that she could leave for America.

What she did for Sorokeh she did with reluctance, regarding it as an imposition. The fact that she kept her distance, and avoided talking to him or looking at him, didn't help matters. His presence was an offense to her dignity. Not only was she puzzled; she was upset by him. What would people say? Was she an easy woman? A strange man in the house!

She was afraid that he might start paying her attention, and she might come to shame. But what could she do? Meanwhile, her mother could see nothing wrong, and the children were fascinated by him and loved to play with him.

As time passed and he made no advances, didn't even engage her in conversation, she took to sitting alone, her eyes fixed on the solitary, unmoving hand of the clock.

"What kind of person is this?" she thought. "What does this man want here?" She couldn't make him out at all.

Once, when Sorokeh had eaten and left, she put her

hands over her eyes and smiled oddly. Then she made straight for her room. In the doorway she paused, both hands pressing on her temples. Her mother came up behind her. "Does your head hurt?"

Freyda didn't answer. She lay down, put her arms around the cushion, and turned to the wall. She tried to think of nothing, to empty her mind, to shut out the world. But thoughts kept coming, memories of her dead husband, an intelligent and educated person of superior character, a man of integrity whose word was his bond. He had left her, and she missed him terribly. Again and again she thought of her husband, who had been a solid person, yes that was the word, solid, so different from this boarder of hers—not that she meant to make comparisons—God forbid, what was she thinking! She simply didn't want to have this fellow around.

She closed her eyes tight and forced herself not to think of anything. But she couldn't help herself. She thought of America, where her future lay. She saw herself walking in a crowd of people on a street in New York, wearing a little caracul hat and delicate leather gloves, when suddenly a man comes toward her, a tall handsome man—is it Sorokeh or is it someone else? No, an older man, better looking, who takes her in his arms. . . .

Just then her little three-year-old climbed on to the couch with her. "Mama, I'm cold."

She covered him with the cushion she was holding and, with the shawl around her shoulders, kissed his two cold little hands, and began to talk to him. Soon they would travel to America, and his uncles would buy him nice clothes and lots of toys.

"A gun, I want a gun. And I want—"

"Yes, what else?"

The little fellow didn't know what to say. He thought for a while, then, "I'll tell you when we get there."

"Yes, yes, son of mine"—hugging and kissing him—"you'll see what you want, and you'll tell me. They have plenty there, lots of bread, and milk, and cake."

Next day, when Sorokeh came for his meal, she looked at him peculiarly, as if they shared some deep secret. When it was time to clear the table, she suddenly asked him when the Revolution would be over, and ships would start sailing to America.

"Soon," he said, "in a little while, two or three months."

She stood there, with the tablecloth in her hand.

"And what about you?" She lowered her eyes.

"Me?" He didn't know what to say.

"You're not likely to stay in Mokry-Kut, are you? What's there to do here?"

"Maybe—" he began.

"I mean, in this loneliness—" She didn't finish her sentence, either.

He thought for a while, then smiled.

"The truth is, I don't know what to do with myself."

At that moment the two little boys came in from outside, threw off their coats, and began jumping all over him. In a twinkling he was telling them a story and crawling on all fours with the children on his back, so that the house rang with their happy noise.

55

The lovers' quarrel between Malia and Shimtze was the subject of much stormy debate among the girls of Mokry-Kut.

Liuba declared Shimtze guilty of violating the canons of

love. "What he did is unforgivable," she declared, her soft blue eyes looking around at the others.

"Yes, it's a crime," said Minna heatedly, her hands aflutter.

Masha, of the tragic eyes, took the opposite view.

"That's a lot of nonsense."

Rosa agreed with her. "Why all the excitement? Can't a fellow talk to another woman?"

"No, he can't!" declared Minna, like a judge pronouncing sentence.

"Another expert heard from!" Rosa belittled. "Look who's talking."

"Bag of bones!" muttered Minna, red to her earlobes, her lips trembling.

Rosa pretended not to hear. "Imagine, she's jealous of Ethel!"

"Don't you think she's got a right to be jealous of Ethel?" asked Liuba. "Isn't Ethel pretty?"

"Nobody has any business being jealous," declared Rosa. "It's a primitive emotion. It reduces human dignity and sullies love."

"On the contrary," Minna jumped into the fray. "There is no true love without jealousy."

On one point the girls did agree. Their respect for Malia was now wondrously enhanced, because of the aura of tragedy that surrounded her.

"You're wonderful!" they whispered admiringly. "You're great! He doesn't deserve you, he's not fit to lick your boots!"

By common consent, none of them would have anything to do with Shimtze.

"I'll thank you not to speak to me!" Minna said to him once, when he tried to tell her something.

Only two of the girls, Rosa and Masha, failed at first to honor this boycott, but on the contrary vied for his attention. They even quarreled with one another on his account. But when he made it clear that he wasn't interested in either one, they joined the rest in turning their backs on him.

"Serves him right," they said, self-righteously.

This did nothing to cool off the angry debate between Minna and Rosa, ostensibly over the theoretical question of jealousy. But Rosa put the argument on a personal level when she challenged Minna as follows: "If jealousy is such an important ingredient of love, how come you're not jealous of your Sukhar?"

"Meaning just what?" Minna's face turned all colors.

"Meaning plenty," said Rosa evasively. "Meaning that there aren't any saints."

"What are you hinting at?"

"Well, if you really want to know—he goes out with other girls!"

"Does he go out with you?" Minna thrust out her chin, like a rooster ready to do battle. "Yes or no? Come on, speak up, does he or doesn't he? You witch! You foulmouth, you!"

Off she ran and poured out an account of the business to Sukhar. He was able to mollify her.

"On my honor as a Bolshevik, the whole thing is a lie. Not a word of truth in it."

He made it his business that very day to seek out Rosa.

"Well, well, Rosatchka," he greeted her. "How are you? And how's the rest of your family? And how's business? Doing all right?"

Rosa stood frightened, rooted to the spot. "Business? What do you mean?"

"Oh, you know, your secret speculations in matches, cigarettes, sugar, flour, and all the rest."

Whereupon he looked her in the eye, and advised her to keep a bridle on her tongue, and not stick her nose in where it didn't belong.

56

The house filled with cigarette smoke as the comrades sat around laughing and talking in the home of Liuba's mother, the widow Brakhah. A small lamp hung on the wall, an iron stove glowed in the corner.

This was the place the young people laughingly called "The People's University of Mokry-Kut." This was where the young men and girls gathered on Sabbaths and festivals, and on those evenings when they weren't visiting Sorokeh. They would read Blok, Gorki, and Mayakovsky, they would sing songs, dance the polka and the quadrille, they would play games, like "Flying Post-office," "Yes or No," and most especially, they would play cards.

On this occasion Mayerke sat beside the stove holding forth on the subject of firearms to an audience consisting of Hillik, Muntchik, and Shayke. He enumerated the relative merits of the Browning, the Colt, the Mauser, the Maxim machine gun with its three hundred rounds per second, the Hotchkiss, somewhat smaller than the Maxim but a prettier weapon, the Lewis with its ammunition fed by disc rather than by belt, the Winchester rifle, and so on and so on.

Meantime, the girls were noisily having fun in their own way. Minna was posing riddles, old ones to which everybody knew the answer, but answered nevertheless, filling the room with peals of laughter.

"What is it," said Minna, looking at the ceiling, "that is

born in the water but fears the water?" "Salt," Kayla shot back.

"Sits in the spoon with its foot dangling?" "A noodle," chorused Liuba and Kayla, laughing loudly.

Malia was busy with Ziame, getting him to repeat a tongue twister, clapping her hands gaily when he stumbled over the words.

Sukhar was telling jokes. "There was this peasant woman on her way to market, and a farmer comes up behind her in a wagon. 'Hop in, granny,' he says. 'No, my dear,' she says, 'I haven't got the time.' "

Yasha roared with gales of high-pitched laughter. Encouraged, Sukhar went on. "A gypsy was asked, 'What's your religion?' and he answered, 'Which would you like?' "

Yasha threw his head back and laughed uproariously, his eyes closed and his white teeth gleaming through the clouds of cigarette smoke.

All through the evening the girls carefully snubbed Shimtze. He wandered from one group to another, listening to their conversation, looking lost. Finally he joined the little audience clustered around Mayerke, who had by this time shifted from weaponry to vehicles, and was discussing planes, tanks, and cars, discoursing learnedly about horsepower and maximum speed. Shimtze spoke up, raising his voice so that Malia and the other girls might hear and be impressed with his scientific knowledge.

"Regarding speed," he said, "I read somewhere that wild geese can fly at a hundred and fifty kilometers per hour. Yes, and the swallow does even better. I understand it flies at ten times the speed of a railway train."

He waited a moment, with a sidelong glance.

"I also read that blood goes through the human heart at the rate of fourteen kilometers an hour. Fourteen kilometers, imagine!"

"An intellectual!" Minna said in a stage whisper to Liuba, winking sarcastically.

"It's really amazing," said Shimtze, turning to her eagerly. "Fourteen. . . ."

Liuba jumped up and called out, "Come on, gang, let's play!" "Right, let's go!" came answering voices.

"What will it be?" Liuba looked around the room.

"Let's play mama and papa," clowned Mayerke in a baby voice.

Liuba ignored him. "We'll play"—she thought for a moment—"we'll play 'Kiss or No.' "

"All right," everybody agreed. "Kiss or No."

Liuba promptly seized Minna and sat her down on a chair in the middle of the room, putting in her hand a long towel that trailed on the floor. Muntchik approached and knelt in front of her, trying to put his knee on the lower end of the towel. But Minna was too quick for him. She pulled the towel up, and Muntchik was left with dry lips. In a tone of mock tragedy he announced, "I was all set for a kiss, and on account of an old rag I lost out."

Then all the other fellows took turns kneeling. Mayerke and Shayke, Ziame, Sukhar and all the rest. Each time Minna pulled the towel.

"No man will ever kiss me!" Minna jumped up, laughing.

"So what," muttered Sukhar.

Liuba rushed over to Malia and pulled her down into the chair, whereupon all the fellows lined up again and knelt before her. Under cover of all this activity Shimtze got his knee on the trailing edge of the towel. There was an immediate uproar. Shimtze stood up to claim his kiss; Malia twisted her head from side to side, laughing.

"Malia, Malia," he whispered, while she kept pushing him away, laughing "No, no, no!" The whole place buzzed with excitement.

"Malia! No fair, Malia! He won, Malia!"

She eluded his grasp and ran to a corner of the room. Shimtze ran after her, caught her and gave her a kiss.

There was loud applause from the crowd. "More! More! Bravo! More!"

Liuba clapped her hands and whispered to those around her. "Nu, at last they've made up, thank God!"

57

Sorokeh had friends in all the surrounding villages, and whenever he went out to visit they trailed around after him like groomsmen dancing attendance on the father of the bride. But with the passage of time the villages changed character. Day after day more and more soldiers returned from the front, most of them still carrying their weapons, some with a rifle slung over their shoulder, others with a couple of grenades at their belt as well, some even carrying a machine gun, and a cartridge belt strapped across their chest.

The villages hummed with activity, like overcrowded beehives in spring. Stormy meetings heard passionate speakers denouncing one another, each speaking up for his particular party program. Some were in favor of the Soviets, others defended the Rada, the Ukrainian National Council. From time to time visiting propagandists showed up: Bolshevik sailors, ordinary Bolsheviks, emissaries of the Rada, Social Revolutionaries, who fanned the flames of political dissension. While all this was going on, the peasants would roast an occasional pig, drink long drafts of *samogon,* and make merry.

The gaiety was not without its ugly side. Drinking and argument led to some violent altercations, with here and there a tipsy protagonist in hot pursuit of his opponent, and the whole village in a turmoil. Or a man in his cups might take the occasion to pay off his wife for her faults, leaving her bruised in face and body.

In the village of Teiteireivka, Yokhim Homanyuk killed the Austrian prisoner who had been consorting with his wife all the time that Yokhim had been rotting away in the mines. It made him feel a lot better.

"I didn't catch up with the enemy there, so I caught up with him here," he told his neighbors with satisfaction, walking around in the gray coat he had taken from his victim.

Sorokeh arrived in Teiteireivka while a public meeting was in progress at the village Council. All kinds of speeches were under way, one by an SR who had been village clerk under the old regime, another by a Ukrainian nationalist, while all the time there was a confusion of heckling from soldiers in the audience. Finally a sailor got up, a tall broad-shouldered fellow with a pockmarked face and two grinning bold eyes. His hat was at a rakish angle over his left ear, and he himself was a trifle tipsy.

"Comrades!" he gestured with his brawny arm. "I'm Petrus, Petro Baranka, that's my name, I'm a sailor from the Black Sea fleet, off the minelayer *Zvonki.*"

He pointed to the letters on the band of his round navy cap, from which two black ribbons fluttered down the back of his neck.

He had listened, said he, to all the oily posturings and tricky nonsense spoken by those old acquaintances—Mensheviks, stinking SR's, and spokesmen for the dear old Rada. Yes, my friends, they're all sons-of-bitches. The Black Sea fleet was infested with them like rats aboard ship, till at last we sent them packing to the mother of devils, them and their dirty politics. Now take General

Kornilov and General Kaledin, what are they after? To liquidate the Workers' and Peasants' government, that's what they want; and who lends them a hand in trying to restore the corrupt old regime, and shove the common folk back into downtrodden poverty? Why, our friends here, the Mensheviks and the SR's and the Central Rada, a thousand curses on the lot of them. They won't be happy till the wolf marries the she-dog, and the owl mates with the cormorant. They want to bring joy to the aristocrats, and make the *pans* happy. Here you've got General Shcherbatchov on the Rumanian front, scheming with the Rada, a plague on it, and there you've got Hetman Dutov, no inconsiderable *pan* himself, cooking up counterrevolution in Oranburg, and the Tatars in the Crimea forming a counterrevolutionary party—*mili firkeh* they call it—and wanting to secede from Russia and join up with Turkey. Not to speak of the Mensheviks and the Georgians out in the Caucasus, and the Armenians and all the rest of those wreckers.

"Comrades!" His hand was raised dramatically, his fingers spread out. "We'll shove a fig in a poppy up their grandmother's nose! Comrades! I serve notice on behalf of the glorious Black Sea fleet, and on behalf of the glorious Baltic fleet! We won't let them bring down the Workers' and Peasants' government! Comrades!"

His fist banged down on the table like a clap of thunder. "Comrades!" he roared. "I ask you, what has happened to you? The Revolution is in danger, and you spend your time swilling and guzzling and lolling around like corpses in the cemetery. Ah-nu, comrades, come and lend us a hand! Turn your backs on the Rada and that declaration of theirs, the 'Third Universal.' Let's cook up a boiling porridge for them, so hot that they'll choke on it. Men! Come roll up your sleeves and let us sweep out the enemies of the people the way you sweep out the granary before threshing time, and let's get rid of all the generals and the het-mans and the *pans. . . ."*

His listeners stroked their big mustaches and nodded their heads. They enjoyed listening to this sailor, they liked his style.

"Sensible fellow," they told one another. "He's all right. Knows what's going on, and lets them all have it."

When the sailor had finished speaking, Sorokeh took the floor. At his first few sentences, Baranka pricked up his ears. "What have we got here?" he whispered to those around him. A few minutes later he was on his feet, arm outstretched, shouting, "Aha, an Anarchist! What business has he got speaking here? Sit down! Nobody wants to listen!"

Scattered shouts were heard from the audience.

"Let him speak!"

"Go ahead, Sorokeh!"

"Let him finish!"

Baranka stuck to his guns. "I know these Anarchists!" he yelled. "We saw enough of them in our fleet, they're the lowest form of counterrevolutionary. Shut your mouth, you bastard! Right now! This instant!"

Sorokeh paid no attention, but went on speaking as if nothing had happened. Baranka pulled out his pistol and aimed it at Sorokeh. Some of the crowd came between them and surrounded the sailor, arguing with him.

"Let the man speak his piece," they said. "That's Soro-keh, he's on our side."

They barely managed to restrain him. He went off to a corner of the room, seething and muttering curses.

When the meeting was over, Baranka and Sorokeh were invited by Sidor Vyun, who was a friend of both of them, to eat at his house. Sorokeh managed to appease Baranka, but when he tried to preach Anarchism to him, Baranka would have none of it.

"Come off it, *kutcheryavi*," he said. "You know where you can go, curly-head."

By the end of the meal Baranka was drunk. He embraced Sorokeh and slobbered kisses on him, even though he was an Anarchist, and everybody knows what a harmful element they are, like a snake in the rafters.

On the other hand, Sorokeh made converts out of Sidor Vyun, and Timukh Kruk, and Ivas Horobetz. They took an accordion and went out into the street singing, and proclaiming that there was no authority or government, no law or statute, but let every man do what was right in his own eyes.

A lecture on the finer points in the world view of Mach and Avenarius was being delivered to the Tseire Tsiyon by their leader, Ruvke, son of the Rabbi, who had once had a reputation as a brilliant student of the Talmud, and had now become quite a scholar in science and philosophy. He stood beside the smoking wick of the solitary lamp and droned on in a boring monotone, about materialism and empirocriticism, space time and motion, energy and impulse, the inertia of light, gravitation, objective reality and empirical perception, the survival of species and natural selection, and more and more. He raised fine distinctions, and tried to reconcile Mach with Marx. It was very hard to understand what he was saying.

Mulye, Mokry-Kut's modernist poet, one of the first in all Russia to follow the style of Mayakovsky, whispered to

Dena that all this scientific talk was giving him the cramps.

"Sit still," Dena whispered back. "Pay attention and keep quiet. Pretend you're listening to the steady drip of gentle rain."

After a while he whispered to her again. "I can't climb after him on those torn guitar strings."

Dena choked back a laugh and forced herself to listen to the speaker, although she understood not a word of what he was saying. Behind the drowsy drone of Ruvke's voice there rose images of the Land of Israel in her mind, like an underground spring forcing its way to the surface.

"Tell me," she whispered to Mulye, "do they have the same regular flowers in Eretz Yisroel as we have here, like violets and daisies and lilacs?"

"Why no!" he answered. "They have the rose of the Sharon, red roses as hot as summer noon."

"Hush!" voices in the room admonished them.

Just then the door opened, and in walked Mayerke, Shayke, and Ziame. They stood in the doorway listening to the lecture, causing quite a stir in the audience.

After a few minutes Mayerke raised his hand and said, "I move we proceed with the agenda!"

Whether because he didn't notice the interruption, or because he chose to ignore it, Ruvke went on with his lecture.

"The difference between Machism and pragmatism," he said in his deadly drone, "resembles the difference between empirocriticism and empiromonism."

"Well, what do you know!" said Shayke to Mayerke with a clownish grin. Mayerke raised his hand again.

"Beg pardon, but what's the topic under discussion?"

Ruvke stopped speaking. Somebody in the audience called out, "Mach."

"Mach? Mach? Who's he?"

"Don't interrupt me," said Ruvke.

Mayerke and his two comrades began to heckle.

"Who's Mach?"

"What did he ever do for the workers of the world?"

The audience was shaken by this behavior. Shouts were hurled back at the three intruders.

"Go away!"

"Get out of here!"

Dena jumped up and turned on them. "Are you drunk, or something?"

"Sober as a rainbarrel," answered Mayerke.

"Well then, what's wrong with you? What do you want here? Why do you come and make a disturbance?"

"You're talking imperialism," said Ziame, pointing at Ruvke. "All we've heard since we got here is imperialism, imperialism. What is this, headquarters for counterrevolution?"

Senye, the son of Ozer Hagbeh, called Senye "Farmer" because he was always arguing that the essence of Zionism is return to the soil, walked up to the three Bolsheviks and said to them in a tone of suppressed rage, "Get out of here, and I mean now!"

"Don't make me laugh!" answered Mayerke with the confident smile of one who has the upper hand.

"Right now!" repeated Senye.

"Go to the devil's mother!" roared Mulye, mounting one of the benches. And then the girls began to scream.

"For shame!" they shrilled. "A shame and a disgrace!"

Near the red flag in a corner of the room stood a blue and white Zionist flag. Ziame grabbed it and tore it. In a flash pandemonium broke loose. Even Ruvke was in the thick of it, waving his fists weakly in all directions.

Senye grabbed the red flag and raised it over the heads of Mayerke and his pals. Mayerke promptly drew his pistol.

"I'll shoot to kill!" he shouted.

"Kill away!" answered Senye, all the while waving the red flag and hitting them over the head. "Go ahead, shoot!"

Misha, a pale scrawny lad with thick lips, lent a hand with the pole of the torn Zionist flag. Before long Mayerke and his buddies were forced out of the house.

Dena gathered up the shreds of the Zionist flag and burst into tears. "What horrible creatures," she sobbed.

"Don't cry, don't cry," they clustered around, comforting.

"We will carry these torn pieces with us to Eretz Yisroel," declared Mulye.

"Yes, yes," they chorused. "They will bear testimony to the shame and degradation of the Jewish Communists."

For a while they debated the meaning of what had just happened. Senye was of the opinion that the Revolution was still in its infancy, but would ultimately find its way. It would not be perfected by hooligans like these, who were not really Communists, but by great revolutionary world figures.

"Then the world will breathe easier," he said. "There will be goodness and blessing for all the nations, and for the Jewish people too."

"Ach, Senka, you're incomparable!" said Dena, purposely adopting a light tone to relieve the tension.

Ruvke wanted to finish his lecture, but the others thought, no, they had had enough.

"Let's all go now," they decided.

Then Dena discovered that she had misplaced her kerchief. Mulye and Sioma helped her look for it, but it was Misha who found it.

"Where were you, naughty one?" Dena addressed the kerchief in that imitation baby voice of hers. "I looked all over for you, and you were hiding behind the cupboard. Is that nice? Is that any way to behave?"

"Dena, come on, let's go!" urged the members of the group who were waiting to take her home.

Outside they were met by strong gusts of wind. They marched off singing in Hebrew, *"Hushu, ahim, hushu—* Forward, brothers, forward!"* and the wind gobbled up their song.

"The wind has gone crazy," said Dena, wrapping her arms around herself.

Mulye said the wind carried with it something from distant lands. "Bits of alien geography," he corrected himself, "in every gust of wind. It's time that is flying, time that has lost its head."

"You're very funny," said Dena, between chattering teeth. "My, it's cold. My fingers are frozen. I'm going to make a run for home."

Mulye and Senye wanted to accompany her, but she would have none of it. "I'm not out for a stroll. I'm running."

"But what if they attack you?" said Senye, softly.

"What an odd notion! Who would attack me?"

She was off and running. The others stood where they were and urged her on—"Run! Keep going! Go!"—until she reached her house.

When Sorokeh came down the street a short time later, there was not a soul to be seen nor a sound to be heard. The houses stood shrouded in darkness. Only the snow glistened in the moonlight.

A shiver passed up and down his spine. "What an unreal town." he thought.

59

The Tseire Tsiyon lived in their own closed little world, associating only with one another, impatiently waiting for word from central headquarters that would signal their departure for Palestine. Somehow, that word was slow in coming.

Meantime, Ruvke the Rabbi's son decided the time could be turned to advantage by learning a trade that would be useful in the Land of Israel. After careful analysis, he determined that he would learn shoemaking, and apprenticed himself to Leizer-Yossl the cobbler. His family was aghast. The Rabbi pleaded with him, the Rebbitzin wept bitter tears, imploring him not to disgrace them. But all to no avail. Not for nothing do they say that a stubborn person is worse than an apostate.

"At least," begged his mother, "study a nice profession like photography."

The rest of the town was just as shocked as was Ruvke's own family. People began to wonder whether the Rabbi's son had gone out of his mind.

It need hardly be added that his comrades encouraged him to stick to his decision. "Ruvke," they said, "stand fast!"

Sioma had no need for special training, since he had already learned his father's trade. He was the son of Kalman the baker. Sounding for all the world like a preacher in the pulpit, he expounded the scriptural verse, " 'Choose life'—this refers to the baker's trade."

Senye, who had agricultural plans, took the burnished

candleholder off the table, put it together with an old pair of his father's boots, a worn-out valise, a few pots and pans out of the kitchen, and five flints that he himself had fashioned, and set out on a tour of the nearby villages. In a couple of days he was back, loaded with precious booty—flour, potatoes, cabbage, beans.

"Good work, Senka," they told him. "You'll make a wonderful farmer!"

Mulye didn't set about learning a trade, and Dena supported his decision. "You'll be a famous poet, like Shneour," she said. "Everybody in the Land of Israel will sing your praises, and you'll be rich and respected."

"After all," Mulye agreed, "poetry is a kind of trade."

Whereupon he sat down and wrote a poem entitled "Love's Imperative Number 1," and dedicated it to Dena. Nothing would do but he must recite it to her, with much halting and many a stammer. He insisted that he was speaking calmly, steadily, like the fire in the smithy's forge, like a locomotive with a full head of steam.

Dena improved on his metaphor. "Like an armored locomotive, with red flags flying?" she asked.

Mulye was deeply stirred by her gloss on his poem, and immediately got busy with his pencil stub, murmuring like one inspired, "Red flags flying."

"And a flower on top." Dena added.

"Yes, yes!" Mulye scribbled excitedly. "With a flower on top."

"Ha-ha!" she laughed, a trifle hysterically. "All this in my honor?"

"In your honor," he answered, humbly.

"And where are we going in this armored steam engine? To the mountains beyond the moon? To—"

"Stop!" he interrupted. "We're in the Central Station of the world, at the great intersection where all lines meet, where events come together, where possibilities converge, destiny and happiness—"

"No, no!" Dena adopted a frightened look, "I have no part in all of this."

"Haven't you?" he whispered. "I love you."

"What?" She burst out laughing. "What else is new? Do you imagine I thought you hated me? Why should you hate me?"

The poor fellow wanted her to be serious, but all he could do was stammer again, "I love you."

"But of course. You love me. And I love you, too."

"No, not like that."

"Well then, how?"

This indecisive game went on for some time, with Mulye declaring his love in farfetched metaphors, and she fending him off; he pressing the verbal attack, and she countering with evasive action—until finally he took her in his arms and kissed her. This proved rather persuasive.

Shortly thereafter Mulye's father, Reb Avrohom-Abba, who regarded himself as one of those rare individuals who support the weight of the world on their shoulders, sent him on an errand to Reb Mordkhe-Leib. The latter was not at home, but his sixteen-year-old daughter, Tania, was. She greeted Mulye as if she had been waiting for him all day, and before they had exchanged more than a few words, she had her arms around his waist. They stood there exchanging passionate kisses, interlocked in the dim twilight.

From that time on Mulye found many occasions to drop in on Tania. Dena sensed that something had changed. "What's happened to you?" she wondered.

His friends began to talk about him, but Dena didn't bring the matter up. She gazed at him reflectively, and saw that he was embarrassed in her presence. Finally she sent him packing.

"Get on with you," she said. "Grow up. You're still a boy. You don't even have a mustache as big as that," holding up a half-covered fingernail. And she refused to see him again.

For two or three weeks he went around like a whipped puppy. Then he took a few household articles and went out to the surrounding villages to prove that he too could help support his family. But he came back practically empty-handed.

Finally he decided to go off to Petrograd. That, he told himself, was where he really belonged, under those white skies, in the artistic bohemian life of the capital, in the coffeehouses, at the art exhibitions, at the masked balls. He pictured himself in the gardens of Tsarskoye-Selo, reading poetry aloud under the stars, on the spot where a student had shot himself.

Freyda wanted to go out to the cemetery, but her mother said no, the snow there was hip deep.

"Who ever goes to the cemetery in wintertime?" the old woman demanded.

So Freyda busied herself around the house. She moved the chairs about, pushed the table from one place to another. She edged her way carefully around the glass objects that cluttered the house. More than once she restrained the impulse to push them over. Something in her wanted to turn everything topsy-turvy, to smash things right and left. She strode about, sweeping, dusting, until there was not a corner that hadn't felt her hand.

Then she lay down on the sofa and stared at the ceiling.

She pushed all thought from her mind, thoughts of her widowhood, her vanished happiness, the heaviness of her heart. Tears caught her by the throat, and she choked them back.

Towards evening Leahtche appeared at the door. "Anybody home?" she called.

Freyda looked up, surprised.

"Come on in, you'll freeze out the house," said old Nehama-Itta, emerging from the kitchen. "Come in and close the door."

Leahtche came in, sat down on the sofa, and looked around the room. "Has he been here?" she asked.

"Who?" said Freyda, blankly.

"Our boarder," put in Nehama-Itta. "What's so difficult to understand? She's asking about our boarder."

"Yes, Sorokeh, Sorokeh," nodded Leahtche. "He eats his lunch here. How is he?"

Mother and daughter exchanged glances.

"What do you mean, how is he?" Nehama-Itta questioned.

"Just asking."

"But why?"

"Because."

"You're talking in riddles," said the old woman.

"I want to know."

"To know?" Freyda echoed.

"To ask—"

"Anything happen?" asked Nehama-Itta. "He was just here."

"No, nothing happened."

"So?"

Leahtche was silent for a moment. Then, "What does he say? Did he have anything to tell?"

When they offered no answer, she spoke again. "What did he come for?"

"What did he come for?" Nehama-Itta weighed her words carefully. "You would know that better than we. After all, your crowd are real close with one another."

"Oh no," said Leahtche quickly, "I don't have the least idea."

"All of you with your 'livolvers,'" Nehama-Itta continued. "All of you walking around with your—what do you call them—portfolios."

Leahtche gave her a look. "Ah," she said. "What I wanted to know is, does he get enough to eat?"

"No." The murmur came from Freyda.

"How do you expect him to eat well," Nehama-Itta chimed in, "when all we can lay hands on is an odd egg, a bit of butter, a drop of milk?"

"Yes, yes."

"Actually, he pays very well," said Freyda.

"That's the kind of person he is," said Nehama-Itta. "Openhanded. A fine young man."

"The young man is . . . a young man." Leahtche's glance at Freyda held a hint of caution. "He's fire mixed with flame."

Nehama-Itta ignored the comment. "He's handed out a regular fortune. Anybody asks, he gives. Must have the riches of Korah."

"What?" Leahtche's eyes opened wide. "Oh no, he hasn't got a thing. Whatever comes into his hand he gives away. He's as poor as can be. No home. No livelihood. Wanders from place to place. A restless soul."

"But why, for goodness' sake?" wondered Nehama-Itta.

"Who knows? He himself wonders why."

Freyda glanced at her sidelong, a weary smile on her lips, a kind of summary of her own loneliness.

Leahtche sensed the smile. "Nu," she sighed. "What really brought me here? I myself don't know. I'd better go now. Please don't hold it against me. Goodbye."

Nehama-Itta saw her to the door. Freyda headed for the kitchen. On the way she noticed her own reflection in the mirror. She paused, and gave herself a knowing nod.

61

Leahtche was wracked by inner torture, thoughts, half-thoughts, guilt, questioning. At times she was depressed, and decided that Sorokeh was a worthless fellow. At other times her mood shifted, and she told herself that he was a wonderful man, one of a kind.

Even more telling were the doubts she began to have about love itself. It had been for her the be-all and end-all. Now, she began to have heretical thoughts. Perhaps love was a delusion; it took more out of her than it was worth; it could lead to no good end. If she had the chance she would climb up on the roof of the synagogue and proclaim for all the world to hear, "Girls, watch out! Beware of love! It can only lead to suffering!"

She laughed at the thought.

Endlessly she cross-examined herself. "What about you? Are you in love? No, I mean really, really in love? For all your life is worth, to the point of insanity? Are you in love till the pain is unbearable, until life is not worth living?"

To these questions she had no confident answer. "Your love," she told herself sternly, "is nothing but a little thing, tiny, insignificant."

No sooner said than she argued back. "But that little thing can be unfathomably deep."

"Nu, don't exaggerate," she scolded herself. "It's really only a shallow puddle."

"No, No! I'd rather die than live without love, without having someone who longs for me, who yearns for me!"

Whereupon she jumped up and ran off to Sorokeh. She arrived breathless, eyes shining, her cheeks crimson with the cold.

"Ach, you rascal, you!" she flung at him.

"What's this, Leahtche?" Sorokeh stood up, smiling. "What's all the excitement?"

"Ach, you rascal, you assassin! Here am I, going out of my mind, pining away all day long, and you couldn't care less!"

No sooner were the words out of her mouth than she checked herself. "Good heavens!" She clapped her hand to her mouth and hunched her head between her shoulders. "No, no! I promised myself! Don't imagine that I meant it. I was only fooling."

She sat herself down on the bench, and leaned against the wall, red-cheeked, eyes sparkling, a half-smile playing about her lips. Sorokeh came and sat near her, his head against the wall beside hers.

Leahtche moved close to him, nudging her shoulder against him.

"Don't touch me. . . ." she whispered.

62

Word went around that Leahtche was involved again with Sorokeh, but she herself was not so confident. On the contrary, she was filled with doubt and perplexity. Her argument with herself went something like this:

"All right, good, so it's a new world, revolution, love. Very fine. Still, a girl ought to plan her life along normal lines, and get married. A husband. What then? Should she stay alone, single, a lonely maiden all her life?"

The more she thought about it, the less was she able to come to any conclusion. Sorokeh was the man of her heart —no, it was Polyishuk—no, back to Sorokeh, and she ended up empty-handed. There were two stalwart trees in her life, but alas, neither one of them was fruit-bearing. What's a body to do?

As for Polyishuk, he paid no attention to her.

"What's wrong with you, comrade Polyishuk?" She had just greeted him, and been ignored. "Have you got something against me?"

"Don't bother me," he scowled.

"But you don't even say hello! Have I broken party discipline, or something?"

"Go to your dear friend the Anarchist," he scowled, bending over his papers.

She shrugged a shoulder and went on her way, smiling to herself. "Nu, this one won't abandon me! He won't marry me, but he's mine, if that's what I want."

With Sorekeh the situation was reversed. He seemed to be paying her court, warm, welcome, friendly, and yet her intuition told her that in the end he would go away and she would never see him again.

"This one," she told herself, "means double trouble. Yes indeed."

So she adopted a whole series of stratagems. She pretended to be angry at him, or she kept him waiting when he expected her, or she stayed out of his sight for a time. All this was more than strategy; it contained an element of fear as well. She was afraid that a moment might come when she would be unable to withstand his importunings; when she might yield to him and find herself in trouble.

"You're playing with fire!" she admonished herself.

But all these calculations of hers were short-lived, though the time she spent under their self-discipline seemed to her like an eternity. Then suddenly, she found herself hurrying to meet him.

"Only for a little while—just for a moment."

Once she was there, her resolution dissolved, and she stayed for a little while, then another little while.

More than once she hinted, now angrily, now gently, what she had hinted at many times before.

"Ach, what a fate it is to be a single girl, with all sorts of hellish dangers lying in wait!"

Sorokeh hugged and kissed her, and spoke soothing words. She contracted in his arms, and spoke sadly.

"How long can we go on this way? Good Lord, what sinners we are! And to think that we could live happily as other people do."

Sorokeh stroked her and talked with persuasive gentleness.

"What's all this about forbidden and permitted?" he whispered. "Are you some pious old lady? The voice of nature is calling to us, from the deeps, from our blood, our very being. After all we love one another. Be my love!"

"Every 'be' except the 'be' of the marriage service," laughed Leahtche, extricating herself from his embrace, a trifle shaken.

A few moments later, calm now, she sat hunched over, looking glum, ruminating aloud.

"How can we make woman truly emancipated? While she's a girl her path is full of pitfalls, and when she gets to be a woman she's dominated by her husband. No, the revolution has a duty to set this right. It's a problem that ought to be high on the agenda. What do you think, Sorokeh, hah? You're the man with all the answers. What do you say?"

63

Every day after morning service, there would be a group of men sitting around in the synagogue, talking over the state of the world. Sorokeh would drop in on them from time to time, and they got so used to his presence that they stopped being careful of what was said in his hearing.

Once he came in just as Reb Mordkhe-Leib was saying, "Hellfire will go out, but their flames will keep on burning."

Yankel Potchtar explained to Sorokeh, "He's talking about your fellow revolutionaries, the Bolsheviklach."

"It's not only the killings they're responsible for," Reb Mordkhe-Leib continued, paying no attention to Sorokeh. "It's the whole climate of bloodshed that surrounds them. They've filled the world with an atmosphere of murder."

" 'They consume both body and soul,' " quoted one man in the group, speaking from the depths of his sheepskin coat, his short-bearded round-eyed face framed by the collar, making him look like a furry cat.

"The bloodshed will not last," said the Rabbi, smiling weakly. "God willing, things will change."

"When?" Reb Itzia Dubinsky asked. "When will they change?"

"The Holy One can bide his time, even if it takes a thousand generations." Reb Mordkhe-Leib was rubbing his hands together. "What does it matter to Him? Does He have a train to catch?"

"From Adam to Noah took ten generations," reflected

Heshel Pribisker aloud. "Another ten generations from Noah to Abraham. The world can't be started at the tenth generation."

"What worries me is the opposite," said Reb Itzia Dubinsky, with a pained grimace. "I'm afraid the generations are moving backwards, from Abraham to Terah."

Heshel blew on his fingertips. "What can you do with Jews who want to force truth, justice and honesty down the throat of this materialistic world?"

Reb Itzia Dubinsky responded with the well-worn refrain, "Alas, we're at the mercy of our children!"

"I can't understand it," said Kalman the baker, stroking the full width of his beard. "What went wrong? The flour was good, and so was the yeast. The dough rose, the oven was stoked. Why then did the loaf turn out so bad?" He spread out his arms, the picture of bewilderment.

"People pray that they have children," muttered Reb Itzia Dubinsky. 'One thing have I asked of the Lord, that will I seek.' What people really ought to pray for is that they know what to pray for!"

Sorokeh intervened in the discussion.

"What do you want from your children? Let's look at the other side of the picture. Have you brought them up to be like you? Do you want them to grow beards and earlocks, to jostle one another in the marketplace over a bundle of pig bristles, to spend their days as petty shopkeepers, waiting for some miracle from heaven, endlessly reciting Psalms?"

They sat silent, every beard pointed in his direction, eyes fixed on him.

"You know that's not what you want," he continued deliberately. "You want them to become doctors, engineers, lawyers, bankers, men of substance. Well then, you and they are on the same footing. You're as much to blame as they are. The only difference is, you're on the inside and they're on the outside."

For a while, nobody said anything. Then Reb Itzia Dubinsky broke the silence. "We're to blame?"

Yankel Potchtar looked around at everybody, with a broad sarcastic grin. "Well, well, he's found us out! It's all our fault!"

From the fringe of the group Heshel Pribisker fastened his gaze on Sorokeh.

"Jews will be what they will be," he said, half smiling, "But one thing remains true. They're always to be reckoned with. It was on account of them that the tablets were broken!"

He leaned forward and extended his hand. "Respect!" he said. "Even the sea stood back respectfully to let the Israelites pass!"

"Very good," the Rabbi murmured. "That's a good thought."

"Yes, it's well put," answered Sorokeh, "But—"

Before he could say another word, Reb Simcha pounced on him. He had it in for him because of Leahtche.

"So you don't like what he said?"

"On the contrary," Sorokeh turned to face him. "I like it very much."

"It would be better if you didn't like us!" flared Reb Simcha, his beard trembling with anger.

"What's the matter?" Sorokeh was genuinely surprised. "I was speaking in all sincerity."

"Don't speak in all sincerity," Reb Simcha interrupted hotly. "Better keep quiet in all sincerity!"

Yankel Potchtar burst out laughing.

"Bogus friends and true enemies," growled Reb Simcha, sitting back angrily, his hands stuck into his sleeves.

Sorokeh turned away from him and addressed the group. The Revolution, he told them, held nothing for them; not land, since they were not farmers, and not factories, for they were not industrial workers. On the contrary, the upshot of the Revolution would be to destroy the

Jewish people, to uproot what little Jewishness still remained. . . .

At this point Yankel Potchtar broke in.

"Nonsense!" he said, shouting and laughing at the same time. "We have a Father in heaven; He will never forsake us. The Blessed Name will have mercy on us. What you say is nonsense! Our number will still come up in the divine lottery!"

"Right," answered Sorokeh, "and you may even win the grand prize. But what good is it if they come knocking on your door, and say 'Hayyim-Yankel, you've just won a million'—but Hayyim-Yankel isn't there to hear it, because in the meantime Hayyim-Yankel is dead?"

They all smiled and nodded their heads. Then everybody got up to go. On his way out, Yankel Potchtar offered Sorokeh a parting shot.

"It's all nonsense," said he. "We have a contract with the *Ribbono-shel-Olam,* a big contract with six hundred and thirteen clauses.

64

Sorokeh was fond of chatting with the older Jews, particularly the more learned ones. With Heshel he had never spoken directly; but the occasional remarks he had heard from him impressed Sorokeh, not so much with their cleverness as with their honesty and originality. It was Chatzkl Kanarik, a plain unpretentious Jew, whom Sorokeh heard applying to Heshel the classical tag: "The tablets themselves, and the pieces of the broken tablets, were both stored in the ark of the covenant."

It happened this way. Sorokeh was in Chatzkl Kanarik's home giving a talk to a group of Zionist boys and girls, at the invitation of Chatzkl's daughter. Chatzkl himself sat in, and listened to the lecture. Afterwards, when the young people had left, Sorokeh sat talking to Chatzkl, whose wife was lying on the sofa trying to keep warm under a pile of rags, and cursing the Bolsheviks with fine abandon.

"He won't speak up," she rasped, indicating her husband. "He's afraid of them, a plague on their heads."

"Do you think I'm afraid because I'm a thief?" Chatzkl defended himself. "I'm afraid because they're murderers."

He looked around fearfully, his beard trembling. "I keep away from anything illegal. I know full well what the punishment is—they take you to the *shtab.*"

"That's right, papa," his daughter spoke up, tugging at her braids, the blood rushing to her face. "Take care nothing happens to you."

"May they be taken care of by trouble and sorrow and all the angels of retribution, *Ribbono-shel-Olam,* wherever they go and wherever they stop," whined his wife, coughing and sniffling. "If this goes on much longer we'll all die of cold and hunger, God forbid."

Sorokeh led the conversation from one topic to another, until finally he asked Chatzkl Kanarik, "Tell me, what kind of person is this Heshel Pribisker?"

Before Kanarik could answer, his wife called out, "Heshel? The *melamed?* Sure, he boards with Simcha. That's the Simcha whose daughter Leahtche is such a precious baggage. Nobody's ever going to profit by her example."

"Leahtche's an interesting person," her daughter protested stoutly. "She has all the best qualities of an intelligent woman."

"You don't say!" The mother's inflection dripped sarcasm. "On all my enemies, *Ribbono-shel-Olam.* Leahtche?

Why, she's one of that gang, she's in her element, hand-in-glove with those rotten murderers."

She launched into a series of lurid curses on the Bolsheviks, specifying the maladies she wished on them, and finishing them off with one all-inclusive malediction: "May they rot, *Ribbono-shel-Olam,* in their lifetimes, and start rotting again after they die."

Sorokeh stood up to leave, and Chatzkl Kanarik accompanied him out of the door. When they got to the foot of the stairs, Sorokeh turned to Chatzkl and asked him again about Heshel Pribisker.

Kanarik tossed his head like a horse in midsummer, and looked at his questioner sidelong. That's when he delivered himself of his classical quotation: "The tablets themselves, and the pieces of the broken tablets, were both stored in the ark of the covenant."

The answer puzzled Sorokeh. He looked Chatzkl up and down from his shabby cap to his badly torn boots.

"What do you mean, tablets and broken tablets?"

Kanarik shifted his gaze, and smiled an embarrassed smile.

"Because the ark is the place of the Torah," he answered evasively.

Just then Yankel Potchtar came toward them, breathing puffs of steamy breath. He stamped the snow off his heavy boots, and walked along with them, asking, "What's the topic of conversation?"

Sorokeh told him.

"Aha!" Yankel brightened, as though he had come upon a promising bit of business. "Let me offer an explanation. The Midrash says that the Israelites carried not one but two arks in the wilderness. In one of them they bore the Torah, while the other held the pieces of the tablets that Moses had broken. The one containing the Torah was kept in the Tent of Meeting, and the one with the broken tablets accompanied them into battle. Now do you see?"

"No," said Sorokeh, "I don't see."

"You don't see. All right," said Yankel, like a patient teacher. "Look, the ark is a parable for students of the Torah."

"Nu?"

"Nu! The ark stays in its resting place."

"So?"

"Where is its place? In the heart of man."

"Because the ark is the place of the Torah," added Chatzkl, repeating what he had said before.

"But what have the broken tablets got to do with it?" Sorokeh asked.

For a few moments the only sound he heard was the crunch of snow under their heavy boots. "Nu?" he pressed.

"How should I know?" Yankel grinned. "There's talk about him."

"Who talks?"

"People."

"What do they say?"

"Not much. Bits and pieces."

"Go on."

"Go on, go on! What should I go on? They talk about him. All right, they say he's infected with the spirit of the times. Not that he's a Bolshevik, God forbid, ha-ha."

"That's all?"

"Well, they say he has women on his mind—since you insist, Leahtche."

"That's a lie," Chatzkl Kanarik shook his head vigorously.

"Of course it's a lie," Yankel Potchtar agreed. "How could it be true? Heshel, that pious Jew, that scholar? Impossible! Still, people talk. How are you going to stop them? They see a man, living apart from his wife, so they talk. Besides, nu, there is such a thing as lust, the Evil Inclination. It wouldn't be the first time in history that a woman caused a falling out between a man and the Holy One.

There was Eve and Adam, there was Cozbi, daughter of Tzur, and Zimri, son of Salu, in the Book of Numbers. Even the angels got mixed up in this business, as we read: 'And the sons of God saw the daughters of men, that they were goodly, and they took unto themselves wives, of whomsoever they chose.' Notice, they chose. They had a choice, and it was women that they chose."

Sorokeh stopped still, looked Yankel full in the face, and burst out laughing. The other two joined in the laughter.

"So you like what I said?" Yankel Potchtar's voice and manner were ingratiating. "A good word, hah?"

Sorokeh's expression changed completely.

"You're a *poyatz!*" His tone was serious.

"What's that you say?" Yankel was genuinely puzzled.

"You're a clown," Sorokeh explained.

"A clown?"

"Yes, a clown of the Holy One. All of you here are clowns for the Holy One."

Saying which, he turned on his heel and left them, a twisted smile on his lips.

65

Leahtche felt like a caged squirrel on a treadmill. The more she thought her situation over, the more she kept going around in circles. Here she was, a mature young woman, and her love life still completely up in the air, and how long could this continue, and where would it all end? Repeatedly she asked herself whether she loved him, Sorokeh that is, with all her soul and all her might, even as it is written in the novels.

"Do you love him?" she asked herself.

"Yes!" she answered, as though there were no doubt about it.

"Does he love me?" she wondered.

"No!" she answered. "Certainly not. He just wants to have an affair with me. What's all this about forbidden and permitted, says he. Nothing could be plainer. All right, very good. 'The demands of nature' and all the rest. Right. Nature calls us. Certainly. But what am I going to tell that selfsame nature afterwards? It's different for him, what does he care? But what about me?"

No, she thought, he's not in love, he's not the kind of fellow to lose his heart. Yes, she knows him well, thank the Lord, she reads him like a book. But even so, this is a very special lad. If "nature" were all that had to be considered, she'd never let go of him. But what can you do? It's not in her power to change the way of the world, to alter the sum of human experience. If it were up to her, love would be abolished, the human race would be freed from it. It leads to no good. Lifts you up on high, then down you fall with a thud. It's like a thatched roof that catches fire. Makes a big blaze for a short time, then leaves a blackened ruin. The time was bound to come, she thought, when humanity would be cured of this sickness. Indeed, why wait? Why not tear it out of one's heart now, and immerse oneself in the Revolution, for the good of mankind and the improvement of the world?

Thoughts like these were her constant companions. Nevertheless, although she consciously rejected Sorokeh's arguments, his words came back to mind unbidden, as though to confuse her. At night, as she lay in bed, she found herself whispering, "The voice of nature calls out to us from the depths, from our blood, our being." Like a patient in fever. "Calls out . . . calls out . . . from our blood . . . from our being . . . my darling, my dearest."

Something else came along to poison her life. Polyishuk

started walking out with Kayla, the eldest daughter of Zalman the harness-dealer, the *liverant.* Leahtche was devoured by jealousy.

In vain she argued with herself. "Fool! What do you care? You've given him up, you're not interested in him!" It did no good.

She went to see him at the Revkom, where she found him sitting at his desk in a surly mood.

"What can I do for you, comrade?" He looked up.

"I have a question." She hesitated, suddenly unsure. "There's something I don't understand."

"What's that, comrade?"

She got hold of herself, and forced a smile. "They say you're going around with that *liverantke.*"

"Nu?" He brought his eyebrows together forbiddingly.

"It's just that I find it surprising." Her laugh was short, embarrassed. "You and that *liverantke.*"

"What business is it of yours?" he barked.

"Please don't shout," she said. "Do you think I don't know that you're tired of me? Nobody has to tell me. I know. I'm not complaining. But why do you want to get mixed up with that good-for-nothing? Must be the horses' tails of her thievish father that attracted you."

"That's not your problem," Polyishuk informed her, stiffly. "I'll do what I feel like doing, and I don't need your advice."

"I'm ashamed," Leahtche persisted. "After all, there was a time when we were close friends."

Leahtche was not to be stopped. On and on she raved, calling Kayla *liverantke,* after her father's occupation, cow, bag of chaff, and other choice names.

Polyishuk waited for an opening, and then remarked, "You're not worth Kayla's little finger."

Leahtche flushed. She threw her head back, her eyes blazing.

"Have it your way. Go ahead and enjoy your bargain!"

She marched out of the room.

Shortly thereafter there was the sound of a shot from Polyishuk's office. Before the comrades could reach his room a second shot was heard. They flung the door open, and there was Polyishuk aiming his revolver at a box of matches hanging on the wall.

"Get out of here!" he bellowed.

Quick as a flash they closed the door, only to hear three more shots in quick succession. They stood around whispering to one another.

"Purim!" Mayerke spat out. "He's beating up on Haman!"

After leaving Polyishuk's office, Leahtche went to see Sorokeh. She arrived at his place still seething.

"What's the matter?" Sorokeh asked.

"It's no concern of yours!" She sounded angry, her lips were trembling, tears stood in her eyes.

"Anything go wrong?" he wondered.

She sat down on the bench, her head bowed, her arms slack and helpless.

"Are you ill?" He took her hand, and bent over her anxiously.

"Yes," she whispered, not looking at him.

"What's the matter?"

"My heart hurts."

"Impossible. You must be imagining."

She put her hand up to her cheek. "I've a pain in my tooth."

"Your tooth too? Oh, you poor thing!"

She turned to look at him. "You—you're a devil!" She gave a forced laugh, slightly hysterical, and burst into tears.

Sorokeh was nonplussed. He didn't know what to say.

"I'm choking!" She put her fingers under her collar and twisted her head from side to side.

"There, there," Sorokeh soothed. "Just rest quiet now."

She bent her head, sobbing.

"What is it?" He was alarmed now. "What's wrong, Leahtche dear?"

Her head went lower and she wept bitterly, uncontrollably.

"What happened? What is it?" He stood there, feeling utterly helpless.

"Tell me—" she managed to get the words out between the sobs that wracked her. "Tell me—"

"Yes? What do you want me to tell you?" he stood uncomprehending.

"Do you love me?"

"Of course!" He put his hand on her shoulder. His face had paled. "Certainly I love you, my child! I love you with all my heart. Believe me. . . ."

In a flash she flung her tear-stained face at him. "If that's the case, tell me what love is?"

Sorokeh was at a loss for an answer. After a moment he said, "My heart and your heart know what love is."

"No!" she cried out at him. "I don't know anything! You don't really love! You're too logical, too clever to be able to love! You think too much of yourself to be able to love! You're too much of an egotist! One who loves diminishes himself, and that you can't do! No, you're incapable of loving, you only know how to make yourself loved! Egotist, that's what you are!"

Sorokeh nodded, as though agreeing with everything she said.

And then suddenly, the storm was over.

"Forgive me, darling," she whispered, "I'm a foolish girl, I've been bad to you, please forgive me, I'm sorry."

They talked quietly now. But just as there is a distant rumble of thunder after the skies have cleared, so she returned to the one topic that was uppermost in her mind.

"A person ought to have some goal in life, some roots. But you keep wandering about, avoiding any fixed purpose, running away from your own happiness."

"Yes, that's me," smiled Sorokeh. "You describe me exactly."

"It's nothing to be proud of, my dear."

"But what can I do? That's the way I am. It's my nature."

Leahtche fell silent, pale, reflective. Sorokeh talked on, his voice a soothing balm. Bit by bit the color returned to her cheeks, her eyes regained their sparkle, she was her usual glowing self. Before long she was all over him, hugging him, covering his face with kisses.

"Take me with you. . . ." she whispered as though in a drunken stupor. Her eyes were closed, her cheeks were flushed, her breath came fast. "Take me, my beloved, my only one. I'll follow you to the ends of the earth."

Sorokeh waited patiently for a chance to speak. "What you said before," he said, controlled, "was the absolute truth. I'm a person without roots and without goals, impractical. I'm not one to depend on."

"Sh, sh!" she put her hand over his mouth. "Don't remind me what I said. Please, please! I was carried away, I was out of my mind."

"But you were right." Gently he took her hand away from his lips. "That is the kind of person I am."

"Have pity!" she begged. "It isn't true, it isn't true!"

He insisted. He was, he said, a creature of paradox, unstable, living only for the moment. One of these days he would fall afoul of the regime, and be thrown into prison.

He might even forfeit his life, but what did that matter? One person, what did that amount to?

He lowered his voice. "I expect to be a lonely wanderer all my life, a rebel fighting for liberty, for a free society, for the dignity of man."

Leahtche sat listening to him spellbound, open-mouthed, her cheeks aflame and her hair in disarray. When he stopped talking, she knelt and put her arms around his knees.

"My beloved! My only one! You—you—"

67

Speaking gently, sadly, Sorokeh told Leahtche what had happened to him during all that time when he was away from Mokry-Kut. He had gone to the Jewish farm settlements in the south with his proposal to convert them into free communes, but nobody would listen. He was equally unsuccessful in getting the young men of the colonies to organize armed bands. Most of them were preparing to emigrate to Palestine, and not much interested in the Revolution. So his dream had come to nothing. On the other hand, he had recruited a group of gentile fellows that called themselves Anarchists into a guerrilla band, and they had stolen some weapons and carried out train robberies. But before a week had passed he discovered that they were not Anarchists at all, just ordinary bandits, so he had left them.

"Mikhail became their leader," he said.

"Who's he?" Leahtche asked.

"A friend of mine. The son of a *melamed.*"

He paused, remembering.

"What a man! One in a million."

"An Anarchist?"

"That's right."

"I see."

"But wait till you hear what he did."

"What was that?"

"The Bolsheviks were chasing his gang, and he was hit by a bullet. He escaped on horseback, found a doctor, and forced him at gunpoint to amputate his wounded hand. Then he jumped on his horse and disappeared."

Leahtche was not much impressed. What do you expect from an Anarchist? She gazed at the melancholy remnants of half light that filtered through the window, and shook her head sorrowfully.

"Poor devil," she murmured.

A wave of pity welled up within her, for Sorokeh, for herself, for the whole world on which the sun was setting. She choked back tears.

"I'm so sorry for you," she whispered, her voice tearful and trembling. "I'm sorry for the way you're wasting your life."

Sorokeh sat silent. Moments passed.

"What a peculiar sunset!" she said to herself, gazing up at the window. "So lonely, so forsaken!"

The sadness of the world at large flowed together with her own inner sorrow, forming one pool of melancholy pity.

"Ach, ach." The sigh came from deep within her.

The cold was unbearable, the more so because of the creeping darkness and the air of an abandoned ruin that pervaded the place. "Cold," said Leahtche, hugging herself.

"I'll make a fire in the stove," offered Sorokeh.

"No, don't bother." Leahtche pressed against him. "Let's go." The warmth of his body enveloped her like a reminder of summer fields, of home and peace and everything good. Sorokeh embraced her, and they lay for a moment in one another's arms. Then suddenly they were no longer two friends, but two adversaries locked in combat. She began to struggle against his advances.

"Quiet, quiet," she whispered, covering his face with kisses. "Hush, darling."

Then suddenly she leapt disheveled from the bench.

"I'm getting out of here!"

Sorokeh got up and followed her silently out the door.

They walked side by side, slowly, neither one saying anything, both of them glum. Finally it was Leahtche who broke the silence.

"How dark the world is! Dark as the human soul."

"The human soul," Sorokeh repeated, mainly to calm himself down.

"Uh-huh," she said uncommunicatively.

Sorokeh decided to imitate her style. "And beyond the darkness, dawn is about to break."

"Yes, yes," she answered impatiently. "But the secret of darkness is not the dawn, but fear, fear—"

"Oh ho, Leahtche!" His tone was light, teasing.

"Ach, you don't understand anything!"

She walked on, ignoring him. "Leahtche," he said appeasingly, but she didn't answer. He stopped still, eyeing the piles of snow as if he didn't know where he was going. She waited, and when he caught up with her she began to scold.

"You're a peculiar person! A girl has to beware of crossing your doorstep. No, not even to talk with you, or to look at a book with you. . . ."

She thought for a while, and then she repeated, "Yes, you're peculiar, strange! You turn everything upside down. You belong in the dark, it suits you."

Sorokeh made no answer. He walked half bowed, as if counting his footsteps.

"Are you insulted?" she asked.

Then she seized his arm and dragged him forward. "Come on! Let's run! I'm freezing. Let's go to the club."

They ran along together, when suddenly she shoved him into a snowbank. She pounced on him and began to rub a fistful of snow in his face.

"Just you wait, I'll show you!" she laughed fiercely, pushing him down and smearing his face. "Wait till you see what I'm going to do to you!

Sorokeh made a point of greeting Heshel Pribisker whenever their paths crossed. Invariably, his greeting was barely acknowledged. Once he even went and sat down opposite him in the study house, and tried to strike up a conversation. All he got for his pains was an occasional monosyllable.

"What's the matter? Don't you know me?"

The only answer was a smile. Sorokeh adopted a biblical tone.

"Thinkest thou me a stranger? Have I become an alien in thine eyes?"

To which Heshel replied, "To me, all are strangers, yet all are brethren." This was mild, compared to his answer when Sorokeh tried again: "I have yet to meet a Jew who is a stranger, or a wicked man who is worth knowing." This brought their encounter to an abrupt end.

Later, when Sorokeh described the episode to Leahtche, she was astonished.

"What Heshel are you talking about? Our Heshel? Surely

not! Our Heshel is a straightforward man; you won't find any sparrows flying out of his mouth."

"That's the one," Sorokeh said. "There's something about him that reminds you of an ancient sage. His quotations sound as if they had just been freshly minted by *Hazal*."

"Hazal!" Leahtche was impressed, unaware that the term means "our sages," assuming that it was the name of a famous writer.

"Heshel is a wise man," she agreed. "It's a pleasure to talk with him."

"He's a fine person." Sorokeh was drawing her out. "Strong, youthful, impressive. A good-looking man."

"Good-looking?" Leahtche sounded dubious.

"Oh yes. And they say he's smitten by you."

"Who says so?" She spoke sharply, flushing to the roots of her hair.

"Oh, so it isn't true, then?"

Leahtche caught the drift of his game, and quickly regained control. "Why not?" she laughed. "Every man has his weakness."

But then her expression changed. "I can't understand what's happened to Heshel." She frowned. "He's always so gentle with people, so soft-spoken. I'll have to ask him. I'll make a point of it."

Then her face lit up. "You know what? I have an idea. Why don't you drop in at our place, and we'll see how he behaves. But tell me, what do you want from Heshel?"

"Nothing special. It's just that I'd like to get to know him. He seems an unusual person, interesting. . . ."

"Interesting?" She sounded puzzled. "I can't imagine . . . Oh, well. Come to our house, and we'll see."

Later in the day Sorokeh arrived at Leahtche's house. He found Reb Simcha and Heshel Pribisker sitting all bundled up, the older man in his bulky old fur, the younger in his overcoat, with the scarf around his neck. Had the visitor fallen through the ceiling they couldn't have been more surprised. Reb Simcha glanced from Sorokeh to Leahtche, as if to say, What's *he* doing here?

Leahtche gestured helplessly. "This is Sorokeh."

Her tone implied, You're looking at a very wise man, one of the world's finest.

With one quick glance Sorokeh took in the room and its contents. He sat down and began to hold forth about the Revolution, describing the places he had been, the people he had met, the things he had seen.

After a while Leahtche tried to intervene in the conversation, but Sorokeh good-naturedly cut her off. "Your opinions we know," he laughed. "But what do you think, gentlemen? What say you, Reb Heshel?"

Heshel looked at the floor and smiled gently. "My saying is expressed in what I don't say."

Sorokeh was intrigued by the cryptic answer. He resumed his analysis of the Revolution, The extremist actions of the Jewish Bolsheviks were their own idea, he said. They were deliberately more oppressive than their own party required them to be.

"The Jewish people," he declared, "is gradually dissolving. Individual Jews everywhere are trying to get out, it's every man for himself. As each Jew improves his personal situation, the people as a whole is weakened."

Heshel Pribisker smiled and shook his head. "The world," he said, "was not created for one particular generation. One generation goes and another generation comes, but the Lord shall reign forever and ever."

Reb Simcha's reaction was different.

"Pheh!" he said. "Idle chatter. Who's to blame for all this but you and the likes of you? It wasn't the Bolsheviks who started the decay. It was people like you!"

Leahtche tried to get into the argument, but Reb Simcha wouldn't let her. "Keep your mouth shut!" he hissed. "You haven't got a brain in your head!"

Sorokeh ignored the interruptions. The Jewish people, he said, had no hope for the future unless it returned to its own land. He gave Heshel a hard look.

"Nu!" he said. "A Jew like you, hah? What do you say? But you won't go to Palestine. No, you'll sit around and wait for the end of days, until the resurrection of the dead takes place, and Messiah the son of David arrives."

"Quite right," Heshel nodded, smiling faintly.

"Dreams!" Sorokeh retorted. "You're dreaming, my friend."

Heshel fingered his beard distractedly.

"I'm not my own master, nor am I master of my dreams. It's my dreams that are master over me."

The answer confounded Sorokeh, and he sat silent for a few minutes. Then he began to quote a poem they all knew:

> *Would I had wings that I might fly to thee,*
> *Lay my heart, broken, on thy broken stones,*
> *Fall down upon my face and kiss thy soil. . . .*

He paused. "If Yehuda Halevi could travel to the Land of Israel, why can't we? If he could long for her with his last breath, why can't we?"

Reb Simcha looked at him, smiling indulgently as at a piece of utter nonsense. Sorokeh's calm self-control began to evaporate.

"What's the use!" he exclaimed. "You're not Yehuda Halevi. You'll never go!"

Heshel looked upwards, addressing his remarks to the ceiling.

"No matter what comes to pass, whatever revolutions, whatever burden of suffering, there is still the promise of Scripture: 'I will restore you to this land.' "

At this, Sorokeh lost his temper. "Verses, verses! You've turned the Torah into a source of dark hints and mysterious allusions, and you think you can answer every problem with a quotation! The Torah has perverted you! The Torah is presiding over your dissolution! Self-deception! Willful blindness!"

He jumped up and strode angrily across the room. At the door he turned and flung a biblical verse in their teeth: " 'The end thereof shall be as a bitter day!' "

He was out the door. Leahtche grabbed her hat and ran after him.

"Crazy!" said Reb Simcha. "Did you hear the fellow?"

"Job's comforters," said Heshel. "Trying to pull the wool over God's eyes! Do you like Job's comforters?"

"Still," said Reb Simcha admiringly, "what a gift of speech! A fiery flame! A heretic, an *apikoros,* and yet. . . ."

Heshel Pribisker began to pace the floor, all the while blowing into his cupped hands to warm them up.

"As long as *we're* around to fear the Lord and keep His commandments," he ruminated, *"they* can allow themselves the luxury of being heretics. But if, God forbid, we were not here, they would have no choice but to accept the yoke and believe in the Name."

Reb Simcha looked at him in astonishment, and decided not to say anything.

69

For Sorokeh the encounter with Heshel Pribisker raised all kinds of suppressed doubts and fears. He had long concluded that the idea of messianic redemption was without substance, that the Jews would never leave the Diaspora. Heshel's whole approach, his appearance and his manner of speaking, reminded him of the frightening simplicity of the Jewish character.

"Useless," he told himself angrily, "it's all in vain. We can hope to survive every affliction, but not this one—this confident faith, this belief that redemption will come from heaven. That's the cruelest fate of all. We've shackled ourselves, there's no way out! What benighted darkness! What self-deception, what folly!"

Bitterly he reflected on the history of the Jewish people, who for two thousand years had pinned their hopes on the supernatural, the mysterious. All these generations they had been waiting for the moment when the Holy One, blessed be He, would personally redeem them, and create His world anew, and rebuild Jerusalem His city, and make death vanish forever. Two thousand years. . . .

"Torah, Torah," he mused, sighing. "A thing that has no parallel in the history of any other peoples, that can't be adequately translated into any other language, or really understood by any outsider."

He began to draw comparisons in his mind between the young people of his own generation, and their forebears.

They're not really so different from one another, he thought. Both of them make the fence more important than the garden. The parents did it with religion, their children do it with their revolutionary zeal. When it comes to redemption, messianic or secular, both generations are equally obscurantist. Well, the end has come, it's plain to see. The dreams have evaporated, Torah is being forgotten, and the final accounting shows a total loss. The end of the Jewish people.

He closed his eyes and tried not to think, but he couldn't rid himself of the pangs of hunger and cold.

"Ach!" He pulled his cap over his eyes. "The devil take it all!"

He pushed away thoughts of his recent misfortunes,

especially of Nadia and the miserable way she had treated him. Childhood memories flooded in upon him. He remembered a blind begger in his hometown to whom he had given all the change in his pocket.

"You can't see at night either?" the young Sorokeh had asked.

"Can't see," the beggar had answered. "Not in the daytime, not at night. Can't see a thing."

"What about dreams?"

No answer.

"But dreams?" he persisted. "Do you see dreams at night?"

"Agh, nonsense." The blind man poked around with his cane. "Go away. Don't pester me."

Then he remembered his Bar Mitzvah day. He and his father had gotten up early, and bathed in the *mikveh.* Afterwards his father taught him the chapter *Kiddush Hashem* in Maimonides' code.

He closed his eyes and whispered the words from memory.

"The whole house of Israel is commanded to sanctify the Holy Name. . . ."

70

That winter all kinds of things happened in Mokry-Kut. Reb Nachman Spektor's Gittel caught typhus, and so did Reiza, the mother of Avremel Voskiboinikov. Reb Avrohom-Elya's Kreina took to her bed. Abrasha, the tinsmith Bunem's eldest, volunteered for the Red Guard, along with

Nyuma, son of Reb Avrohom-Abba, Eisik Koysh's Nissel, and four or five other young men. So far, nobody had heard a word from any of them.

On the other hand, the local dramatic circle put on a play at the Bolshevik clubhouse, before a packed audience. It was called "New Life," and was the work of a gifted comrade in the provincial capital. The play poked bitter fun at the Rabbi, the *melamed,* the Jews who studied Torah, the merchants, and just about everybody, but the audience didn't seem to mind. For one thing, this was their first experience of theater. And besides, who were the actors, the dancers, the singers? Their own, their very own local talent.

The most enthusiastic person in the audience was Yankel Potchtar. He was completely under the spell of the actors, jumping up and down in his seat, clapping his hands, yelling "Hooray!"—utterly carried away. For several days thereafter he went around glowing, praising the actors, talking about their talent, analyzing the performance to anybody who would listen.

To his mind, the star of the piece was Sioma, the son of Kalman the baker.

"Listen," he told him. "You must go to Kiev and study at the university. You don't realize how talented you are. You're sure to become famous. Why, what you can do with a twist of your mouth, with one flutter of your eyelid! God willing, you'll become world famous, and rich and honored besides!"

When it came to Dena, Yankel was speechless with admiration.

"You rascal!" he said to her fondly, winking and nodding his head. He opened his mouth to say more, but nothing came out. So he closed his eyes and smiled, like a Hasid in religious ecstasy.

Yankel's praise fell pleasingly on the ears of Kalman the baker. He remarked that he hadn't recognized his son on the stage. "That gray hair, and the white beard they hung on him!" He laughed till the tears came. "He looked older than me!"

"And remember how he swayed to and fro over the Talmud?" Yankel chimed in. "And how he led the prayers—like an accomplished cantor!"

Kalman shook his head in amazement. "What a job they did! They scraped the whole pot clean, that clever bunch of rascals!"

Kalman's wife, Tzeitl, took up the theme.

"Do I need you to tell me about my Sioma?" she said to Yankel Potchtar. "He's a jewel, that boy, a diamond. There isn't another like him in the entire province. He knows the whole Bible by heart, dashes off Hebrew poetry without blinking an eye. Now he's interested in the *dramkruzhok,* the dramatic circle. Why, he himself is the whole *dramkruzhok.*"

As a result of this well-reported conversation, Sioma became known as "*dramkruzhok.*" His pals would say, "Come here, *dramkruzhok*! Listen, *dramkruzhok*!"

This self-same *dramkruzhok*, a boy of fourteen who had been a biblical scholar and Hebrew poet, and had become a budding genius of the theater, this lad boldly informed his mother one day that there is no God.

"He doesn't exist!" the boy declared. "Only ignorant people and reactionaries believe such nonsense."

Tzeitl was horrified.

"Scholar mine, genius mine, what are you saying?"

He said it again. Whereupon Tzeitl cried out, "Kalman! Kalman! Where are you? Come hear what your son is saying!"

Kalman the baker came on the run. When he heard what had happened he exploded.

"You'll pay for this!" he warned his son. "Do you hear what I'm telling you, you stupid ox, you horse's head!"

Tzeitl sensed that things were getting out of hand. She

knew her Kalman. From angry words to angry blows was but a short step for him.

"Wait!" she said. "He's only a child. He doesn't know what he's saying."

"Then I'll teach him!"

Having said which, Kalman became somewhat calmer. But he was still heated enough to offer a postscript.

"If I ever hear you say that again I'll break your neck."

Sioma bore the tirade with a look of injured innocence. After a few minutes, he took his coat and started to leave.

"Where are you going?" said his mother, worried.

"To the library." Sioma sounded downcast. "Today it's my turn to mind the library. After that I go to the literary section. I'll be home late tonight."

"And when will you eat? Come, eat something first. You're not going to miss anything important."

When he had finished his stint for the day, Sioma headed for the bath-house, to see Sorokeh.

"Greetings, comrade," he called out from the doorway. "I haven't seen you in a dog's age."

"Come on in." Sorokeh pushed aside his pencil and paper. "Nu? How are you?"

"There's something I want to talk to you about. In fact, quite a number of things."

He sat down beside Sorokeh and began to speak. First about the newer literature, poetry especially, Bialik, Tchernikhovsky, Shneour, Blok, and others, Hebrew and Russian. Then he addressed himself to theatrical matters, repertoire, acting, production; and finally he broached the dispute with his parents.

"Morally," said he, "I should be considered an adult, yet my father treats me as if I was still a child."

"What's the issue?"

"God."

"God?"

"Uh-huh. They still believe that there is a God. Such foolishness."

"Whether there is or isn't, as long as faith exists, it exists," was Sorokeh's answer.

"What does that mean?"

"It means, all is not lost."

Sioma wanted to debate the matter, but Sorokeh stopped him.

"Where's the gang?" he asked.

"Outside sledding," answered Sioma, in a deprecatory tone.

"Aha!" Sorokeh nudged him. "Come on!"

Sorokeh joined the crowd of noisy laughing youngsters, seated himself on a sled, and careened down the sloping street a couple of times. The children found him great fun.

"Ride with me, comrade Sorokeh! Mine's the best!"

Sorokeh took a turn with Tania, Reb Mordkhe-Leib's daughter. She put her arms around his waist and they flew downhill, the wind whipping their cheeks, their eyes closed, laughing uproariously.

"Again," she said.

On the third trip down their sled turned over and they fell into a snowbank. All the youngsters stood around laughing.

"Enough," said her little brother, taking his sled away from them. "My turn now."

Tania stood up and brushed the snow off. Her cheeks were on fire and her eyes shining. She turned from Sorokeh and looked up at the massive display of twinkling stars in the clear night sky.

"The world is still wonderful," she said. Then, after a moment and half to herself, "Some people remember a night in springtime, but I'll remember this winter night as long as I live."

71

Polyishuk agreed reluctantly to debate with Sorokeh at the Bolshevik clubhouse.

With head held high Sorokeh faced the comrades and launched into a critique of Marxism. He attacked the dictatorship of the proletariat, claiming that it was an elitist concept, representing the dominance of the few over the many. Tyranny was tyranny, he argued, whether it was the tyranny of capital or the tyranny of the commune. A revolution founded on despotism could not lead to liberty. The state would become one big garrison, and all the people would be slaves.

"Dictatorship of the proletariat to what end?" he asked his audience. "Who dictates, and who is dictated to? Who constitutes the commune other than the proletariat itself? And how does this form of government work? Is it to be headed by the whole proletariat, all those hundreds of millions of people?"

He went on to explain the theory of Anarchism, the idea of free communes in free partnership, the notion of a society in which force is absent, in which the individual is free from all sanctions, all coercion, in which there is utter and absolute equality, along with freedom of thought, of speech, of creativity.

The comrades listened intently, some of them apparent veterans of the ideological fray, others looking like beginners who were finding all this difficult to follow.

"Ach!" they whispered to one another admiringly. "What eloquence! What an outpouring!"

Polyishuk took the floor. He began by disavowing all intellectual pretensions. No, he was no expert in weaving elaborations on impractical theories, he hadn't the honor of belonging to the intelligentsia, not everyone is lucky enough to have a background of fine family, wealth and learning—at the expense of the working class.

His contempt and sarcasm were obvious as he stood there, one hand clenched in a fist, his eyes fixed on the table.

He himself, he continued, was a simple man. He had not studied the doctrines of Kropotkin or Bakunin, he knew nothing about their complicated sophistry. He would presume, nevertheless, to tell the comrades that these were not the ones to guide the Revolution, and to give direction to the proletariat. Not they, but Karl Marx, Lenin, Trotsky. Anyhow, he went on, the fine words spoken by comrade Sorokeh were like soap bubbles, without substance. Could anybody tell him, he asked, spreading his palm out in a gesture of triumph, how any people could survive without a government, without law and order? How could the Revolution fight off its enemies without an army, without leaders? What would be happening to the Revolution right now, if it were not for Lenin and Trotsky? On the other hand, wasn't the speech just made by comrade Sorokeh downright subversive? He himself, he repeated, was no theoretician, he was a practical man, a man of action. As such, it was clear to him that the dictatorship of the proletariat was an absolute necessity. And why? To safeguard the Revolution. It was the Revolution that counted above all; from it would come salvation, it would bring blessing and happiness to the Russian proletariat, and not only to them but to the proletariat of all countries, to all humanity, to the whole world from one end to the other, and from now through all the rest of history.

At this point his argument became disjointed, and he began to repeat himself. He wanted to finish, but he didn't know how. Just then he glanced at Sorokeh, sitting there grinning at him, and that reminded him of counterrevolution. Suddenly he was in control of the situation again.

"Let the bourgeoisie and all enemies of the people take warning!" His fist came crashing down on the table. "Up against the wall! We'll destroy them! We'll wipe them out!"

On this note Polyishuk reached a triumphant conclusion.

Sorokeh wanted a chance for rebuttal, but Polyishuk would have none of it. "Agh, you've said your piece. What more is there? We know what you are—a counterrevolutionary!"

He headed for the door, like a robber who has stripped his victim and has nothing more to take. At the door he turned and called back, "Just you wait, we'll take care of you, you can be sure of that!"

The comrades applauded loud and long. "Good speech!" they called out after him. "You hit the mark!"

Once Polyishuk had left, they gathered around Sorokeh and listened while he took apart the arguments of his absent opponent. They liked listening to him, even though their minds were made up not to agree, since after all they were committed Bolsheviks. The honor of the Communist party required them to refute his words.

"Nu, Sorokeh, you went too far! That proclamation of yours was out of bounds."

Sorokeh went over the ground again, with much rhetoric and many a clever argument. He was indefatigable in his efforts to convert people to Anarchism, and sure that the time would come when everybody would see the light. On this occasion he struck an added note, arguing that Jewish Communists had a special responsibility, one inherited from their forebears. It was for them to be specially concerned with the moral core of the Revolution, its ethically mature character, for were they not the children of an ancient people that had dreamed the dream of social justice at the dawn of its history? Nor was there any people so poor and persecuted as the Jewish people, or any that had waited so fervently and so long for the day of redemption. What was most important, he said, was that they should concern themselves for the sanctity and purity of the Revolution, for these two qualities had characterized the Jewish people throughout the ages.

"The Revolution is becoming perverted," he warned. "It's wallowing in blood, immorality and arrogance, turning drunken, stupid, and cruel. It's becoming Russian rather than universal. It's beginning to look like a revival of the old cossack uprisings, another *pugatchovshtchina,* a renewed *zaporozhie.* Fierce abandon, an enjoyment of violence, aimless, without limit. . . . Mark well, comrades, you're dancing at the wedding of strangers!"

"Why not?" they laughed at him. "Where else should we dance?"

72

The comrades made their way noisy outside, and found themselves in the middle of a blizzard.

"I can't see a thing," said Leahtche, doubled over, turning her face into her collar.

Sorokeh took her arm and pulled her along.

"Uch, what a blizzard!" The words seemed to come from Ziame. The wind carried them away.

Whistling and wailing, the blizzard blew the clouds of wet snow into the faces of the comrades, who bent their heads and fought their way against the howling elements.

"The whole world is blowing away," said Mayerke, and his laugh was cut short by a blast of wind. The comrades jumped, ran, laughed, and pushed one another playfully into the snow.

Leahtche elbowed her way through the crowd, and pulled Sorokeh into a run. "Hey, hey," she shouted.

The wind howled and screeched. Leahtche pressed against Sorokeh and said, "Tell me something."

"Hah?" He turned his face in her direction.

"Tell me. . . ." in a cajoling whisper.

"I. . . ." The wind snatched the words out of his mouth and blew them away into the swirling white maelstrom.

Sorokeh bent his head to let a particularly strong gust pass, then he took Leahtche's hand and started to run, shouting into the wind, "Oho, ho, ho!"

When there was a momentary lull in the storm, Leahtche pulled him to a standstill.

"I didn't like your speech at the club today," she said.

"No matter," he answered. "It's not words that we need."

"The trouble is, you're not a Communist," she interrupted.

"What we need is to make a great outcry," he finished his own sentence.

Leahtche stood up tall, spread her hands, and shouted into the night, "Hurray! Hurray for us!"

The world around them wailed and whistled. The snow flew. The comrades pranced about in youthful horseplay. Leahtche slid along leaning close against Sorokeh. He bent over and kissed her wet cheek.

"Darling," she whispered when the wind would let her, "what did you come for?"

"Imagination," he shouted into her ear through a sudden gust.

"No, but really. . . ."

"My imagination convinced me," he managed between blasts of the wind.

"What?" She had no idea what he was talking about.

"It's all imaginary," he puffed. "The revolution—Mokry-Kut—I myself. Just imagination. This storm must be intended to let us know how far gone we are."

She could hear only fragments of what he was saying.

"Mokry-Kut doesn't exist." He waved his hand at the houses, by now almost totally obscured by the snow. "No sound from any house, no light to be seen, nobody around . . . and everything that you can see . . . separated from the earth . . . mixed up with the sky . . . with the four winds . . . chaos . . . all of us. I'm not me, and you're not . . ."

Leahtche simply pressed closer and kept her head down.

Two wailing gusts of wind clashed right over their heads, one of them pitched low, like a man's voice, the other high, like a woman's.

"You and I," Sorokeh shouted into her ear, "are nothing but two winds keening in the night."

Suddenly they heard a voice down the street. It sounded like a man chanting a chapter from the Prophets in the Bible.

"Who's that?" Sorokeh stopped in his tracks.

"Sounds like a ghost calling," said Shimtze.

"Who's there?" Ziame called out into the darkness.

The voice came nearer. The comrades stood still, huddled against the wind. In a few minutes they made out a human shape, all ghostly white, swaying in the wind, stumbling and falling and rising and moving erratically.

"One-third of you shall die of the pestilence"—the wind blew the words in their direction. It sounded like a preacher of doom—"and shall perish of hunger in your midst, and a third shall fall by the sword round about, and a third will I scatter to every wind, and the sword shall pursue them."

"Who's that?" the comrades asked one another. "Who's yammering there?"

"Oy!" Leahtche clasped her hands in amazement. "That's our Heshel!"

"Aha!" cried Mayerke.

"That's who it is!" shouted Shayke. "The devil take him!"

"What's he up to?" said Ziame.

By this time Heshel had reached the group.

"Where are you going?" demanded Mayerke, with the voice of authority.

"I'm just . . . just on my way." Heshel spoke appeasingly. His head was pulled into his scarf, his hands deep in his pockets.

"What was that you were yelling?" demanded Mayerke gruffly. "From what I heard, it was counterrevolutionary propaganda!"

"No, no!" answered Heshel Pribisker hastily. "I was only talking with Ezekiel."

"What Ezekiel? Are you trying to pull the wool over my eyes?"

"Ezekiel, comrade. Ezekiel the prophet."

"Who? What prophet?"

"Back there"—he pointed behind him—"he asked me what I made of the verse 'A third shall fall by the sword'?"

"Nu?" Sorokeh came closer.

"Prophet, prophet. . . ." Leahtche interrupted. "He's got Satan dancing between his eyes!"

"Just like a Hasid and holy man," laughed Mayerke. "May his merit stand me in good stead before a plate of noodles!"

"Leahtche? Is it you?" Heshel was astonished. "Why, it's you I'm looking for. Your father asked me . . . he's worried about you!"

"Papa asked," she said sarcastically. "Big news! Go on, go back where you came from."

Heshel Pribisker bent over, turning his face away from the wind.

"Don't you laugh," he stammered. "Don't laugh."

BOOK TWO

73

Like rows of covered sepulchres in the cemetery, the houses stood on either side of the street, half buried in the snow, each one tottering under its sloping burden of white. It was a sunless day. The wind had died down, and heavy clouds hung in the sky.

Sorokeh wandered aimlessly through the streets and alleys. His eyes were glazed, his lips taut, his fists clenched in his pockets. He was in a deep mood of depression, but none of the passersby seemed to notice. On the contrary, men and women came up to him as usual, to pass the time of day. Most of them managed to exchange a few sighs, and to complain that the times were more than flesh and blood could bear. One man declared that there could be only one explanation—the good Lord must have some mysterious calculations of His own. Another offered the opinion that there was really nothing to fear but the truth, and the only trouble with that was that the truth was greatly to be feared.

Sorokeh walked on. He himself could not understand what had come over him. In the middle of the main street he stopped in his tracks and asked himself why he had ever come to this out-of-the-way hamlet, this miserable Mokry-Kut.

"So as to be alone," he told himself.

"No, to overcome loneliness," he countered.

Finally, "Neither."

He continued walking. The snow creaked loudly underfoot, an accusing counterpoint to his thoughts. A feeling of guilt weighed heavily on him, not specific, but bleakly real nonetheless.

He came to the edge of the town, where the street crested a hill, and suddenly there were no more houses, only the silent white emptiness of snow-covered fields as far as the eye could see. The world that stretched before him was coldly forbidding, unfriendly.

He turned around and headed back into town. His mind was a turmoil of reflection and memory; thoughts of his people and of what destiny might hold in store for them; memories of the early months of the Revolution; of the women he had known; of rivalry and jealousy and heartbreak.

Nagging at the core of all his thoughts was the memory of Nadia. She had left him and gone off with his best friend, Sasha, and then after a while had come back to him all smiles and laughter. Not many days had passed, however, before Sasha enticed her away again. That's when Sorokeh had pulled a gun on his friend and wounded him. Now the memory haunted him, intruding on his every thought.

He turned into one of the narrow streets that led to the old bath-house. Suddenly the white snow called up the image of Nadia's gleaming teeth, that time she had come back to him open-mouthed with laughter. He choked back tears.

Inside the bath-house he got the fire going, and sat down to warm himself. The vaulted chamber of the old furnace filled up with flame and color, with the sounds of crackling wood and flying sparks. Sorokeh held his two chapped hands over the fire.

"How cold the world has become!" he thought. "There's nothing any more to warm yourself up with, no light to sit by." A moment's distracted silence, shot through with thoughts of Nadia, then he repeated half aloud, "Light to sit by—to sit by."

He straightened up, with a grimace of distaste. "None of it matters," he decreed, like a judge pronouncing sentence. He made a deliberate effort to take hold of himself, to think rationally.

"The trouble is," he reflected, "there's no peace anywhere in the world, no blessing, no goodness. Nowadays the only place you can find *shalom* is at the end of the mourner's *kaddish.*"

This last wry witticism he had once heard from an old Jew, and he liked the sound of it. He smiled to himself.

"That's what it is with these Jews of ours. All they've got to fall back on is their words and their wit."

He picked up a few bundles of twigs and threw them into the furnace. For a moment the fire darkened.

"That's why we're such nay-sayers," he thought, "the eternal critics and dissenters. more revolutionary than anybody else. It's because we have so little stake in things as they are. We've got nothing to lose."

He recoiled from a great billow of smoke that took him unawares.

"That's why we're such extremists," he ruminated, rubbing his eyes. "Always and ever the extremists. In everything. In politics. In art. We have to be the modernists. The first to take up any new notion, every passing fad. Right up there in the thick of things whenever there's any ferment, any turmoil in human history. No, I've had enough of this people! I'm sick and tired of the whole business!"

By now the fire had taken hold and the ruddy glow of the flames imparted a look of sunset to the interior of the old bath-house.

74

Ordinarily of a gregarious nature, Sorokeh was now in no mood to see anybody. He was out of patience with the older generation of Jews, with their moaning and groaning and even with their acid cleverness. He was sick of the young Bolsheviks, with their constant mouthing of the party line, and the strutting arrogance of their newfound power. He was weary of his own debating and lecturing and the whole frenetic hubbub of the Revolution. He sat alone in the bath-house, oppressed by his thoughts, most of all by the thought that the Jewish people was finished, done for.

He tried, without much success, to talk himself out of that conviction.

"Look," he told himself. "Things can't stay the way they are. The Revolution will either come to an end, or it will change direction. Either way, the Jewish people will survive, as it always has. In fact, we can't help but be better off no matter how things go, because we are the poorest and most persecuted of all peoples!"

Yes, that was the logic of the situation. Unfortunately, it was not the reality of the situation. He just couldn't shake the sense of impending doom, and it weighed heavily and persistently on his mind.

Since there was no one there to talk to, he sat in front of the cold stove and addressed his agony to the One above.

"Ribbono-shel-Olam! Yes, yes, I know You don't exist. Even if You did, I wouldn't be trying to talk to You. But Your people, the Jewish people, have been claiming for a long time that You do exist, as the eternal Lord of the universe, great, mighty, and awesome. So, on the basis of the faith my ancestors have had in You for so many generations, I presume to address You. I know—You're not listening to me. The fact is, even human beings who ought to understand won't listen, because what I have to say is a pill too bitter to swallow. It's this—the Jewish people is at the end of its rope! I see the whole thing clearly. Just as once the Temple in Jerusalem was destroyed, so now is the people doomed to be destroyed. True, the world will be the poorer for it. Humanity will be orphaned. The *Shechinah* will depart from the world, the Holy Spirit will be gone, nothing will be sacred any more. But there's no help for it, because this is the end.

"From the moment that men began to doubt Your existence, You were done for—and so were we! Because if there's no God, there's no Jewish people. If there's no God, there's no Messiah, no redemption, no hope of renewal for the world, nothing left to look forward to. From which it follows that the Jewish people has no right to survive, no reason for being. Anyhow, we're in the process of destroying ourselves, doing it by our own efforts. All those dreams and hopes of ours—all bankrupt! We put our trust in You all these thousands of years, generation after generation—while all the time You weren't even there! Come to think of it, why should You have been? Why bother being God? What's the use of all this feverish drive to exist, this hot divine will-to-be? Especially nowadays, when being God is a bad business, just as being a Jew is a bad business. See, we're in the same boat, You and we.

"Still, none of that matters, since You were never anything but an illusion of ours. If not for us, the world would never have heard of You. It wouldn't have been You that created the world, but some other God. If not for us, You wouldn't have been forced to perform all those miracles for us—nor, by the way, to inflict all those misfortunes on us! Like destroying our homeland, and sending us into exile among the nations! Aren't You ashamed of Yourself, turning us into homeless exiles like that? We gave You the whole world, and how did You reward us? With dark and bitter exile. If that's how You treat us when You don't exist, imagine what You would have done to us if You did exist!

"Well, it's a good thing that You don't, You and that Messiah of Yours. Because if Messiah arrived today, he wouldn't find any of us to follow him. You see? Time's up, for You and for him. It's all over."

He spat angrily into the cold ashes. Adjusting his cap, he got up and went outside.

He made his way to the river's edge and started walking across the ice, slipping and falling every once in a while, until he found himself at the place where a water hole had been chopped in the ice. The sight of it reminded him of his grandfather. That saintly Rabbi, it was said, used to immerse himself in the water hole during the winter months, instead of going to the *mikveh.* Sorokeh crouched down and watched the dark swirl of the icy current.

"Br-r-r," he shivered, as though he had glimpsed some awful danger, and quickly turned away.

Like a driven man he strode back through town, shifting

from street to street without purpose or destination. Finally, as the day wore on, he made his way back to the old bath-house. There he stood still for a long time, gazing at the doorway on the western side of the building. It glowed in the rays of the setting sun, so red you might have thought there was a great conflagration somewhere.

A massive stillness hung over the place. It was not the kind of evening peace that floods the human heart with yearning, and makes man feel a partner in the grandeur of the departing day. No, this was a stillness lonely and desolate, the kind that walls a person off from the world, and makes him feel an alien in the universe, alone and without hope.

75

The bath-house lay dark, except for the glow of a few embers in the furnace. Leahtche came in, tired and hungry, shivering with cold, and saw Sorokeh sprawled on one of the benches. Was he ill? Or was he pretending to be asleep? She bent over him.

"What's the matter?" she whispered. "Why are you stretched out?"

"No reason," he answered, lying there, not even removing the cap from his eyes.

She had been carrying a cooking pot. She put it on the bench and sat down beside him.

"You keep it awfully cold in here, with the wind seeping in through the window, and the floor like ice. Aren't you stoking the fire?"

Sorokeh sat up, slack and dispirited.

"Nu!" she urged. "Pull yourself together! I've brought you some porridge."

He gave her a wan smile. "I don't feel like eating."

"Do me a favor," she ordered, "and stop the nonsense. Come on, eat."

She kept after him until he finally took up the spoon and began to feed himself.

"Have you had anything?" he asked.

"I ate, I ate," she answered, a bit too quickly. "Don't worry about me."

Between mouthfuls Sorokeh asked after Heshel Pribisker.

"Heshel?" She was surprised at the question, a little pleased. "Same as always. No different."

"Fine person," said Sorokeh through a mouthful of porridge.

"Why, what's so special about him," she wanted to know. "A Jew, like all the others of his type!"

"No, no!" he waved the spoon for emphasis. "He's the best of us all. He's helped me understand each one of us Jews better."

Leahtche's eyebrows shot up; she was astonished. "Each one of us? I grant you, he's a prime example of the religious Jew, the Hasid. But what's that got to do with you and me?"

"Each one of us," Sorokeh insisted stubbornly, letting the spoon fall into the now empty pot. "There's no difference between us and those other Jews. The same fate awaits us all."

"Everything you say is a puzzle," murmured Leahtche.

"We're all in the same boat," Sorokeh went on between clenched teeth. "You, me, the rest of us. We're all doomed."

He paused for a moment, bent, despairing. "It's hopeless," he said. "The Jewish people will disappear. All the fences are down, everything's falling to pieces."

Leahtche looked at him wearily. "You're possessed," she said. "Some Jewish dybbuk has gotten hold of you."

Sorokeh kept silent.

"All of a sudden you're more of a Jew than anybody else. Peculiar! I can't figure it out."

Sorokeh still said nothing.

"Well," said Leahtche in a subdued tone, "I see you're in a bad mood today. I'll run along."

She made a move to get up, but changed her mind. Instead, she sat gazing at the floor, looking like a rejected wife.

A heavy brooding silence hung over them for a few minutes, then finally she did get up.

"All right," she sighed. "See you some other time."

"Yes, yes," he nodded. "Some other time."

"All right, then." She picked up the empty pot, and stood uncertainly, shifting her weight from one foot to the other. "Well, then"—with a sad little smile—"goodbye."

As soon as she had left Sorokeh stood up and started pacing restlessly. Then he sat down again. Suddenly he remembered that he was supposed to give a lecture to the Tseire Tsiyon. He pulled out his pocket watch.

"Now," he muttered, and set out for the meeting.

He walked unhurried through the twisting alley. It was a pale gray day, the sky heavy with clouds. No sooner was he out of the alley than it began to snow, tufts of white drifting down aimlessly, giving the whole world a mottled appearance.

A young girl on her way to hear his lecture caught up with him from behind. With her was a small boy who looked to be no more than ten years old, wrapped in a long heavy coat, from his head to the patched outsize boots on his feet.

Sorokeh looked him up and down.

"And where," he asked, "is this gosling headed?"

The girl was abashed. "My brother. He wants to hear the lecture."

"You a Zionist?" Sorokeh addressed the boy with mock severity.

"Sure!" The youngster brushed his nose with his fist.

"Will you go to the Land of Israel?"

"God willing."

"God won't be willing," said Sorokeh sternly, like a judge handing down a verdict.

"What do you mean?" the boy said.

"God won't be willing if you won't be willing."

"Oh, that!" The boy's face broke out in a pleased smile. "I'll be willing! I'll be willing!"

"Nu, in that case, it's a different story. But what about the rest of the Jews? They're not willing. They don't even want to hear about it."

"Don't want to hear?" The boy brushed the snowflakes off his eyelashes. "If God listens how can Jews not listen?" Actually, he spoke the words in Yiddish: *Oyb got hot derhert veln yidn nit derhern?*

His sister was embarrassed. "Don't be silly," she blushed.

But Sorokeh was enchanted. His face lit up, as though he had just heard good news. He put an arm around the little fellow, lifting him a few inches off the ground.

"Good boy!" he said. "We'll act and God will listen! Right?"

"Right!" the youngster echoed.

76

Karpo tried his hand with Polyishuk once again.

"It's like this . . . I mean . . . you understand. . . ."

"What's wrong?" Polyishuk asked over his shoulder, absently.

"The laws have been twisted out of shape."

"Laws?" Polyishuk swung around and looked at him. "What laws?"

"People are ignoring the statutes of the Revolution."

"Which laws are they violating?" Polyishuk's suddenly solemn manner was a surprise, and Karpo was taken aback.

"Well," he said, "there's a lot of talk, reports, directives, but nothing comes of it. They turn a deaf ear to the decrees of Lenin-Trotsky. Yes. Who would have thought that bloody musclemen—may they choke on their ill-gotten gains—would be given priority over the poorest of the poor."

Polyishuk's expression changed. His eyes began to flash ominously. "Who gave them priority? Where? Who conducted the investigation?" Karpo averted his eyes, and the muscles of his face stiffened.

"The tough peasants in the village got hold of most of the squire's property," he said. "Nice for them, hah?"

"That's an old tune, I've heard it before," retorted Polyishuk, an angry sarcasm creeping into his voice. "The thing is, you're wrong about it. It's not the tough ones who took possession. Ilko and Mitri and Halka, they all got their share. And Cosma Kvasha got his, and Andrei Zhivohlaz and Stepan Zelenetz and Timokh Zavertaillo. And you yourself, with all due respect, got hold of a pretty good share."

"Me? What are you talking about! Two or three bits and pieces! Why, I know one fellow who got the horses with their first grade harness, along with the carriage and all its furnishings, and another who took the cows, and a third who got furs, and rugs and mirrors, and saddles, and riding boots!"

"So? You got a silver samovar, and the ikons with their silver ornaments."

"And what good do they do me?" Karpo retorted bitterly. "Look at Domna Bistrukha and her brood of bastards. They've filled their house with flour, while we have to push our kids' knees into their hungry mouths. Our bellies are sticking to our ribs."

Polyishuk turned away from him. The fire had gone out of his eyes. Karpo pressed on with his argument.

"Nobody's concerned for the people's property," he complained. "That's what's gone wrong with the Revolution. Look here, it'll soon be spring. The farmers will go out into the fields, but the lands haven't been divided up yet. So you can just imagine what a mess that will be—ee-ee! God preserve us! Before we catch our breath, retribution will jump us from the other side of the fence! We'll get caught with our—"

"Don't worry." Polyishuk had stood up, and gave him a kindly slap on the back. "Never fear."

"But you did say we'll think about it. That's what you said."

Karpo stood there a few more minutes, downcast, his eyes fixed on the hem of his tunic. Finally he shot a gob of spit expertly into a corner of the room, and walked out.

". . . *sorokeh bielobokah,*" he called back. "We're off to see the crow, with the shins white as snow."

He found Sorokeh in, and proceeded to describe the encounter with Polyishuk, chapter and verse. "The fellow tried to fob me off with all kinds of twisting arguments, damn his mother's eyes, fetching whole pailfuls from the Don and from the sea. But when I put my just case, which is that I've got my rights, because I'm the poorest of the poor, on top of being a Communist and a Commissar, why then he went into a rage, and started to spout crazy talk, like a mad capitalist."

Sorokeh sat there and listened, enjoying himself hugely.

"Nu?" Karpo pressed him. "What do you say? I've got my rights, no? What do you think? Was I right or wasn't I? Come on, what's your opinion? Do me a favor, explain it all to me."

"I'll tell you what," laughed Sorokeh. "Let the whole bunch go to hell. Send the lot of them off to the mother of evil spirits!"

Whereupon he launched into an exposition of the entire theory of Anarchism, from alpha to omega. Karpo listened attentively, and understood no better than he had on many previous ocassions, which is to say, not at all.

"I listened to every word." He scratched the back of his neck reflectively. "This time I made up my mind to understand, come hell or high water. I thought, Now I'll become smart. But no! Oh, there's nothing wrong with your explanation. You do a good job, no two ways about it. It's just that I can't get it all straight in my mind. No. I lose the thread somewhere. Anyhow, listen. There's something I want to tell you, something I've been thinking about."

He fell silent for a moment, gazing reflectively at the ceiling of the bath-house. Then he spoke.

"How would you like to come in on our side, and help us plain folks out?"

"Nu?" Sorokeh waited.

"Will you?"

"Nu?"

"All right, I'll tell you what you ought to do. Make a deal with us."

"Meaning?"

"Get yourself admitted to the Party, and we'll all back you up. Wait till you see what we'll do for you—you'll become a general, no less! And those others, damn and blast them, what we won't do to them! That Polyishuk—one kick in the ass and he'll be gone! You won't be able to smell a trace of him around here!"

Warming to his subject, Karpo went on about how the Revolution would be fulfilled, and the poverty-stricken masses lifted up at the expense of the selfish kulaks, while he, Karpo, would at last get his share of those lovely horses and those fine cows they had looted from the squire, not to speak of the carriage, and the harness, and the saddle, and the double-barreled shotgun.

"Eh-heh!" he exclaimed gleefully. "I'll be crowned with everything good in the world, like an ear at the harvest wrapped in its corn silk!"

Sorokeh looked at him fondly. "Karpo, you talk with the magic voice of a bard."

"All right then, let's get going. This scheme doesn't allow for the *potchekai* of the *pan* or the *zaraz* of the Jew. Neither 'wait' nor 'presently'—but right now."

"It doesn't allow for that either," Sorokeh answered soothingly. "It's just impossible, out of the question."

"But why?" Karpo implored him. "Come on, my friend, give it a try. Be a man! Nu, old buddy, together we can bring it off . We'll set the whole village seething!"

It was no use. When Karpo finally did leave, he was in a black rage. "Mud-son-of-dirt!" he spat, rolling out a string of curses. "The two of them tarred with the same brush, both from one field, the same breed, seed of Judas both of them. A plague on them both! A cholera!"

77

Karpo wasn't wrong. The booty from the looted manor-houses really had become a bone of contention among the villagers. Arguments led to fistfights, peasants stole the loot from one another, and some openly seized what they reckoned was their fair share of the spoils. People began to predict that there would be bloodshed.

"By the saints, blood will flow!"

Karpo kept drumming his complaint into Polyishuk's ears.

"The village is buzzing like a swarm of bees in a field of millet. . . ."

"Get down to cases, man!" Polyishuk cut in sharply. "Who's buzzing?"

"The whole village, from one end to the other."

"I'm asking you, who's buzzing?" Polyishuk raised his voice angrily.

"Well"—Karpo began ticking them off on his fingers—"Netchiporenko, and Zhmenya, and Piven, and Makar Trukhliyoe, and Savko Horiholovo. They don't like the way the political situation is going."

At this Polyishuk jumped to his feet in a rage.

"Go to the devil!" he shouted. "You know as much about politics as a one-eyed chicken!"

Karpo eyed him with suppressed fury, but when he spoke it was in a level tone.

"The chicken lays an egg, and the egg hatches into a chicken. Don't dismiss it so lightly."

Later, when Ilko came along with more or less the same

story, saying, "Well yes, things are kind of stormy," Polyishuk decided that he had better see for himself. Taking along Prokop Mikitov, the Party Secretary in Mokry-Kut, and the militiaman Stetzko, he set out for Proshibino, the nearest village.

Within a few minutes after his arrival the village Council House was packed from wall to wall. The Council Chairman led off with a high-flown speech. Capitalism, he declared, had breathed its last, done in by the regime of peasants, workers and soldiers. The corpse of capitalism lay sprawled on the ash heap of history. Finished. Now a plan was being worked out, there would be equality and freedom for all. But right now, comrades, the main thing was to preserve discipline. Just let everybody hew to the line, and be careful not to upset the applecart, God forbid.

Prokop, the Party Secretary, then took the floor and spoke in a similar vein. He was just warming up to a fiery panegyric on the Revolution when he was interrupted from the audience. The heckler wore a sheepskin cap askew on his head, a sly grin on his face. His scraggly beard waggled upwards as he called out, "Where is this 'Levorution' you're talking about? Is it far away? From here we can't see it at all."

Prokop paid no attention, but plowed ahead at his most oratorical. A moment later somebody shouted from the last row.

"What about the fields? When are we going to divide up the land?"

"Right!" Voices called out from different parts of the hall. "Stop beating around the bush!"

"Comrades!" With an effort, Prokop made himself heard. "Comrades! The October Revolution nationalized all the landed estates, and is going to divide them up among the poor. It's all written down, signed and sealed in the statutes of the Communist party. . . ."

The crowd laughed in his face. "Don't give us that stuff!" they scoffed. "The pen scratches and the horsefly hatches. Soon it'll be spring, plowing time."

"That's right!" Shouts came from every side. "Spring is breathing down our necks!"

At this point one of the poorest peasants, who happened to be standing near one of the most prosperous, turned on his neighbor.

"Who's breathing down your neck?" he asked sarcastically. "You short of acreage? Or maybe you got a raw deal at the squire's?"

The other eyed him coldly. "I'm entitled to what I got."

In a flash the place was in an uproar of argument. One fellow turned on his neighbor and taxed him with the pigs he had taken from the squire's farm. "Why you and not me?" he screamed.

In another corner a peasant who had helped himself to three of the squire's cows was under attack by another who had made off with only the bull.

"What good is he to me?" he argued. "Do I bring him over to your place so he can have fun with your cows?"

One villager was demanding a share of the sacks of flour his neighbor had looted. What he got was a dusty answer.

"I'll let you have a large fig under your nose. You can sniff it or suck it, take your choice."

The tumult spread throughout the crowd. The room was filled with angry shouts, yells, screams. The place was seething.

At this point Polyishuk stood up and let out a mighty roar.

"Comrades!" he shouted, with palms outspread in a demand for attention. The room fell silent, the crowd stood watching him expectantly.

"Comrades!" he shouted again. "You know that the agrarian question has been settled by decree. You can depend on the Communist party to keep its word, and see to it that everybody gets his proper share of land. However, comrades. . . ."

He paused and surveyed the entire assemblage for a moment.

" . . . however, our victories still have to be firmed up. We have to move forward to a new stage in the people's economy. The Revolution hasn't reached its full growth yet."

"What's the matter, is it still a baby?" an old peasant called out mockingly. He was dressed in a heavy sheepskin coat, with a black lambskin hat on his head. His big beard was shaped like a baker's shovel.

"What's the matter with the *revolutzia?*" he asked. "Is she still in the cradle, or what? And what will she be when she grows up? A calf, for example, becomes a cow, a colt grows into a mare. Now, what's the Revolution going to grow up to be?"

"Just wait for her to grow up!" yelled a man in the crowd. "In the meantime they're grabbing everything for themselves!"

"Ah, those sons of the devil!" shouted the man next to him. "A curse on their mother's privates! Fattening themselves on the people's property!"

"Who put them in charge?" yelled a voice. "Did they hold a secret meeting behind the barn? Nine cockroaches and one frog, plus one *zhid!* That's a new one—a *zhid* lording it over us!"

Polyishuk tried to calm the crowd down, but it was no use. The storm grew louder, it began to engulf them. Sensing that they were in danger, they left their places at the table and started to push their way through the crowd. Somebody shouted, "Beat them up!" They headed toward the door, but the way out was blocked. An ominous silence fell on the crowd, broken only by the sound of heavy breathing.

Gates of Bronze | 228

Polyishuk pulled out his revolver.

"Ah-nu," he said, his voice controlled. "Let us pass."

Prokop also drew his gun.

"Make way!" he shouted. "One side, whoever isn't looking for a bullet!"

Wordlessly the crowd separated. Polyishuk and Prokop passed between them, waving their revolvers, followed by Stetzko, and the Council Chairman. As soon as they were outside, the crowd poured through the door and stood in the snow alongside the building, filling the air with angry curses and catcalls.

78

The reception that Polyishuk had met with in Proshibino was deeply gratifying to Karpo, who could now barely conceal his hatred for his chief. In spite of this, he remained on friendly terms with all the other comrades. "Those others are fine fellows, good Communists, not at all like that poisonous so-and-so."

He got a lot of pleasure out of describing in detail how Polyishuk had gotten his wings clipped down at the village.

"What more can I tell you, dear friends? They certainly gave him a whiff of the people's power. Now he knows about the strong right arm of the peasants. If he hadn't leapt out of there like a scared rabbit he would have been a goner. Yes, don't look so surprised. They were ready to tear him limb from limb."

And now, he went on, what's the result? Why, those sons-of-bitches have cast off all authority, they thumb their noses at the Soviet regime, they talk against the government, morning noon and night, and all you've got in the villages is downright *kontra,* unvarnished counterrevolution. The administration is soviet, but the tune they sing is straight *burzhui.* And what's the cause of it all? Why, because nobody in power pays attention to the underdog. Look, they burned down the manor-house and seized everything belonging to the landowner. Fine, that was a good law. But what then? Who got the benefit? Only the few strong-armed, the ones with the sharp elbows, while the village poor were left out. It's just not fair. That's why the peasants are acting antagonistic to us. They've been handed the dirty end of the stick.

"How about it, comrades," he pressed. "Am I right or not?"

The comrades agreed with him. They even added their own indignation to his.

"You're absolutely right," they said. "What business have those greedy fellows helping themselves to the people's property? But see here, comrade Karpo. It's winter now. The fields are buried in snow, so the estates can't be subdivided because the surveyor's *strument* doesn't work in the snow. Besides, the soldiers aren't all back from the front, So you see, that's what's holding things up."

As far as Karpo was concerned, a plot of land could be measured quite well enough by the practiced eye of a farmer, or if need be, by pacing it off. Still, he was willing to grant for the sake of argument that a surveyor was needed.

"Have it your way," he said. "But how does the snow prevent you from writing?"

"Writing?" they asked, baffled.

"That's what I said. Is it possible in the winter, or not?"

"Nu, it's possible."

"Well then, write down that I'm to get thirty or forty *desyatin* of land, and register the water mill in my name, free and clear, and put me down as the owner of two of the squire's horses, the ones Omelko Masliuk has in his possession. And as for provender, three or four sacks of flour out of those that were stolen from the squire. Do this, comrades, to strengthen the hands of a faithful Communist. You'll get a lot of credit for acting so generously."

After presenting this proposal a number of times, Karpo began to realize that nothing would come of it. At this, he lost patience with his Communist comrades.

"What's the good of complaining?" he asked himself, uttering a string of curses that consigned all the Jews to the same purgatory, noting too that every one of them was tainted with the sin of Judas, their great-grandfather. "What in hell's the good of this whole revolution if it doesn't produce any practical results?"

In this frame of mind, it was natural that he should look for sanctuary in Spod, the gentile section of Mokry-Kut. Whenever he had any free time he would go there and comfort himself with a bottle, meanwhile telling his tale of woe to all who would listen.

At first he met with less than unqualified sympathy.

"What about you?" they objected. "Didn't some of the squire's property stick to your fingers?"

"Damn right," he answered. "After all he was *our* squire, one of us. First there was his father, Andrei Petrovitch. He died. After that came his son—Nikolai Andreyevitch was his name. One of *us.* You know that."

This answer convinced his listeners, and they gave him no further argument.

Between one glass and another Karpo complained about the Jews. They were running the show, and that was hard to take.

"Worse," he grumbled, "than the worst kind of slavery."

The others agreed. "That's it. You hit the nail on the head. Everybody else has to do without, while they live off the fat of the land."

They examined the subject from every angle, and talked about the Revolution and the troubles that had come in its wake, and the hard times, and the fact that a man couldn't earn a decent kopeck.

"There isn't even a nail to be had," complained one.

"And not a drop of kerosene to light the house with," chimed in another. "We have to sit in the dark these long nights, as if it wasn't winter, as if these were the summer nights before St. Elias Day, when you can eat your supper out of doors while the sun is setting, and go to bed when it's still light enough to see. But the main thing is the hunger, nothing in the house to eat, no bread, nothing in the pot, and all the time your teeth are chattering with the cold."

"And it's all on account of them." Karpo's tongue was thick with drink as he hurled the usual catalogue of obscenities. "All on account of them."

Mikhailo Katchan, the town philosopher of Spod, spoke up and said, "Let me tell you, gentlemen, what's behind the whole business. I know a little something about what's going on under the sun. All this, mark you well, comes from the power of evil that has the upper hand in the world just now. Antichrist. He, and none other. Look you —there's not a candle burning in the church, because there are no candles to be had, any more than there is incense for the eucharist. What do you say to that, hah? But *he* won't last long. He's bound to come crashing down. Because falsehood has no staying power. No. Never had. Never will."

79

It was *novye god,* New Year's eve in the Julian calendar. As night fell, the young people gathered at Sorokeh's place to celebrate. Each one brought something—a loaf of bread, four or five potatoes, a bit of cabbage, a slightly moldy herring. Most of all they brought *samogon*—lots of *samogon.*

A lively fire was burning in the furnace of the old bathhouse. The flames leapt outwards, licking at the blackened row of bricks in the vaulted mouth of the firechamber. A few candlewicks flickered here and there in the barnlike interior. Far from giving light, they served rather to emphasize the darkness, making the place crawl with flitting shadows. Some of the people were seated on the bench alongside the wall, some sat on upended old pots, others milled about noisily, filling the big room with the smoke of their cigarettes.

Comrade Ziame had his pistol out of its holster, and was showing it off to Liuba. A Mauser, he boasted, an officer's weapon.

"I took it from a sergeant-major in the early days of the Revolution. One of those things that happened on the battlefield. Don't ask. Lovely weapon, isn't it? Not many like it around."

Comrade Hillik was hanging by his knees from a ladder, showing off his muscles to three girls who stood by.

"Look at the balance!" he yelled, dangling head downwards, his arms outstretched.

Comrade Sukhar sat astride a wooden trestle that had

been left in the middle of the room. He was addressing Minna beseechingly, paying court to her. "The person you agree to share your life with will be the luckiest of men," he said.

On the board where the bath-house keeper had formerly taken up his post, Sorokeh sat ensconced. He was deep in argument with a group of young fellows.

"How is it possible?" they asked. "Aren't anarchy and social order mutually contradictory concepts?"

This was their constant argument, the opening gambit in every discussion they had with him.

"What a tiresome subject!" said Mayerke, looking around the room. "Is this a holiday or isn't it? Come on, gang, how about a song!"

"Let's have 'Marusia.'" Comrade Shayke seconded the motion.

"Liuba! Ethel! Malia!" Mayerke called out. "How about it?"

Liuba sang the opening bars of 'Marusia, Don't Cry'—*Nye platch ti, Marusya.* Everybody joined in with gusto. Then somebody started *Razluka,* and then *Zets-zets-zets,* followed by *Pupsik.*

At this point the *samogon* began to flow, and things really warmed up. Everyone present did his best to contribute to the general merriment. One stood up and recited, another delivered a monologue, someone else told funny stories. Comrade Sukhar, Mendel Sukhar that is, the militiaman, danced a Ukrainian *kozatchok,* with all the customary flourishes, including full-throated shouts of "ee! ekh! hoo!" He was followed by Comrade Muntchik, who did a Jewish dance, a *hossidl*—all, of course, in a spirit of mockery and fun. Then the girls started a series of partnered dances—polka, waltz, quadrille. In the lead, bustling about noisily here, there and everywhere, was none other than Leahtche, who grabbed Sorokeh and pulled him into the dance.

Looking on at all this was Masha, who was nicknamed "Tragic Eyes." She was a black-haired girl, with small features, an oval forehead, big round eyes. She sat in a corner and waited for the fellows to come by and chat with her, all the while wearing a fixed sweet smile that signified absolutely nothing.

"Just look at the way Leahtche is carrying on!" she whispered to Rosa, a thin, sallow, somewhat spinsterish maiden on whose nose perched a pair of pince-nez.

"What are you so surprised about?" Rosa shrugged. "First the available Polyishuk, and now the charming Sorokeh."

At midnight comrade Mayerke took a glass of *samogon* in hand and strode into the middle of the room.

"Comrades!" he announced. "Happy New Year!"

"Hurrah!" everybody shouted, glasses held high. "Hurrah! Happy New Year!"

"Sorokeh!" comrade Shimtze yelled out. "Stand up and say something for the occasion!"

"That's right!" came shouts from different parts of the room. "Speech! Speech!"

"Something good!"

"To the point!"

Sorokeh stood and held up his hand. A hubbub of silencing filled the room. "Sh! Sh! . . . Quiet!"

Bit by bit the din subsided.

"Comrades!" Sorokeh's hand was raised in a dramatic gesture. "At this midnight hour, this very moment, the whole world is crossing a frontier, traversing a line that divides all of human history into two. Everything that has gone before, the entire past for two thousand years, four thousand years—all of that lies to one side. And whatever is going to be, the whole future of humanity from this moment forward, lies on the other side of the line. The sun of capitalism has set—a new world has come into being— a world of social justice, of freedom and happiness, a world celebrating the grandeur of man. But comrades! This new world, struggling to be born, faces a grave danger. The Revolution is in the grasp of dictators. . . ."

A stir swept through the audience.

"What's he driving at?" they whispered to one another.

Mayerke fingered his holster and gave a short cough.

"Nu-nu, comrade, watch what you're saying."

But Sorokeh had caught fire. Rising to a pitch, he sang the praises of liberty, individual and social, absolute and unfettered, freedom unchecked by restraint or authority. Finally he reached the point of demanding that the comrades declare themselves independent of the Soviet government.

There were shouts from the crowd.

"Enough!"

"Shut your mouth!"

Undaunted, Sorokeh launched into a denunciation of those who had seized power, present company included.

"Look at what you've done to this poor unhappy little town, to these inoffensive Jews! What have you got against them, what crime have they committed, that they should be so sorely punished?"

"It's the process of history!" Hillik shouted hoarsely. He was a short, squat fellow, standing on tiptoe so as to be seen.

"What?" Sorokeh strained to hear.

"That's right!" Hillik looked around for approval.

"But what do you want from these miserable people? How do you propose to straighten them out?"

"Eh! The dregs of yesterday's chicory!" Mayerke shrugged his shoulder and spat on the floor. He was supported by comrade Sukhar, who had just fed a few pieces of kindling into the fire.

"Capitalist propaganda!" He straightened up. "Just because they're Jews are we supposed to betray the Revolution?"

"But who are you, and who are they?" Sorokeh argued.

"We're Communists," Mayerke flung at him, "while they are capitalistic bourgeois. Understand?"

"All right," Sorokeh answered. "Let's say you're Communists, but does that automatically make you renegades, *meshumadim*? In times gone by, it was always the *meshumad* who gave us Jews the most trouble. Once a Jew became an apostate, he turned into an anti-Semite, and that made him an important person in the outside world. Every blood-accusation, every anti-Jewish persecution, if you look closely you'll always find a *meshumad* had a hand in it. Are Jewish Communists the same kind of anti-Semites?"

Catcalls assailed him from every part of the room. Suddenly Leahtche jumped up and yelled, "What's going on, is this a meeting or something? We're supposed to be celebrating!"

"No matter," said Mayerke coolly. "Let him talk, I'm not afraid of his arguments. I've got a few good answers that will shut him up."

Sorokeh didn't spare his audience. He told them they were leaves fallen from the family tree, subject to every passing gust of wind. Rootless individuals, he called them, with no people or language of their own, emptied of ethical sensitivity, blind and deaf to any hint of the sacred, devoid of the capacity for self-examination.

Finally he ended his speech with a rousing peroration: "Long live Communist Anarchism!" At that point Leahtche leapt into the middle of the room, arms outspread.

"Enough! Enough!" she called out. *"Karahod,* comrades! Let's dance a *karahod!"*

"Karahod! Karahod!" came the answering shouts, as the crowd surged forward, joining hand to hand in the swirling dance.

80

How much *samogon* comrade Ziame had put away was anybody's guess. Now he stood facing Sorokeh, the remnants of a cigarette dangling from the corner of his open mouth, his cheeks flushed, eyes bloodshot, the veins on his forehead pulsing.

"You certainly let us have it," he swayed. "Put us through the wringer, hah? Spoke against the Workers' Council—the, uh . . . program of the . . . uh, Bolsheviks. Let me tell you, right here, in this historic bath-house—beg pardon, in this historic hour—I could answer you back on . . . uh . . . every point . . . but for the, uh . . . time being let's leave that conversation alone. Let's leave it for the time being. Instead, let's have a drink together. Do me that little favor, will you? Let's drink *lehayyim!*"

They sat down together and knocked back three or four glasses.

The party grew noisier, shriller, more confused. The comrades pushed one another around, drank more than they could hold, and pressed drinks on the girls, some of whom were willing, some reluctant. Everybody was animated, every voice high-pitched. Some of the fellows strutted around, doing their best to act like lusty young Russians. Others started arguments about old remembered slights, demanding satisfaction. Some were even seen to be wrestling with one another. Some were laughing, others crying, and still others were fondling girls and whispering enticements into their ears.

Leahtche attached herself to Sorokeh, sitting beside him in front of the blazing furnace, talking busily. He sat there listening to the fire, its crackle sounding like a field full of cicadas; sat there nodding with a drunken smile on his face, murmuring whenever she paused, "Grasshopper, grasshopper. . . ."

"Me? A grasshopper?" She glanced at him uncertainly.

"Grasshopper, grasshopper," he repeated tipsily, running his hand across his burning cheek.

"Oh, I see, it's summer," Leahtche played along. "Cornflowers, violets, poppies. . . ."

"Poppies, yes, cornflowers. . . ."

"The wheatfield is baking under the blazing sun, while I chirp away. Here you come walking down a path between the rows of standing grain. Suddenly you hear me and stop, listening while I chirp on and on."

Sorokeh sat attentively, as though it were all in dead earnest. Then all of a sudden his face sagged.

"Dear heart," he whispered. "Where? Where are you?"

"Who?" Leahtche was dismayed. "I'm here, beside you."

"Grasshopper." Sorokeh reached out his hand, and it fell heavily on her shoulder.

"Me?"

"Little grasshopper," Sorokeh babbled on. "Hot summer's day . . . noontime. . . ."

Leahtche sat for a few moments, pensive. She breathed a heavy sigh. "Nu, so be it. What's the good of useless talk? You—a question-mark, me—a next-to-nothing, a little grasshopper. Too bad! In the end, this grasshopper will go out of its mind. Ah well, there's nothing to be done. That's the way things are."

"Don't worry, you won't go out of your mind," Sorokeh gave her a friendly pat on the shoulder. "Jewish grasshoppers don't go out of their minds."

Just then comrade Ziame pranced over, singing aloud, a bottle in one hand and a cup in the other.

"What's this, you two sitting all by yourselves like a romantic couple in the moonlight!"

"Why, what's wrong?" Leahtche bridled.

Sorokeh intervened, soothingly. "Pay no attention to him."

"Look at him!" Ziame retorted. "Gazing at her like a *rebbe* examining his Succoth citron, his *esrog!*"

"What's it to you?" Leahtche glared.

"It's not right. You're cutting yourselves off from the rest of the crowd. How about a drink, comrade, hah?"

"You've already got a skinful," Leahtche chided.

"What's that you say?" Ziame tipped the bottle and filled the cup with *samogon.* "You're talking in riddles today, Leahtche. Anyhow, Sorokeh, *lehayyim!*"

Sorokeh upended the cup, while Ziame drank straight from the bottle.

"I've got a bone to pick with you!" Ziame closed his eyes and pursed his lips, blowing out like a horse snorting into the feedbag. "I remember, don't imagine for a minute that I've forgotten. One of these days you and I are going to have a serious discussion, comrade. All I've got to do is ask you one question, and you'll be left without a leg to stand on. But not now, no. This isn't the time for it. Agreed, Sorokeh? How about another drink?"

Leahtche put her hand on Sorokeh's knee. "Don't drink."

"It's all right," Sorokeh spoke in a gentle, drunken voice.

Ziame glanced from one to the other. "Is she in a position to give you orders?" he grinned.

Leahtche averted her face. "Agh, a lot of nonsense."

Ziame clinked his bottle against the cup in Sorokeh's unsteady hand. *"Lehayyim!* Long live the Socialist World Revolution!"

Quite a few other comrades came by, and Sorokeh had

a drink with each of them. Then Mayerke was standing in front of him, arrogant, challenging.

"How come you didn't invite comrade Polyishuk?"

"Oh, go away," Sorokeh answered, wearily.

Leahtche interjected, "Comrade Polyishuk has gone to a conference. Didn't you know?"

"Better than you," Mayerke wrinkled his nose at her. "What I'm asking is, why didn't he invite him?"

Addled with drink as he was, and with no clear idea of what he was saying, Sorokeh fixed his eyes on Mayerke, and managed to sound quite rational. "Who is this comrade of yours, this Polyishuk? A Jew? A Russian? Oh, I see, neither. A fictional character, a figment of your imagination!"

He got up and walked as steadily as he could into the middle of the room, where the crowd was thickest and the merriment most intense.

"Mr. Rabbi," Mayerke grinned. *"Gospodin rabin."*

Leahtche stood up, and started to follow Sorokeh, walking abstracted, head bent. Then she became aware of Muntchik alongside her.

"Leahtche," he begged, "come dance with me."

"No thanks."

"What's the matter?" Muntchik was offended. "It's beneath you to dance with anybody but Sorokeh?"

She shrugged one shoulder. "I wouldn't give an onion for you and him and all the men in the world put together."

Meantime Sorokeh had pushed his way into the gay confusion in the middle of the room, and started roaring out a *niggun,* a melody he remembered from the study house. In a flash a pulsing circle of dancers was whirling around, pounding the floor, like a summer thunderstorm suddenly drumming on the roof, and just as suddenly breaking off. Then a new circle formed, dancing a *freilachs* with rising tempo and ever-increasing abandon. Again, and again, until finally they came to a stop, everybody out of breath, everybody sweating. They all drank a toast, panting, talking, laughing hysterically, each mightily pleased with himself.

A circle of girls gathered around Sorokeh, letting him know by tone and smile and indirection what a wonderful fellow they thought he was. He felt very tired. He was dizzy, short of breath, utterly befuddled.

"What a tiny hand, soft as silk!" He was holding Ethel's hand in his. "What lovely sculptured fingers!"

Ethel stood beside him, face aglow, her eyes fixed on him adoringly, as though she owed him her very life.

"How lovely!" he murmured. "How happy you will make somebody! What tears, what laughter, what joy!"

"Oh, but it's good to be alive!" He put both hands on Leahtche's shoulders. "A beautiful world! High . . . I want to fly to . . . to . . . you girls are all so lovely . . . to warm myself in the glow of your beauty. . . ."

Masha came by with a drunken grin on her face and started putting out the candles one by one.

"What are you doing?" Leahtche screamed at her.

"Hurray!" the fellows all cheered.

Sorokeh walked to the door and went outside. She waited for him to come back, waited some time before she followed him out of doors. He was nowhere to be seen. She stood on the doorstep, peering right and left. Suddenly she heard a piercing cry from the direction of the river. "He-elp! He-e-elp!"

Leahtche opened the door behind her and shouted into the room. "Accident! There's been an accident! Hurry! Somebody's shouting for help!"

"What? Who? Where?"

"On the river! Oy, gevald!" A thought struck her suddenly. "It must be Sorokeh! Save him!"

In a flash they were all pounding their way down to the river. It took them no time at all to find Sorokeh immersed in the water hole, only his head and neck visible above the ice. He was trying to get himself out, but the ice had formed around his shoulders, and was holding him firmly under.

They pulled him out and rushed him to the bath-house. He was shaking all over, his face lilac blue, his teeth chattering uncontrollably. Inside the bath-house they took him into the steam room, stripped off his clothes and put him on the top shelf. A pot of water, dipped out of the *mikveh* pool and poured over the hot stones that encircled the firebox, was enough to fill the room with steam.

Comrade Mayerke stood by, pouring *samogon* down the victim's throat. "Drink!" he yelled at him. "A swig of the strong stuff goes good after a dip in the *mikveh.*"

Sorokeh began to revive.

"Nu, what do you say?" laughed Ziame. "Wet yourself, hah?"

Sorokeh grimaced. "Ah, good," he whispered through chattering teeth. "J-j-just like m-my g-g-grandfather. . . ."

A few minutes later, teeth still chattering, he added, "One t-time he s-said t-to m-me: m-mind you d-don't shame m-me in the n-next w-world!"

"Who?" Ziame was puzzled. Sorokeh didn't answer.

"What don't you understand?" Mayerke explained. "His grandfather, that's who."

81

There was a considerable stir in town over the events of New Year's eve. Whispered reports spread swiftly, mingling fact with fiction, fleshing out the explicit with insinuation.

Anybody who went out that morning and met a fellow townsman would stop him and say, "Did you ever hear the likes of it?"

The other, pretending not to understand, would draw him out, all innocence. "Nu?"

"You mean you haven't heard? I'm talking about what happened in the bath-house."

"Yes?"

"Don't ask! Awful things, the Lord preserve us!"

"For example?"

"Well, they were swilling *samogon* the whole night long. Got drunk, the lot of them. Boys and girls together, in the bath-house. Nu, you can imagine what goings-on."

The imagination was helped along by a wrinkle of the nose.

The girls especially came in for criticism. "It's all a punishment for our sins. Jewish girls getting drunk! Nu-nu, what honor the good Lord has bestowed on us!"

The episode involving Sorokeh was of particular interest, and gave rise to a variety of interpretations. Some said, "An accident, nothing more. He was crossing the river blind drunk on *samogon*, and he fell in."

Others said, "That was no accident. He did it deliberately. Tried to take his own life."

Another school of thought speculated, "There's more here than meets the eye. Polyishuk must have had a hand in it."

Reb Mordkhe-Leib listened indulgently to all the theories, a sardonic smile half hidden in his mustache. "Neither this, that, nor the other," he finally said, leaving room for doubt as to whether he was being serious. "The truth is, he was following in the footsteps of his grandfather, Reb Yitzchak-Eisikl, the memory of the righteous be blessed. This young fellow was so enflamed by the holy fervor of the Revolution that he ran out and plunged into the river. His grandfather, of blessed memory, used to take fire with the holy love of the Creator, and he made it a habit to practice ritual immersion in the river during the winter. Exactly as the Talmud says: *t'var gezizi d'barda u-nhat u-t'val.* And the proof that that's what happened last night is that when they pulled him out of the river and got him into the bath-house, they stood over him chanting the verse from the Second Book of Samuel: 'He smote the lion in the pit on the snowy day.' "

"Yes, yes," chimed in Reb Avrohom-Elya. "They put him into the steam room stark naked, and they say some of the girls were there tending to him—Leahtche, Malia, Masha —woe to our ears that hear of such doings!"

The women folk clucked to one another about the affair, exchanging many a malediction. Whenever there was a chance they would get hold of one of the girls and begin to interrogate her.

"What's new at the bath-house?" The barbed question was put in the sweetest of tones. "Did you have a wedding party there last night?"

"What wedding? We celebrated *novye god.*"

"*Novye god?*" The rising inflection conveyed total amazement. "What have you got to do with *novye god*? Don't we have enough holidays of our own? How come you were celebrating a Christian holy day?"

"*Novye god* isn't a Christian holy day, it's a civic holiday."

"Civic holiday? Nu, have it your way. So tell me, what's the custom on *novye god,* is it the custom for fellows and girls to spend the night together in the bath-house, drinking liquor all night long?"

82

Bluma was a busy, talkative old widow, the sister of Reb Itzia Dubinsky. She had raised a large family, sons, daughters, grandchildren, but now she lived all by herself. It was she whom Leahtche, on her way to visit Sorokeh, heard calling after her.

"Wait, wait, Leahtche"—waving her hand, beckoning—"I want to talk to you."

"What's the matter, Grandma Bluma?" Leahtche stood waiting.

"Come here, come. All day I've been hoping for a chance to talk with you."

"What is it?"

"Come closer, don't be afraid. I only want to ask you one question."

Leahtche turned back. The old woman took her by the hand, gently pulling.

"Come into the house with me, it's terribly cold outside. My feet are like two blocks of ice, may you and the whole household of Israel never know what it's like."

Once they were indoors and seated, Bluma addressed her subject in a relaxed, grandmotherly manner.

"Let me ask you, dear heart, to explain one thing that has me puzzled. What's come over you?"

"Who?"

"You, my little pigeon, you girls."

"Why, what's the matter with us?"

"That's just what I'm asking, my little minnow. What's the matter with you? Ach, ach, dear Father in heaven, our sins have caught up with us! I was a young girl myself once, and no pitz-mitz either, let me tell you. I was a pretty one—if you'll forgive me for saying so, prettier than you, tall, nice figure, rosy cheeks—fiery, like the noonday sun. But the Lord be thanked I was modest and chaste, pleasing to God and man, like a proper Jewish girl should be. And I was a smart one—oo-oo was I smart! I wasn't about to be led up the garden path for a bushel basket of nonsense— no indeed! I never looked at boys, you hear. Leahtche? And as for love—perish the thought, the idea never crossed my mind, much less my lips, no, not so much as one scale on a whole fish. I certainly didn't go out walking until cock-crow! That fashion had not yet been heard of. And still, I wasn't left sitting in my parents' house, God forbid, until my hair turned white. One day before I was full sixteen years old my mother came home from the market and says, 'Bluma, my daughter, you know what? God willing we will have guests at home this Sabbath.' 'What sort of guests?' I ask. 'Good guests,' she answers. Right away I understand which way the wind is blowing, so I say 'What's it got to do with me?' 'And if a young man comes to visit?' 'If he comes, we'll take a look at him.' 'That's what I meant by a good guest.' 'Oh, good for his intended.' 'And if that happens to be you?' 'Well then, he'll be my bride-groom.' I was smart, hah? A real sharp customer, no? And what do you think, a few days later I was engaged, and before the year was out, married. Without love, without midnight strolls. *Ribbono-shel-Olam,* would that the same fortune befall all the daughters of Israel, God preserve me! Nu, and what's with you girls? Always searching for love, running after desire, out walking the live-long night, and in the end left spinsters, your world frittered away, not even the lame watchman of a cucumber patch to ask for the hand of any one of you. A hundred *ukhazhors,* but not one bridegroom. What is this? What? Where are your eyes? Where's your good sense? Help me out of this puzzlement, my dearest heart."

Leahtche deliberated for a few minutes before answering.

"Grandma Bluma, what do you want me to say? Those were the olden days you're telling me about. Nowadays things are different. We have to plan our lives according to the times, we have to follow the spirit of our own generation. But don't worry, our girls aren't going to produce little bastards, you can depend on that."

Bluma was horrified. "Who said anything about bastards? Tfu-tfu!" she warded off the evil eye. "God be with you, what kind of talk is that? But since you did mention it—well, now we come to the heart of the matter! Don't take offense, dearest darling, but people are talking, scandalous things are being said, Leahtchenyu. They say you girls are secretly involved in depraved goings-on. Hah? Is that nice? Nice?"

Stung, Leahtche jumped to her feet. "That's a downright lie!" Her cheeks were flaming. "We're not mixed up in any depraved goings-on, openly or secretly. But even if we were, what business is it of you people? Those who sin will take their beating in the next world. Whatever we do, you won't be blamed!"

"Don't be angry, Leahtchenyu, don't be angry, darling. I'm sure all of you are decent daughters of Israel, but people will talk, you know that. Why should you give them food for gossip? What do you think, it will improve your marriage prospects? You've eased my mind somewhat, dear heart, somewhat but not altogether. Ach, ach, Father in heaven, what business have maidens with young men in the bath-house? One thing is certain—it's not proper behavior."

"Bath-house, bath-house," Leahtche flung back at her. "So what? It's nothing to do with depraved goings-on. The bath-house happens to be where comrade Sorokeh lives, and lots of people drop in, fellows and girls, whoever feels like it. Now you tell me—what's so terrible about that? You'd think it was the sin of the Golden Calf, or something."

"You're right, you're right, I know it," Bluma nodded, her wrinkled old cheeks quivering. "But just listen to what I'm saying. You young girls, take good care of your honor, for God's sake, take care. Because if not, you'll get a bad name, God forbid, and then what will become of you? Papa-mama won't help, because what do papa-mama count for these days? If you don't take care of yourselves, nobody will. Protect yourselves, avoid like the plague giving cause for gossip. Watch out! Take care!"

Leahtche got to her feet and started to leave. "You can tell folks to tend to their own faults before they start worrying about ours. Anyhow, Grandma Bluma, I've got to be going. I'm on my way to the bath-house to visit comrade Sorokeh. He's lying there sick, you know. Goodbye, *bobbeh,* keep well."

83

For one whole week Sorokeh lay on the long bench in the bath-house, covered with a greatcoat, a woolen scarf around his neck. He had no lack of visitors, who would sit and chatter with him. "Alive and kicking, Sorokeh?" They would pretend to be surprised. "What happened? Were you out there fishing or something?" This was invariably followed by gales of laughter.

"Ye-es," Sorokeh would drawl, playing along. "Something like that."

"Well, watch out," they would say knowingly. "Since you were not fated to pay for your sins by water, you're probably destined to get yours by fire."

The girls would come singly or in groups, at such times as they reckoned that Leahtche was not likely to be there. They would sit in his presence shyly, looking at the floor a lot, laughing at inappropriate moments. Some tried to draw him into ideological discussions with instant philosophizing on every subject under the sun. Others preferred to talk about themselves, bemoaning their dark and helpless fate.

"This isn't living," they would sigh, "it's only half living." These and similar complaints gave them a certain self-flattering satisfaction; and having uttered them they could sit there smiling in silence, the kind of silence that is in itself a means of communication. They seemed to be waiting for something to happen to them.

Leahtche, of course, was at Sorokeh's place every free moment she could find. She cooked his food and patched his clothes and did his laundry. He on his part kept up his usual edifying discourses, laying down the law of Philosophical Anarchism. She didn't hesitate to disagree, so they argued.

"All right, all right," she would counter. "But what happens to your theories in the world of practical reality?"

She had become contrary, almost cantankerous, and would put him down in sudden bursts of fury, brushing aside the whole structure of his ideas with a few words.

"You're not consistent!" she flung at him, and there was resentment in her voice. "No, you're not consistent, and the sooner you realize it the better. Your mind is a jumble of mixed ideas, with enough to supply a whole *minyan* of socialists, bourgeois, and counterrevolutionaries!"

Sorokeh smiled at her fondly, with that mischievous twinkle in his eye, and put his arm around her. "What's the matter, Leahtche? Why so angry, hah?"

"Ah, leave me alone." She twisted out of his embrace and turned her back on him. "You people are no good for anything."

"You people? Who's that?"

"All of you. Polyishuk, you. . . . Between the two of you I've been left standing."

"What do you mean?"

"You know what I mean!" She turned on him suddenly, flushed with anger. "Why do you pretend to be so innocent?"

"Has something happened?"

"That's the whole trouble, nothing's happened." But even as she spoke she burst out laughing, forced, too loud. Then she came and sat down beside him, calm suddenly, eased.

"Bad mood gone?" Sorokeh put a comforting hand on her shoulder. "Never mind. Your turn will come, you'll get married, have no fear."

"Yes," she answered, only half amused. "Here comes the

crowd, each one impatient to take me to wife! No, I don't expect to get married until I'm a grandmother!"

"A grandmother?" Sorokeh laughed.

"Why so surprised? I'm already twenty years old, well, almost twenty. An old maid, on the shelf. That's no joke, my dear."

"On the contrary, it's a colossal joke, my love." He took both her hands in his. "It's absolute stuff and nonsense."

"Anyhow," she said, with a curious little smile. "What's marriage, after all? A petty-bourgeois convention. . . ."

He laughed aloud.

" . . . or else a sort of mania that afflicts bachelors. No, I'll marry no man. Especially since I have a steady *ukhaz-hor,* a permanent suitor like you, so charming and brilliant. What can I do? It seems my fate has already been decided."

84

All the while that Sorokeh lay ill, he kept up a steady stream of exposition of Anarchist doctrine, arguing with those comrades who came to see him. The latter, whose learning left something to be desired, were unable to debate with him on the substance, so they were reduced to mouthing the usual party slogans, or to baiting him with the standard epithets reserved for deviationists.

Occasionally he veered the talk from social theory to Jewish problems, and then things really got furious. The comrades were upset with him for finding fault with the Revolution because of what was happening to the Jews.

"What's the matter with you?" The pitch of their voices

would always go up a notch, as though faced with especially dangerous ideas. "Why are you always harping on the Jews, the Jews, the Jews?"

"Well, just look how the Jews have been done in by the Bolshevik regime."

"Come on, don't talk nonsense, will you? What's the importance of the Jews to the Revolution?"

"Nu, and to you?"

"No more to us."

At this Sorokeh would gaze at them fixedly, as though he had just seen an apparition, and say, "Who taught you that?"

"Nobody"—preening themselves—"we're self-taught, just natural born revolutionaries."

"Have you ever met a Russian Bolshevik who doesn't love his Russian people?"

"Proof from the *goyim* is no proof," they laughed, pleased with their cleverness.

"But that's exactly what I'm asking—how are you different from the *goyim?*"

"Why, we're the atonement for Israel." They might well have been in full earnest. "When the *goyim* make a revolution, they have their own good in mind. They're out to benefit their own people, their own country. But when Jews join hands with them, it's out of pure disinterested idealism, for the sake of heaven you might say, for the benefit of all mankind."

"You're right when you say that the gentiles do what they do for their own interests. Nu, and who'll look after the interests of the Jews?"

"What's good for Russia will be good for the Jews. The good of the majority embraces the good of the minority."

"Wait a minute!" Sorokeh kept at them. "Not everybody's in the same boat. What's good for one may be bad for the other. Now, take the Jews—for the most part neither workers nor peasants, but middle-class people, small storekeepers, artisans, peddlers and the like. The Revolution was not made for their sakes."

"So let them turn themselves into workers and peasants."

"And who, I ask you, is going to see to that? Ivan and Stepan aren't going to be bothered, and the young Jews haven't a thought to spare for the survival of their own people, oh no, they've got no time for Jewry, they're busy saving humanity as a whole."

They had an answer for him. "For the Revolution, nothing is impossible."

"Not so!" Sorokeh retorted heatedly. "Some things *are* impossible. What's more, there is a streak of cruelty, a spirit of perverse tyranny in the Revolution. The Revolution won't try to remedy the condition of the Jewish people, it's just as likely to make an end of the Jewish people. Look here: this is no charade you're involved in, no fun and games dressed up in a belted tunic and military breeches, with a pistol on your hip. You're involved in national suicide, physical as well as spiritual! What all our enemies through all of history couldn't do to us, what Christianity couldn't accomplish, what anti-Semitism in every age and every land was unable to do, what persecutions and pogroms and expulsions failed to bring about—this Revolution will succeed in doing, and very quickly at that! Think about it, if you have minds to think: you're busy destroying the Jewish people, and history will hold you to account for it!"

"Idle chatter," they mumbled, nonplussed by his tirade.

"No, it's not idle chatter!" Sorokeh blazed at them. "Don't fool yourselves!"

"But you want to have your cake and eat it! You want the Revolution, and you want a Jewish future!"

"Why not?" Sorokeh exploded. "Certainly! Yes, I want social revolution *and* Jewish survival, the one no less than the other. The way things are now, the Revolution is a

Gates of Bronze | 254

purely Russian phenomenon, authoritarian, shot through with cruelty, with unrestricted despotism. And you— you're its lackeys, its obedient servants; *prikaztchiki,* that's what you are, miserable shop assistants, insignificant clerks doing what you're told, without will or purpose of your own. How can young Jews be so stupid?"

They defended themselves. "But it's for the sake of the great ideal!"

"Ha!" Sorokeh laughed in their faces. "Ideal? What a joke! It's for the sake of power! For the sake of feeling your finger on the trigger of the *nagan!* But you would rather hide your heads in the sand. All right, in the end reality will catch up with you, you'll have to pay for your illusions. The bill will be paid by the Jew each of you carries hidden within himself. These *goyim* will take it out on him with axe and pitchfork, as they have from time immemorial!"

Karpo took to drinking more heavily than usual. When he was well into his cups, he would sing ditties he had learned in his childhood, or talk to himself, quoting peasant proverbs remembered from his youth. "Two Yehori are they, one for cold and one for hunger." It took no great imagination to see the association with the two days of Saint Yegori. No doubt he had a similar thought in mind when he muttered, "Kosma-Demyan bridges the space, while Mikola drives the nail in place."

Sometimes he could be seen awash with drink, rolling big balls of snow into one another, bending over, straightening up, clowning about, beating his breast and proclaiming that he had been bilked of his share in the people's property. Was he not a pauper-son-of-a-churchmouse? Had not the spoils been unjustly divided, giving the undeserving too much and the deserving too little? Where are Tchubari and Gneidko, the two choicest horses of the squire, hah? Tchubari, the princeliest of them all, with his piebald flanks and his small-sized head and his flaring nostrils and his adorable little hooves; and Gneidko, the golden one, his shining russet coat set off by the jet-black mane and tail, a star-shaped spot of white on his forehead between his slanting eyes, his slender knees so very white—who's got them now? Why, a fellow with more clout than him, than Karpo, a soldier who spent three years rotting in the mines, him, Karpo, a Communist loyal and true.

Then he would straighten up, knee-deep in a snowbank, arms outstretched, and yell at the top of his lungs, "My Gneidko! My Tchubari! Omelko Masliuk has got them! My darlings!"

He was going to pieces, drunk more often than sober. He started grumbling publicly against the Communists, as well as against the Jews, those enemies of God, and of the holy Church, and of the fatherland.

"There is a God!" he proclaimed. "There is a God, accursed Jews, may you burn in hellfire! Just wait, your time will come! The Lord will take notice of our shame, for He is merciful and just!"

The comrades treated him indulgently, because they didn't hold him responsible. "Let him be, pay no attention, he doesn't know what he's saying."

Some tried to have a bit of fun with him. "Listen, go tell the dog that the Messiah is coming."

Others wanted to talk sense with him, to sober him up. "Shame on you, Karpo. The devil alone knows that's coming out of your mouth."

Then Karpo would beg their forgiveness, and tearfully

swear undying friendship. The next day, sober once more, he would vow to turn over a new leaf, on his honor as a Communist. Before you could turn around he had broken his resolution, and was out on the street shouting, "Hell-bound devils, may evil diseases take you! Wait, you'll get what's coming to you! We'll show you where the crab spends the winter!"

One evening when the young people of Spod were having a party, Karpo barged in among the dancing couples and broke up their polka. Then he began pestering the accordion player, and tried to take his instrument away. When that didn't work, he stopped the music.

"What kind of celebration is this?" he roared. "I declare this party counterrevolutionary!"

They tried to calm him down, and brought him a drink, and then another. But the more he drank the nastier he became. Finally the young fellows ganged up on him, fists flying, and beat him bloody. They threw him into a deserted areaway, where he was hidden by high banks of snow.

As a result of this unpleasantness, Polyishuk issued an order depriving Karpo of the right to carry a revolver. At the same time he gave him a warning. "You can lose your Party membership. Watch your step!"

86

The removal of his side arm was a serious blow to Karpo's pride. Anger and resentment never left his face.

Most of the comrades had something to say in his defense. Mendel Sukhar spoke up for him, as did Shimtze and Hillik and Ziame, but most of all Timoshenko and Korotchkin and Zabolotni, three scions of Spod who were his best friends.

"He has a passion for horses," they explained. "Tchubari and Gneidko have gotten under his skin, and you'll have to admit they're no ordinary horses."

On the other hand, Ilko felt that Polyishuk had done the right thing. How can you let a drunkard go around armed? He might have an accident, he could kill somebody.

"But he's a Commissar!" argued Timoshenko. "Same as us!"

"So what?" Ilko answered calmly. "Let him keep his nose out of the glass. It's no credit for a Commissar to drink himself out of control."

"That may be so," Zabolotni agreed reluctantly. "But how can you have a Commissar without a gun? It's his duty to go armed, because if not, where's his sign of authority? Without a revolver he's the same as anybody else. We can't have that. Impossible!"

This view was shared by Korotchkin. "A ruler without a gun? No use at all. You're right, it's out of the question."

Polyishuk's answer to all this was a compromise; he declared the expedient temporary. "Don't worry," he said. "Let him walk around empty-handed for a few days. After all, he's under a cloud, let's see how he acts."

A few days later Karpo showed up at the bath-house. He didn't want Sorokeh to know that he was seething inwardly, so he assumed a hard, set expression. Nor did he mention his predicament; it was Sorokeh who made the first move.

"Nu, Karpo," he said, "what do you think you'll do?"

Karpo was silent for a while. Finally, he spoke. "I don't think. Why should I?"

"Too much of an effort?" Sorokeh tried to banter.

Karpo offered no answer. Apparently he hadn't understood.

"Well now," Sorokeh tried again, "what are your plans?"

"Whatever God turns up," Karpo answered. "The Lord will not desert me, the boar will not devour me."

"Why don't you join up with us?"

After a long pause, Karpo addressed his answer to the stove. "Between demons and evil spirits there isn't much to choose. One's as holy as the other."

He broke off, and sat there depressed. "Anyhow," he finally growled, "what's the use of those fancy ideas of yours?"

"We'll get you a revolver," Sorokeh smiled.

"Who needs it?" Karpo spat expertly between his teeth into the open stove. "I'll be the same fine fellow without a revolver."

Then suddenly he was talkative. "I'll take care of my needs in another way, I will. Don't worry about me. I'll pull up a choice sapling in the forest, and all I'll have to do is wham it crisscross on somebody's head and poof! He's in the next world."

That left both of them silent. Finally, Sorokeh, for want of something better to say, urged, "Yes, go on."

"Go on what?" Karpo was beginning to take liberties, and Sorokeh made no attempt to answer. "I'm not altogether helpless." Karpo twirled his mustache, an impudent smile playing around his lips. "I got seeds planted in my field, never fear."

Silence.

Karpo swept the room with his eyes. "It's cold in here. Listen, you got a swig of liquor for me? Do me a favor."

As it happened, Sorokeh didn't have a drop in the place.

"Not a drop?" Karpo was astonished. Somehow, it seemed like a dirty trick. "I don't understand you."

"Why, what's the matter?" Sorokeh tried to make his

laugh sound easy. Karpo surveyed him, as though seeing him for the first time.

"What kind of life have you got? Worse than a Gypsy. No house, no table, no bed. I'll tell you the truth, it's a sorry life you lead." It sounded as though Sorokeh had given him cause for complaint. "To all appearances a regular fellow, but look what's happened to him." He paused, but got no reaction.

"Look," he pursued his theme, "you've got all kinds of girls to choose from, all desirable; just pick one out, the one that suits you down to a tee, grab her off, and make her your wife. Or maybe you'd rather have one of our girls? What do you say?"

He squinted at Sorokeh with a sly, mocking grin. "Now take your dear friend Ilko—he's got a sister, a big one, broad in the beam. How about her?"

"You're a clown." Sorokeh was making the best of a distasteful situation.

"But no, come to think of it, not one of ours would take up with you." Karpo spoke as innocently as could be. "Not even if she's ugly as sin, because after all a *zhid,* a kike. . . ."

Sorokeh sat very still, a fixed smile on his face.

". . . because you people are twisters, slippery. . . ."

Sorokeh got to his feet. "What's the use of wasting words? Just get up and leave."

Karpo bent his head and remained where he was.

"Get out!" Sorokeh hissed. "Now!"

Karpo sized up the situation. Slowly he stood up and edged toward the door.

"Get out and don't come back!" Sorokeh was very pale, his hands were clenched in his pockets. Karpo glanced at him sidelong.

"Big hero!" he said. At the door he turned for a parting shot. "Your kind won't be lording it over us for long. No sir!"

Sorokeh waited for him to be gone. "Just a fool blathering," he told himself, and sat down depressed, thinking long thoughts that rolled in on him like gray clouds coming to blanket the black clouds that were already there in the first place.

87

It was plain that Karpo was not doing his job at Party headquarters. One day he would show up, then no sign of him for two or three days at a stretch. And drunk, always drunk.

Polyishuk tried to look the other way. "Let him go to hell!" Actually, he was glad to be relieved of his constant pestering complaints.

Meantime, Karpo was getting more and more involved in questionable activities. To the poor peasants in the village he lamented as usual about the loot from the manor, topping off the oft-told tale with a tirade against the Jews, the chief obstacle in the way of peace and plenty. One thing led to another, and soon he was fulminating against the Communists. This so affected many of the peasants that they formed a mob and swarmed after him to the village Council House, where they proceeded to break all the windows and smash the furniture, tearing up the files and ripping down the pictures of Lenin and Trotsky. The confused rabble then headed back to the village, venting its rage at first in angry yells, then in a spate of noisy quarrels, and finally in actual hand-to-hand combat. They cast about for weapons, one seizing a fence picket, another a shaft that his young son had run to fetch, while others used pitchforks or whatever came to hand. Before long the square in front of the church was one big battleground.

The following day Karpo was back in Mokry-Kut, with no hint in his bearing that he had fallen from grace. He carried himself as befits a Party member of long standing, as though nothing had happened. He wanted to see Polyishuk, but he was intercepted on the way by a group of comrades. One look was enough to show them that he had been in action. His eye was swollen, all black and blue, his lips were puffy, and the wounds where his face had been cut open were covered with dried blood.

"Eh-eh!" they clucked. "Somebody did a beautiful job of decoration on you! Who did it?"

"Who?" he echoed. "As if you didn't know! Enemies of the people, that's who. They certainly gave me the business. On account of the *politika*. Yes. Wrecked the Council House, damn them!"

He didn't get in to see Polyishuk. The militiaman on sentry duty had been carefully instructed. "Sorry, comrade Polyishuk can't see you. He's busy."

Later in the day Karpo tried again. By this time he was slightly tipsy, in the best of humor, meek and mild. He found Polyishuk's door unguarded, and walked right in.

Polyishuk looked up at him, a pen dangling between his fingers.

"What now?" He pretended not to see the bumps and the bruises.

"Take a look, comrade." Karpo sat down and pointed to his swollen eye. "I fell into a pretty mess of porridge."

"And who was it that cooked up the mess?"

Karpo eyed him carefully, trying to guess how much he knew. Then he shrugged one shoulder. "It's obvious. Ivan and Khvoma and the likes of them. The people, in other words."

Polyishuk stared at him and waited.

"The people are complaining." Karpo fingered his purpled eyelid. "Let me tell you a bit of what's going on, and when you hear what I have to say, you'll understand the rest. It's like this: the people are dissatisfied. Oh, the Revolution as revolution—no argument. And the people as people—ignorant as ever. Still, the power of reason has been given to man, and why, I ask? Why was it given? Let's take the peasant, after all he was there before the Revolution, what's he got on his mind? Land! Yes, sir, that's the only thing that interests him. He wants to cut off his piece, get hold of his own little plot. To each his field, his small corner of mother earth. That's how they are, the peasants, all of the same opinion: divide up the lands, and the Revolution will be over. Finished, done with. Once its goal is reached, who needs it any more?"

Karpo took a deep breath. He felt better already. A peculiar smile twisted itself around his swollen bluish lips.

"Nu?" Polyishuk pressed.

"I've already given you 'nu.' "

"So you say there's no more need for the Revolution?"

"That's right, no need, no need at all. Once a man's got his piece of land, what does he need any other headaches for?"

"So-o-o!" Polyishuk drew out the syllable.

Karpo saw that there was need for further elucidation.

"See, once he's a property owner, that's it. What bothers them is, they haven't got the land yet. Item number one, the Revolution is too slow for the good of the people. Wait, you say, till she gets moving? 'Ulita the snail is on her way —when will she get here?' Item number two, before you can turn around spring will be here, and not only has the land not been distributed, but there's no seed either. All the while the granaries are empty, clean as a whistle. See? That's where the dog lies buried. What's going to become of us? The little we have to eat isn't enough to make the trip from our jaws to our guts. A child who could eat a whole loaf gets a bite the size of a sparrow's head. And no supplies at all—no kerosene, no hemp-seed oil, no fodder, our animals are starving. You can see we're dying of hunger. What's to become of us?"

"Cut out the blind-beggar song and dance," Polyishuk broke in. "It's taken you only a few minutes to settle all political questions, and to polish off the Revolution. Finished! Done with! A real artist!"

Karpo began to protest. "But I'm faithful to the political line. . . ."

"Drop it," Polyishuk cut him off. "We know all about you, how you messed yourself up in the village."

"Me?" Karpo protested.

"What you did at the Council House."

"Not me!" Karpo protested. "That was the people! They're the ones! They attacked the Council House. The people. . . ."

"Who gave them the idea?"

"It was their own idea! Because they want their share of the land—that's at the bottom of it all!"

"And what were you doing at the Council House?"

"Who, me? I would never . . . I didn't . . ." Karpo began to stammer. "It was the people . . . they went crazy . . . smashed things up . . . I tried. . . ."

Polyishuk stood up. "I'm placing you under arrest." He was scowling, his two bushy eyebrows forming one straight line.

Karpo was thunderstruck. "Arrest? . . . You arresting *me*?"

Polyishuk picked up the bell on his desk and rang it. The prearranged signal brought the two militiamen, Stetzko and Ivas, marching in, followed by Mendel Sukhar, Shimtze, Hillik and Ziame, with Zabolotni, Korotchkin, and Timoshenko bringing up the rear.

Karpo jumped up. "Take him," Polyishuk ordered quietly.

"Nu, nothing doing!" Karpo's face was contorted, his

swollen lips were twisted, the half-closed eyelid was plum purple. "You can't mean it. You'll never take me!"

Stetzko put a hand on Karpo's shoulder, but it was thrown off. "You can't do this to me!" He was shouting now. "For three years I fought! It was we who made the Revolution, where did you show up from?"

Stetzko and Ivas both took hold of him, but he grappled with the two of them.

"We made the Revolution!" he glared at Polyishuk, even as he wrestled with the two guards. "We! The soldiers ... the peasants! The Revolution is ours ... the soldiers and the peasants ... not yours!"

"Get him out of here!" Polyishuk pointed at the door.

". . . . our Revolution! . . . you've got no part of it! . . . you!"

He was still shouting as they twisted his arms behind his back and propelled him through the door.

Something that Sorokeh had once told Leahtche stuck in her mind. It had to do with the young people of the Jewish agricultural settlements, who were planning to settle in the Land of Israel. Once, when she was paying him a visit, she brought it up.

"Those agricultural settlements you spoke about, what are they like? Villages like any other? Do the farmers there work in the fields just like gentile peasants? Do they plow and plant and harvest? Are the fellows anything like the farmers around here, the girls like the *shiksas*?"

His answer, when it came, was an ironic one. "How can

you ask such a thing? The whole distinctiveness of the Jew lies in the fact that 'He hath not made our destiny like that of the nations.' Every morning the Jew thanks God 'for that He hath not made me a gentile.' Mind you, not 'made me a Jew,' but only 'not made me a gentile.' And you come along and ask whether they are just like *goyim!*"

"No, really," she persisted. "Do they work all day in the fields, men, women and children, and come home in the evening with hoe and pitchfork over their shoulder?"

"But of course! What did you think?"

"And the fellows and girls sit singing in the pasture down by the stream on a springtime evening?"

"Naturally."

"Oh, how I envy them!" Her voice was full of longing.

For several minutes the two of them sat silent, each sunk in his own thoughts.

"And with all that," she wondered aloud, "they want to leave everything and go to Palestine!"

He let her words hang in midair, so she repeated the thought. "Seems to me that's what you said? That they intend to go to Palestine?"

"Yes," he nodded, and began softly singing to himself, to the chant of Lamentations. Leahtche was not deflected.

"Why should they want to leave Russia?" she wondered. "Must be the Revolution they're running away from."

"*Zion, wilt thou not seek . . .*" Sorokeh intoned in Hebrew. It was Yehuda Halevi's famous elegy.

"What's the matter with you?" She turned to look at him. "What's that you're moaning?"

"Accept from them their greeting from afar./Their greeting and their longing and their ache"

Leahtche was unfamiliar with the Hebrew words. She returned to her own train of thought. "The proverb that says 'Never trust a peasant' is right. The village is reactionary by nature."

". . . would dream away thy manacles,/And be the harp melodious for thy song!". . .

"One thing I'll never understand," Leahtche mused, ignoring him. "What sense does it make for them to exchange village life here for village life in Palestine?"

Sorokeh stopped his chanting and looked at her in amazement. "They're not exchanging one exile for another, are they? They're exchanging *golus* for the Land of Israel?"

"Who are these people?" she asked. "Zionists, I suppose."

"*Halutzim.*"

"What's that?"

"Pioneers."

Sorokeh's answer was addressed half to himself. "Something new in Jewish life. Nobody can be sure what it will lead to. It may be the beginning of a new birth, or it may mark the beginning of the end. Either the Revolution will sweep us away, or the Land of Israel will save us from extinction."

He took her hand in both of his, and told her about the wave of enthusiasm that had swept through Jewish youth in Eastern Europe, a fever to go to Palestine and build it up, to plow and plant and reap, to build a Jewish homeland. The big question now was whether the Jewish people would shake off its lethargy and respond to the challenge. On that, everything depended. So far it was only the youth, and a minority of them at that.

He was talking reflectively, thinking out loud. "But then, we've always been like that, a nation of individuals, the chosen few."

He didn't release her hand, but sat there lost in thought for quite some time. Finally, with a deep sigh, he looked away.

"I myself might go to Palestine. It's possible. Yes, a new people is being created there, a new society, free associations of groups of workers, that can serve as a model for the rest of the world. That's something we alone can accomplish, only the Jews."

"Oh!" Leahtche jumped up like one transported. Her face was aglow, her eyes shining. "Take me along! I want to go too!"

89

From time to time Tania would slip in to see Sorokeh. He enjoyed her visits—her bright young face, the gray eyes that would light up and seem to turn blue whenever she became animated, the sudden shyness in her smile.

The two kept their distance from one another, almost as if they had agreed to observe the proprieties. But the barrier was a fragile one, not quite solid enough to keep the atmosphere from being charged with unspoken feelings, little hints of mutual attraction, unacknowledged overtones of seductiveness. Sorokeh found pleasure in this covert minuet of approach and withdrawal, a thing more of form than of substance.

Tania talked about a lot of subjects, Turgeniev for example, and Korolenko, both of whom were behind her, so she said. The same for Gorki—a voice now of the past.

"He's the drummer in the ensemble," she said, proud of her sophistication. Then she was silent for a moment, waiting for his reaction.

There was no reaction.

Hastily she turned to another topic, the usual plaint of her generation, bemoaning the boredom of being stuck in that miserable little town, where life had no grandeur, and the human being no dignity, where nothing ever happened, no romance, no drama, no tragedy, none of the wonderful things one had a right to expect out of life.

"Could you by any stretch of the imagination"—there was a twinkle of mischief in her eye—"picture my father involved in an affair of the heart?"

"I forget," he apologized. "Who's your father?"

"What's the difference? Mordkhe-Leib. Mordkhe-Leib Segal."

"Oh," said Sorokeh, blankly.

"Or take Yankel Potchtar, or Avrohom-Elya. Imagine, Reb Avrohom-Elya going off the deep end for love of a woman! It's absurd, inconceivable. Now, you take the typical Russian. . . ."

She let the thought hang in midair, as though meditating on it. The pause, the silence, was freighted with danger, and Sorokeh stepped into the breach. "A Russian"—he glanced into her eyes—"when a Russian man loves a woman he's loving Mother Russia at the same time—all of her, the cherry tree in his orchard, the river, the steppe. But when it's a Jew's turn, all he's got to love beside the woman is his exile."

She interrupted him. "No, he doesn't love a woman at all. What he loves is his family. Yes, that's it. His children."

"You may be right," Sorokeh nodded.

"How can a woman love men like that?" she shrugged. "That's why we're such sorry creatures leading such sorry lives. All you see around here is narrow little people, with lives to match. Empty. Suffocating. If the heart makes demands, they're denied, smothered. But the heart doesn't even make any demands—it remains empty and desolate."

How she longed to see the big wide world, she said, great cities, streets full of people, parks with fountains, like you see on picture postcards. How wonderful to go to the theater, to attend a lecture, a concert, all sorts of exciting things.

Sorokeh nodded. Easiest thing in the world, he told her, to go and see these places. Nothing easier.

"Nothing easier?" She looked at him sidelong. "What would I do there? How would I support myself?"

"You'd manage."

They both fell silent, and the silence was a charged one, part anticipation, part apprehension.

"Will you take me with you?" She covered the question with a quick, forced laugh.

"Why certainly," he answered with elaborate courtesy. "Please do come."

After a pause, he added, "Out there, in the great world, there's a man who has been dreaming of an unknown girl, slim and straight-limbed, who will transform his life, and bring him inexpressible happiness. That girl is you."

Tania's eyelashes fluttered. "Really?" she murmured. "You mean it?"

"Come," his voice now held a slight tremor. "We'll go to Odessa by the sea. The sea is always beautiful, especially on a summer's day, all blue as turquoise out to the horizon, as far as the eye can see."

He stopped talking, and his eyes swept over her body. She bent her head, her fingers fluttering in her lap, her face a little flushed.

"The sea," he said, "is like a girl."

"A girl?" Tania wasn't looking at him.

"No," he corrected himself. "Like a young woman. A girl is a sprig of lilac."

He stood up, and started pacing up and down, Then he approached her. She pulled back, he bent over her, and suddenly they fell into one another's arms. Quickly he picked her up, and walking very tall carried her to the doorway, his face glowing. At the doorway he kissed her hard and then set her down.

"This is the boundary between us," he pointed to

the threshold. She looked at him with an odd expression.

He opened the door. His voice had become husky. "Run," he said. "Run home. Don't lose a minute."

90

It had been a dream of Sorokeh's to create an armed force of Jewish Anarchists, but nothing had come of it. Now he had a different idea—to organize units for Jewish self-defense in the small towns. The need for such a step was becoming daily more apparent.

The threat of civil strife had darkened the sky of the Ukraine from the very beginning. There had been tension between the Ukrainians and the Russian Provisional Government, and when the latter had been ousted in the October Revolution, between the Ukrainians and the Russian Bolsheviks. The situation deteriorated steadily as the Ukrainian nationalists gathered more and more power into their hands, and began to talk of seceding from Russia and creating an independent republic. Within a few months the dikes of social order had been breached, and the whole province became a seething caldron. It was then that Sorokeh made up his mind that the Jews ought to take steps. He was convinced that a time of great social disturbance was at hand, and that the Jewish population would suffer from it more than any other, since they were the element that would be caught between the hammer and the anvil. Besides which, Jew-hatred was deeply rooted in the Ukraine: its people had been anti-Semites since time immemorial.

It was while Sorokeh was still convalescing in the bathhouse that the Bolsheviks declared war on the Ukrainian Republic and its legislature, the Central Rada. Hearing that actual civil war had broken out, Sorokeh roused himself from his sickbed and went to see the local comrades, to broach the matter of Jewish self-defense. They looked at him in astonishment.

"Hullo! Where have you been all these months? Has it perchance reached your ears that this country has a government? A regime of soldiers, workers and peasants?"

His answer was, "Let's not depend on the government, let's depend on ourselves."

"What makes you talk like that?"

"Because the country's in a state of confusion, and there's danger of pogroms against the Jews. The usual way of the world at times like these."

They laughed in his face. "The usual way of the world has been abolished. Besides, we're in charge of the world now."

"Mere words. You can't get off that cheaply."

"Not mere words—real deeds. For one thing, everything's going our way, and for another, we've got the upper hand over the *burzhui*. You yourself can see that the Jews are still ensconced on their own dung heap, with none to make them afraid."

He tried again. "The peasants of a miserable little village like Bielosuknia set fire to your town. What more do you want?"

"That's a thing of the past," they answered. "Why bring up old stuff like that?"

"Because it's all the more likely to happen again in the future!"

Sorokeh drew on every argument he could think of, and

on all his considerable powers of persuasion. He stormed against their skepticism until their disbelief began to crumble. But they didn't dare give him their assent, because after all, they were afraid of Polyishuk. So they answered him lamely, some of them quite humbly, looking for all the world like penitents at afternoon prayers on a public fast day. Some mumbled, "We can't help you, because it would be considered counterrevolutionary." Others had even less of an answer, so they merely said, "It's not right for us to defend ourselves."

He was equally unsuccessful with the Jewish townspeople. As soon as they understood what he was driving at they recoiled, their eyes darting fearfully from side to side, their faces clouded, frowning.

"Leave us alone," they said, "before you bring great trouble down on our heads, God forbid."

"Jews!" he warned, "there isn't much time before the storm breaks!"

"Don't get yourself involved in what's not your responsibility," they answered, somewhat sadly. "Then perhaps what you fear won't happen at all."

"Jews!" he persisted. "Don't take this lightly! The only thing that stands between you and catastrophe is self-defense!"

"The good Lord will protect us."

He tried hard, but he got nowhere. He walked away feeling sad, defeated. "A quixotic people," he whispered to himself with a sorrowful shrug. "A nation of dancers before the moon!"

The Jewish townsfolk also walked away, outwardly satisfied that they had handled him well. "Ach-ach!" they sighed. "Such concern on our behalf! How fortunate we are to have such saviors and defenders, may fire consume them! Nu-nu, we're being punished for our sins. Who roused up the *goyim* in the first place, and led them astray with lies, so that they burned and robbed and looted? Now he comes telling us what to do—may hellfire know what to do with him!"

Reb Itzia Dubinsky nodded sagely and dropped a comment about Sorokeh. "One of his kind can burn up the whole world!"

Reb Ozer Hagbeh tugged at his trousers and offered a comment on Polyishuk: "One of his kind can destroy the whole world!"

Kalman the baker stroked his beard and smiled. "One to knead the dough, one to upend the vat, and one to do the baking."

91

Sorokeh managed to assemble a group of ten lads, members of the Tseire Tsiyon, and to get Itzik Yapontchik to drill them. Itzik had earned his nickname in the Russo-Japanese war, from which he emerged with a limp in one leg. There were three additional recruits of no special distinction: Berel the meatcutter, Shaylik, Velvel the blacksmith's boy, and Yoellik, youngest son of Zanvill the wagoner who was noted for his regularity in studying a chapter of Midrash or *En Ya'akov* every Sabbath between the afternoon and evening services. It was this selfsame Zanvill who proudly proclaimed that he was a driver-son-of-a-driver, and that his father too had been a *balagoleh,* son of a *balagoleh,* all the way back to Jonadab the son of Rechab in the Bible. The recruits let it be known that they had organized for self-defense. They were able to put their hands on seven rifles that had been brought back from the front by local Jews who had served in the army, and whose military careers had been broken off by the Revolution. These men did not join the self-defense group, but they did say they could be counted on as a reserve, "God forbid you should need us."

An hour before it was time for the afternoon service a crowd was observed running toward the synagogue. "What happened?" folks called out from the doorways.

"It's the Yapontchik and his regiment!" the runners panted. "The Yapontchik is mobilizing his troops!"

In the spacious snow-filled courtyard of the synagogue the members of the self-defense squad labored away at their basic training. Itzik Yapontchik was putting them through their paces, in the best parade-ground fashion.

"Left, right!" his voice rang out. "One, two! Hup, hup!" His squad swung their arms and marched off double-file.

"Hey, take a look at that wooden stick!" said one vastly amused spectator to another, pointing to a nearsighted skinny fellow.

"Ruvke!" Somebody recognized the Rabbi's son, and tried to grab hold of his coattails as he shuffled past, weighed down by his heavy flannel boots, panting and puffing like a goose.

They had a good deal of fun at the expense of Itzik Yapontchik, claiming that he must have studied his sergeant very carefully.

"Look, look at him! Watch how he bangs his feet down!" They laughed, holding their sides. "One, two! A veritable scholar! A commanding officer!"

Sorokeh made no attempt to hide his displeasure at all this levity. Finally he turned on them angrily.

"What's the big joke?" he shouted. "It's yourselves you're making fun of, mocking your own fate, your own lives!"

He turned away from them, still seething. "What a people!" he muttered to himself. "When they're not crying, they're laughing!"

92

What he had done in Mokry-Kut was, Sorokeh felt, only a drop in the bucket. He envisioned a self-defense unit in every Jewish town; and as he thought about it, it occurred to him that all the units could be joined under a central command, forming a mighty force for the protection of Jewry in case of need. The magnitude and simplicity of the idea excited him, and he thought it over in exhaustive detail, whipping himself into a fever of enthusiasm.

"There you have it," he whispered to himself as he sat on the big wooden block in front of the furnace. "It's exactly what the times call for, because whenever there's social disorder, the Jews get attacked."

For quite a while he sat thinking, tackling various problems, imagining battles and deeds of heroism, seeing in his mind's eye an end to anti-Semitism everywhere in the land. Finally, all this heated thinking exhausted him. Bit by bit his enthusiasm evaporated. He began to see the difficulties, to be assailed by doubts.

"Ach-ach-ach!" he shook his head worriedly. "Who's going to stand up for the Jews, who'll devote himself to their battles, travel around from one little town to the next, mobilize the manpower, find the arms and the money and everything else that's needed? Who?"

He tried, but without much success, to quiet himself down. "Eh, nonsense. What's it to you? Who do you think you are, the guardian of Israel?" It didn't work. Once he had gotten himself worked up, he couldn't put out of his mind the dark premonitions that were always at the back of his thoughts. The more he tried to suppress them, the more they came to the surface. Bolshevism, a regime that denied elementary human rights, boded nothing but ill for the Jewish people, of that he was convinced. Over and over, in his mind he denounced those young Jews who had joined the Bolsheviks, and with the power in their hands, had proved to be arbitrary and cruel, quick to use force, insensitive and hardhearted, given to every kind of abomination that had never been typical of Jews.

A little while later Leahtche came in, all bundled up against the cold, her rosy cheeks peeking out from between the fringes of the kerchief that covered her head.

Once inside the bath-house, her face fell. "What's the matter, Sorokeh?" she worried. "Still sick?"

"No. I'm all right."

"Then why do you look so strange?"

"Oh, nothing."

"Bored?" She approached him, uncertain.

From outside came the sound of feet crunching in the snow. The door was flung open, and in came comrades Mayerke and Ziame.

"You've got visitors," comrade Ziame announced briskly, rubbing his hands together. "My, Sorokeh, but it's cold here."

"Yes, the stove's gone out," Sorokeh answered civilly.

Ziame sat down, pushing back from his head the hood of his greatcoat. "You seem to be in a melancholy mood today," he said. "They been beating you with the bath-house switches?"

Sorokeh didn't answer.

Ziame looked at Leahtche. "What's the matter with him?"

Leahtche shrugged silently. Awkward in her many layers of clothing, she moved like a pregnant woman toward an inverted pail, and sat herself down.

Mayerke pulled a pouch of tobacco out of his pocket.

"The Yapontchik and his boys," he said, rolling himself a cigarette, "they're kicking up a commotion."

"Those boys are doing a useful piece of work," Sorokeh answered.

"I see you have no faith in the Soviet regime," Ziame wagged a finger at him. "Tsk, tsk, Sorokeh, you should know that as long as the Soviets are in power your Jews are quite safe from harm."

"I'm not so sure."

Mayerke drew on his cigarette, screwing up his eyes against the smoke. "It might be worth our while," he said, "to expend a couple of *zolotniki* of lead on you."

Ziame intervened, speaking with perfect calm, slowly. "There's no reason for concern, no fear of pogroms. Why all of a sudden pogroms? Who? What? Where? That kind of thing doesn't happen any more, there's no need for self-defense."

"What do we care?" asked Mayerke, straddling the wooden trestle in the middle of the room. "He wants the Yapontchik to play soldier? Let him play. Either way the Revolution will know how to choke off the hydra head of counterrevolution. The real question is a different one, and comrade Sorokeh has already formulated it. Suppose, comrades, that pogroms become necessary for the Revolution? What then, hah? Which side will you come down on —the Jews, or the Revolution? That, comrades, is the question."

"Are you putting the question as an issue of principle?" Ziame asked with a short, embarrassed laugh.

"An issue of principle!" Mayerke pushed his lambskin cap back from his forehead and flicked the stub of his cigarette into a corner of the room. "Let's put it this way: either, or. Either the Revolution is undermined and disappears, while the Jewish people continues to exist; or the Jewish people disappears, and the Revolution stands firm. Well now, comrades, what would your judgment be?"

He waited for a minute, then went on. "All right, I'll tell you how I would rule: Let Jewry perish and the Revolution remain! Yes, sir, that's the way a loyal and responsible Communist sees it, and anybody who thinks otherwise is a renegade and a counterrevolutionary!"

"As a matter of principle?" Ziame repeated, his laugh somewhat tentative.

"As a matter of practical principle!" declared Mayerke, with an air of finality.

Sorokeh spoke tonelessly. "You're miserable creatures," he said. "A bunch of maniacs."

"And you're a counterrevolutionary!" Mayerke's voice rose, filled with venom. "You're a chau . . . chau . . . chauvinist, that's what you are! Hired lackey of the Jewish bourgeoisie! Chauvinist! Counterrevolutionary!"

"What's the matter with you fellows?" Ziame was taken aback. "What's biting you?"

"Chauvinist that he is!" Mayerke jumped off the trestle. "Traitor that he is! And he dares call us maniacs!"

"Come on, now!" Ziame tried to quiet him down. "Why so angry?"

"Miserable creatures," Sorokeh repeated with a grimace of distaste. "Psychological cripples. Repulsive unfortunates."

"Wait, just you wait!" Mayerke wagged a finger at him. "We'll see to it that you pay for this! We'll take care of you, you can be sure of that!"

"You're talking nonsense," Leahtche broke in. "Plain nonsense."

"One thing I don't understand," said Ziame to Sorokeh. "If you're so concerned about the Jewish people, how come you involved yourself with the peasants in seizing the farmlands, instead of busying yourself with the Jews?"

Sorokeh sat as though he hadn't heard the question. After a while he raised his head and spoke sadly.

"To each his own, in accordance with his condition. To

the peasants, land; to the Jews, self-defense. Because there's nothing else to offer the Jews but their lives, and right now their lives are hanging in the balance."

Leahtche gave a deep sigh. "It doesn't take an expert to see that self-defense can't do any harm." Her cheeks were on fire, sparks flashed from her eyes. "We all know how they hate us, and what damage they can do to us. But there's something I want to say to you, Sorokeh. It seems to me that the Revolution can't be judged by ordinary standards of morality. Say even, if you will, the Revolution represents a colossal injustice. Well and good; that's its strength; that's a necessity. I can't explain it, but that's the way it is."

She paused for a moment, blinked her eyes a few times, and spoke again, giving voice to the thoughts that were agitating her.

"After all, there simply has to be justice in the world! Maybe even more than justice!"

93

Polyishuk started something new: a committee to look after the interests of women. Most of the girls were made members: Liuba, Masha, Kayla, Malia, Rosa. Only Leahtche was left out.

Impressed by the importance of their assignment, the girls held meetings with Polyishuk to discuss ways and means of involving the womenfolk more closely with the Revolution, of educating them in the tenets of Communism, and preparing them to become dedicated and loyal comrades of the Soviet regime.

The line was defined by Polyishuk at the very first meeting. "Comrades!" he said. "Anybody who knows history knows that you can't have a revolution without the feminine element. Every Communist is aware of the extent to which a revolution succeeds in direct proportion to the participation of the women. Comrade Lenin has said it: 'No social revolution can last unless the majority of women in the population are on its side.' Absolutely right. Now comrade Trotsky has said. . . ."

Then Mayerke took up the theme, and went on to blame the women for the present vulnerability of the Revolution. Yes, it was their fault, seeing that the vast majority of them stood aside from the work at hand.

Comrades Ziame and Hillik, waxing dialectical, offered more of the same. Comrade Ziame laid at the door of the Communist party the responsibility for achieving full equality for women, and freeing them from the yoke of capitalist subjugation. Comrade Hillik raised his voice against the women of Mokry-Kut, who had failed to acquire a class viewpoint, and had absented themselves from the ranks of those fighting the battle of the proletariat.

Then Rosa took the floor with a fiery denunciation of inequality and prejudice, of clerical fanaticism and bourgeois dictatorship, demanding the emancipation of women, urging the importance of educational efforts. Her pince-nez quivered as she shook her fist, insisting that something be done for the poverty-stricken elements at the bottom of the social heap.

Malia was not to be outdone. Ranging across a variety of issues, she touched on Katyusha Maslova and Sonia Marmaladova, quoted from *The Lower Depths* by Gorki, and from *Anathema* by Leonid Andreyev. Rising to a pitch of excitement, she went on and on, not knowing how to finish. Finally comrade Shimtze helped her out, and she extricated herself from the complexities of her long speech with a ringing declaration: "All power to the Soviets! Long live the Revolution! Equality for all, irrespective of sex, race, or creed!"

She was out of breath. Her face was flushed, her eyes darted unseeing from side to side. She breathed deeply and added in a sharp, preternaturally high voice, "Workers of the world, unite!"

The committee caused quite a stir. Half a dozen or so women in Mokry-Kut who had been considered ineligible because they came from families of too high a social status volunteered humbly and were allowed to attend a meeting. Polyishuk made the opening remarks in praise of the Soviets. He was followed by those comrades whom the Revolution had transformed into spokesmen, who treated the ladies to generous helpings of Marx and Engels, Lenin and Trotsky, leaving their helpless listeners somewhat confused.

A handful of illiterate women, of the most deprived element in the community, were formed into a class to study the alphabet. Some of the girls organized a study group, led by Rosa, who gave them heavy doses of Gorki and Andreyev, Kuprin and Artzybasheff, so that in short order they were stuffed with culture and knowledge, instant intellectuals.

The townspeople made bitter fun of these women. Any time one of the local citizenry met one of these girls on the street, he was likely to stop her and say, "Tell me, comrade, in your own gifted words, about your great teachers, fountainheads of wisdom."

If he got any answer at all, it was usually, "What's it to you?" When that happened, the questioner would don a mask of innocence, explaining sweetly, "I'm asking because you are a proletarian woman, a pillar of the Revolution."

Then, when she had walked on, the questioner would usually break out into mocking laughter, nodding his head and muttering, "Put to the test and found repulsive, a plague on her!"

Meantime, the women's committee was formulating all kinds of plans, a public dining hall, a community laundry, a central nursery for children.

"Sooner or later," they reassured one another. "The time is bound to come."

94

Leahtche became the object of much talk. The other girls whispered about her, and when anyone quoted, "How the mighty have fallen," everybody knew who was meant.

"The merits of Kropotkin are not much help to her now," Rosa whispered with a satisfied smile.

"There you have the difference between Communism and Anarchism," declared Malia.

"A different brand of tobacco," Mayerke agreed, with a broadly knowing wink.

Leahtche noticed the stir she was causing, the gossip and the whispering, and she felt miserable about the whole thing. "Pity the person," she sighed to herself, "who has one cloak and two claimants."

Nevertheless, she wore a cheerful face, as if nothing had happened. The girls had an explanation for this, too. "It's an act," they said. "She's putting up a front."

Occasionally one of the comrades would stop her and say, "Listen, how come you're not taking part in the people's welfare projects?"

She would regard him with utmost amazement, and answer, "Are you speaking out of fever, or are you moonstruck? I, not involved in the people's . . . ? Whose welfare do you think I'm involved in?"

If that didn't settle the matter, and he persisted, she would change her tune. "Birds of a feather flock together," she would retort, breaking out into gales of laughter.

And to herself she would add, "Bad teeth are no excuse for not laughing."

Her thoughts were confused and unhappy, thoughts about Polyishuk, thoughts about Sorokeh. She reviewed each of them from every angle, but it was all old stuff. It seemed to her she had made a big mistake. But maybe not. . . . Still, they had one thing in common: what happened to her didn't matter to them. Why should it bother the storm if a tree gets uprooted?

Sorokeh noticed that a change had come over her. "Nu," he said, "what happened?"

She turned her face away.

"Troubles?" he said, with a knowing smile. This brought her quickly to the boiling point.

"I've got troubles because you don't have troubles!"

Sorokeh laughed. "What do you mean?"

"What, what," she echoed angrily. "Things. Episodes."

"Come now." Sorokeh was amused. "Episodes? What episodes?"

Silence.

"Have the comrades got something against you?" he ventured. She glanced at him.

"Who's responsible?" he said gently. "Come, Leahtche, tell me."

He got an answer faster than he expected. "Mr. So-and-so, such-and-such a poison. Maybe it's the man, maybe it's the poison, maybe it's you."

"Me?" Sorokeh looked surprised.

"You, you." She gentled her voice, pretending to be apologetic. "You, the crown of my head."

Sorokeh was at a loss. "I see what you mean," was all he could think of to say.

"You see? But of course. Certainly!" She turned on him with all the fury of a sudden storm wind. *"You see* indeed! Maybe you can tell me why you ever took the trouble to come here, and what I'm doing in this place? It could only have been evil demons that pushed me."

The outburst stopped suddenly. "I'm in such a turmoil," she started to say. She bent her head, and choked up with tears.

Sorokeh put his hand on her shoulder. "Leahtche," he whispered. She bent her head lower.

"Leahtche, do you hear?" he whispered and said no more, as if those words were enough to convey something that was deep in his heart.

They sat there silently for a while. After a while Leahtche stood up, walked to the door, and was gone.

95

From one day to the next Leahtche grew more and more tense. The other girls said she was burning up. "A fire has gotten into her," they said. Occasional quarrels broke out between them, and the girls traded sharp words.

Sorokeh added to her troubles by going off to make the rounds of the villages. "I'll be back a week from today," he comforted her.

But she was not that easily comforted. She felt miserable, and it showed on her face. After work, she went home and threw herself fully clothed on her bed. She lay there thinking about her relationship to Sorokeh, wondering whether she loved him. Indeed, she wondered whether there was such a thing as love.

"What is love?" she pondered. "What? . . ." It seemed to her that it was a bad business, more like an affliction than anything good, a flimsy thing blown away by the slightest puff of wind. Love was proof, she thought, that the human being is by nature an evil creature, given to jealousy and vengefulness, mercilessly cruel, and blind withal—that is, until disillusionment comes and opens his eyes.

But after a while a wave of feeling washed away all the logic of her thoughts, and she was left with nothing but her longing for Sorokeh.

"My beloved," she whispered, feeling faint, her eyes closed, her heart dying a thousand little deaths.

A week passed, but Sorokeh did not return. Leahtche was restless, in a constant state of turmoil.

Once, after the day's work, when all the comrades were getting ready to leave, she entered Polyishuk's office.

"Comrade Polyishuk." She stood there with head held high, a smile fixed to her lips. "I've come to straighten out my affairs."

He lifted up his eyes and looked at her. "Your affairs?" he said, with elaborate calm. "What are they?"

Leahtche sat down facing him on the other side of his worktable. "Kindly tell me why I'm treated with contempt. Have I earned it?"

"What are you trying to say?"

"Isn't there a single item in my favor? The least little one?"

He stared at her steadily. Only his mustache quivered.

"Or do you want to tell me that I've been disqualified?"

"Come out with it." Polyishuk leaned on the arm of his chair in a listening attitude. "What's on your mind?"

"All right, I'll tell you what's on my mind." She pulled her chair closer to the table. "You know me well enough, thank goodness, to realize that I'm not looking for honors. I'm not that kind of a person. But once you started something for the good of the Revolution, why keep me out of it? Me, of all people? Everybody else, yes—me, no. Do I lose out because I'm not shortsighted and long-nosed like Rosa? Because I'm not conceited like Malia, or a silly fake tragedienne like Masha, or a half-pint like Kayla?"

Polyishuk tried not to show his pleasure at her annoyance. He held his gaze.

"So why did you include them and shunt me aside? Am I not as good a Communist as they are? As much of an intellectual? Don't I know the abc's as well as they do?"

"Don't turn your nose up at the abc's," said Polyishuk, sounding very official. "No subject is in itself more important than any other except in terms of the people's needs, and the struggle against illiteracy is a need of the people."

"Well and good." Leahtche's tone was a mixture of conciliation and complaint. "Then why exclude me?"

"You know why," he said suddenly severe.

"Yes, I know!" she answered exultantly. "I guessed what was on your mind, and now I see I was right!"

Polyishuk looked at her, surprised.

"It's personal!" She leaned clear across the table and fixed him with her eyes. "I can see it! I read your heart like an open book!"

"You've got it wrong," Polyishuk said with an unpleasant little smile. "You must be thinking of somebody else's heart."

"No," she laughed in his face, "I'm not wrong."

"It seems to me"—he got up slowly and came around to where she sat—"it seems to me that you were thinking of the Anarchist. By the way, how is he?"

"All right," she answered. "Just fine."

"I hear he's making the rounds of the villages."

"Uh-huh."

"When will he be back?"

"Tomorrow or the day after." Having him stand over her like that made her uncomfortable. She pushed her chair back and stood up.

"Aha," he said. For a few minutes they looked at one another, not speaking. Then he blurted out, "Leahtche!"

She waited.

"Leahtche!" he lowered his voice. "Drop him."

She thought he might have something more to say. Instead, he put his hand on her shoulder.

Quietly and firmly she removed his hand. "No," she said. Suddenly he seized her and held her tight, trying to kiss her. She twisted her face from side to side, fighting him off, finally pushing him away with both hands. As soon as she was free she made for the door.

"I told you, you're an open book!" She laughed in his face.

She walked with long strides down the middle of the street, inwardly seething. "What an artist!" She rubbed her hand across her mouth, as though trying to erase his kisses. "Knows his way around!"

That's what she whispered to herself. But she couldn't help feeling the glow of pleasure that had invaded her when Polyishuk had held her tight, the thrill that had flowed through her entire body.

"What a creature is man!" she said, nodding sagely, and the thought was two-edged, referring on the one hand to Polyishuk, on the other to herself.

96

It was around this time that Leahtche ran into Dena on the street. Dena was quite cordial, and as the two of them walked together they hit it off so well that they were soon exchanging confidences, as if they had been lifelong friends. Leahtche brought up the subject of Sorokeh.

"You work with him, so you know what he's like. You I can trust, you're not a *koketka* like all the others. What can I tell you. He'll be the death of me."

"Sorokeh?" Dena was astonished. "Why, he's a wonderful fellow!"

"You're right," answered Leahtche. "That's the trouble. I wish he wasn't so wonderful."

"Ah, what are you saying?" Dena turned her face away because of the glare of the sun on the snow.

"The more I think about it, the less I understand," said Leahtche, her voice troubled.

"What seems to be the matter?" Dena asked.

"Why are things this way?" Leahtche avoided a direct answer. "I could make somebody happy, so very happy. What did I do to deserve this?"

Dena didn't need any diagrams. Instead, she tried to offer some comfort. "Times are changing," she said. "It's the same with all the fellows. No more sudden falling in love, like a storm breaking out, or a fire, not even like a flash of light on the shiny lamp in the big synagogue. . . ."

She broke out laughing. "Ha-ha, like the lamp in the synagogue, what a comparison! No, it's more like the cleft flame of a smoky little wick."

"No, no," Leahtche protested.

Dena went on sagely, "Nowadays, the fellows are more straightforward, simpler. They're men of action, they've all got official duties. . . ."

"No, no," Leahtche broke in. "A girl like you doesn't have to swallow that line."

"They're all alike," Dena persisted, "except, of course, for the exceptions, ha-ha-ha!"

"Trouble is, he's an exception," said Leahtche seriously.

"Except for the exceptions!" Dena laughed uproariously, vastly amused at herself.

The next day they made a point of meeting again on their way home at nightfall. Dena told Leahtche about her dream of settling in Palestine, in a cooperative settlement in *yokhdanskaya dolina*, her version of the Jordan Valley. There, she said, by the shores of Lake Kinneret, she would build herself a house, and have a flock of sheep, three or four cows, a couple of horses.

"The world is really beautiful," she said. "And still quite young. If there are such big animals around, cows, horses, even camels. . . . Strange, isn't it? The world is so young."

Just then Mulye came toward them. "Good evening," he said. "You're headed . . . ?" Without waiting for an answer, he changed direction and fell in beside them.

"Where to?" he asked. "Under these stars, tens of thousands of planets lighting up the void of space? Down here, who needs them? Once upon a time they were useful to ex-poets, but now they're just a waste. . . ."

"Really?" Leahtche teased.

"And as for that miserable satellite, tagging along all the time"—he looked up at the moon, and the girls exchanged glances—"he never gets anywhere."

Dena came to a stop. "Good night, Leahtche," she said, and turned off in the direction of her house.

Mulye walked on beside Leahtche, head down, lost in

thought. After a while he spoke. "Leahtche," he said, "make peace between us."

"You and Dena?" she asked.

"Yes."

"What happened between you two?"

"She's got it in for me because I kissed . . ."

"Who? Who did you say?"

"Tania. But that's just between us, Leahtche."

Leahtche stood stock-still. "Ah, you miserable creature! You're all miserable things, every last one of you! Tfu. . . ." She spat out in disgust. "And you think she can be won over? A girl like her, and you think she can be wheedled?"

"You're right," Mulye whispered despairingly. "She's flint. . . ."

"She's flint?" Leahtche jibed at him. "And what do you think you are? You're a *shmatte,* that's what, a rag, and nothing else!"

She turned away from him, and walked on alone to her house.

97

Word got around that Karpo had broken into the stable of Omelko Masliuk, and had stolen Sokol and Krasotka, two horses formerly belonging to the squire. The animals were none other than the famed Gneidko and Tchubari, the very same.

Sorokeh, on his return from the village, confirmed the

report, adding that Karpo was a Jew-hater and an un-doubted counterrevolutionary.

"There's a Bolshevik for you," he said, "a typical Bol-shevik."

Leahtche heard that Sorokeh was back, and she couldn't get over to his place fast enough, the minute her day's work was done.

"Sorokeh!" The one word seemed freighted with all the unexpressed longings and yearnings of her entire lifetime. She didn't know what else to say. Even after she had calmed down a little, she was still in a state of euphoria, her face shining, the joy evident in every word she uttered, every laugh, every nonsense syllable.

Sorokeh was tired from his trip, and in a depressed mood. No matter how she tried to cheer him up it didn't work, and bit by bit her own mood slid downhill. She tried to enliven the conversation.

"Did you think of me, Sorokeh?"

"Naturally."

"How did you think of me?" She put her hand on his shoulder.

"Intentionally and unintentionally."

"No, really, Sorokeh."

"Really."

"It's a good thing you thought of me," she said, only half in jest. "Because if you hadn't, I'd have been sort of non-existent."

"You exist, you exist," he said, putting his arm around her.

"And I suppose you'll remember me in the future as well?"

"Certainly," Sorokeh answered, ignoring the implied sarcasm. "What then?"

"Yes," she said, spelling it out. "You're an expert at remembering." He didn't answer.

"Do remember me, Sorokeh." She took his hand in hers. Their hands were so cold that neither felt the other.

"Remember me," she was begging now, "but don't leave me."

"You want it both ways?" he bantered. "Why, it's a contradiction in terms."

"What of it?" she retorted. "You yourself are a contradiction in terms."

He looked at her, astonished, then nodded his head. "You're absolutely right, that's exactly the way it is. I'm a contradiction in terms."

"You see?" She waggled a finger at him triumphantly. "You see?"

"I see," he said thoughtfully, "that you've got something against me."

She laughed, a quick forced laugh. "You've never told me about the women you have loved."

"Which ones would you like to hear about?" he grinned.

She reversed her tack. "And it's a good thing you never told me about them, because that makes them nonexistent."

"Nonexistent," he humored her.

"Yes," she nodded. "Tomorrow, woe is me, I'll be like them."

He sagged wearily, overcome by depression.

"Tomorrow," she said, "you will either have forgotten me, or you'll remember me."

The twilight had been deepening gradually, and now the place was in complete darkness. Leahtche and Sorokeh were swallowed up in the shadows, invisible, as though they were nonexistent. Finally Leahtche sighed. "Nu, all right. What difference does it make? Come on, take me home."

He got up, went over to a bag standing on the bench in

a corner of the room, and took out a loaf of bread. "Here," he said. "I brought it from the country."

The moment they were outside Leahtche became a different person. Now she was all vigor, stamping her feet on account of the cold, taking brisk steps, almost dancing. "Nu, Sorokeh!" she urged. "You're dragging your feet as though you had brought back a load of sloth from the village!"

"I'm tired."

Scattered clouds scudded across the sky, making it look as though the moon and the stars were sailing at a fast clip. Leahtche suggested that the heavenly bodies were having a celebration, that they could raise your spirits and make you hopeful.

"Ah, my dearest. . . ." She craned her neck toward him, whispering.

Sorokeh twined his arm around hers, and their faces came close together. Suddenly she realized how defenseless she was. Her knees felt weak, and all the strength ebbed out of her.

On one occasion Sorokeh was walking along the street when he heard the sound of singing. Glancing around, he realized that it was coming from the *kloyz,* the small study house, so he peeped into the window. What he saw was Heshel Pribisker pacing up and down, singing softly to himself. Sorokeh went into the vestibule and listened closely at the inner door. He could make out the words *"b'rikh rahmana di m'sayan ad kan*—blessed be the Lord who has helped us up to now." Soon Heshel raised his voice and began to dance, clapping his hands.

"Ki gadol hashem," he sang. *"Oy-oy-oy,* for the Lord is great!"

Sorokeh opened the door stealthily and stepped inside, watching. Heshel didn't sense his presence, but continued his ecstatic dance.

"Oy gevald, oy gevald!" He clapped his hands over his head, singing all the while. "In the midst of sorrow to rejoice from the depths of one's heart, *ki gadol hashem!* Oy, for the Lord is great!" Just then he caught sight of Sorokeh, and stopped in his tracks, astonished. It was Sorokeh who spoke.

"What's making you so happy?" He stepped forward out of the shadows.

"It's on account of my sufferings."

"Sufferings?" Sorokeh was nonplussed.

"You see," Heshel explained, gesturing with one chapped, frozen finger, "when suffering gets you down, deep deep down to the lowest level, that's where you find essential joy."

Even as he said this he left Sorokeh and resumed his pacing up and down, singing, sighing, groaning, humming, until he came to a stop before the prayer stand near the ark.

"Ah," he said, striking his palm to his forehead. "All I've got left is my head, and even that is good for *kaporos,* useless."

He went back to his study-lectern and sat down. "The only thing is to start from the beginning, from *kometz-aleph!"*

He bent over the big open folio of the Gemara, shifting his eyes to the inner margin of the page for a glance at Rashi's commentary, sweeping across to the outer margin to see where the Tosafot differed, and before long he was swaying to and fro, audibly sounding the scholar's chant as he wrestled with the talmudic argumentation.

Sorokeh went over to the bookcase and took down the first volume that came to hand. It happened to be a tattered old copy of the *Yalkut Shim'oni*. He sat down and began to read at random. A few minutes later he jumped in astonishment. "Look what it says here!"

He walked over to show the passage to Heshel, but the book accidently closed, and he lost the place. He began to flip through the pages, looking, searching. " 'Alas for the generation whose heroes are low!'—it was something like that, very striking." After much leafing through the volume, and failing to find the passage, he came and sat down beside Heshel.

"Sorry I lost it," he said. "It was exactly as though the *Yalkut Shim'oni* was addressing our generation. Golden words, I tell you!" Then, after a pause, "Heroes. . . . The masses, in their laziness, exalt the energetic individual, the man of action, the one with the drive to power, and make a hero out of him."

He was trying to draw Heshel into conversation, but Heshel kept his eyes fixed on the page of the Gemara.

"The people pride themselves on the leader they have created," Sorokeh continued. "It gives them pleasure to place their necks under his heel, they even enjoy the sacrifices he extorts from them!"

Heshel glanced up, and smiled faintly. "Scripture says, 'Choose men to lead us.' It says 'men,' not angels."

Sorokeh showed his astonishment. "Men, you say? You call the Bolsheviks men?"

"What then?" Heshel deliberately baited him.

"I call them devils!" Sorokeh spoke heatedly. "Cruel sadists, the wicked of Israel, murderers!"

Quietly, hand on beard, Heshel repeated something he had said more than once. "If it weren't for the commandment, 'Thou shalt not kill,' I'd have become a Bolshevik long ago."

Sorokeh looked at him, flabbergasted. "You ... you ... ," he stammered.

Heshel simply smiled. After a moment, Sorokeh recovered his composure.

"But the Jewish Bolsheviks are the worst kind," he insisted. "They're the most evil, the cruelest of the lot."

"They're being true to their ancestral tradition," Heshel granted the point. "They're doing the will of their Father in heaven: truth, right, justice. All the other nations were baked in a cool oven, but we were baked in the iron furnace of slavery and suffering. They fried us, they roasted us—"

"Yes," Sorokeh broke in. "They fried us, they roasted us, but these Bolsheviks will destroy us, they'll 'blot out the remembrance of us from under the heavens!'"

Heshel's answer was slow in coming. Reflectively, he slipped his fingernail under his beard and scratched his chin. "The Torah is older than us and stronger than us. It is stated explicitly in the Talmud, in the tractate Menahot: 'Just as the leaves of the olive tree do not fall off, neither in the dry season nor in the rainy season, so is it with the people of Israel: they will never be effaced, neither in this world nor in the next.'"

"The Torah. . . ." Sorokeh's lips were twisted in a bitter smile. "The Torah can be interpreted in many ways. Add to the seventy aspects of Torah interpretation one more: the aspect of mockery! No, Rabbi Yosé and his olives won't help us much. The sickle has been raised over our heads! Do you understand what I'm telling you? Our generation has become the generation of doom for all Israel."

"The Torah is more powerful than all the generations put together." Heshel used both hands to adjust the scarf around his neck. "If this generation has lost its way, then the next generation will repent. The world has not been handed over to one generation, not even to two or three. As Koheleth says, 'One generation passeth and another generation cometh.' It's like Rabbi Yosé's description of twilight: the twinkling of an eye—one enters, the other exits."

Sorokeh lost patience. "Torah, Torah!" he expostulated. "You Jews of the old school! . . . Containers for the Torah, nothing more. . . . Lead people astray by quoting Scripture, settle everything with an aphorism from the Talmud! Misleaders, that's what you are!"

Heshel didn't answer, but shook his head sadly. He closed his book and stood up.

"Time to leave the *kloyz*," he said, addressing the world at large. *"Shalom."*

He pulled his ragged coat tightly around his shoulders, bent his head and walked out.

99

Sorokeh remained seated, thinking about Heshel, and about the whole Jewish people. A people of the past, he ruminated, with faint memories of a dim and distant past, with a system of values and views belonging to the past, a people whose joys and sorrows were echoes of the ancient past—all past, all past.

"What do they want, and what have they got?" he tortured himself. "They don't ask for anything, and yet they have nothing of their own, no country, no language, no culture, no soil under their feet, nothing that a normal people should have. All they've got in the world is their Torah, and their millennial hopes, two things that distract them from their present urgencies and their immediate peril. They nourish their minds on the Torah, twisting its words with great subtlety to apply to any and every situation. As for their messianic hopes—nothing will ever come of them."

The volume of the Talmud that Heshel had left on the reading lectern caught his eye. He opened it, and bent his head over the folio.

"Everything has already been said," he uttered, as though reading from the book. "They've nothing new to say, so they take apart what their predecessors have put together. A great chasm has opened up between the earlier and the later generations, between fathers and sons. The merit of the fathers has been used up."

Meantime, his eyes darted to the Rashi commentary, then to the Tosafot.

"The only thing that keeps them alive," he mused, "is the trouble and persecution they experience. The troubles produce hope, the hope leads to inaction, but woe betide them when their troubles cease."

The *kloyz* was deserted, a smell of dust and mold, tobacco and decay filled the air. Benches and study lecterns were strewn about, most of them ready to fall apart, squeaking and squealing at the slightest touch, seemingly held together only by the sacred purpose to which they were dedicated. In the middle of the room stood the *bimah*, twisted and misshapen. Brass candelabra hung from the ceiling as though hanging in thin air. To one side stood the bookcase, heaped with torn and tattered volumes. In front of the holy ark, with its big gilded Star of David, stood the prayer lectern, its two candlesticks obscured by the inscription: "I have set the Lord before me at all times." The charity boxes obtruding in every corner gave the room a funereal aspect, as though it were the headquarters of a burial society.

Sorokeh put his head in the curve of his arm, in the posture of one reciting the penitential *Tahanun* prayer.

When he heard people coming in for the afternoon prayers, he raised his head, shivered with the cold, and forced his eyes to focus on the open volume. Snatches of conversation reached him from the entranceway.

". . . chief of all the bandits," a voice said, apparently referring to Polyishuk. "They act like the lowest of the low!"

Sounds of washing of hands at the laver, and then the speaker continued.

"I didn't answer him a word. Just like the Good Book says: 'For all this, Job did not sin with his lips.'"

When they became aware of Sorokeh sitting in front of the open tome, they were amazed. "Look . . . ," they whispered.

Three or four men entered, and then the Rabbi. He paused at the spot where Sorokeh was sitting and glanced at the open page.

"Hm, a difficult passage, I see," he commented, looking searchingly at Sorokeh. Without waiting for an answer he continued on, and sat himself down at the end of a row, curled up between his sheepskin hat and his sheepskin coat, shoulders hunched high, each hand thrust into its opposite sleeve. He didn't take hold of a book, he didn't whisper a prayer, he simply sat there, waiting for the service to begin.

Soon the place was filled with the hum of conversation, coughs, groans, occasional laughter. A skinny little Jew, somewhat shorter than a man but taller than a boy, roamed around the room reciting Psalms in an audible chant. He brought to mind a nightingale that ignores its cage and bursts into song.

"Oy-oy, behold the Guardian of Israel doth neither slumber nor sleep!" the Psalm-singer poured out his heart, in sweet lament. It brought Sorokeh to his feet.

"Neither slumber nor sleep!" he shouted. "Yes, the Holy

One can't find anybody else to look after His people, so He has no choice but to do it Himself, to be our shade at our right hand. Good! Fine! But what about you? Why are you asleep? Why do you slumber? Scripture says, 'Thou shalt surely help Him.' Him! Help *Him!*"

Even as he spoke he ran toward the door, turning from side to side, shouting at the thunderstruck congregants, "What do you think, you're doing God's will?"

He slammed the door behind him in a rage. The people looked at one another.

The Psalm-sayer grinned. "Crazy as a loon."

Out on the street Yankel Potchtar ran into Sorokeh.

"So you people have improved the social order?" he said in a mocking but friendly tone. "What a job you've done! Really fixed it. A new world, eh? Left nothing of the old world, not so much as a slice of bread. Almost no 'this world' left at all."

"Good night." Sorokeh was in no mood for conversation. He turned his back on him and walked away. He walked for a long time, first toward Spod, then toward the water mill, then back to Spod.

The sun was setting, and the western sky glowed red. Atop the church the cross glittered like molten gold. The snow, piled up at the side of the road and on the roofs of the houses, changed color from one moment to the next. Ravens flew past in black disorder, seeking out their night-time roost.

Bit by bit the sunset faded. The sky filled with stars, bright, twinkling fiercely. Now the snow looked whiter. Mokry-Kut lay blanketed, with night and with silence. No voice or light; it seemed an uninhabited place. The only sound was the creaking of the snow under Sorokeh's feet.

He turned around and swept the town with his eyes. "Almost no 'this world' at all," he said, repeating aloud the words he had just heard from Yankel Potchtar.

100

Hesbel Pribisker awoke before sunrise. He was in good spirits, even though he had been up studying past midnight, something he had not done in a long time. Soon Reb Simcha and Leahtche were up and poking around in the gray murk of early morning.

"Oo-wah, cold!" Reb Simcha rubbed his hands together. "What a frost!"

Heshel began to chant, "Be strong as a leopard and swift as an eagle, fleet as a hind and brave as a lion, to do the will of your Father in heaven."

"For goodness' sake, what are you singing there?" Leahtche said testily, talking through a mouthful of hairpins as she stood in front of what was left of the mirror.

Heshel glanced at her, continuing his chant. "Judah ben Tema says—"

"Who said?" Leahtche interrupted.

"Not said, says," Heshel smiled at her. "He still says, he says it now, right up to this moment he says."

"Gemara, Gemara," Leahtche grumbled at her reflection in the mirror. "That's all they do with their whole lives, sit over the Gemara, go over it a hundred and one times. Better for you if you took Marx in your hand instead of the Gemara."

Reb Simcha exploded. "She goes to bed with Marx and gets up with Marx! Day is here—Marx is here! Marx, Marx —the devil with Marx!"

He went over to the window and glanced outside. "I'm faint with hunger."

"I'll have tea for you in a minute," said Leahtche, quickly putting the finishing touches to her hair.

"Huh, tea. . . ." Reb Simcha smiled forlornly, a ray of the rising sun glinting off his beard.

The "tea" they drank was made from dried carrots, taken with a bit of fruit-drop as a substitute for sugar. As soon as they were done with it, Leahtche left for work.

"Keep an eye open today," she instructed her father on her way out. "They might distribute bread."

Heshel Pribisker watched her leave. "Buzzing about, busy as a bee," he marveled.

Reb Simcha looked at him angrily, some sharp word trembling on the tip of his tongue.

"Those Marxists with their twisted ideas!" he finally said. "The Gemara isn't good enough for them. . . . *She* knows what Gemara is! But they hate everything Jewish like poison."

He was quiet for a few moments. Then, before Heshel could answer, he wrinkled his brow and raised both shoulders in perplexity.

"There's no way of understanding what they're after, no way in the world. What are they thinking of?" He was speaking to himself as much as to Heshel.

"They are the righteous." Heshel held his head high, looking radiant. "I believe it was the Rebbe of Lublin, may the memory of a just and saintly man be a blessing, I think it was he who said, The distinguishing mark of the righteous man is that he does not love himself; and of the penitent, that he hates himself."

"Righteous ones . . . ," Reb Simcha growled. "A bit more than is required, I don't think!"

"Seed of Israel," Heshel insisted. "True to the heritage of their ancestors. Even though they have their being in the secular—revolution, Marx, and all that—still, their inner essence comes from a sacred source, from the Besht and his saintly disciples, may their merit protect us. They rise to great heights, to the loftiest realms . . . fervor and wonder . . . the divine fire . . . almost to the ecstasy of self-effacement . . . and . . . and . . ."

Reb Simcha looked at him searchingly.

". . . and I'm afraid we'll have to sit at their feet and learn from them how to serve the Lord."

Reb Simcha sprang up, pale with anger. "You're worse than they are! You . . . you're ten thousand times worse if you can let such words pass your lips!"

Heshel tried to soothe him. "The Holy One remembers the virtues of the fathers to the credit of their descendants." He was smiling affectionately. "You see, whatever good deed we do, out of love or truth or justice, even though the format of the act is very different from the deeds of our forebears, the *mitzvah* itself stirs up the divine source of the action, and fans the flame of ancestral merit. That's the meaning of the promise given us by Moses our teacher, peace be unto him: 'And He chose his seed after him.' "

"What an advocate!" said Reb Simcha sarcastically, planting his hands on his hips. "Come on, now, you know they're mired deep in the forty-ninth level of impurity! The world has never seen a generation so benighted, so depraved. . . ."

"Exactly," Heshel broke in. "Just like the Israelite slaves in Egypt." It sounded as though he had been there, and was giving an eyewitness report. "As the Midrash says, at the last moment before the Exodus they were at the lowest point in all time, down to the forty-ninth depth of impurity, yet somehow in the end it was all transformed, and turned into great salvation, a light to the world."

"Ah, leave me alone!" Reb Simcha closed his eyes and stopped his ears with his thumbs. "What do you want from my life?"

Heshel stroked his beard for a moment, then his hand fell away. He put on his overcoat, wrapped a scarf around his neck, and took his *tallis* and *tefillin* from the top of the bookcase.

"The sun's up," he said, and hurried off to the synagogue.

101

It was a beautiful morning, cold and bright. The snow sparkled in the blinding sunshine, refracting the light into rainbow colors, like so many diamonds. Every branch and twig glittered with its decoration of jeweled frost. On either side of the street the houses peeped out in innocent silence from under snow-covered roofs, crystal icicles hanging from the eaves. The sky seemed bluer than usual, wider and deeper, in the sharp cold stillness.

Heshel walked with head held high, his feet crunching into the crusted snow. The radiance of the morning filled him with deep satisfaction, and he thought, This day is like a luminous mirror in which a man can see his very soul. A day, he thought, to keep pure and unsullied.

Joy stirred within him unbidden, the kind of childhood happiness a person sometimes experiences all of a sudden. "They must be thinking of me up above," he explained to himself as he strode along with bouncing steps. He looked up at the clear blue expanse.

"Do you know what?" he admonished himself. "You're attached to the upper spheres, away up there."

Mayerke and Shayke came up from behind him, and Heshel called out cheerily, "Good morning!"

"Good morning." Their tone was casual, condescending. They drew level with him.

"Where do you think you're going?" Mayerke asked, in the manner of one whose authority is taken for granted.

"And where would a Jew be going at sunup?" Heshel's smile was ingratiating. "To serve my Maker."

Mayerke glanced at the *tallis* and *tefillin* under Heshel's arm. "This too is called service?" His grin exposed two rows of yellow teeth. "Workers like you, my friend, ought to be locked up in the clink."

It was Shayke's turn to speak. "You're kind of high today." He spat out from between his teeth. "Sort of tipsy."

"But of course," Heshel smiled. "What else, on a day like this?"

"Like this? How do you mean?"

"Clear and clean, like the good side of a person's character, or like the joy of performing a *mitzvah.*"

Shayke simply didn't understand. "So what's making you so happy?"

Heshel's answer was slow and deliberate. "When I see there's a God in the world, joy takes hold of me. That's the meaning of 'I will greatly rejoice in the Lord.'"

"And what makes you think you see that?" Mayerke interrogated.

"I see it when I look at you."

"From what I hear," said Mayerke significantly, "you're not such a saint yourself. They say you've got quite a bundle of sins to your credit."

"I'm sure of it," said Heshel quietly. "But I learn about the glory of my Creator from my sins, too."

Mayerke winked broadly and gave a coarse laugh. "Seems that in your book the Holy One and the female sex have gotten tangled together." He and Shayke turned off abruptly, and took a path between two piles of snow.

Watching them go, Heshel blinked in the hard bright light. "Infants!" He smiled, shaking his head.

A few minutes later Ziame came hustling by on his way to work. Running along beside him, trying to keep up, was

Reb Avrohom-Elya Karp, his beard fluttering like the tail feathers of a hen caught in a crosswind. He panted a remark to Heshel as they passed. "Good morning, I'm working on him to nationalize a few rubles for me, so that I'll have something to eat for *Shabbos.*"

Ziame tossed at look at Heshel and called out after him, "To synagogue? Don't you know there is no kingdom in heaven?"

"Ha-ha-ha!" Reb Avrohom-Elya's laughter trailed behind him.

They were gone, and Heshel continued on his way, his face shining and his eyes darting over the sparkling expanse of snow. He had not quite arrived at the big synagogue when Reb Avrohom-Elya caught up with him again, and rumbled in his ear.

"Did you transact some business today? Earn anything?"

"No business at all."

"No? So what are you so happy about?"

Heshel looked around at the morning landscape. "When you see a vessel of fine quality, it makes you happy."

Reb Avrohom-Elya thought the reference was to himself, so he replied with all due modesty, "That applies only to an undamaged vessel. But when, for our sins, the vessel is broken?"

"Actually, the good Lord has a special love for broken vessels," Heshel explained gently. *"Manin tavirin,* as the Kabbalah puts it. What can I tell you? 'The Lord is nigh unto them that are broken of heart.' "

"Yes, yes, broken of heart. . . ." Reb Avrohom-Elya turned the idea over in his mind. "This is a generation of bitter deeds, bitter as gall. They hate doing a Jew a favor, like you and I hate pork."

"Nu, to work!" Heshel smiled as he pushed open the door of the synagogue. "We're day laborers in the employ of the Holy One, blessed be He!"

102

Yankel Potchtar managed to get to Poritchki, the district capital, by pushing his way on to a train packed with soldiers returning from the front. They were crushed together inside the cars, hanging from the windows and overflowing at the doors, clinging to the ladder and crouched on the roof. It was no easy trip for Yankel, who could neither stand not sit, but had to make the journey crushed between the soldiers, half suspended, scarcely able to breathe. He thought he would never get out of there alive. One soldier did fall off the steps, breaking his ribs. Another lost his hold on the roof, fell to the tracks, and was run over. At Voloshki, a railway junction, the chatter of a machine gun kept the crowd in the station away from the train. Even so, some of the people broke through and made a run for it. There were casualties.

Yankel risked his life to this extent, not so much for business purposes as for the sake of seeing something of God's big wide world, in order to find out what was going on in those changing times. After all, his principal avocation was talk, conversation, newsbearing. He was a sort of town crier, which is how he got his nickname in the first place, for Potchtar means "Postman," he whose sack bears something new each day. To a man like that, what greater deprivation can there be then to be confined to a little town where nothing ever happens? And what does happen repeats itself, like *Ashrei* repeated three times daily in the prayers? So he made the trip, and was gone for some time.

When he returned he was like a new person, a man-of-action who had been to the big city and mingled with the crowds and looked into recent developments, and could answer any question about what was going on in the world. In short, he filled a public need, and was entitled to public esteem and admiration.

The most important news he brought back was confidential. It had to do with those local merchants whom Polyishuk had arrested and sent to prison in Poritchki. Yankel reported that they were out of jail, free as the birds and in the best of health, all busy trading in the marketplace and doing quite nicely, thank you, every single one of them: Hayyim-Meir Shklianka, and Reb Shimen-Yossel, and Reb Yitzhok-Yakov, and Reb Nachman, and Reb Osher Zaslavsky. Yes, their wives have known about it for some time, but pretended not to know, and quite rightly too, considering the dangers involved. What's more, the men have managed to get money to their wives several times, to keep their households alive. Even Reb Yakov-Yosef Lifshitz, who had been sent all the way to the capital of the province, was now safe in Poritchki. Oh yes, you can add to the list the three Mensheviks: Hirshel the clockmaker, Avremel Voskiboinikov, and Nachman the tailor; they're there all right, wandering around the marketplace like horses out of harness, pouring fire and brimstone on comrade Polyishuk. You ask, Why then don't they return to their homes? For fear of Polyishuk!

The people stood around wide-eyed with astonishment. "Nu! . . ." The exclamation held a note of doubt.

"Upon my word," he took his oath to them, waggling his newly trimmed beard. "So may you and I live in peace, as it is true that I saw them and spoke with them. Why, I even . . . well, all right, I'll let you in on a deep dark secret, on condition that it remains strictly between us. I brought letters and a little money to their womenfolk."

Another thing he told them was that the market in Poritchki was open, and trade had not been forbidden. No, merchants sit in their stores and sell quite openly, and nobody objects, nobody lets out a peep.

"What the comrades have established in our community is not in force over there," he rolled his eyes at them meaningfully.

"Not in force there?" His listeners looked at one another dubiously. "What are you saying? Why are you telling us such fairy tales? What do you mean, not in force there? So what is in force?"

"Everything as it always was." He spoke softly, like a spy passing on secret information. "The market is in operation, the merchants are in their stores, the vendors are at their stalls, everybody is at his post. The only thing is, it would be nice if they had some merchandise to sell. See, the Revolution hasn't made trade illegal, it's only in our town that the comrades are stricter than need be, because they think they're better Communists than Lenin and Trotsky. But it's not something the Revolution ordered. No, there's nothing to show that all these things are ordered by the Revolution."

"You mean to say they have no law of *kontributzia?*"

"Absolutely not."

"And no nationalization?"

"No nationalization. True, I heard speculation that it's bound to come, but so far, there's no law. For the time being, it hasn't been enacted. The thing is, our local authorities follow the ancient motto *z'rizin makdimin*—enthusiasts start early."

"So then, the Revolution hasn't changed anything?" They sounded incredulous. "Folks there are living in a regular paradise enjoying the fat of the land?"

"What? Enjoying the fat of the land? May the enemies of Israel know such enjoyment, *Ribbono-shel-Olam!!* What the people there have is *tsores*, nothing but troubles. Business is absolutely dead, buried nine cubits in the ground. Sure, the stores are open, but what good is that? There isn't an earthly thing to sell. You doubt it? All right, you tell me, what should they sell? Troubles? Headaches? Used poultices? Why, ten dealers compete for one handful of sugarlumps, and twenty merchants vie for a bit of saccharin. Finished fabric? None to be had. Notions, drygoods? Forget it. And do I have to tell you there's no sign of a nail, a hoe, a rake. As for food—not even a leftover crumb. 'Fat of the land' indeed! Don't make me laugh!"

"So how do people live?" they asked more gently now, attuned to the familiar symptoms of despair.

"Barely," he answered. "It's a bitter life, bitter as gall. Whoever has a few rubles in cash lives off it, and manages to keep body and soul together, but that applies to very few. Most of them never had any ready money. Why do you have to ask? They drag themselves along painfully in God's good world. Not to speak of a new affliction, to round out an already full inventory: requisitions."

"Requisitions?" voices protested from every side. "But didn't you say they don't have requisitions there?"

"Who, me?" Yankel put his hand on his heart and looked around at them. "I said no requisitions? Nothing of the sort. I said: no *kontributzia,* no *natzionalizatzia.* But requisitions? As much as your hearts desires! And do they squeeze, my, oh my, do they bear down! All the authorities at the same time, each one for itself."

"What do you mean?" they wondered, protesting. "How many authorities are there?"

"Ho-ho-ho!" Yankel's hand reached high, with a rising inflection to match. "All kinds of authorities, nine bushels of demons, all vying with one another, all at odds with one another, disputing noisily like a cloud of starlings coming down on one tree. They've got the Ispolkom, the Executive Committee of the Council of Soldiers, Workers, and Farmers—that's number one. Then there's the Voyenrevkom, an Army outfit, that's number two. Plus the Staff Against Counterrevolution, that's number three. Now, all of these get their authority from the same Bolsheviks, but they're all independent of one another, so each one is a boss in its own right. But wait, I'm not finished. There's also the Commissar of the Rada, plus five bigshots called the Piatyorka, who scare the daylights out of everybody, but don't ask me what they're for, because nobody knows. In short, one's a goat and the other a sheep, but they've got one thing in common—requisitions! They show up and put their hands on everything that isn't nailed down. To top it all off, you've got the Anarchists. They're in a class by themselves —outright murderers, God preserve us! Cruel, merciless. No requisitions for them. No, my friends. They're specialists in something called 'ex.' What is it? Let me explain. An armed band comes flying up in an automobile and all of a sudden they stop and break into a house. First off they hang out a black flag. Then they haul out the owner, and plunder the house, loading the loot into the automobile. After that they make an announcement all up and down the street, inviting everybody to come and help himself to what's left. Then they're on their way, singing, whistling, shouting, firing shots into the air. A job like this is called 'ex.' People are scared to death of these fellows. As soon as they see one of those black flags on a house the whole street panics, and people begin running around in confusion, every which way. Such fear! Absolute terror! Believe me, I'm not handing you any hearsay, I'm telling you things I've seen with my own eyes. One morning, last Thursday it was, a big automobile drives up to the house of Reb Baruch Rapaport—you know, the one who used to be rich, people said he was worth quite a few thousand rubles. Anyhow, they stormed into his house and took out everything—the big mirrors, his gold and silver bric-a-brac, all sorts of precious items. They cleaned the place out like the tailbone of a herring, and off they went. I should so live in peace as I'm telling you what I myself witnessed. Other people told me about a lot more happenings, and that's only part of what's going on. Awful, terrible things, God preserve us!"

He would wind up his report with a few gems of irony, and conclude hopefully, "But we have a merciful God in heaven!" The truth is, however, that he was never really finished. He always thought of something more to say, and he always found someone else who had not yet heard his report, so that he was like a perpetual fountain. He described a meeting at which Bolsheviks, Mensheviks, SR's and Anarchists had contended with one another, all of them wise, all of them orators, all of them as full of Marxism and other such Torah as a pomegranate is full of seeds. They debated, they disputed, they argued, they beat one another over the head with their texts, until finally the Anarchists pulled out their revolvers and started shooting. The Bolsheviks returned fire, the Anarchists threatened to blow the place up with hand grenades, the whole audience screamed and yelled and pushed and stepped all over one another—in short, a situation described in the Good Book: "The mountains rose, the valleys sank down."

He remembered another episode. The Bolsheviks had dragged Reb Shmuel Moreino off to the cellar of the *shtab* and murdered him, down there in the cellar, for nothing, nothing at all, the man was innocent, but the way things are now, there's no judge and no justice. Some say the murder was done by Volko, son of the old *shochet* by his second wife, but others claim it was a *goy* who killed Reb Shmuel, a certain comrade Kirilo, son of a priest or a deacon, or some other offspring of the *dukhovnoye zvaniyeh,* the Orthodox clergy.

Another incident involved the Anarchists. They raided a nunnery on the other side of the river, and what they did there shouldn't be mentioned, some of the nuns are already in a delicate condition. Those Anarchists, they're living it up. Made themselves at home in the beautiful big courthouse building, with two machine guns set up at the main entrance, eating and drinking and making merry, and they say some of those nuns don't need any urging to drop in.

"To sum it all up," he said with a knowing wink, "they're living the life, like God in Odessa."

"However," he went on, "there are all kinds of fishponds, and not all Anarchists are cut from the same cloth. Now take Sorokeh, he's a breed all by himself. If you listen to the people in Poritchki, it's Sorokeh who's responsible for the whole plague of Anarchists. According to them, he's the fountainhead of that brand of impurity, the dean of them all, the bearer of the true doctrine of Anarchism. He started his career by paying a visit to his uncle, Reb Moshe-Yitzhok Sorokeh, his father's brother. He, as the whole world knows, was a wealthy trader and contractor in Kolobrod. Well, his nephew held him up at gunpoint and robbed him of ten thousand rubles cash, keeping only a little for himself, but turning most of it over to the band of Anarchists he organized as a commune. These were a motley crew of young fellows, a mixed bag of activists and lazy good-for-nothings and cripples. In this way there came to pass the beginning of the Anarchists, according to their habitations.

"Now, they say that before very long there was a falling-out between Sorokeh and the rest of the gang, especially between him and a certain Sasha Anarchist, a murderous, cruel, violent fellow. Nobody knows for sure what they quarreled about. Some say it was over a matter of principle, a regular dispute for the sake of heaven, like between the schools of Shammai and Hillel. But some say it was over a woman, a pretty little thing, scarcely more than a child, Nadia, her name was. How they did fight over her! One was like flint and the other like iron; one a true-blue Anarchist and the other a double-dyed Anarchist. They say that in the end it was Sasha Anarchist who won, and expelled Sorokeh from the commune, and even took his machine gun away from him, the gun that Sorokeh wanted to shoot up the commune with."

Having reached this climactic point, Yankel stopped, well satisfied with his performance, and calmly picked his nose, coughed a few times, and blew on his cupped hands. Then, when he felt he had brought his audience to the right pitch of suspense, he resumed.

"I suppose you think that's it? The story's over? Not at all, my friends! Sorokeh's not the kind of person to take this sort of thing lying down. He waited until Sasha Anarchist was busy with the rest of his gang carrying out an 'ex,' then came along and caught him unawares, and *trakh!* He shot him with his *livorvet. . . .*"

"Killed him?" his listeners asked fearfully. "Killed?"

"Almost killed," Yankel answered calmly. "Wounded him. He still hasn't recovered. That's how Sorokeh happened to come to our town."

Yankel had more to tell, and he played his role for all it was worth. His listeners stood around with mouths agape, rolling their eyes, sighing deeply.

103

Mokry-Kut was abuzz with rumors. Nobody knows who started them or how they spread, but the whole town was whispering. Not that anybody had any real information, just a general feeling that something was about to happen. What? That depended on who was doing the whispering.

Some said, "A great liberation is in the offing."

Others, "A great catastrophe awaits us."

The predictions reflected their authors. Yankel Potchtar

was the most self-important. He walked around like a man with a great secret, a smug look on his face, his lips tightly compressed, a knowing smile barely concealed. Wherever he saw a group of people he would join them, and in a trice take over the conversation.

"They're on the verge of bankruptcy," he would whisper, looking about to make sure the coast was clear.

"Everything points in that direction," the others would agree.

"Just . . . you . . . wait!" he would draw out the words. "They'll pull them down from their pedestals, that they will! No doubt about it."

"Who will?" All eyes were upon him. "Who'll bring them down?"

"There are those who will. Never fear."

"The Ukrainians?"

"The Ukrainians too."

"And who else?"

"What do you mean, who else? What about Kerensky? Do you take him for a dog? What do you think, he's sitting around doing nothing? No, my friends and brothers, he's been negotiating with all Europe, he's been rousing the whole wide world, America, England, France! It's no laughing matter, what the big fellows are doing. There's still some order in the world."

"Nu, and Leibele"—referring to Trotsky—"will he just sit and take it?"

"Eh!" His gesture was like brushing off a fly. "What's Leibele, in the face of all that power? Why, they have huge armies, tanks, planes and those big artilleries."

They were impressed. "How do you know all this?"

"A little birdie told me," he fended them off.

"So you mean to say they'll break off their war with Fritz and come to fight the Bolshevik?"

"And why not? They'll even join hands."

"With who? With the Germans?"

"What then, with you?"

"Eh, that's a lot of nonsense."

Whereat Yankel put out his palm and whispered, "Want to bet? How much?" And seeing that none cared to risk money, he adopted a high and mighty tone. "We'll see who turns out to be right."

"We hope you're right!" they replied. "One hard fact is worth more than all the imaginary curtains of King Solomon."

Reb Simcha wanted to hear the latest news, so he went out into the street. He discovered Yankel Potchtar holding forth to a group of men gathered behind the house of Mordkhe the liquor dealer. Reb Simcha listened for a while to Yankel's prognostications. Then he challenged him.

"Wouldn't you be willing to settle for less?" Yankel had no idea what was meant, so Reb Simcha spelled it out. "Nu, without the Germans, for example?"

Yankel glanced around fearfully. "Oh no," he said. "They'll all form one alliance!"

"You don't say." Reb Simcha wagged his head. "And who, pray tell, gave you this information?"

"It's well known. Everybody says so."

"Aha. Everybody says so." Reb Simcha surveyed him contemptuously. "Don't be such a blowhard, Yankel. You hear? You'd better keep your mouth shut, or you'll get into trouble with the powers that be. Take my advice: go. Go home and keep quiet."

What Reb Simcha had warned about came to pass that very day. Mayerke and Shayke seized Yankel Potchtar and took him to the Revkom, marched him into an inner room, and beat him within an inch of his life. His screams could be heard from one end of the street to the other. Then they picked him up and threw him outside, bruised, battered, bloodied.

"Go be a hero to your wife," they told him. "Boast to her that you got away alive!"

104

Yankel Potchtar was beaten so badly that he took to his bed. The whole town learned of the outrage, and wherever people gathered it was the prime topic of conversation.

"Imagine, they hit people!" Eyes were raised to heaven at something so unheard of.

The women cursed Mayerke and Shayke without stint, and lumped the rest of the Bolsheviks in with them. "May their hands wither, *Ribbono-shel-Olam!*" they whispered.

Surrounded by a company of sympathetic women, Hindel Potchtarnitza, Yankel's wife, wept softly and steadily. She was a little woman, shriveled and sickly, her face the color of wax, her nose sharp and shiny, her eyes a constant drip.

"They found the right customer for a beating," she wailed like a sick hen. "A poor man like him, with all kinds of ailments, a quiet person who never harmed a fly, woe to my days and years! When the nanny-goat is little, the fences jump all over her!"

Old Bluma posted herself on the street in front of her house, and waited to catch Mayerke and Shayke on their way to work. They came along whistling a song, caps at a jaunty angle, revolvers on hip, boots shining in the sunlight like burnished mirrors.

She intercepted them. "A good morning to you, boys."

"A good morning and a good year. What can we do for you, granny?"

She spoke in a tone of gentle reproof. "Tell me, if you don't mind, where do you get the nerve to beat up a poor Jew? What is this? Is this any way to behave? Beating up a poor man with a wife and children! Who are you, anyway? Hooligans, God forbid? Ruffians? Aren't you Jews?"

"The dog deserves the stick, granny."

"But what did he ever do to you? Did he break any of your laws? He didn't do a thing, except maybe talk too much. So what? It's human nature to talk when you're with people."

"There's talk, and there's talk," they answered. "You'd better watch your own tongue, granny, and don't stick your nose into what's no business of yours. Be a smart old lady, and keep quiet."

"And if not, what will you do to me?" She adjusted her kerchief and smiled in amusement: "You going to arrest me? Hale me into court? Ha-ha-ha! . . . Aiee, boys, boys! Don't you know that the good Lord notices the suffering of the poor, and sees to it that accounts are balanced? Why, He makes it rain for the sake of one blade of grass, one petal of a flower. Don't get any ideas, dear boys. There's justice, and there's a Judge! Yes, indeed!"

The boys showed her their teeth in a broad, coarse laugh, and went on their way. She remained standing for a few minutes, nodding her head at their retreating backs.

"Oy, how shameful!" she muttered. "Something new they've introduced—beatings! . . . Nu-nu, big heroes! Authority suits them like a pearl fits a sow!"

105

The peasants hardly ever took their produce to market any more. Instead, they would go into the houses of familiar townspeople, to barter for household goods and groceries. Some called on Reb Mordkhe-Leib, others on Reb Ozer Hagbeh, some knocked on Reb Simcha's door.

One fine morning, a day all snow and sunshine, Yokhim dropped in on Reb Moshe-Meir the Ladder and his wife, Dobbe. The couple welcomed their peasant visitor as though he were a long-lost relative, sat him down in the kitchen, inquired after his health, his family's health. Yokhim sat there enveloped in his huge white sheepskin, looking like his own white oxen, stolidly chewing their cud after the day's work.

"What's doing in Varnitsa?" Reb Moshe-Meir asked.

"Doing?" Yokhim measured his words. "Happenings. Yes. All sorts."

"You haven't been around in a long time," Dobbe joined in.

"Why should I show my face?" Yokhim answered quietly. "I've got nothing to show."

"We think of you as our friend," said Dobbe, ingratiatingly.

Yokhim sat for a while in solemn silence. When he spoke, he seemed to be changing the subject. "All kinds of piddling deals, but no real business."

"It's the bad times," Reb Moshe-Meir lowered his voice. "Dangerous."

"Uh-huh," Yokhim agreed. After a few moments, he

added, "Seems they're in charge. Every lazy nobody, every misfit. The tough guys, ours and yours, a plague on them."

Again a silence, and again it was Yokhim who spoke. "They stopped the war, now they've started up again. Stopped and started, it seems. They said, they were going to parcel out the fields. Yes. When we die, they'll give us six feet of earth. But meantime, there's no *makhorka* to smoke, no kerosene, no hemp oil, no thread, no nails. Not a thing. God in heaven, you can't find anything in the market!"

Reb Moshe-Meir signaled his wife, and she left the room.

"What time is it?" asked Yokhim.

"Time?" Reb Moshe-Meir looked around. "It's still early. I did have a watch, but I gave it to Svirid Rudy for a sack of flour. Today I could get three sacks for it. . . ."

Dobbe came back into the room. She brought two little bags of *makhorka* and a small package of black thread.

"Here you are." She put them down in front of him, like somebody sharing a deep secret. "Hide them in your pocket, don't let anybody see, God preserve us."

Yokhim slowly pocketed the hoarded merchandise.

"Kerosene?" he asked. "Oil . . . ?"

"No kerosene," Reb Moshe-Meir answered. "No oil."

"How about salt?"

Dobbe again left the room and returned with a fistful of salt. But now it was her turn to ask.

"What did you bring?"

Yokhim didn't answer. She waited patiently as he sat there unmoving. After a while he got up and went outside, returning in a few minutes with a sack in his hand. Dobbe put her hand into the sack and pulled out some cabbage stems, a few beets, a black radish, a bunch of onions.

"No flour?" she asked, disappointed.

"No flour," Yokhim answered calmly.

"Millet? A little spelt?" Then she launched into her bargaining speech. "Do you realize how high thread is these days? *Makhorka*? Salt? . . ."

That was the moment that Eisik Koysh chose to walk in. He had seen Yokhim's team of horses standing out front, and he had a pretty good idea what they were doing there.

"Greetings," he said ceremoniously, rubbing his hands, his eyes taking in Yokhim and Dobbe and the sack on the floor. Dobbe lost no time in pulling the sack out of the kitchen.

"How has God been treating you?" Eisik inquired.

"I thank the Lord above," was Yokhim's calm response. "We take the rough with the smooth. That's the way it goes. Winter. No work. No way to earn a kopeck. The sugar factory's closed, the horses are unemployed. What can a body do? It's God's will."

Dobbe returned. Her face was dark with anger.

"Why did you have to barge in?" she complained.

"What's the matter? Did I make you lose a treasure?"

"You butted in between us and our *goy*."

Eisik laughed hugely. "Yours?"

"At the moment, he's in our house."

"What's that supposed to mean?"

"The meaning is plain: Go, go home."

Eisik Koysh was flabbergasted. A scowl spread over his face. "What's she chewing her cud about?" he said to the ceiling.

All this time Reb Moshe-Meir had been occupying Yokhim's attention with small talk in Ukrainian, while his wife and Eisik quarreled in Yiddish.

"I'm chewing my cud?" Dobbe was incensed by the insult. "Get out of my house! Now, right away!"

No longer able to ignore the racket, Reb Moshe-Meir glanced at his wife. "Quiet!" he scolded. "Shut your mouth, stupid cow!"

Yokhim looked at them with a smile which might have

signified astonishment, but might just as easily have indicated pleasure.

"So that's the way it is?" Eisik Koysh lowered his voice and addressed Dobbe. "All right. But don't think for a minute that you're going to swallow that mouthful so easily."

"What are you going to do to me? Hale me into beggar's court?"

"You'll see. By the time I'm finished, you won't want to ask for a better stew. Everything will rise to the surface of the pot."

"What's going on here?" Reb Moshe-Meir turned on Eisik. "What surface? Whose surface? Which surface? What are you threatening me with?"

Eisik Koysh didn't answer him. Instead, he turned to Yokhim. "Come with me," he said to the farmer. "Come to my place. I'll have something for you." And so saying, he stamped out of the door.

106

All kinds of reports continued to reach Mokry-Kut, some explicit, some vague. They were like distant echoes, distorted rumbles. Nobody came forth to explain them, to offer a commentary. Yankel Potchtar still lay confined to his bed, and none could replace him. So the townsfolk remained in the dark about the meaning of it all.

One report had it that there had been a clash in Poltava between the armed forces of the Rada and the Council of Workers and Peasants. It was also reported that the Bolsheviks had been completely pushed out of Odessa, where power was now in the hands of a coalition consisting of the Central Rada, the Mensheviks, and the Social Revolutionaries.

The people grasped at these Job's-comforters' tidings.

"Sounds like *they* are on very thin ice."

"Certainly sounds like it."

They were especially encouraged by what they heard about a certain General Shcherbatchov, who was said to have disarmed the mutinous troops on the Rumanian front, and arrested their officers and Commissars, and what's more, sent a force of ten thousand officers and men to Odessa, in support of the Rumtcherod, a Council representing the army group on the Rumanian front, the Black Sea fleet, and the Odessa district.

When this report reached them, they nodded sagely, and exchanged knowing looks, and exclaimed, "Aha!"

Suddenly, the said general, whose name they had never heard before, became their hero, a great leader who could do no wrong, and against whom no force could prevail.

"Ah, General Shcherbatchov!" they whispered to one another. "He'll show them! With God's help, he'll put an end to them! Just you wait and see!"

In this fashion the people sustained themselves from one rumor to the next, each report providing them with the desired proof that the downfall of the Bolsheviks was imminent.

They also quoted a certain Bird-Son, in support of the proposition that the Bolsheviks were in trouble. Sorokeh, which means "crow" in Russian, had been given this code name as a measure of security—walls have ears, you know. Word was passed along the grapevine, quoting him, that in most of the urban centers, and of course in the villages, the law of the Bolsheviks no longer obtained, and where it supposedly did, it was being disregarded. Kharkov was in a state of confusion, Ekaterinaslav in a turmoil, the Bolsheviks were fighting for their lives in Lozovaya, in

Pavlograd, in Sinelnikovo and other cities, not to speak of the Don Basin.

When the news arrived about General Shcherbatchov, the townspeople sent a small boy to the bath-house to find out Sorokeh's opinion. After a while, the lad returned with a message.

"Bird-Son says thus: One insect breeds many, and one worm is the father of a host of worms—Krasnov, Kornilov, Kaledin, Alekseiyev, Dutov—them and their progeny, them and the likes of them, but all of them malignant growths spawned by the counterrevolution, and all of them boding nothing but evil for Israel, for all of them will turn around and take out their frustration on the Jews."

The recipients of this intelligence passed the word on, whispering excitedly. "You hear? You hear? All generals, all commanders, and they're all warring against the Bolsheviks! He knows what he's talking about, he gets all the newspapers. Too bad he has that one-track mind, God preserve us, and all he can think about is self-defense. But the main thing is, all those generals!"

107

One evening the whole crowd was over at Liuba's, some of them playing cards, others fooling around with experiments in hypnotism. Ziame was making particular efforts to put Masha into a trance, when suddenly Kayla burst into the room with a queer expression on her face. "Come," she gasped. "Come and see what's wrong with Ethel."

"What's the matter?" they looked up, astonished. "Where is she?"

"In the kitchen. Lying on the floor. . . ."

Everybody ran to the kitchen. They found Ethel doubled up in a corner, her hand over her heart, her face twisted. "What's the matter?" Luiba bent over her. "What's wrong, Ethel?"

"I drank . . . I drank . . ."—choking and grimacing between one groan and the next.

"What did you drink?" For a moment Liuba thought Ethel had found some *samogon* and gulped it down.

". . . that." Ethel's eyes indicated a bottle of kerosene that was lying beside her.

Minna promptly shooed everybody out of the kitchen, leaving only herself and Liuba, along with Masha, who refused to leave. The widow Brakhah got out of bed to lend a hand. She turned Ethel over, face down, put two fingers into her mouth, and forced her to vomit. When Ethel had recovered from these exertions, Brakhah managed to get her behind the curtain and up on Liuba's bed, where she sat consoling her in whispers.

"Foolish child," she whispered.

Liuba, Minna, and Masha went back to the rest of the gang, who jumped up and began pelting them with questions. "What happened? What happened? Why did she drink the kerosene?"

"She was trying to commit suicide," Liuba whispered.

"But why?" Ziame was upset, even more than the others. "Such a shy, quiet girl."

At this, Minna flew off the handle. "You have some nerve to talk!" she scolded. "What right have you got to offer sympathy?"

"What's wrong?" Ziame was the picture of puzzlement. "What's the matter?"

"The matter, the matter. . . ." Her voice dripped sarcasm. "You're to blame, and you're sorry for her!"

"I'm to bl—?"

"Yes! Yes! You!"

Ziame looked around helplessly at the comrades, silent spectators at this drama. "Me?"

"Don't play the innocent fool!" Minna lashed at him. "You know perfectly well that she's crazy about you!"

"Crazy about me?" Ziame repeated.

The comrades burst out laughing. "So that's it!"

"What's all this you're pinning on me?" Ziame tried to understand. "I haven't the least idea."

But by now the comrades were making him the butt of their amusement. "Ziamke!" they teased. "Don't play hard to get!"

"But I swear it, as I live, I don't know what this is all about. She never said a word to me, not even half a word, no hint, even."

"Nu-nu, tell us some more fairy tales!" they mocked. "We already know how much you don't know."

Masha decided that it was time for her to get into the act. "For the past several weeks I've noticed that haunted look in her eyes," she breathed. "This evening I watched her sitting there, and her eyes were popping out, she watched every move he made."

"Really?" Ziame was astonished. "I had no idea, I must have been blind."

"Ha-ha-ha!" the comrades roared with laughter.

"Whinnying like a bunch of horses!" Minna whispered with suppressed resentment. "Low creatures!"

Sukhar noticed how upset she was. "Don't worry," he said. "It'll be all right. She won't come to any harm. Kerosene isn't a dangerous poison."

Ziame was still in a state of shock. "What a strange thing. What could have happened to her? I'm not worth any of this, I give you my word on it. Oh me, oh my! What could have come over her?"

In a little while Ethel was recovered enough to leave, and Minna and Liuba escorted her home. Shayke watched them go, and he seemed to be doing some deep thinking.

"Liubov nye kartoshka," he said, half to himself. "Love is not a potato."

"It's a lucky person who passes the test," said Masha reverently. "Many hearts are broken, but only a few have the courage to take the step. What can you do?"

"Well, it's time to get going!" said Mayerke, giving Shayke a slap on the back, and proceeding to pull down his earlaps and put on his gloves. "Nu, who's coming along? Let's go!"

108

Ethel was now famous. She was celebrated by the young people, denounced by the older generation.

Her contemporaries were all agog. "That's what you call love!" they said. "Ready to die for it, to commit suicide!"

The older folks rumbled angrily to one another. "Plumb out of their minds, those girls! The world's gone crazy, a plague on our enemies. So she drank kerosene, hah? What do you say, I ask you? Kerosene she drinks!"

Some tried to turn it into a joke. "Now we know why the price of the stuff has gone up."

It was the womenfolk, naturally, who took it hardest. They shook their heads and hurled their imprecations and spat to avert the evil eye, pooh! pooh! pooh!

The widow Bluma was most deeply pained by the episode. "Oy!" She rocked to and fro, keening. "Oy, she's taken my head off!" The old lady made it a point to seize hold of the girls, wherever she could, and engage them in conversation, pleading, reproving.

"Listen, my darlings, listen to what I'm telling you. Love

is good for nothing. All you get out of it is a bellyache. Listen to me, my daughters. Leave the Revolution alone for a while, and go get yourselves married to husbands."

Meanwhile, Liuba and Minna busied themselves with Ethel, hovering over her, showering her with affection and sympathy. Soon the three girls became fast friends, bound together by a pact of loyalty. They spent all their time together, sharing confidences, exchanging views, indulging in fancies.

Minna decided to keep her distance from Sukhar for the time being, until she was sure of her feelings.

"I want to probe my innermost being," she said, "to the utmost degree."

One idea that came up in the course of their intimate talks was that they might all go to Palestine together. As youngsters, they had been members of a Zionist club called Children of Zion. The Revolution had taken them onto a different track, but now their earlier interest was reawakened, partly under the influence of Sorokeh, but more especially under the influence of Dena. They became convinced that the self-realization and inner wholeness they sought, the spiritual completeness and the life of idealism they so longed for—this awaited them in one place, and one place only, in the Land of Israel.

"There, there . . . ," murmured Minna, half closing her big blue eyes, her voice filled with yearning, as though she were seeing in the far-off distance a Land of Israel already rebuilt and resettled.

However, the three did not become members of Tseire Tsiyon, claiming that they preferred the rival Hechalutz organization. They were joined by Yasha, who informed them that he was a secret Zionist. He began teaching the girls the Hebrew language. Now all their dreams were centered on the Land of Israel. "Palestine, Palestine . . . ," they repeated at every other word.

They knew every little about this Palestine of theirs, a

bit about Degania and Kinneret, the new communal settlements, something about the Jewish laborers and watchmen. But their lack of knowledge was offset by the great love that burned in their hearts, a love informed by the dreams that reached out and converted that far-off land into a legendary habitation.

"Do you think we'll ever see the Land?" Liuba sighed to herself.

Ethel sat there lost in thought, her pale round face and quiet eyes bespeaking a sad troubled world of inner reflection.

"How will we ever get there?" she pondered.

"We'll get there, we'll get there!" Minna's rosy cheeks shone like the pink of a cold winter morning. "We'll be like the storks that fly off in the fall to sunny lands. We'll spread our wings and fly."

109

The introspection and the boredom got to be too much for Sorokeh. He pulled himself together and went outside.

It was not much of a day. The dark sky was like a solid gray prison wall. The air hung murky and damp. Sorokeh made his way through the snow that overflowed onto the footpath, wondering what a person could do with himself under such forbidding gray skies.

He emerged on Post Office Street, and walked along aimlessly. In the meantime, it had begun to grow dark. There was no sunset, the sun not having put in an appearance all day. Night simply came on, the horizon disappeared, the snow looked whiter than before. He walked slowly, as if strolling with a companion, deep in conversation. Then he stopped, as though the invisible companion had gone on, and he himself was left standing alone in the heavy silence.

Here and there points of light appeared in the windows. To Sorokeh they failed to suggest scenes of family warmth. On the contrary, he told himself, blessing has vanished from Jewry; no longer do parents sit with their children around the table, eating and drinking and rejoicing in one another.

Loneliness.

Out there in the middle of the street he felt with a special sharp stab of poignancy how bereft and forsaken was his people, how absolutely alone, with no one to turn to.

Slowly he moved on, his feet sinking in the soft snow, until he came to the edge of town and could go no further. He turned back. By this time it had begun to snow, heavy flakes falling slantwise, making it hard for him to see where he was going.

Sorokeh straightened up, thrust aside his melancholy reflections, and strode along briskly, turning and twisting his head to avoid the snowflakes, which in spite of his efforts kept catching him, now on the nose and mouth, now on his eyelashes, now on his neck or behind his collar. He laughed out loud. It was as if the snow was playing a game with him.

It occurred to him it would be nice to drop in on someone, but he couldn't think of anybody suitable. Then suddenly he remembered Piltch. "Hah!" he exclaimed aloud. "That's it! The old bachelor."

It didn't take long to get there. He found the pharmacy closed, but a ring of the bell brought Piltch to the door, growling as he opened up. "Whom has the devil blown here?" He put the lamp down on the table and peered out.

"Greetings, old bachelor!" Sorokeh called out lightly.

"You?" Piltch was taken by surprise. "Where from, you footloose wanderer? Nu, come on in."

He led Sorokeh into his living quarters, behind the pharmacy. It looked like a regular middle-class dwelling, the kind that a son might inherit from his father. A round table, topped by a kerosene lamp, occupied the center of the room. A big wide couch stood against the wall, with four upholstered chairs scattered about. There was an ornately carved cabinet in one corner, an overloaded bookcase in another. The fire burned gaily in the stove, a chirping cricket seemed engaged in competition with the big heavy clock that ticked away on the wall.

Sorokeh spread his hands over the stove. "How comfortable," he said. "Not at all like a bachelor's quarters."

"My dear sir," Piltch answered with a straight face. "These are not a bachelor's quarters. These are the quarters of a pharmacist."

"Ah . . . ," said Sorokeh, for want of anything better, and sat himself down on the sofa. He waited a few minutes, looking around the room. "Signs of a woman's hand," he said.

"Of course. Odarka."

"The maid?"

"Uh-huh. . . . Care for a bite?"

"No, thanks."

"Waiting till you people finish creating the perfect society? Nu! So be it. But you'll drink some tea?"

"Pour."

Piltch set a kettle of water on a small alcohol burner. The water soon came to a boil, and the two of them sat there drinking camomile tea, sweetened with mints.

Their conversation ranged far and wide. Piltch took the occasion to poke fun at those young Jews who had become stalwarts of the Revolution. As far as he was concerned, he had no faith in these young heroes, nor in the idea that it was possible to create a just society.

"The Jews of old postponed the perfection of mankind to the days of the Messiah," he said. "And not for nothing: they were realists."

This remark gave Sorokeh an opening, and he proceeded to pour forth his concern for Jewish survival.

"What will become of this people?" he said passionately. "It has been forsaken by its own children, they've dedicated themselves to mankind as a whole."

Dressed in a brown robe open at the neck, Piltch sat relaxed beside him, his heavy lower lip slack, his bulging eyes looking at the floor.

"What do you care?" he asked.

"I'm not sure I understand you." Sorokeh used his sleeve to wipe the sweat from his forehead. "This camomile of yours is powerful stuff! . . . As I was saying, how can a people survive the loss of its next generation? And what can it possibly expect for itself out of all this confusion?"

Piltch made it a point to keep silent, and Sorokeh went on. "The economic base of the Jewish population has always been precarious, but now it's been cut right out from under their feet. This people hasn't got a leg left to stand on. There's a total break between fathers and sons. You're not dealing with two generations, but with two opposites, two worlds that have nothing in common."

"You see things very clearly," said Piltch, taking one foot in both hands and tucking it comfortably under his thigh. "So?"

"It's a tired people you're talking about," Piltch said with a sigh. "Tired of itself, tired of others. All it wants is to rest."

"What do you mean?" Sorokeh broke in sharply. "When you say rest like that, it can only mean death."

". . . tired, weary. . . ." Piltch seemed not to have heard.

"You can even say, it's not a people we're talking about, it's a religion. A religion on the way out. Both individually and collectively. Yes, my friend. Not one of them is concerned about national survival, but all of them are concerned about religious survival. Well, almost all, all except a handful of Bundists and dried out Zionists, but they hardly count. It's a religion we're talking about, and religion by its very nature stands above time and place. It's fixed; if you will, frozen. No past, no future, unchanging in great things as in small, whether the commandment be major or minor. Unalterable in tradition and custom. If you lay a single finger on any part of the whole structure—"

"Wait, wait, not so fast." Sorokeh interrupted.

Piltch looked at him with a cool eye.

"All right. What word of wisdom have you got to offer?"

Sorokeh was thrown off balance, and could offer only a protest. "According to you, then, it's all over, we're doomed?"

"That's not up to me, and not up to you. In any case, you can't help them, because you've left the fold. You've stopped observing the religious commandments. You're an outsider now."

Sorokeh was thunderstruck. "What are you saying?" He looked at him, wide-eyed. "What are you trying to tell me?"

"Just that. Do you wash your hands before you eat? Put on *tefillin?* Say grace after your meals?"

"Therefore, you mean to say I'm not a Jew?"

"Therefore, therefore . . . ," Piltch echoed sarcastically. "Correct. Therefore you're not a Jew. You nationalists, you Yiddishists, you Zionists—all of you want to be Jews and gentiles at the same time. That's just not possible. You've got to make a choice, it's either one thing or the other. This whole concern of yours for the survival of the people comes from the non-Jew in you, from the part of you that denies its own essence, from the self-despising element in you. Unlike the youth of other nations, young Jews don't love their own people, and never have. Certainly not like the young Russian intellectuals, the *narodniki,* who went out to serve *their* people with heart and soul. No, our young intellectuals judge their own people harshly, and find them wanting, either rejecting them, or trying to change them, to improve them. Forget all that nonsense. It's a wornout people, all its got is *bitokhen,* blind faith. It has the destruction of the First Temple, and the destruction of the Second Temple . . . and it has *bitokhen.*"

"But that's not faith, that's fatalism, a counsel of despair. It's irresponsible."

"All right, all right, but it's all they've got. Anyhow, it's no business of yours. Go busy yourself with the problems of the Russian people. Burn down manor-houses, burn down anything you can find."

"The fire you're making is more destructive than any fire I ever started," Sorokeh retorted bitterly.

Later, on his way back to the bath-house, he thought over his conversation with Piltch.

"There isn't a word of truth in anything that he said. But notice, the Jewish people doesn't need outside enemies to destroy it. It carries the seeds of self-destruction, all kinds of them, within its own body!"

110

Sorokeh's mind was a fever of disjointed reflections. The sum total was the story of his life—disintegration, chaos, meaninglessness. Never very far from the center of his unhappiness was Nadia, who had left him for another man. Yes, she who had loved him so completely, she who was beautiful, so very beautiful, she had walked out on him. How was it possible? Where were her feelings? All of a sudden her power of resistance had evaporated. How had it happened, how? Was this Nadia? The Nadia he had once known? Had she changed, become somebody different? Or had she been different all along? Still, what had made her do it? Well, nothing, really. Whatever had driven her into his arms in the first place had driven her into the arms of . . . of . . . *that one.* Not her fault. Nobody's fault. If anybody's, then his, Sorokeh's. Yes, his own fault that she had left him. The very fact that he had shot *him* showed up his weak, flawed, twisted character. For her sake he had been willing to give up, not his own life, but another man's life! She was right to have walked out on him.

The more he examined himself, the more negative were his conclusions. He discovered that there was no substance at all to his cherished certainties, including his intellectual Anarchism and his emotional love of his people. He decided that there was no hope for him, no future, just as Anarchism had no future, in the face of the fierce tide of the Revolution. . . . Ach, there was no way out. Emptiness and chaos. He himself was just a casualty of the breakup of Jewish existence. As a matter of fact, that explained everything about him: his rebellious nonconformity, his skepticism, his alternating bouts of determination and defeatism, his utopian impatience, and his lack of spiritual moorings. So that's where his Anarchism came from—it was a legacy from his forebears!

The revolver in his pocket pressed against his thigh. He took it out and began to toy with it. His eye fell on the trigger. Aha! One squeeze—and all his problems would be solved. How easy. One squeeze—and after that nothing. Finis. . . .

The barrel glinted in the light of the fire. He remembered the glint in Nadia's eyes, the arch of her eyebrows, her sidelong glance. Wherever she was now, was she thinking of him? Now, at night, in her bed, wherever, remembering? Ah, memories, memories. . . . The memory of Israel is the memory of mankind, from earliest times. The nations of the world have short memories. . . . Every kingdom and state has its allotted span, but Anarchism is exempt from the life-and-death cycle of states . . . it can go on and on, to the end of time. . . . Maybe after all he should leave everything behind and go to the Land of Israel? That's where the world got started, maybe that's the best place for a fresh start? It would be a good place to try out Anarchism as a way of life. . . . But no. The people won't go. They're a people of optimists, depending on miracles, trusting in the millennium. . . . A decrepit people. All old folks. Mired down in their Mokry-Kuts, the way he is stuck now in this abandoned old bath-house, sitting there creating a new society. . . . Critical times. The fate of the world is hanging in the balance. The Bolsheviks have chosen the way of violence, and they're getting the upper hand. They've dispersed the Constituent Assembly. Good, they deserved it. . . . One day he's sure to walk out on her. Wait, what's that? Only a gust of wind. . . . When it does happen, will she come back to him? Certainly! It can't be long now before *that one* deserts her. Probably by the time the snow melts. Oh, absolutely! . . . Then what? She'll come back to him. . . . Will he take her back, or reject her? . . . He'll take her back! Of course. She'll be the old Nadia again, from the happy times . . . radiant as sunshine, with her full moist lips, tossing her head from side to side gaily, like a young mare. . . . He won't hold her to account. Far from it. No matter what happened, he'll forget everything. He'll take her the way she is. And yet . . . ultimately, he's bound to put her to shame. Oh, not deliberately, not on purpose, certainly not. It'll just happen by itself. And when it does, she'll find a way of taking revenge—on him? Yes, on him! . . . It's not logical, makes no sense, but that's how it will be. Nu! So she'll take it out on him. How? Wouldn't be surprised if she killed him. Or herself. Or maybe both of them. . . .

Outside the wind moaned louder, filling the vast expanse of snow with its despairing lament. An express train rushed by in the darkness. To Moscow? Petrograd? To Petrograd! That's where he should go! To Lenin and Trotsky —to shoot them down! Aha! That's the answer! That's what he had been looking for, without knowing it. It all falls into place. What do those others amount to, those generals, Kaledin, Dutov, the others? What value has all this petty sabotage? Lenin and Trotsky, they're the ones—destroy them, and put an end to all this cursed turmoil! Of course, Nadia will help him. She'll jump at the chance, eyes closed, no questions asked. It's just the kind of action she would go for, tailor-made for her. . . . Afterwards? Oh well, who knows how long he's got to live? Sure, they might be seized on the spot, torn limb from limb. Or maybe put on trial and sentenced to—

"Eureka!" He put the gun back in his pocket, a beatific expression on his face. Now that the scales had fallen from his eyes, he could tell the difference between the inconsequential and what was really important. Odd, it was his isolation that had given him this perspective, yes, the solitude and the snow and the long nights—and more than anything else, this abandoned old bath-house, never intended as a place of human habitation, and now become a sort of ruin standing in the middle of this sad Jewish town, itself a miserable half-burned ruin. Here, in this place, he had been able to withdraw into himself, to find out who he really was. It was here that he had turned inward and organized all those ideas that had been racing through his brain, and here that he had come to terms with all his doubts and disappointments and frustrations. Imagine, from this lonely spot he had reached out by the sheer power of thought, and been able to put his finger on the very pulse of world history!

And what a great plan he had hit upon! It was to be a deed commensurate with the grand sweep of his ideas, a blow struck for liberty and the betterment of mankind. It would guarantee him a place in history, his name would be enshrined for all time in the annals of heroism and glory.

He went over the plan in his mind very carefully, analyzing its every aspect, and finally deciding not to use a bomb. No, a revolver would be better. Shoot them while they were on the platform at one of those big public meetings. Better still, catch them beforehand as they were entering the hall, or afterwards while they were on the way out. The plan was sure to succeed. He was confident that he and Nadia could carry it off. Granted, something might go wrong, they might get caught. Certainly, it was a risky business, dangerous. Ah, but that was just the thing: the grandeur of the act was in direct proportion to its danger. As for death, he wasn't afraid of it; this wouldn't be the first time in his life that he had looked death in the face. All his days he had been like a tempestuous river, rushing along between an intense love of life on the one side, and the intoxicating allure of the decisive act on the other. In any case, he was living dangerously every minute of the time; that went automatically with being an Anarchist.

In the excitement that now took hold of him there was still another ingredient, perhaps unacknowledged. Thoughts of suicide, explicit or suppressed, were a not insignificant part of his makeup. These tendencies made his scheme seem all the more attractive.

Now he knew what he had to do. He would carry out his plan with the help of Nadia. Of course, there were details to work out. For example, which of them would shoot Lenin? He could almost hear Nadia exclaiming eagerly, "Me!

Me!" All right, let her have her way. Let Lenin fall by her hand. It would bring her back to him . . . if they lived. And if not? What if death was in store for them? So be it. But wait—maybe he should keep Nadia out of this danger, not let her risk her life, take *him* along instead?

"Salka da'atakh?" he said aloud, using a familiar phrase of talmudic reasoning, as though he were back at the yeshiva studying Torah. "Is this idea conceivable?" His answer was immediate. "No, only Nadia! No one else but Nadia!"

The combination of love with the thrill of mortal danger swept over him in a wave of certainty. "She," he murmured, "she." Images of Lenin and Trotsky filled his mind's eye and helped harden his resolve. Now he was possessed, as with a dybbuk, on fire with his idea, his spirits soaring, his heart beating fast.

111

Freyda went out to the marketplace. No sooner had she left than Hillik came to the house, simply opened the door and walked in. Nehama-Itta was taken aback, and stood rooted to the spot. Still, she gave him a civil greeting.

"Good morning," she said, with a questioning look.

"Good morning," he answered.

"What can I do for you?"

"You the mistress of the house?"

"Why, what's the matter?"

"Oh, nothing." He pulled up a chair and sat down. "I was passing by, so I dropped in."

It occurred to Nehama-Itta that she might unwittingly

have fallen afoul of the authorities. She decided to brave it out.

"Thank you for doing me the honor," she smiled.

"You have a daughter," he announced. "And she has two children."

"That's right." Nehama-Itta fluttered her eyelids.

"You see"—his tone was officious—"nobody hides anything from us."

"Yes," the old lady answered. "I have a daughter and two grandsons. What's to hide? Everybody knows it."

"She's a widow."

Nehama-Itta said nothing. She just stood looking at him. After a pause, her visitor continued.

"Quite," he said. "Quite. . . . And then, there's somebody who takes his meals here. Is that so?"

"Nu, there is somebody. Sorokeh." Hastily she added, "Not that he gets much in the way of meals. Our table is empty, our cupboard is bare."

"That's just it," said Hillik. "That's what puzzles me."

"What puzzles you?" She raised her eyebrows.

"Oh nothing," he said. "Still, it can't be easy . . ."

"You're right," she assented. "It isn't easy."

". . . these days when trade isn't allowed."

"But we do earn a little something from him. A bite to put into the mouths of the children."

Hillik got up to go. "If I were you, I wouldn't take in any boarders these days." Having delivered himself of this remark, he bade her goodbye and went on his way. He left Nehama-Itta wondering what it was all about.

Before long Freyda was back, empty-handed and unhappy. "Not a thing," she said. "What am I going to give him?" She looked around as though confronted by a decision she didn't know how to make. "The whole world is being punished," she complained. "How does a body cope with this? I'd be willing to flee to the Mountains of Darkness!"

At noon Sorokeh arrived, bringing with him a loaf of bread, a horseradish, and three onions. The women were overjoyed.

While Sorokeh was at the table Nehama-Itta came and told him about her uninvited visitor.

"Who was he?" Sorokeh asked.

"How am I supposed to know?" she answered testily. "I didn't ask for his pedigree. All I can tell you is, he was one of theirs, a real pleasure to behold, with a 'livorvet' on his hip."

"Short fellow? Tall?"

"Well, he had a long horse-face and high shoulders."

This left Sorokeh completely in the dark.

"It's a mystery," said the old lady. "What could he have been after? It's very strange."

"They've got something against me," Sorokeh explained.

"Who has?" The old lady was astonished.

"The *livorvets*," Sorokeh joked. "They want me out of the way."

"Let them only not find something to charge us with," said Nehama-Itta doubtfully.

"Don't worry, grandma. They're a bunch of good-for-nothings."

A few days later he went off to the village. When he returned, he had something to eat. Then he asked if anybody could go to the pharmacy and get him some aspirin. This was most unusual, since he had never before asked for anything. Freyda went on the errand, leaving him alone with Nehama-Itta.

"They say you're not a Bolshevik," the old lady stated.

"No, I'm not a Bolshevik."

"What then?"

"An Anarchist, grandma."

"What's that?"

"An Anarchist is a person who rejects all laws and regulations."

She found this difficult to comprehend. "What do you mean? He doesn't come under the law?"

"That's right."

"No law at all?"

"None at all."

She turned that over in her mind, and gave him a sidelong glance. "How is that possible?" she asked. "Everything in the world comes under some law. The whole of human life is one law after another. Look at me. I'm old —old age is a law. Everybody dies. Death is a law, one that never changes."

Sorokeh was nonplussed. He had no answer for her. Then he burst out laughing. "See how bad law is? It even kills people!"

The following day Nehama-Itta told him that the pharmacist had been there, asking for him.

"Where?" Sorokeh was surprised.

"Right here, at our house."

The next day she repeated the message. "He was asking for you again."

"Who? The pharmacist?" Sorokeh was astounded. "He was here?"

"Yes."

"When?"

"At nightfall."

Before the week was out a rumor had swept through town that the pharmacist wanted to marry Freyda.

112

The course of events threw Sorokeh into a state of great agitation, and he scarcely knew what to think. The fixed points in his universe had come unstuck. He would have to leave Mokry-Kut and plunge into the maelstrom of confusion that was sweeping the country, to see what he could make of it.

As between the Bolsheviks and the Whites—the generals who were trying to overthrow the regime—his choice was clear. He would side with the Bolsheviks, because the Revolution had to be given priority over everything else. Willy-nilly he must favor his ideological enemies. But he would extract a price for his support. He would insist on a supply of weapons, and a sizable war chest, to equip and support the Jewish self-defense. Whether they liked it or not, even against their will! To be sure, he had no idea how he was going to accomplish this, and he spent a lot of time thinking up schemes and laying plans.

On the other hand, Polyishuk and his comrades were quite unperturbed. They went about their business as usual, and as usual some of them dropped in on Sorokeh to argue with him. He kept a rein on his tongue, and didn't tell them what he was planning to do. But they persisted in drawing him out, until finally he revealed the trend of his current thinking. It took them by surprise.

"Ha!" they laughed triumphantly. "Now you're singing the same tune as us!"

"Not because I favor Bolshevism," he resisted stoutly.

"Only for the sake of the Revolution. Everybody must rally 'round to save the Revolution."

"Exactly," they replied. "Bolshevism is synonymous with the Revolution. Every revolutionary must end up by becoming a Bolshevik. It's the only way." Mayerke gave him a nudge of the shoulder. "Your program is bankrupt, comrade!"

Shayke drove the point home with one chapped finger. "We've cornered the market!"

"They're right," comrade Ziame told Sorokeh in the friendliest kind of way. "When all is said and done, you're going to find yourself at one with us, shoulder to shoulder. You can't help it—it's the inescapable logic of the Revolution."

In a little while Leahtche came to see Sorokeh. She was in a turmoil, fear in her eyes. "Sorokeh!" Her screech was like that of a gull skimming the waves on a stormy day.

"What's wrong?" he asked.

"You . . . you're . . ."—she was breathing heavily, she couldn't speak.

"What? What? What happened?"

". . . going away?"

"Yes, Leahtche." He put his hand on her shoulder, with a helpless smile.

"What? You're going to leave me? . . ."

"It's what the Revolution demands." An ultimate reason, unanswerable.

"But why?" She touched his hand and looked him up and down, as though begging for mercy. "It would be so easy—"

"No, Leahtche," he interrupted gently. "It's not easy."

"It's only . . . only . . . the force of circumstances. . . ." She scarcely knew what she was saying.

He led her to the bench and sat her down and tried to calm her.

"All right, all right," she nodded, with a vacant smile. "But I'm not sure you're right."

She spoke rapidly, as if there wasn't a moment to lose. "Yes, I understand that political events dictate what we must do. Yes, the Revolution takes priority over love. Don't think for a minute that I don't understand. I do! I do! But at the same time, I think your calculations are all wrong. Just as I wish good fortune for both of us, and that you and I may live in peace, so am I convinced you're making a big mistake. Everybody says so. Polyishuk says there's no ground for all those nervous fears of yours. The proof is, the Red Guard has been sent here to help, from Moscow, from Petrograd, from Minsk. Before you can turn around there won't be a hint of counterrevolution left in the whole area."

Sorokeh insisted that she was wrong, that they were all in great danger. "What more proof do you need? You yourself said it—they had to send in reinforcements from Moscow and Petrograd! No, it's our duty to step into the breach and help save the Revolution. There's no time to lose! Everybody has got to do his share!"

"But you're mistaken!" Her hands were spread out, pleading; there was a suppressed sob in her voice. "If it was what the Revolution needed. . . . But it isn't! Polyishuk said so, and he knows what he's talking about, he has access to sources of information—"

"Ach," he interrupted her. "Don't bother me with the likes of Polyishuk!" His face was twisted, as though he were in physical pain. But now the floodgates were open, and he was unable to keep his thoughts to himself. "Those miserable creatures. The only reason they're Bolsheviks is that the Bolsheviks are winning. If the SR's had gotten into power, they would be SR's. It all depends who has the upper hand. They're despicable, the lowest of the low. All they've got is their stupid cruelty, the pleasure they take in pushing people around, that's all there is to them!"

Even as he talked, Leahtche whispered his name forlornly. "Sorokeh." He seemed not to hear.

"Tfu!" he actually spat out. "They've turned cruelty into an ideology, they've made a system out of it, a policy. A lot they care about the Revolution, those miserable reptiles! Socialists! Don't make me laugh! Revolutionaries! Ha!"

"Sorokeh!" she threw herself tearfully into his arms. "You're leaving me, and I'll never see you again! Don't leave me! My darling, my life! Don't leave me. . . ."

113

Leahtche alternated between rage and resignation. Her whole being was now caught up in a confused storm of inner conflict, in which everything she had ever thought or experienced, every feeling whether acknowledged or suppressed, all her dreams and longings—all clamored within her.

She was bad company for herself, but even more snappish with any of the comrades who came near her. She was constantly involved in petty quarrels, flying off the handle, throwing on the floor in helpless rage her pencil and ruler and whatever else came to hand.

"What's the matter with you?" the comrades asked, in tones of innocent inquiry, meantime exchanging significant looks. "What's happened to you, Leahtche?"

She didn't answer them, but whispered her anguish to herself. "Ach, everything's gone sour for me. I'm out of luck."

She tortured herself endlessly with gloomy and despairing thoughts, and with a mental bill of particulars against

Sorokeh. Yes indeed, he was a useless idler, unwilling to accept responsibility, a footloose intellectual without roots, unreliable, insubstantial, and much more of the same, all of which was ground she had been over many times before.

"I was a fool to believe him," she lectured herself. "All he was ever interested in was a bit of fun. But you—you got what was coming to you, serves you right. You can't blame him, he never pretended to be anything more than a fellow interested in girls. But you're a thousand times worse than he is. Serves you right, nobody forced you, nobody held a knife to your throat. You did it yourself, with your own two hands!"

Having worn herself out with all this self-flagellation, she changed her tune. "Eh," she comforted herself. "It's my good fortune that he's leaving. After all, what would I have to look forward to with him? A home in the bath-house? Or following him around like a Gypsy from one place to another, one village to the next? How lovely! . . . It was a mistake on my part to prefer him to Polyishuk. Polyishuk is worth a dozen of his kind! Why, Polyishuk is a clear-cut person, you know where you stand with him. He's a straightforward revolutionary, responsible, disciplined, it's men like him who are the backbone of the Party. Ach, too bad, too bad!"

Her thoughts were also laced with scorn on the whole idea of romantic love. A useless business, she told herself sternly, a snare and a delusion invented by idle wastrels to beguile petty-bourgeois men and women, a plague on them. They had nothing better to do with themselves, since their lives were empty of honest toil and real-life problems.

"We don't need all this empty foolishness," she declared to herself. "We've got enough of a challenge in the Revolution, and work, and . . . and . . . and a plague on all of them!"

The truth is, all these efforts to talk herself out of the misery of her unrequited love were useless. Her heart was heavy, and her misery rose up in her throat as if to choke her.

"There's no hope for me," she whispered, as though condemned to death. "I'm doomed, woe is me!"

And then—to the devil with all this calculation. Throw it all on the rubbish heap, and run to Sorokeh, run. Close your eyes and leap into the whirlpool and let yourself be swept away! The thought took hold of her like a fever, and gave her no rest. Her whole body was atremble, she was like a caldron brought to a boil.

She sat with her eyes closed, her heart pounding, her cheeks red. Nothing was clear to her any more, she just couldn't think straight.

114

Looking and acting as though she had taken leave of her senses, she rushed off to Sorokeh—but he wasn't there. Compulsively, she ran back to his place a second time, and a third, and still he was nowhere to be found. She stood in the empty, frigid bath-house and clasped her hands in anguish. "Ach! Where is he? Where can he be?"

She went outside and walked around the back of the bath-house, along the river, pushing her way through the piles of snow, while the thoughts in her head went round and round, swinging her from one pole to the other.

One minute she was telling herself, "I'll find him, come what may, and whatever happens to me will happen!"

The next minute she was thinking, "If that's the case, decide right here and now how you want to die. People will tear you limb from limb."

In the debate that followed she was both advocate and antagonist. "What do you care what people think? Aren't you a free person? I should be answerable to my own will, not the will of others. I ought to live while I'm still alive!"

"It won't be living, it'll be ruining your life. All in one moment, ruining it."

"I don't care!"

"Don't say that! You certainly do care!"

She passed in front of the bath-house again, knocked on the door, got no answer, and went on her way. Slowly she proceeded along the narrow alley, between the humble houses with their snow-covered roofs. Her feet threshed a path through the piles of snow now trodden into dirty slush.

"Ach-ach," she sighed. "Human beings have fenced themselves in with all sorts of prohibitions. People just don't know how to accept happiness!"

She made her way out to Post Office Street, and went into the Bolshevik clubhouse. It was empty. She started to leave, but before she could open the door, in came Muntchik.

"Ah, Leahtche!" he exclaimed, surprised and pleased. "What are you doing here at this hour?"

"Nothing." Her face still reflected her state of mind.

"Good that you came!" He couldn't conceal his pleasure. "I'm so happy. . . ."

"What makes you so happy?" she retorted, her hand on the doorknob.

"Don't go," he begged. "Stay a little. . . ."

"What's the matter with you, Muntchik?" She acted both puzzled and concerned. He didn't know what to say, but stood embarrassed, not looking at her, a guilty smile on his trembling lips. Leahtche looked him over, raised her eyebrows, and gave a quiet sigh. Then she opened the door and went out quickly.

Muntchik followed her out. "Leahtche...." his voice was barely audible.

She walked on, oblivious.

"Leahtche...." She stopped, turned around, and looked him full in the face.

"What do you want?" she asked. "Why are you following me?"

"I wanted to tell you"—his smile was apologetic— "maybe you haven't heard about it.... They're starting a commune. Next week they start—"

"Who?" her whole expression changed. "Who?"

"Quite a few."

"Tell me who?" she insisted.

"Well, Polyishuk, Ziame, Sukhar, Shayke, Mayerke, and—"

"And what about girls? Not a single one?"

"How can you ask? A commune without girls! We're not talking about a monastery! This is going to be a commune!"

"So, which ones?"

"It hasn't been settled yet." He wanted to keep the conversation going. "There's been a lot of discussion about it. Some say Kayla—"

"That stick of wood!" Leahtche interrupted.

"Ha-ha-ha! That stick of wood!" laughed Muntchik, trying to curry favor. "And some say Masha...."

"Nu," she prodded.

"And maybe Rosa. I know they're discussing it with Liuba and Malia. And maybe you too, Leahtche. Hah? What do you say?"

She shrugged one shoulder. "Goodbye," she said, with ill-concealed anger.

Muntchik blinked as he stopped in his tracks and watched her disappear down the street.

115

A circular arrived from Zionist headquarters, calling on the members of Tseire Tsiyon "to mobilize all hands able to work, for the rebirth of the Land." The circular declared, among other things, that unless Jews performed the actual industrial and agricultural labor in Palestine, the country would never become Jewish.

A lot of young men and women joined the movement. It was their intention to go out into the villages as soon as spring came, to learn how to become proper farmers.

Dena shared her secret with Leahtche. "I'll soon be leaving for Dzhankoi," she whispered, all aglow.

"Where's Dzhankoi?" asked Leahtche.

"I haven't the least idea," laughed Dena. "They say it's somewhere in the Crimea or the Caucasus. But don't worry, I'll find it."

"Why are you going? What'll you do there?"

"*Hakhsharah!* Agricultural training! I'll work in the fields. There's somebody or something there, I don't know, maybe a farm or an estate."

"Will you be traveling alone?"

"Oh, no. With Senye 'Farmer,' and Sioma. And of course my brother, Yasha."

"Yasha?" Leahtche was astounded. "You must be mistaken, Yasha is one of ours."

"Not so much yours as you think. Our movement is growing fast."

Leahtche was silent for a moment, then she spoke up. "It's all a mistake, a fatal error. . . ."

"Not at all! You Bolsheviks are planning to change everything, and we'll change everything too."

"How can you compare!"

"I'm comparing," Dena retorted. "We'll make our own revolution, I promise you."

Leahtche looked at her as if she were seeing her for the first time. "Don't go, Dena," she said. "Listen to me, don't go. I beg of you."

"Sorokeh thinks we're doing the right thing."

"Sorokeh? You listen to his opinion? Why, he's a regular pendulum."

Dena burst out laughing. "Pendulum. . . . Sorokeh a pendulum . . . ha-ha-ha! A human being hanging inside a clock like a pendulum. Imagine! Ha-ha-ha!"

"He moves to and fro between yes and no," Leahtche explained. "Now you understand?"

"Oy, Jews, Jews." Dena wiped the tears from her eyes. "Too bad Ruvke isn't here. He would explain to you that what you call a pendulum, moving between the poles of yes and no, of temporary and eternal, is just a synthesis. I heard him say something like that once. *Synthesis!* You understand? That Sorokeh of yours is not a pendulum, and not a human being, he's a synthesis. Get it?" And again she laughed uproariously.

When she had caught her breath, she asked a question. "What do you think, Leahtche, is a synthesis good or bad?" She thought about it for a while, then said, "I'll have to talk that one over with Sorokeh."

"No, don't do that," Leahtche said hastily. "Don't do it."

"Why not?" Dena was puzzled.

"Because . . . because . . . the pendulum will stop swinging."

The two girls looked into one another's eyes and burst out laughing.

"All right," Dena gasped when she could. "I won't talk to him about it. Too bad about the pendulum."

After a while, Leahtche, her laughter completely evaporated, hinted darkly, "As a matter of fact, you'd be better off to avoid talking with him altogether."

She interrupted herself, and when she resumed, it was more like thinking out loud.

"The truth is, he's a hunter, if you really want to know. A hunter out after game. He's a nomad, like any hunter, he never stays put. What excites him is the chase, the prey, whether it's big game, or small. He lies in wait, spreads his net, makes the catch, kills his prey. End of game."

"All right," Dena answered humbly, "I'll talk to him as little as possible."

Leahtche didn't answer her. Instead she whispered to herself, "I'm going out of my mind."

116

She ran around everywhere looking for Sorokeh, but couldn't find him. "He's not here," everybody replied to her inquiries. Freyda added, as though speaking of one prematurely departed, "He's already gone from us."

The fact however, was that Sorokeh had found much to do in the few days before he was to leave. He and Dena were busy with the schoolchildren, now that the teacher had deserted them to follow his wife to Kharkov. He also occupied himself with plans for Jewish self-defense, restated his views to a group of interested comrades, consulted with the Tseire Tsiyon on matters connected with their projected departure for Palestine, toured the nearby villages to pick up rifles from returned soldiers, so that he could turn them over to the Jewish self-defense corps.

Leahtche had been looking for him everywhere, but when she finally found him, the meeting was accidental. One day she ran into him on the street, as he went rushing by on one of his errands.

"Wait a minute! Wait!" she called out.

"Ah. . . ." His face lit up with surprise.

"Seeing you these days has become a rare privilege," she said formally, a note of complaint in her voice. "I eat no bread and drink no water, but run around looking for the day before yesterday. Where did you disappear to?"

"Busy, Leahtche, busy," he smiled. "I've had a million things to do, but today I finish up. I'll be free soon, in a couple or three hours—"

"No, my dear," she interrupted. "Make yourself free right now, and come along with me. Don't worry, your business won't run away."

"All right, all right." He took her arm and walked beside her. "How are you, Leahtche?"

"One drags oneself along," she answered, like an old woman. "And you, how've you been?"

"Busy, terribly busy."

Their conversation was halting, they didn't seem to have anything to say to each other. Finally Leahtche asked calmly, "Nu, when will you be leaving?"

"When?" he echoed, as though he hadn't given it much thought. "Tomorrow, the day after. To Moscow, Petrograd!"

"Already tomorrow?" Now there was a slight tremor in her voice.

"I'm waiting for news. There's a major undertaking. . . ."

"That's how I'm repaid for my honest penny." She said it to herself, eyes fixed on the ground.

They walked in silence for a while, she seemed to be concentrating on the sound of her steps in the snow.

"You're leaving me," she said in a low voice, "And I don't know which . . . what. . . ."

They negotiated two or three winding alleyways, and started to return. "I know," she finally whispered. "You're going away and you'll never come back."

"What makes you say that?" Sorokeh stood still, with a most peculiar expression on his face. "Of course I'll come back!"

"No, no." She shook her head and smiled wanly. "My heart tells me. Nu, let's leave that alone. It's a big wide world . . . yes. And the Revolution is big, too. . . . I'll remember you. I . . . I . . . ."

"Don't talk like that." Sorokeh looked at her imploringly, as if begging for her mercy. "I'll be back. Two or three months from now, at most."

"Yes, yes." Her choked whisper implied that she had expected him to say that.

Little by little she regained control of herself. They arrived at an intersection, the parting of the ways.

"Nu, Leahtche, I'll leave you now." There was an amber glint in the pupils of his eyes. "When it gets dark, come over to my place."

Leahtche looked at the ground. Her legs felt weak, her heart trembled, she said nothing.

"Will you come, Leahtche? Come, it's our last time. . . . Will you?"

He waited for her answer, but she didn't speak. Her lips parted, then closed again. Clearly, she wanted to say something, but didn't know how.

He bent close and whispered. "I'll wait for you! All night!" Then he turned, and walked quickly away.

117

She stood rooted to the spot, breathing heavily, her heart pounding. After a while she bestirred herself and went home. "What an operator!" she said to herself. She tried to make light of the encounter, even as tears welled up in her eyes.

In the house she found her father crouched over the stove, trying to get a fire started. His beard wreathed in smoke, he turned on her as usual.

"What's the matter, are you too delicate to tend to the stove? Look at her, running around from pillar to post, like an idle mare!"

She paid no attention to him, but went into her room. Even though it was still daytime, the room was bathed in the dull gray of twilight, filled with the wornout boredom of many years. The old commode stood there broad and bulky, as it had stood from the time of her mother's mother. Her own desolate bed, a big wooden thing with high headboards, also dated from that earlier generation.

Confused, heart-sore, weary of soul, she moved aimlessly around the room, glancing at the broken piece of mirror on the wall, and finally flinging herself on the bed just as she was, in her heavy overcoat and shawl. From under the pillow she pulled a book of Lermontov's poems, and glanced at a line here and a line there. From the adjoining room she could hear the sound of her father reciting the afternoon prayer. It was a desolate sound, as irksome as a fly's buzzing. She turned over and lay face down as though in a faint. A few moments later she jumped up and rushed out of the house.

She walked along the street at a rapid clip, in such a state of inner turmoil that she almost failed to notice a twelve-year-old girl carrying a pail of water in a hand blue with the cold, bent sideways by the weight of her burden, her tongue hanging out of the corner of her mouth.

"Greetings, comrade," the girl said adult-fashion, her little face glowing with pride and dignity.

The widow Bluma tapped on her windowpane. Leahtche looked up.

"Leahtche! Leahtche!" Bluma came out of her doorway. "Where are you going in such a hurry?"

". . . . Hurry!" Leahtche echoed without slackening her pace.

"Busy? . . ."

"No time. . . ." Leahtche shrugged one shoulder and moved on out of earshot. In order to get away from people she turned into Station Street, which led out of town to the railway station.

Beyond the town the fields were still blanketed in deep snow, one broad open expanse. It was colder here, and the winds blew stronger. The scene, the solitude, made her feel contemplative, rather like a thinker or a poet.

"Love can't be tamed," she sighed deeply. "Man has mastery over everything else in the world, but not over love. Even the Revolution, which has gained the upper hand over all comers, and turned everything topsy-turvy, hasn't managed to bring love into line, to control it the least little bit. By authority of the Revolution I can help myself to any piece of bourgeois property, or any rich girl's jewelry, rings, golden chains, pearls, anything I like. But what's really mine, the main thing, the essence, what I'm dying for, that the Revolution can't give me. . . ."

A cloud of powdery snow, caught up in a gust of wind,

swirled in the air like smoke. She bent her head down and turned her face aside.

"He doesn't love me. Quite the contrary, he's my opponent, almost my mortal enemy. I should come to his place! On his last night here I should come to his place, for God's sake!"

The sun started to set, and Leahtche turned back. "It'll soon be dark," she thought.

A sudden blast of wind from behind blew her forward three or four paces. She accompanied each step with a shout.

"No! I won't!"

Her anxiety increased as she got near town. She was sweating. "I won't go! I won't go to him!" Now she was whispering, her hands clasped together.

But in spite of putting all this determination into words, she was still not sure of herself, and the whole issue remained up in the air.

Out in the open spaces there was still some light, and the western sky slowly turned crimson. In the town itself, some shadows were tentatively red and blue and green, but most were unequivocally violet. Houses seemed mottled with colors running into one another, the piles of snow were turning gray, then blue, and the whole world seemed sunk under a heavy burden of bereavement.

As though she had something to be ashamed of, she bent her head and slipped quietly into the house.

118

Heshel Pribisker was pacing up and down the room, chanting a passage from Isaiah. *"Ranu shamayim . . .* oy-oy-oy . . . Sing, O heavens, and be joyful, O earth . . . *ranu-ranu-ranu,* bim-bam-bam . . . and break forth into singing, O ye hills, *rina-rina-rina,* oy-oy-oy. . . ."

He caressed each word lovingly, repeating it several times over, entwining the heavens with the earth and the earth with the hills, clapping his hands in Hasidic ecstasy, all fire and flame and feeling.

"Bim-bam-bam, bam-bam-bam, sing, 'sing, O heavens, rejoice, O earth,' oy-oy, Sweet Father! 'Break forth into song, O hills,' song-song-song, because You Yourself say it, *Ribbono-shel-Olam,* 'For the Lord hath comforted His people, He will have compassion on His poor ones.' "

At that moment Leahtche came into the house. A quick look at her, and his chanting ceased. He cleared his throat several times and coughed.

Reb Simcha was just finishing the concluding *olenu* of the evening prayer. "Leahtche," he turned to her. "Would you bring in a few pieces of wood for the stove?" She went outside.

Reb Simcha busied himself with one thing and another, then he lit the wick of the lamp. Meantime, Leahtche returned with an armful of wood, and dumped it on the floor. Reb Simcha bent over and put several pieces into the fire.

"Let there be heat!" He smiled contentedly into his beard. "Today we're going to have a feast worthy of King

Solomon in all his glory. Slaughter the bullocks, prepare the sheep!"

"Why, what's going on?" Leahtche asked supiciously.

"Heshel has brought us a herring and a whole loaf of bread." This with a broad wink at Heshel.

The warmth of the stove and the taste of the herring combined to induce a feeling of well-being in Reb Simcha, and he became more like his old self. Genially he presided at the head of his table, taking care, as a good host should, to keep Leahtche and Heshel involved in the conversation.

"Has something gone wrong today?" he asked Leahtche solicitously, speaking through a mouthful of herring and bread, sensing her sour mood, but not really expecting an answer.

When they had finished, he drank a glass of cold water, and wiped his mustache. "Thanks be to God," he smiled. "We have eaten our fill. I swear, no millionaire in America can be feeling the contentment that is ours at this moment!"

Leahtche took the lamp and went into the kitchen to wash the dishes. Reb Simcha and Heshel sat warming themselves in front of the stove.

"I wonder what's wrong with her?" Reb Simcha said, all compassion and concern. Heshel Pribisker made no attempt to answer.

Reb Simcha sighed to himself, and switched the conversation to the Bolsheviks. "You know what occurs to me?" he said.

"Nu?"

"Well, harking back to what you said, when you claimed that they have some of the characteristics of Hasidim, it occurs to me that what they really are is Misnagdim."

"Who?"

"Them, the Bolsheviks. Everything about them reminds one of the Misnagdim. Strict adherence to law, no mercy, without a drop of the milk of human kindness, of love, only the law itself. Iron and brass! Dyed-in-the-wool Misnagdim. Them and that Marx of of theirs, it's like a Misnaged in the presence of the Code of Laws. Dear me, the 'honor of the Torah,' tut-tut! No joy in them, not a spark. Even when they sing their tunes, they sound like Misnagdim, no sweetness of melody, no yearning of the soul. . . . Ach, if only the Revolution had been made by Hasidim, disciples of the Besht."

Leahtche came into the room, bringing the lamp back.

"Are you going out, or will you be staying home?" Reb Simcha's tone was placating.

"I don't know," she shrugged.

"Stay home, my daughter, stay home. It's warm here, nice. Why not make it an early night?"

Leahtche did not answer. She went into her room and closed the door.

119

As soon as she was in her room, she began to stiffen her resolve not to go to Sorokeh. "You're to be confined to this room for the rest of the night!" she admonished herself.

She sat in the dark and tried hard not to think of him, to make believe that he didn't exist. She forced herself to think of various matters, political issues, the course of the Revolution, the Constituent Assembly; Polyishuk and his crude manners; Shimtze, who would soon be leading Malia to the marriage canopy; Hillik and Liuba, who might soon follow.

Accompanying these thoughts was an unacknowledged but powerful yearning, stormy, restless.

"Patience," she told herself. "You'll get your share, your time will come, just so long as you pass this test. Tonight, just let tonight be safely over. . . ."

But it was no use. "He's leaving tonight, and he'll never come back," she whispered.

She went over and pressed her forehead against the frosted windowpane. All she could see outside was darkness, and the occasional glint of starlight on the snow. She turned away and walked slowly, with deliberate steps, her hands outstretched.

"Maybe I should go to the club?" she tried to fool herself.

"You won't go," she told herself, but with little conviction. "You will not go!"

She threw herself on the bed and buried her head in the pillow. "I'm lost, I'm lost," she sobbed.

After a few minutes she stopped crying, and lay there, buffeted by thoughts and imaginings beyond her control. The darkness and silence washed over her like some black ocean, filled with images of desire pressing against her flesh, of the touch of eager, probing hands, the delirium of bodily contact.

She jumped off her bed and rushed out of the house.

It was a cold blue night. The streets were deserted. The houses brooded in silence, their shuttered windows peering blindly at the world. Here and there an occasional sliver of light showed through. From off in the distance there could be heard the shouts of boys coasting on their sleds down some hilly street.

Leahtche walked as though stealing away. She was in a turmoil, confused and conflicted, wondering what would happen to her, feeling as though her entire life hung in the balance.

Halfway down a narrow street she stopped short. "Where am I going?" she asked herself.

She turned into an alley that led farther away from the old bath-house. "I won't go to him," she told herself firmly. "No matter what, I won't go!"

The night cold had failed to sober her, and her heart was still pounding, her breath coming fast. Every once in a while her footsteps turned toward the bath-house, but each time she caught herself.

"I don't care if you burst, you're not to go to him!"

Wandering through the alleyways like a woman pursued, she wanted to cry out, a bitter cry for the love that was leaving her, the happiness that was to be shattered forever. She raised her head to the moon, her throat choked with sobs, her eyes filled with tears. She discovered that she had wandered into a dead-end street and she had to turn back.

It occurred to her that Sorokeh was waiting for her. "Let him wait!" she told herself vengefully. "Serves him right, let him wait!"

Other thoughts followed in confusing succession. How strange, she wondered, how strange to be wandering the streets in the middle of the night, running away from my own happiness. Then she considered the possibility of going off with Sorokeh and following him wherever he went, and being with him always. Then she hurled accusations at herself, saying that she had a head stuffed with nonsense, and that she was unworthy of the Revolution, the Party, or anything in the world. In this fashion she proceeded from one street to another, until, wittingly or unwittingly, she found herself walking down the alleyway that led to the old bath-house. She stopped, looked around, quite surprised that her steps had led her to this spot. She lifted her chin and listened intently, but all she heard was the silence. Slowly, she took a few fearful steps and stopped again. Back and forth, back and forth, she didn't know what to do.

"Go back, go back." Her lips actually moved.

"It's all right, don't worry," she countered. "I'm only going as far as—"

"No, no. . . ."

"Yes, just up to that spot over there."

She stepped forward on tiptoe, listening carefully to her own footsteps. Soon she stopped within arm's reach of the bath-house and stood looking at the door. She went behind the building and stood in the shadows in a corner of the wall.

The bright stars seemed to be winking at her. She was reminded of the stars in a poem by Lermontov, and in her distraction whispered half aloud, "Solitary I go forth upon my way. . . ."

Stealthily, still on tiptoe, she went up to the door and put her hand on it. "One step," she thought, "one step and I'm in there with him."

She stood there, not knowing what to do, as though waiting for some miracle to make up her mind for her.

"I'll only tell him goodbye," she lied to herself. Once, twice, and again her hand went up to the door and retreated. Then she heard Sorokeh cough, and the sound of his footsteps as he walked across the floor inside. Fear took hold of her. With her head bent, still on tiptoe, she turned around and ran, ran all the way home.

120

She rushed into the house, panting. Her father was asleep. Heshel sat in the parlor, studying Torah by the light of the lamp. She took in the scene at a glance and went to her room. Her turmoil had not subsided. She wasn't sure whether she had just escaped from danger, and ought to feel relieved; or whether she was now doomed to a future of unhappiness. Perhaps putting it into words might solve the dilemma. "I'm lucky, it was an escape," she tried to tell herself.

But her whole being was filled with pain and yearning, and she was nagged by desire. How could she be sure that she wouldn't run out again, and rush back to him, to Sorokeh? Extreme measures were called for, so she decided to take refuge in the parlor. Stealthily, so as not to waken her father, she tiptoed out of her room and sat down near Heshel Pribisker.

"Don't be angry at me for interrupting," she whispered. "I can't stand being alone just now, let me sit here awhile."

Heshel lifted his eyes from the book, and pushed the lamp away from his elbow. His beard trembled, he was very pale.

"I'm afraid to be by myself." Leahtche was looking at the floor. "Talk to me, say something."

"What do you want me to say?" He looked at her searchingly.

"It doesn't matter. Anything."

"Did you just come in?" He didn't take his eyes off her.

"Yes, just now. It's a starry night. . . . Speak. Don't just sit there, say something."

"Were you with *him?*"

"Who? Oh, no. I wasn't with anybody." She was silent for a moment, then she added, "You don't like them, do you?"

He answered, speaking sadly, slowly, as though to himself. "In our long history we've had Prophets, and Sages, and Geonim, and Rabbis. We had the Holy Ari and his disciples, and the Besht and his disciples, and so on. And finally now these Bolsheviks: murderers, atheists. Sorokeh, Polyishuk and his crowd. . . . They, and gentiles of the same stripe, they think the world can be improved by means of bloodshed. But this world can only be improved by kindness and compassion. One word of love can purify the whole universe."

Leahtche was only half listening. She sat there absorbed in her own turbulence, cheeks flushed, eyes flashing. Heshel's eyes followed the shadows dancing on the wall and the ceiling, and he continued.

"This Revolution began because of the love of mankind, but it has turned out to be cruel, bloodthirsty, drowning in human tears. If it had been started for the sake of heaven it would have been full of love for people, full of joy and grace and lovingkindness."

"Keep talking, keep talking," said Leahtche, her fingers fluttering in her lap. Heshel regarded her with concern.

"Taken by itself, love of mankind amounts to nothing. On the other hand, the love of heaven, taken by itself, is the same thing as the love of our fellow-men. When God's in His heaven, Israel exists in the world. If, perish the thought, there is no God, then there's no Jewish people."

He was silent for a few moments, bowed in thought. "In this unbelieving generation," he resumed, "with the loss of faith among us, as well as among the *goyim,* the very existence of the Jewish people is in grave danger, God forbid."

"Nu?" The fact that she uttered the syllable was no proof that she was paying attention. He glanced at her.

"Unbelief is not so much a denial of God as a denial of man. It does not threaten the existence of the Blessed Name, but it does threaten man with extinction."

Leahtche fixed her gaze on the little flame of the wick, as it smoked and flickered and sent shadows crawling up and down the wall. Nothing had happened to calm down her thoughts, or her body for that matter. "If only I would get sick!" she sighed inwardly. "Ach, *Ribbono-shel-Olam!*"

Heshel was immersed in his own train of thought. "I think about it constantly," he whispered. "The whole thing is clear to me, it gives me no rest, but there's nobody I can tell it to. Your father won't listen to me, and I suppose he's got his reasons. Polyishuk and Sorokeh won't hear me out, for reasons of their own. Maybe I can talk to you, you're the only one. . . ."

He took her hand and whispered. "Never mind, it's enough for me that you're willing to sit with me, and let me see your face. Even that little bit of happiness is immeasurable. . . ."

Leahtche pulled away, guarded. She was trembling all over. "What's the matter with you?" She gave a forced, artificial laugh.

He leaned over and put his hand on her back. "Please" —she turned toward him—"please sit still. Don't talk nonsense."

He began to stammer endearments. "Beloved of my soul . . . beloved. . . ."

"You mustn't." Her voice had gone hoarse, as though she had suddenly caught cold. But there was a nervous smile on her lips.

"I think of you all day," he whispered, his head close to hers. "All day I see your face, you are with me, inside me. You are with me when I study, when I pray, when I am alone, sorting out my thoughts."

"Well, you certainly found something to say!" She fingered the fringe of her kerchief nervously.

"I don't know how to talk to you, how to tell you what's in my heart." His eyes had grown big, his face was pale as chalk. "I'm talking to you the only way I know how, the way I pour out my heart to Him. I love you with my last breath, I love you to the outer limits of my being, to the point of no thought and no feeling, so much that I don't know where I am and what's happening to me."

She was bent over, she could hear the unnatural pounding of her heart. Heshel Pribisker continued to pour forth endearments. He put his arms around her and kissed her neck, her lips, her eyes.

Silently she struggled with him, pushing him away with both her fists, writhing like a snake, turning her head from side to side, even biting him. And yet, unwillingly, she clung to him, and her lips touched his. A wave of desire engulfed her, and she was swept along. She could no longer think, her eyes were closed, her cheeks burning. It seemed that she was on fire, her body, her hair, her clothes. All of a sudden she stopped struggling. Her arms went around his neck, she pressed against him, and the two of them fell onto the sofa, locked in embrace.

"Let me alone. . . ." Her lips clung to his.

121

A stranger came to town, and asked where he could find Sorokeh. He was a young man, spare and quick-moving, wearing a sheepskin cap and big boots, a rifle slung across his back, a revolver and two grenades attached to his belt.

His progress through the town was watched from almost every doorway.

"Any idea what he's doing here? Who is he?" Since nobody knew, they had to fall back on speculation. Some guessed, "Probably one of that Anarchist bunch." Others speculated, a courier with a message for Sorokeh.

Chatzkl Kanarik fell into step alongside the stranger. "Who you looking for, comrade? Is it Sorokeh?"

Almost at the same moment he dropped his voice, and said out of the side of his mouth, "What's new? What's happening in the world out there?"

Chatzkl reported on the encounter: "Big doings very soon. A regular wedding-dance. 'Come along,' he said, 'rejoice with us, you'll be guests at the wedding. We'll be beating all the drums.' That's what he said, 'We'll be beating all the drums!' "

A few hours later Sorokeh and the stranger left town together. The townsfolk, undeterred by lack of evidence, were quite ready to draw conclusions. They exchanged many a knowing wink and enigmatic smile. "Nu . . . ?" They were certain that what they had seen was of major significance. The jig was up for the Bolsheviks, they were riding for a fall.

"It's clear," they said. "If you want proof, look at the sudden way Sorokeh disappeared, before you could say *shema yisroel.* And what about that young fellow, armed to the teeth? No, all this is not just coincidence."

Yankel Potchtar had not given up his avocation as the local interpreter of world events, but now he went about it a little more discreetly. He picked up reports and passed them on, launched a few good rumors and speculations of his own, and started whole whispering campaigns of inside information on politics, diplomacy, and military strategy. His general conclusion was an optimistic one:

"I'm not ready yet to trade in our chances for a sack of onions!"

The local authorities, meantime, went about their business as if nothing had happened. But the pundits weren't fooled, not for one minute. "Keeping up appearances," they comforted themselves. "They don't want the public to lose confidence."

The fact is, the government even tightened its reins. It outlawed the self-defense organization, and went around knocking on private doors in search of boots, blankets, linens, furs, and other supplies needed by the Red Guard. This affliction took the people unawares. The women stood about on the street like victims of a fire, like people burned out of house and home, complaining bitterly about the invasion of their houses by "that murderous robber," and cursing Polyishuk to a crisp.

But that was not all. Polyishuk now turned on the shopkeepers, demanding to know what had happened to the inventories he had listed.

"Where's it all gone!" he roared at them.

After talking it over among themselves, the merchants made counterclaim, demanding to know what *he* had done with their merchandise. One complained about his stock of groceries, his vanished notions, another bemoaned his lost textiles, his missing metal goods. Each insisted that he had turned over a big supply of merchandise that couldn't be replaced nowadays for ten pair of horses.

Polyishuk wasn't going to be drawn into any legal arguments. He simply waved his riding crop and said very slowly and deliberately, "I'll give you three days, from now until Friday noon. By that time you'll put back all of the missing merchandise. I don't want to find a single button missing!"

As they were leaving, a confused and murmurous group, they heard the gallop of a horse's hooves. It was none other than Karpo, mounted on the squire's Krasotka. He sat tall and proud in the saddle, his cap at a jaunty angle, his cowlick tossing in the wind.

"Down with the commune of the *zhids!*" he shouted. "Long live the rule of the Soviets!"

He reined in his mount in front of Revkom headquarters, pulled out his revolver and fired three shots in rapid succession through Polyishuk's window. The people inside poured our through the door. "Look!" they shouted in amazement. "It's Karpo!"

Even as they spoke Karpo applied the whip to the horse's flanks, right and left. The beast reared, whisked its tail, and broke into a gallop, sparks of ice and snow flying from under its hooves. As Karpo rounded the corner there was the sound of a single shot. Immediately an outcry filled the entire street.

"Chatzkl! He's killed Chatzkl Kanarik!"

122

Reb Moshe-Meir denounced Eisik Koysh as an informer.

"He tattled on us," he told his neighbors, citing as a motive the quarrel he and Eisik had had over the peasant Yokhim.

At first Eisik Koysh denied the whole thing. "I don't even know what you're babbling about," he insisted. Pressed to the wall, he finally admitted what he had done. "I only meant to get even with the 'Ladder,' but they put two and two together."

The whole community turned its back on him. The men showered him with abuse and contempt, calling him informer, criminal, reptile of the reptiles. The women resorted to richer curses, wishing that he might be shrouded in bedsheets, that worms might eat his flesh, that hellfire be extinguished while he continued to burn, and much more of the same.

On the Sabbath day he came to the synagogue and wrapped himself in his *tallis*. Whereupon three or four men picked him up and threw him out. From that point on he began making the rounds, asking for forgiveness. He went to see Reb Itzia Dubinsky, and Reb Mordkhe-Leib Segal, and Reb Simcha, pleading for mercy. "Don't take vengeance on a fellow Jew," he cried.

They wouldn't look at him.

All week he stayed away from the synagogue. On the following Sabbath he showed up again. As soon as he put on his *tallis,* they grabbed him again and threw him out. He lay down in the snow and stayed there until the service was over.

The widow Bluma passed by, and tried to get him to rise, but he refused. "No," was all he would say, lying there in the snow, shaking his head.

The congregation stood off to one side, watching.

All in a fluster his wife and sons arrived, and tried to talk him into getting up. He told them to go away. "Let them forgive me," he said. "I won't budge until they forgive. Otherwise, I'll die right here."

His wife let loose a stream of maledictions, invoking cholera, fire, the breaking of arms and legs on a straight path. Her youngest son, Mendel, a lad of about twenty, shouted to the silent spectators, "Hey, you capitalistic burghers—"

No one ever found out how he would have finished the sentence, because he was silenced by his father: "Keep quiet!"

Reb Moshe-Meir stood there tall as a ladder, his puzzled face towering above the crowd, his eyes fixed on the snow under his long legs. Finally, he left the spot where he had been standing between Reb Itzia Dubinsky and Reb Mordkhe-Leib Segal, and went and stood over the prostrate Eisik Koysh.

"Get up, you carrion!"

Eisik Koysh turned his head and looked straight up at the clouds. "Have you people forgiven me?"

"We forgive, we forgive, the devil take your father's father's father!"

At this, Eisik Koysh stood up, brushed away the snow, adjusted the *tallis* he had been wearing all the time, and having missed the communal service, walked into the synagogue with head bowed, to say his prayers in solitude.

The spectators nodded their heads and smiled. Reb Mordkhe-Leib turned to Reb Itzia Dubinsky and Reb Ozer Hagbeh.

" 'Happy the man who hath not walked in the council of the wicked,' " he quoted from the first Psalm. "How in the world does King David know so much about the council of the wicked? It's amazing, it's a mystery, but he knows. Yes, it seems he knows."

123

Like a clap of thunder on a clear day, the news hit Mokry-Kut that the Bolsheviks were besieging Kiev. The authorities issued a proclamation: "The Revolution is in danger!" The whole town spluttered like a frying-pan over the flame. People walked the streets looking like astrologers whose business it is to predict the future, outwardly unhappy but inwardly rejoicing. With deliberate ambiguity they sighed to one another, "God will have mercy."

Indoors, where it was safe to talk, they whispered to one another all sorts of good tidings of salvation and comfort. They took turns predicting to one another that *they*—the Bolsheviks, that is—were on their last legs. "The same befall all the Lord's enemies," they congratulated one another.

Yankel Potchtar was now in his element, spreading news, rumors, predictions. "Just you wait!" he winked, with the smile of a man who has information denied to ordinary mortals. "What you see now is only the appetizer, the main course is yet to come!"

"Namely?" they tried to draw him out.

"Namely? Don't ask! See how they were driven out of Kiev? That's how they'll be driven out of every place else, out of Petrograd and Moscow and the whole country, driven out with song and rejoicing, until there won't be a trace of them left."

In his usual way he went on at length, alternating veiled remarks with explicit statements. In one respect he sounded convincing. He lumped America with England, France and Germany, and poised them against the Bolsheviks.

"What do you think, they'll stand idly by? All the nations? The whole world? No, they won't. You can be sure of that."

He had still another card to play: "Muraviov."

Or rather, he never would mention the name without giving him his rank: "Polkovnik Muraviov!"

He had a lot to say about this military paragon, this Muraviov, whom he praised to the skies.

"He's nothing to sneeze at, Polkovnik Muraviov! Oh, Colonel Muraviov will show them!"

Hearing all this, Reb Avrohom-Abba was unable to conceal his surprise. "Seems to me you've got things kind of backwards. This Muraviov you're praising so much is a Bolshevik."

"Muraviov a Bolshevik?" Yankel Potchtar was taken aback.

"But of course."

"Nu-nu!" Yankel made a quick recovery. "What are you saying, if I may ask? Do you know what you're talking about?"

"Oh come on. . . ."

"You're right as far as you go," Yankel interrupted. "Let me explain the mixup. At first Polkovnik Muraviov was a Bolshevik, as you say, the real article, heart and soul. Then when he saw what kind of people they are, when he realized that they're thugs and hooligans and robbers, he changed his mind. . . ."

"The only trouble with your explanation is that he's in command of the Red Guard at Kiev!"

"Nu, so what?" Yankel smiled. "So he's commanding. But first you must ask yourself, how is he commanding, why is he commanding? You see, my friend, some things are far from obvious. . . ."

Polyishuk issued an order for all men eighteen years old and up to report for military duty. Comrades Timoshenko, Zabolotni, Ziame, Mendel Sukhar, and Muntchik reported voluntarily, and were joined by Mulye, yes, Mulye the poet. They all hurried off to the railway station.

Three days passed, but not a single additional man showed up. Polyishuk ran out on the street and leveled his revolver at anybody of military age who was around. "You're drafted!" he yelled like a drill sergeant. "Report for duty, you sons-of-bitches!"

The "draftees" ducked their heads low and scattered in every direction. "I'll shoot to kill!" he roared, giving chase.

In this fashion he caught five men and marched them

off to Revkom headquarters. Then he went out and brought in eight more. But by evening they had all managed to get away, and he was left without a single one.

124

Leahtche was a changed person. All of a sudden her whole world had crumbled, and she walked around like a lost soul, troubled, afraid, in despair. She felt that her youth was over, that all her dreams and hopes had evaporated. Nothing mattered to her any more, not the Revolution, now embroiled in war with the Ukrainians, not the new commune that had been set up in Polyishuk's quarters. She couldn't care less; her mind was on other things.

At night, in bed, she cried a lot, and worried in the dark about what would become of her. In a very few months her shame would be plain for all to see. "Gevald, gevald, *Ribbono-shel-Olam!*"

Without success, she tried to talk herself into a reasonable frame of mind. "It's not all that serious! You aren't some petty-bourgeois girl. . . ." Right. To be sure. But how was she going to be able to face people with her belly between her teeth?

"Ah, that's a matter on which we can get guidance."

"Guidance? How? Where? From whom?. . . . Ach, you unhappy thing! Unhappy now and for the rest of your life!"

During the day, she tried to hide her agony, and to go through the routine motions. But people sensed the change that had come over her, and interpreted it as a combination of longing for the absent Sorokeh and resentment over her exclusion from the commune.

It must be admitted that the girls who worked with her were happy to see her in such a state. "She's broken her back over the commune," they sniffed smugly. "She's jealous of Kayla. Serves her right!"

The membership of the commune consisted of Polyishuk, Shimtze, Hillik, Shayke, Mayerke, and two girls, Kayla and Malia.

The town reacted like a volatile mixture put to the flame, seething, hissing, making all kinds of noises. Some tried to analyze the phenomenon, others joked about it, everybody according to his nature and inclination. The womenfolk cursed Kayla and Malia, some of them even weeping as they lamented about the doings of the younger generation.

The widow Bluma stopped Leahtche on her way home from work, and spoke to her about that very subject. After Leahtche had left, the old woman stood there on the street singing her praises.

"In spite of everything, still her father's daughter, hah! To all intents and purposes a thorough Bolshevitchka, and yet she hasn't besmirched her honor, God forbid. Not like those two promiscuous pieces of carrion!"

Leahtche walked along the street lost in thought, until she caught sight of Heshel Pribisker standing some distance away and watching her, his head bent, his fingers nervously clutching at his beard. A wave of bitter hatred engulfed her. Her heart pounded, and she felt warm sweat on her neck and back.

"Wretch!" She ground her teeth and clenched her fists. *"Menuval!"*

This was the first time she had seen him since she had driven him out of the house, on the morning after the incident that she felt had ruined her life. She had come into the parlor, faced him, and whispered, "Get out of my house!" Then turned her back on him and walked away.

She didn't hear him pleading, stammering, saying that he wanted to marry her. "Leah," he said, not Leahtche, as usual, but Leah, with humble respect, "let's get married . . . please . . . I have nothing in life but . . . Leah. . . ."

That very day he moved in with Pesach Yossem. Reb Simcha was puzzled, perturbed by the whole thing. "What's going on?" He spread his questioning palms. He put the question to Heshel himself.

"How should I know?" Heshel stammered. "Just like that. No special reason. It's more comfortable. . . ."

Reb Simcha asked Leahtche, and she answered him darkly. "He's been with us long enough. Let him go to Pribisk, or wherever!"

Reb Simcha shrugged his shoulders, pursed his lips, and uttered an odd sound: "Pu-pu-pu. . . ." After a while he turned to her again. "Still, something must have happened. Why should he move out all of a sudden?"

She met his question this time with silence, but it was a loaded silence, filled with hatred.

125

By midday on Friday none of the shopkeepers had returned any of the missing merchandise. Polyishuk announced an extension. He would wait until the time for lighting the Sabbath candles, but no longer.

As dusk approached he marched out, leading a detail of four men: Shayke, Mayerke, Hillik, and Shimtze. They were armed to the teeth, just as though they and their fathers before them had been highwaymen since time immemorial. They marched in step, erect, stern-visaged, bringing down the wrath of the law on the quiet houses now wrapped in twilight and twinkling with the modest glow of the Sabbath candles.

Their first stop was the home of Reb Moshe-Meir the Ladder, where they began conducting a search. Reb Moshe-Meir was already at the synagogue with his young sons, and there was nobody home but his wife. She lost no time in rushing out into the street and raising her voice in a mighty wail.

"Ge-va-ld! Help! Ge-va-ld!"

In one split second the street was filled with women who had come running out of their houses, and men pouring out of the synagogue and the small prayer houses, everybody rushing about in confusion, asking, "What happened? What happened?"

Reb Moshe-Meir came panting into his house, followed by a crowd of men and women who choked into the doorway and stood watching.

"Comrades!" he faced Polyishuk and his men, breathing heavily. "What are you doing here at this hour? What are you looking for in my house?"

"Merchandise!" barked Polyishuk. "The merchandise you stole from the store."

"Comrade!" Reb Moshe-Meir pleaded. "I didn't steal any merchandise. I don't know a thing. I'm just a poor Jew. What do you want from my life?"

"Merchandise!" Polyishuk repeated curtly. "We know that you smuggled out merchandise. We have a reliable witness."

The men standing in the doorway growled their protest, while the women called down retribution on the heads of Polyishuk and his men.

"*Goyim!* On the Sabbath. . . ."

"They're doing it on purpose!"

"Evil men! May their hands wither and their eyes rot, *Ribbono-shel-Olam*! May they be struck deaf, break all their bones, be ground to dust! Let them be destroyed in one swift punishment!"

The search party descended next on Reb Avrohom-Abba, then on Reb Avrohom-Elya Karp. From there they went to the house of Reb Itzia Dubinsky, where they demanded to investigate his garret. They told Reb Itzia to take the lamp and show them the way.

Reb Itzia looked at them wide-eyed, in a state of shock. His bushy eyebrows seemed to be standing on end, his heavy beard wagged in protest.

"Are you fellows crazy, or just plain stupid? Don't you realize today is *Shabbos*?"

Mayerke shoved the lamp into his hand, and barked angrily, "Don't be insubordinate! Do as you're told!"

Reb Itzia recoiled, clasping his hands firmly behind his back. "*Shabbos!*" he said. "You can kill me, but you won't get me to desecrate the Sabbath!"

"Let him alone," Polyishuk ordered Mayerke. "We'll get rid of these superstitions in due time. Just give us time. Just give us time"

When they got to Reb Simcha he was already in bed.

"Ha!" he welcomed them expansively. "Good *Shabbos* to you! I was beginning to be afraid that you might overlook me. . . ."

"Where's the merchandise from your store?" Polyishuk cut him short.

"Ach, get on with you," answered Reb Simcha. "As the king of Sodom said to Father Abraham, 'Give me the persons, and take the goods for thyself.' Search, go ahead. Turn the house upside down, be my guest."

"Don't worry, we'll search," growled Polyishuk. "Come on, show us where your hidden treasures are."

"I'll tell you one thing." Reb Simcha forced a grin, pulling his fur coat tighter around his shoulders. "After length of days, when I arrive in the next world, and if, God forbid, they sentence me to purgatory, I'll ask them for one favor: Please, demons and evil spirits, don't pile hot coals on my heart. Anywhere else you like, on my whole body, just not on my heart. The same way I'm asking you a favor, comrades: don't pile hot coals on my heart. Search my place any day of the week, only not on *Shabbos.*"

"You old fox, you!" Polyishuk growled, "Trying to put us off with your talk."

Leahtche emerged from her room. "Ah, Leahtche," Mayerke greeted her. "Look, you've got company."

"What's happening?" She looked around the room. "A search?"

"Figure it out for yourself, comrade." There was a tinge of nastiness in the mockery of Polyishuk's tone. He didn't look at her directly.

"A search. That's it exactly," laughed Mayerke.

"Be my guests." She threw the cupboard doors wide open.

They searched the bed, looked under it and behind it, then turned their attention to the cupboard and sideboard. "Why are you standing around?" Shayke laughed at Leahtche. "Come on, help us search."

Reb Simcha straightened out his bedclothes and lay down again silently, his face to the wall. The others left the bedroom and went into the parlor. "Where's the *melamed?*" Polyishuk wanted to know.

"Not here," said Leahtche, shortly.

"Where'd he disappear to?"

"The devil knows."

They started turning things inside out, poking around in every corner. While this was going on, Polyishuk found a moment to have a word with Leahtche.

"Aren't you at all interested in the commune?"

She thought for a moment, then said, "No."

"Why not?"

"I'm just not interested."

"Too bad. . . ."

"Not for me. On the contrary."

"What do you mean, on the contrary?"

"I'll soon be leaving here, anyway." It was un-premeditated, but she needed an answer. It took Polyishuk by surprise.

"Leaving?" he asked. "Where to?"

"Oh, we'll see. Maybe to Kiev. . . ."

She paused, her face lit up with the idea that had come to her out of the blue.

"To Kiev!" She was suddenly more positive. "I'm fed up with this dreary Mokry-Kut. I've had enough! I'll be off to Kiev, and from there to Moscow, to Petrograd, to the big wide world. . . ."

126

Reb Simcha sensed that Leahtche had become extremely unhappy. He ascribed it to the unsatisfactory state of her emotional life, the fact that she was not yet married. This was a very serious problem, but there was nothing new about it, he had agonized over it many times and had tossed through more than one sleepless night, awake with worry. But what could he do? Where can you find a bride-groom these days, with the whole country in a turmoil, and the air filled with uncertainty? Meanwhile, one day follows another, the months and the years pile up, and before you can look around, time will have passed her by, God forbid. The thought saddened him greatly, and he sighed deeply and often.

In the evening, when Leahtche was about to go to bed, he tried to engage her in conversation. "Nu," he said, with a forlorn smile. "What's happening with you?"

She swung around and looked at him uncertainly.

"It seems to me, uh . . . uh . . . ," he hemmed and hawed, then took the plunge. "What will be the outcome?"

"What outcome?" She pretended not to understand.

"Perhaps"—he groped for a word of affection—"perhaps, my daughter, I should send for a matchmaker?"

"Really, father!" But she was looking at the floor.

"I don't know." The poor man was pleading. "Maybe you have somebody. I thought a *shadchan* might help things along."

"How can he help? By this time, no man in the world can help me."

"Don't, dearest, don't. God forbid. We have a merciful Father in heaven." He looked up at the shadows chasing themselves across the wall and ceiling. "A *shadchan* might call on the head of the yeshiva at Novoseltsovo. Hah? What do you think? He might expedite matters . . . bring things to a conclusion."

"Oh, papa."

"What's the problem?" He was trying hard to be nice. "There's no question about his being of good family. Quite the contrary, his father's a rabbi, a head of a yeshiva. . . ."

"That's enough!" she cut him off. "Don't interfere in what isn't your concern."

"Not my concern?" There was a suppressed sob in his voice. "My brains are dried out from agonizing over this."

She didn't answer, but gave a long drawn-out sigh.

"It's all the fault of that Revolution of yours, plague take it. It's the source of all our troubles."

Leahtche went to her room.

After a while Reb Simcha recited his bedtime *shema* and lay down. But he couldn't sleep. His thoughts nagged away at him, and besides, he was painfully cold. He took the larger of the two pillows, the one that had belonged to his late wife, and put it over his feet. The second pillow was his own, the one his mother had made him for his wedding-day. In accordance with custom, she had put into it, along with the feathers, locks of hair she had saved from his first haircut, on the day he had turned three years old. The memory of his mother's act flooded in on him as he lay there curled up. His heart ached, his tears dropped silently onto the pillow.

127

Polyishuk's searches turned up next to nothing: a small amount of wormy flour, five or six sacks of grits, half a barrel of hemp seed oil, a little kerosene, a bit of saccharin, some toffee, and other things of equal insignificance. This led people to believe that the wave of searches was safely past, so that they greeted one another with knowing winks and suppressed smiles of sly satisfaction. But only two days after that Black Sabbath, Polyishuk resumed his searches, going through every Jewish house in town.

"I'll find the stuff no matter what!" he insisted stubbornly. "Even if I have to dig up the ground!"

When they started turning everything upside down at Pesach Yossem's, Heshel Pribisker spoke up. Heshel had had one drink too many, and was in a slightly irresponsible frame of mind.

"Just imagine what they would find if they were to conduct a raid on the Holy One, bless His name. Do I have to tell you? Seems to me they would find all kinds of juicy contraband—destruction of the Temple, exile, evil decrees by the score. . . ."

"Who're you?" Polyishuk raised his head, speaking with the voice of authority.

"Who am I?" Heshel acted confused, as though he had been asked the most difficult question in the world. "Yes, who am I?"

"What do you do?" Polyishuk raised his voice.

"What I do?" Heshel pondered the question.

"A speculator?"

"Oh no, I'm not a speculator, and no merchant, and I don't have anything. What I do have, that is, my 'mine,' is not enough to displace my 'me,' that is, what I am."

"Don't talk so much!" Polyishuk ordered sharply. "Just tell me where these people have got their stuff hidden. Hurry up, speak!"

Heshel shrugged, offered a smile, but no answer.

"Let's see," Shayke intervened. "You're not a speculator, not a trader, not a shopkeeper, and you're no longer a *melamed*. So how do you make a living? By the Holy Spirit?"

"Don't believe him, he's a speculator," Shimtze spoke up. "Every last one of them is a speculator."

Before the day was out Polyishuk had arrested Avrohom-Elya Karp, and Reb Avrohom-Abba, and Reb Itzia Dubinsky.

"Terror!" he declared. "Let the bourgeoisie get its just deserts!"

Lamentation filled the town from one end to the other. The women cried out to heaven, and the men defended those arrested, arguing that Polyishuk had made a very doubtful accusation.

"God forbid," they argued. "That 'terror' he talked about,

these men never did anything like that in all their lives. They're innocent."

Polyishuk declared that he didn't like Heshel Pribisker, there was something suspicious about him. So he sent Mayerke and Shayke to arrest him.

Heshel walked along between the two of them, smiling his slightly tipsy smile. "You, you the ones arresting me? *You*, a couple of Jewish boys? *Ai-ai*, little brothers!"

"Nu-nu, keep quiet," they silenced him. "Come along like a man."

" 'All may slaughter,' " Heshel quoted the Mishna. "All may slaughter, at any time, with any means." He smiled a drunken smile. "Everybody slaughters, whoever has God in his heart. To be sure, no person can bring the dead back to life. But slaughter, that anybody can do."

When they got to the Revkom headquarters he saw a lot of people outside, crowded together noisily, like a tree full of starlings at twilight. He raised his voice and called out to them.

"Jews, seed of Abraham! I'm ashamed of you, every single one of you."

"Heshel, Heshel!" The voices came from everywhere in the crowd. "You too? Woe to us! They took Reb Itzia and Reb Avrohom-Elya. . . ."

He looked around at them. "When a Jew arrives, the Judge of the whole world asks him, 'Where's your "love thy neighbor"?' I'm coming, here I am, *Ribbono-d' alma-kula!*"

"Heshele, Heshele!" The women burst out crying.

Shayke and Mayerke cleared a way for him through the crowd. "Don't drag your feet," they ordered. "Go right in to the Revkom office."

"How much is the admission ticket?" Heshel's grin was more like a grimace.

"Go ahead, go on in," answered Shayke. "It's free for nothing."

"Nu, and how much is the exit ticket?"

In the crowd, there were some who burst out laughing, and others who burst out crying.

"Master of the universe!" Heshel raised his voice. "Thou knowest my shame and my disgrace, my affliction and the soreness of my heart. . . . My people, my brothers! I accept my fate without bitterness, my suffering with love. . . . *Ashamti, bagad'ti* . . . I have sinned, I have dealt treacherously. . . ."

Before he could finish his confession, they took hold of him and dragged him inside.

A shudder ran through the people, as they stood rooted to the spot, unable to utter a word. The only sound was a collective sigh that rose from the crowd, and hung trembling in the air.

128

Accompanied by Korotchkin and Ilko, Polyishuk went out to the villages in search of recruits for the Red Guard. All three were armed, Korotchkin and Ilko with rifles slung across their backs, while Polyishuk carried a *nagan* on his hip. They picked up a few volunteers, here a Party member, there a landless farmer.

They arrived in Varnitsa at noon.

It was a bright day, and the icicles were dripping in the gleaming sunshine. Children were sledding on the village streets, accompanied by barking dogs racing alongside. As soon as the children became aware of Polyishuk and his men they stopped, watching warily. The dogs barked at the strangers, three or four brave salvos, and then retreated. From somewhere came the sound of a drum and a fiddle. Two drunken peasants appeared on the scene, supporting between them a third, whose nose was dripping blood. The man in the middle was dragging his feet in the snow, waving his hand like a choir-conductor, and singing a song.

"They've been loaded since sunup," Ilko hazarded.

"Looks to me like they've been at it all night," remarked Korotchkin, with a mixture of contempt and admiration.

The peasants became aware of their visitors. "Come and join the fun," said he of the bloody nose.

"You fellows had a few?" laughed Ilko.

"Uh-huh," nodded Nose with satisfaction. "And so can you. That's what the Revolution is for."

"And to the war, say finished, amen," said his buddy.

"Commissars?" The third one pointed his questioning finger at them.

"Uh-huh," said Number Two, ignoring Number Three. "Amen. Kaput."

After Polyishuk had conferred with the headman of the village, the church bell was rung, and the villagers gathered in the Council House.

Polyishuk sensed from the start that he didn't have the crowd with him. Still, he kept himself under control, stood up and spoke his piece. He began with a homespun example. If the farmer is lazy, and spends his time lolling at the hearth, without planting at seedtime, how is he going to bring in a harvest? The same with the Revolution. Because, see, there's a life-and-death struggle between the landed gentry and the peasants, between those who own the plow and those who work the land. True, both these and those are people. But these aim to spend a luxurious life of idle debauchery, while those seek a life of toil and dignity, and ask for an honorable reward for their labors. So the battlelines are drawn, and it's a difficult struggle against a bitter, relentless enemy. But there's no choice. The people have gone forth to battle, because their fate is being decided at this time.

"It's the hour of decision for all who toil, for all farmers and all workers. And it's everyone's duty to declare, 'My place is in the ranks of the Red Guard!' "

"Ready and willing," mocked a voice in the crowd.

Polyishuk pretended not to hear. He went on to say that it was the people's duty to provide food for the army.

"Mobilization of the army, mobilization of labor, and mobilization of food supply—victory depends on these three, which are really one."

"Sure, bring your bushel-basket and start measuring," heckled a peasant, as he shot the spit from his mouth. "Being buried in the trenches for four years wasn't enough for you, hah? Looking for more war? Smart fellow!"

"They're all smart fellows," called out the man next to him. "And so are we, three wise men—you and me and my billy goat."

The crowd roared with laughter.

From that moment on Polyishuk couldn't say a word without having it turned into a joke by somebody in the audience. The head of the Village Council tried to restore order, and two members of the local Communist cell also shouted at the crowd. But they were countered by the Ukrainian nationalists. Every time one of the speakers roared, "Let us be a shield of protection for the Revolution!" the opposition yelled back, "Nothing doing! Your Revolution made us lose our Mother Ukrainia!" Other voices answered, "Ukrainia is not lost! Ukrainia's not a needle!" Still others shouted, "You'll find her in the hands of the *zhids* and the *russkis*!" From the front came the cry, "Long live Lenin-Trotsky!" only to be met by a roar, *"Slava!* Long live Free Ukrainia!" Before very long the two camps were at one another's throats, and the fighting soon spread outdoors. They thrashed around in the snow, some two by two, others in larger battling groups. Small boys joined the fighting, trying to help their fathers. Women ran out of the houses, wailing at the top of their lungs.

Polyishuk saw that the situation was hopeless, and he started to leave the village, accompanied by Ilko. Korotchkin wasn't with them. They couldn't find him, and they had no time to look.

"A murderous crew!" Ilko raged. "Go try to keep a Revolution going with people like that! It's *kontra,* out-and-out counterrevolution!"

They strode along, half blinded by the glare of the noonday sun on the snow.

"Murderers!" Ilko repeated. What you've got here is no Mokry-Kut. Murderers, God preserve us!"

While he was speaking they heard the sound of a shot.

"They're shooting!" Ilko couldn't believe it.

As the two of them turned in the direction of the shot, a bullet whistled between them. Two figures darted across the street, took up positions behind a gate, and fired at them. Polyishuk and Ilko quickened their pace, guns at the ready. When they got to the edge of the village, they paused. The sound of firing had increased, and shots could be heard from every corner of the village.

"They've gone plumb crazy," said Ilko, as he rolled *makhorka* and a bit of torn newspaper into a cigarette held between two chapped fingers. Then they both lifted their heads sharply. The sound they heard was the rat-a-tat of a machine-gun.

Korotchkin showed up just as it was getting dark. He gave a lengthy account of the battle. Seven men had been wounded, and as for the doctor, she had given up the ghost.

"What doctor?" Polyishuk asked sharply. "What are you talking about?"

"Nu, the lady doctor. She had come to see the priest,

Father Andrei; you know how sick he is, on his last legs, they say."

"What!" Polyishuk cut in. "Doctor Stephanida Dmitrievna?"

"Who do you think?" Korotchkin retorted. "Of course, she's the one, Stephanida Dmitrievna. Who else could I be talking about?"

A few days later everybody in Spod turned out to accompany the doctor to her grave. Four days thereafter Odarka found Piltch lying lifeless on the floor. Mokry-Kut was deeply shaken by his death, and gave him a big funeral. Not a person in town was absent. Some said he had died of a heart attack, some said he had taken his own life.

"Wasn't he a pharmacist?" they argued. "You know as well as I do that you can always find poison in a pharmacy."

129

The Bolsheviks took Kiev. In Mokry-Kut the news was treated as a kind of Job's tidings.

"There you are!" they said, bitter, hopeless. "The wicked have all the luck. The plague does not take them, the fire does not consume them, a *kholerye* on them!"

Yankel Potchtar was a man dismayed. "Nu, Yankele," they nagged at him. "What's happened with your predictions?"

"Sheer happenstance," he answered miserably, chewing at his beard. "Bad luck."

"Muraviov?" they teased. "Muraviov, hah?"

"Alas, I am found out," he nodded, grinning sheepishly.

The Bolsheviks declared a holiday to celebrate the victory. The town was decorated with red flags. The comrades strutted around, congratulating one another, flushed with the joy of victory.

Polyishuk called a public meeting and delivered an impassioned speech, exalting the Revolution and shaking the fist of the proletariat in the face of the hydra head of counterrevolution, not sparing the enemies of the people in Mokry-Kut either, and denouncing the violent hooligans in the surrounding villages.

That evening the Communist club was the scene of a happy celebration, with much singing and dancing. Leahtche was there but she kept to herself, standing off in a corner. The girls looked at her, whispered to one another, and giggled behind their hands. They sent Hillik to test her out.

"What's the trouble, Leahtche," he asked. "You're usually in the middle of things when there's singing and dancing. Are you sore, or something?"

A couple of times Mayerke went over and tried to draw her out in a friendly way.

"Come on, dance with me. How about a polka or a waltz?"

She didn't want to dance.

"Nu, Leahtche, on a happy day you ought to be in good spirits!"

Polyishuk too went over to her. He asked if she still intended to go to Kiev.

"Certainly," she answered.

"Don't go," he said. "Stay here."

Kayla came over and draped herself on his arm. "What have you got to do with her?" she asked. Polyishuk stood there, caught between the two of them, until he let Kayla pull him away.

"Comrade Polyishuk!" Leahtche called after him.

"What?" He turned around. Without answering, Leahtche gave him a funny look. He detached himself from Kayla and came back.

"What is it?" he asked.

"Dance a waltz with me."

"Ach, to hell with it! I don't know how. I never danced in all my life."

"That's nothing, I'll lead. All you have to do is follow." Without waiting for an answer, she put her hand on his shoulder and pulled him out onto the floor. Everybody was watching. Polyishuk got his feet tangled up, pushed and pulled, and found it all very awkward.

"Comrade Polyishuk!" Mayerke, who was dancing with Liuba, turned his head. "Looks like making a revolution is easier than dancing, hah?"

They went around the floor three or four times, then stood by the window talking. Repeatedly he asked her to stay in Mokry-Kut.

"Stay on. Please. You'll see, things will be all right. Please. . . ." He persisted. "At least, don't go away just yet. For the time being. After that, maybe I'll join you and we'll go away together."

Leahtche glanced across the room. She saw Kayla, standing by herself in a corner, short, bulging in all the wrong places, red-faced, downcast, looking miserable. Suddenly, Leahtche felt better.

"Go on over to her." She indicated Kayla by a motion of her eyes. "Go and appease her. She's just about ready to burst with jealousy."

He didn't want to go. "Let her burst."

Leahtche took his arm and started walking him across the room. When they came to Kayla, Leahtche looked her up and down with a slight smile of contempt, then suddenly called out to Mayerke. He came running.

"What, Leahtche?"

"A polka."

"Polka?" He was flabbergasted. "With me?"

Quickly he turned, clapped his hands a few times, and called out, "Polka! Hey, *harmoshka!* Let's have a polka!"

A little while later, when the dance was finished, she stole out of the club and went home.

That same night Polyishuk called the comrades together and appointed Mayerke to head the Revkom.

"I'm joining the Red Guard," he explained, deliberately casual.

The comrades were astounded. Kayla burst into tears. Quickly he slung a rifle across his back, said goodbye to each of them in turn, and headed for the railway station. They started to go along with him, to see him off.

"No," he said. "No need to."

They stood watching him until he was almost out of sight.

130

From the day that Heshel Pribisker was arrested there wasn't a moment's peace in Reb Simcha's house. Nothing but arguments, accusations, recriminations. Reb Simcha became withdrawn and bitter, brooding sorrowfully for hours at a stretch. He was now unusually exacting in the performance of his religious duties, spending much more time at prayers, and especially at reading the Psalms. On the other hand, he neglected the study of Torah. He never opened a Gemara, never glanced at the Mishna, as if these were part of the world that had treated him so badly, and on which he was turning his back.

Of course he had it in for Leahtche, because she hadn't spoken up for Heshel in his hour of need. It became the cause of a nonstop quarrel between them.

"How could you let yourself see him arrested by those criminals without lifting a finger to help him?" he raged at her, his face contorted, his lips agitated.

She answered calmly. "He wasn't arrested for nothing."

"What did he ever do to you? Did he slit your purse? Did he do you any harm? What did he do?"

"He did, he did," enigmatically.

"So? Let's hear! What's his sin?"

She looked at her shoes and said nothing. He pressed for a specific answer, and when he didn't get any, his rage boiled over.

"You don't know a single thing against him, I swear it!" He began to cough, clawing at his collar, choking. "Evildoers. . . . Cursed ones. . . . Don't you have any obligation to me? Why am I any different? Have me arrested! Go ahead, arrest *me*, the same as you people arrested him! It's all my fault! He's suffering on my account. Go on, go to those fine comrades of yours, a plague on you and them, and see to it that they let him go!"

All his shouting was no use. Leahtche simply refused.

"I won't go," she said, calmly.

"Yes, you will, you'll go!" he raised his voice, his lips quivering, his beard shaking. "Immediately, right now!"

"Not even if he was on his deathbed." She was still controlled. "Not even if he was bleeding to death under my eyes."

"Shut your mouth!" His fist came down on the psalter, his eyes glazed over. "Get out of my house! I don't want to see your face around here!"

"Don't worry, I'll leave." Her voice was subdued. "It won't be long now. You'll see."

Such scenes were terrible, but his silence was worse. For hours at a time he would sit wordless, enveloped in a heavy, oppressive, silent rage, paying no attention to Leahtche, as if she had ceased to exist.

Leahtche resigned herself to the situation, and started making preparations for travel. She washed her clothes, she sewed and patched. She figured to leave soon, right after Passover, because after all, she told herself, there wasn't much time to lose.

131

In due course the Bolsheviks and the Germans signed a peace treaty at Brest-Litovsk. The news sent the townspeople of Mokry Kut scurrying about like agitated ants. Some of them thought it was good news, some of them took it as a bad omen.

The optimists said, "Now the Bolsheviks will feel more secure and leave us alone."

The pessimists said, "Now that their hands are free, they'll turn their full attention on us, and destroy the world."

Nobody knew the nature of the peace treaty. One school of thought said, "Some peace! An abomination, not a peace!"

Another theory offered details. "The Germans carved out a big helping for themselves! They're taking over the Ukraine, Poland, Lithuania, Latvia, and Estonia. A mere bagatelle, hah!"

A third opinion advised, "America, England, and France

haven't recognized the Bolshevik regime, they're still to be heard from. So you see, it's not all that simple, definitely not!"

Altogether, they agreed with a sigh, quite a kettle of fish. . . .

The comrades, on the other hand, boasted about strikes and demonstrations in Germany and Austria, and predicted that social revolution would soon engulf Europe.

When the news reached Reb Simcha, he interrupted the Psalm he was chanting, spread his palms on his knees, and bent over like a man worn out, exhausted.

"It's a world full of futility." He spat on the floor and slowly ground his spittle under his foot. His face registered a grimace of disgust.

Then he returned to his chant, swaying to and fro, his voice a cracked and weary protest, as though he was complaining to the prayer book against the Holy One, blessed be He.

132

Spring arrived unheralded. The snow softened, within a few days it melted and was gone. Like the fences and the gates, the walls of the houses turned black from soaking up so much rain, and the edges of the garden plots dripped constantly. Muddy rivulets gurgled down the sides of the narrow streets.

One day the river threw off its icy straitjacket. The sound of the ice breaking up was like the noise of distant thunder. That night the river broke its banks and flooded the pasture land.

Day by day the light grew stronger. People emerged tentatively from the doorways, coming out to enjoy the sunshine, looking like convalescents just up from a sickbed, their faces pallid, their eyes blinking in the unaccustomed light.

Leahtche found no pleasure in any of this. The season seemed to have come only to mock her. It was as if all the sadness, all the unfulfilled yearning in the world, all the melancholy returning even now with the twilight and the shadows, had seized hold of her, enveloped her.

Every free moment that she had, she walked along the road that led to the isolated railway stop. She took in the smell of the earth, black and moist. She watched the crows at play in the treetops, the noisy convocations of swallows, the skittering of the season's first squirrels, and the vanguard of wild geese flying in formation back from southern lands.

As she walked alone in the half light after sunset, or by the light of the moon and stars, she imagined herself in Kiev, busy working for the Party, associating with all the great Bolsheviks, famous people. There she is, going off to a conference in Petrograd, making a speech in front of a huge audience, who rise to their feet in tribute and fill the hall with thunderous applause. Lenin and Trotsky are present, and they shake her hand and praise her to her face. Now her fantasy shows her striking up a friendship with a comrade, a man of action as well as a famous theoretician, and they fall in love, and he marries her, and her days are filled with happiness. And then by chance she runs into Sorokeh. . . .

One night, shortly before midnight, as she was walking down the street, the frogs croaking and the nightingale singing, everybody asleep in bed and the houses all sunk in darkness, she suddenly sensed someone approaching, as if hurrying on urgent business. She hid behind the fence of the commune, and watched. The figure turned out to be Muntchik, back from the front. He bounded up the steps, kicked in the door, and shouted into the house.

"Asleep, you devils? Wake up, wake up! The Germans are coming!"